To the boundless absent presence

Tony Parsons

Contents

Thank you

A word of thanks to unconditional
Love, from itself, appearing as the forms
Silent, shouting, softly singing lyrical
Secrets of life – free as skies, or in norms –
As simple being, scrolls untouched by writing,
Yet pointing to the freedom present, is;
As life donning varied roles, yet dancing
As immediacy, past limits of bliss;
As appearing relations and the friends
Displaying warmth, support, or jealousy,
And, finally, the reader on whom depends
The seeming author's fiscal activity.
Yet none exists to choose to write or buy
The book, or sing, or long for untouched skies.

Acknowledgements

This book has come into being with the help and contribution of many, all of whom have contributed in their unique manner.

Immense gratitude for and thanks to Tony and Claire Parsons (https://www.theopensecret.com) without whom this book would not have been possible. Thanks to Jeff Foster and Richard Sylvester.

Special thanks to Dr Sukbir Singh Kapoor (World Sikh University) for being a wonderful teacher and guide in the study of the Sikh scriptures; to Dr Wazir Singh Sidhu for his support, and guidance; to M N Nandakumar (Bhartiya Vidya Bhavan) for teaching Indian scriptures; and to Nicholas Sutton for being my tutor at the Oxford Centre of Hindu Studies. The late Dr Satyanaryana Sastry's contribution is ineffable, he imparted the essence of *Advaita Vedanta*, philosophy, and the non-dual meanings prevalent in the Indian scriptures. He sent me to Tony Parsons to experience their essence, only for there to be the illumination (for no one) that there is no one, no path, and no experience.

Heartfelt thanks to the immensely talented Raghav Rayasam for bringing this book to life with his creative design, and to Andrew Cook for redesign. A huge thank you to Aniket Athalye and Tim Hyde for copy editing and feedback, and to the artistic photographers Joseph Monk and Abhishek Khanna for their fantastic photography.

Thank you to Ajay Sharma for teaching miniature art; Ikoko Aso for her detailed explanation of Japanese cuisine; Misorez for introducing the phrase *seijaku wo kiku* and help with Japanese calligraphy; to Rachel O'Driscoll, Haruko Sair, Andy Li and Alexander Greze.

Special thanks to Sudhir Seth for his invaluable guidance; Suvir for support; Sumaera for her mountain painting; Laksh Anand for design ideas; Rehraas for providing her colourful creative corn in clay, and Sumita for her impeccable artwork, colour coordination, and guidance in the other illustrations. Thanks to Parvati and Jagdish Rathore. Heartfelt thanks to all my friends for their assistance and support.

Finally, thanks to my family, whose contribution is priceless. They have patiently and painstakingly listened to endless monologues; scrutinised the finer details of the book; offered invaluable counsel and encouragement while being very liberal with ridicule, criticism, and irritation throughout the apparent endeavour.

DES
23 & 25
DE
MÉDAILLE D'OR
1889
Ingrédients
150g de farine familière
1 jaune d'oeuf
1 cuillère à soupe de sucre sucré
cl de lait tiède

Life's but a walking shadow, a poor player that struts and frets his hour upon the stage and is heard no more. It is a tale told by an idiot, full of sound and fury, signifying nothing.

William Shakespeare, *Macbeth*

Introduction

Businesses, books and individuals try to promote products or stories, offer solutions to problems, or opportunities to grow, or simply provide entertainment. The advocates and recipients involved in the activity feel they have benefitted in several ways and find the results worth their time and money. If you think this book will motivate you to become better, make you spiritual, or benefit you in any way, you are mistaken. This book has nothing to offer; rather, the book questions the self's very existence and the apparent collective beliefs of society. Moreover, this work has no intention to teach or establish a doctrine. It does not aim to bring about a change of any sort and certainly cannot lead you to enlightenment. On the contrary, it simply illuminates the dream of individuality and highlights the Oneness of formlessness and form. Nevertheless, this message is not exclusive to this work but is present in some scriptures and a few *Satsangs* (translated literally as 'alive presence').

This book can be referred to as a song sung from the heart, a message that has flowed for no apparent reason, purpose, or motivation. However, in my apparent story: life, glimpses, and the translation of the scriptures led me to seek 'liberation' in life. Little did I realise: one can neither be liberated in life nor from life, for all is life. On meeting Tony Parsons, there was a deep resonance with the song of nothingness shared by him. Yet the illusory sense of self lurked in the shadows for a seemingly long time, with certain glimpses making an appearance. Finally, the illusion of the self seemed to unravel, though there was no experience of it, for there is no one to experience it. There was simply a recognition that one cannot be liberated, for there is no individual and no liberation. The illusory self thus cannot acquire a special state, cease, or become enlightened. Moreover, to call it as an 'event' or an 'experience' would be completely erroneous; not only there is no individual to be liberated but there is no occurrence either, as life alone appears as it is, without a continual flow. So, this song of freedom is simply an appearance of creativity.

Being fascinated with the scriptures, I read many manuscripts, attended several courses, interacted with experts, and taught the essence of the scriptures at the World Sikh University for many years. Research and intuitive resonance revealed that the message of Oneness, or non-duality, has always been around. Even though some texts express it clearly – though most of it has been interpreted dualistically – in others it is veiled by symbolisms or is articulated in poetry, implying it is open to interpretation. As Joseph Campbell aptly states, traditional doctrines or scriptural messages are symbolic or metaphorical; to take them literally is reading them in prose instead of poetry – that is, it is reading the metaphor in terms of the denotation instead of the connotation. In many of the verses in this book, I have included my renditions and translations of the non-dual verses from various ancient and modern scriptures and texts. Nonetheless, I would like to add that no translation or rendition of any scripture can be termed as right or wrong, for not only do perspectives differ, but one energetic presence alone prevails or appears as everything. Moreover, a language is like a confluence of rivers – there are several dialects of the same language at the same time – and being alive it seems to constantly change. This makes it rather difficult to translate words where the import shifts over time. Likewise, poetry, and imagery give the scriptures an ethereal quality, and local connotations make it difficult to decipher or convey the essence of the songs of freedom.

For those verses in this book without references, either I am unaware of their presence, or I have exercised my artistic license to highlight the essence of their message. Such unreferenced songs have been found in the scriptures across timelines and geographical locations – for instance, similar phrases have been used in Zen Buddhism and the *Upanishads*. Parallels of the *Advaita Vedanta* and the *Guru Granth Sahib* are also found in the works of many modern-day guides unaware of the existence of those scriptures. These similarities appear because the song of freedom emanates from the same formless source.

The poems and stories in this book echo and illuminate the workings of the seeming collective mind or its apparent seeking in a creative and light-hearted way, while pointing to the Oneness that is. Thus, while illuminating the workings of an apparent self – which seemingly lives in a parallel appearance (of space and time) and adds layers to its presence by creating concepts of systems, cultures, or nations – this book also highlights that the absolute alone appears as the relative. The verses also unravel the subtle claims of the seeking self where it pursues spirituality or non-duality and believes it can attain the formless presence and creates levels to attain it. This is because the seeming self is convinced it is real and not an illusion (though this self can never apprehend that it is illusory, for an illusion can never recognise that it is an illusion). The message also illustrates that the illusion of separation is an appearance of the energetic presence alone, not distinct from it, for all there is is energy appearing as everything, and yet it is untouched by its appearance – like how the shadow of the light is made possible by the presence of light alone, yet light is untouched by its dark shadows.

At this point, one may wonder what exactly is meant by 'Oneness'. Oneness implies all that appears and does not, is the formless forming, nothing appearing as everything or emptiness singing. However, the formless neither creates this creation, nor does it come into existence. It is not born so does not die and does not even occur. It simply appears as what is appearing and is not, and so is impossible to define. Moreover, this formless is too alive, immediate, and intimate to be confined in words as it appears as everything – the galaxies, earth, clouds, thoughts, feelings, food, you, me, and its illusory pilgrimage. This Oneness, though one as formless and form, also appears as the one which is dual. Therefore, not only is it indescribable, but there is no other to define it, or understand it. It is the formless dressed as form as it is and is not. However, I would like to take the opportunity here to emphatically state that it is easy to speak of Oneness, cite its perception, claim it as an experience, and consider it to be spiritual or holy; but everything collapses at the altar of life, its appearing presence. Nevertheless, it is the presence alone that continually reminds itself that all there is is the infinite singing the finite song.

Does this Oneness imply that there are no individuals with their life stories? Simply stated, there are no individuals but only an appearance of seeming individuality, which is nothing but a play of the one that hides from itself by being everything, and then seeks itself in diverse ways. I know this paradoxical message is impossible to understand – nor can it ever be understood – for the self cannot know its own absence. So, simply dive in the book, be as bold as the sheep, seek *Nirvana* with the bamboo, have a good laugh with the fig, fall in love with the tomato, or dream of a friend like the bird. You may also wish to see through the mind, relate with the rebellious rose, feel at home with the chicken, adore Professor Nutty Cream, or wonder with the potato.

You may agree with the message or not. Love it or hate it. Find faults in the poetry and art or interpret it as you wish. Simply remember: all is as it is and, as Tony Parsons emphatically states, 'Nothing is significant for nothing matters.' This message of freedom is neither the ultimate truth nor can it be bound in any theory, but if it appeals to you and there are glimpses, then relate with the verse of the famous Punjabi poet Bhai Veer Singh: 'In the dream you met me and I embraced you tight, in manner swift; there was a glow alone, you were ungraspable, kept quivering my longing wrist.' If the message permeates deep and there is a clear seeing of Oneness, just remember that there is no individual to see it and no cause to bring an effect, but life alone appearing as it is. So, read through, skim, or dive deep and see how the one appears as this myriad manifestation and wonders at its own marvel, or maybe not.

Darpana

01

Ingress – Egress

The open gate
Invites, abates
The absent one
In pathless run
To home unknown,
Immense, alone.

The unstruck sound
Appears, abounds:
As form sublime,
And rhythmic rhyme,
As breeze and blaze,
And ocean's plays,

As seen, unseen,
In ceaseless scenes;
As stars that cease,
And space in ease,
As riven grace,
Which it encases;

As grand demise,
And rearing guise,
As seeming death,
And tending breath,
As valour's core,
In silent roar;

As mind aware
That craves and shares,
Inside the urn,
Until it burns.
Endeavoured mess
Is boundlessness.

Arrive to merge,
Can one converge?
For ceaseless song
To none belongs.
One endless verse
Appears diverse.

Receives the gate,
Seems to abate.
Yet none exists
To cease in tryst,
Or end in womb
Of life in bloom.

Appears the light
As every bite,
For life is this,
Unanswered quiz.
In wonder tastes
The essence placed.

Alive, unknown,
The presence owned,
As life it glows
In wondrous shows;
Apparent, lone,
Silence, alone.

02

The Enlightened Tea

They said, ‘Make a lasting impression,
Be known, remembered as an icon,
Achieve your dreams, eternal life,
Be special and leave what is rife.’
I asked: ‘Can trails be left on waters
Of life, will not the waves them scatter?
Would I know of the colossal fame
On the cessation of my name?’

They looked and said, ‘You’ll lose the game
With your ambivalent claims.
Summits demand seminal strength,
And not a quixotic, tepid bent.’
‘Oh, don’t I have the skills to sail?
Or shallow is the worldly vale?
From whence to where does this life go?
Or, truly, does it ever flow?

From where does all thus rise?
Where does it fade or demise?
Are all forms merely an appearance,
Like a dance or a song in silence?’
They gave up hope, in certainty,
That I’d be a liability
For pragmatic individuals,
Marked me a failure: ‘Typical!’

‘Do I resume to start the climb?
Do questions mean I’ve lost the time?
Or do I complete the task at hand,
Or maybe not, but defend my stand?
Let’s just forget the mental games,
The ridicule or imagined fame.
Just enjoy a cup of tea:
Taste the joy of simplicity.

A sip of tea, a biscuit bite,
Freedom from black and white.
A gateway to eternity
Seem these scones, biscuits, jam, and tea.
They’re free of vertiginous degrees –
The biscuit crumbs and the spilt tea

That surround and mesmerise,
Impromptu, natural in guise.

Is there a further to unmask?
Or there's no time, or tea, or mask
But this immediacy alive,
Where there is no beyond, to thrive.
The simple joys of life
Surpass all claims of afterlife,
For in the errands, fare, and drink
Rests acclaim, freedom to the brink.

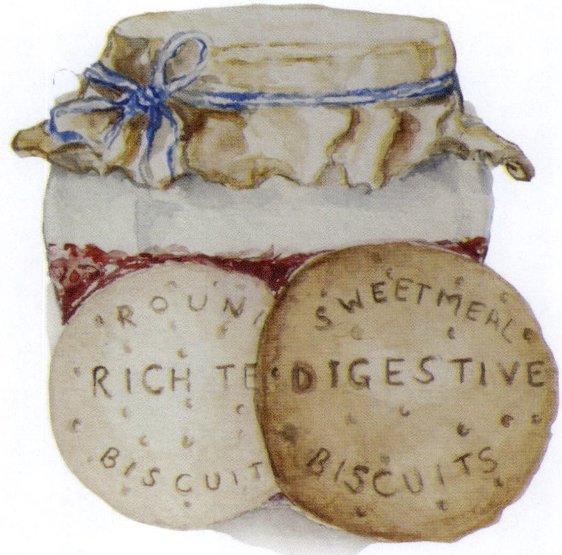

Though liberation seems to abound,
Yet is untouched, for none is bound,
And words seem trivial, confined,
In front of the flavours truly fine,
Yet nothing's vital in this game,
Tea or achievement just the same:
One is the flow and static stream,
And nothing is wrong with the dream.

Yet I won't trade my cup of tea
To leave my footprints on waters free.'

03

A Perfect Shape

An aloof and shy aubergine
Often cried for not being lean.
She sought those moments to escape,
When mocked for being out of shape,
For courgette, spinach, the French bean
Constantly made a stagy scene:
'Plain, fat with lowly taste,
Stout, shapeless, hefty waist!'
They whispered when she was around,
And in the taunts, she appeared drowned.

Dejected with her imperfect form,
The aubergine wished to reform,
Modify her persona, renew,
Conform to the regular view.
So she tried several techniques
To change natural hue and physique,
But failed to turn to 'normal' greens,
Was pained for not being trendy and lean.
She then advanced to witness her state,
But failed to sadness dissipate.

Pained by her plight – the pumpkin wise,
Finally, gave her good advice:
'O, rise above this issue small,
You don't know how you enthral all.
Untold is your being, your essence,
Endearing your flavours, influence.
See, how shaming is disguised jealousy,
A show of spurious supremacy,
For prevails insecurity,
A seeming split from totality.
It's like a beggar looking down
Upon the other beggars around;
So why feel sad for what they say?
The one's lost in the worldly play.'

Then changing tones inspirational,
He spoke in a tenor radical:
'Ponder, who leads, as in a herd,
To define 'normal' standards,
For nature appears as all its forms,
Doesn't set ideals, to conform;
So can a tree with a smooth bark
Be the archetype, defining mark?
Is thin and green the way to be
When there's no epitome of beauty?
You cannot grade an oak and bamboo,
Then why revere a shape or hue?

The caw of the crow is as divine
As nightingale's song or deity's shrine;
The cacti and the vivid rose
Are nature's own expressive shows;
And nature follows no decrees,
Is free to defy even this policy,
Appears as all forms, is free
To be structured or artless naturally;
So all that presides is perfection,
For all is one in its expression.

Illusions are all gauging scales,
For they the alive presence veil,
And make the view relative and confined,
While all that appears is the undefined.
So thin and smooth mere words alone,
With none existing on its own,
As for a day to be termed a day
Must have the night in its shadows stay,
Hence words are mere contrasting labels
Of an apparent dreamy fable.'

Continued the pumpkin his advice,
As the aubergine stayed mesmerised:
'Besides, observe the ones who tease,
Create a scene, but seem at unease.
Don't they reflect their pain
By being mean and inane?
And when they know not what they are,
Can they define your core, or mar
You? What they opine, an insular view,
How can it see the vast or true?

Yet those who bully know it not,
For they repeat the beliefs taught,
And like acquired are flavours, tastes,
By being regionally placed,
So they mime the paradigms,
Which are nothing but seeming grime.
For principles, whether old or new,
Even if shared are not true.
And none can say what is seen or heard:
It's too alive to be bound in words.'
...

Relaxed seemed the aubergine,
Listening to the song pristine,
So asked about the pumpkin's composure,
In contrast to her mental enclosure,
Probed him to clarify her din,
And serenely replied the pumpkin:
'Thoughts are being fat or thin,
To be diverse or akin,
Perfect – imperfect in the skin,
But they are simply thoughts arising
In the vast space, thy home, which stays
Unperturbed, untouched by their play.

Though at the core of suffering and long,
I am distinct from life, its song,
And life seen through the self's chasm
Curtails the vast, boundless in stratums.
And empty is this self's abyss,
Always owns or escapes what is,
Is insatiable and split
Like a bottomless pit.

Addiction is at times pursued,
Be it to me, substances, or food,
Yes, 'me' and 'mine' too an addiction,
Which seeks ceaseless admiration,
Therefore, the need for constant praise
Is the desire to calm this seeking blaze;
And more the shortage, more is sought,
And more the seeking, more the fraught.

As flowers don't need admiration
For hues, or birds for their oration,
So your censure too will fall away,
Of self and others in the play,
On seeing there is the play alone,
Without characters acting, on its own.
But recognise the self – the chase,
While you are the formless in form's grace.
Hence, the self is not your creation.
So now, do not pursue that station.

Your worthiness is your existence,
Not your silhouette or influence,
And unparalleled is every form,
So how can the perfect reform?
And nothing is useless or useful,
And none incomplete to grow full.
So do not fall for this inane game,
For love is the essence and the frame.'

Then pondered the aubergine
About the self, its ravine,
Of the radical inference –
A fusion of relief and offence.
Yet external guidance cannot aid
Silence, or calm the self's parade,
Nonetheless, it seemed to commence healing –
A shift seemingly revealing.

Later requested the aubergine
The pumpkin to advise the greens,
But quickly professed the pumpkin:

'I do not uphold any doctrines,
Or instruct how to end scission,
Nor wish to palliate anyone,
Nor intend worldwide bliss,
But say what is, as it is.
And there is no authority
To decide one's value, set one free.
All is an energetic play,
Seemingly bound or free in display.
To give an exact illustration:
Look at us gourds, our celebration;
A few are bitter, some sweet, others grey,
Some impolite, a few carefree stay,
Yet one, as a stunning applique.
And we've no guru to guide the way.

Heed, even if none admires the taste
Of the pumpkin, it is not a waste,
For it will sing its song,
Does not relate or wish to belong
To the halls of name and fame,
For life is but a game.
And, oh, Aubergine, don't forget
This general precept:
That which appears the perfect shape
Is emptiness dressed in flawless drape.'

Then shaken seemed the aubergine,
But ceased conditioning of cuisines,
Recognised life as roles unfolding,
And praise or slander nothing holding,
For none, exists, to be hurt
By a discordant concert.
So her need to change her views
Was love too, in spontaneous hues.

Though life appears just the same,
Apparently with, without the names,
A perfect shape, with none to please,
With no peg to hang the drape of unease.
Appears the one alone that is, and not,
Is not in form or formless caught:
Apparent scenes with none to choose,
Life on its own in varied hues,
Appearing as it may,
With none to follow or guide the way.
And the same remarks but none to sway
– A flawless aubergine in boundless play –
'Plain, fat with lowly taste,
Stout, shapeless, hefty waist.'

04

Home

PART 1

The Chicken Tikka Masala at JFK International Airport, New York:

The Chicken Tikka[1] weary did grow,
Awaiting his flight to Heathrow,
Which was delayed for the second time;
Now bored, he stared at the skies sublime.
Surrounded by the careless sounds and smells,
Each trying a story to sell,
Fragrances fused with the aromas of food.
While the Dior and doughnuts seemed in feud,
The announcements screamed for attention:
Peanut ice-cream sought affection.
In the seeming din and alarm,
And the range that seemed to swarm,
The coffee's intensity brought calm
To his senses, as did the psalm.

A story then captured his mind,
Remote rush inner calm did find.
Though his agreement brought felicity
– With a skilful chef from New York City –
Past visions consumed his expanse,
Images as an account did dance,

1 An abbreviation for Chicken Tikka Masala.

And though these were thoughts in the present,
They seemed like a tale of real events.

'He hailed from the north Indian cuisine,
Rooted in values of the local canteen,
And was raised heeding ancient tales
Of fearless men on vivid trails.
Celebrated was his ancestry too
For taste, philanthropy, and sinew;
His father – the Chicken Tandoori –
Was prized for succulence and fury
By most locals, and the army,
Who adored his spices stormy.

However, the Tikka never did progress,
For lack of support brought regress;
His lineage too could not accomplish
Means, as his cousins clout did establish,
For favoured were his creamy cousins –
The butter chicken and the mutton –
Over his parched versions
And small lean portions.
Then years of struggle made him take
A chance that would make or break,
So distant shores and lands he sought
To display talents, skills untaught.

He moved to London, started anew,
And a unique set of trials did ensue;
Staggered was his regular gait,
Relaxed ways, habit to delegate;
A shock to his system it did feel,
Yet to none could he his state reveal;
When locals prayed for a sunny day,
He wondered how summers could outweigh
The monsoon season, its eminence,
Crucial for life, its sustenance.[2]
He marvelled how the landscape wasn't feral;
It wasn't chaotic even in peril,
And how the clan integral
Was dwarfed by the individual,
How being curious, inclusive
Was impolite and intrusive;

To add to this, the mild, bland tastes
Of food, with volumes of food waste,
Constantly made him compare lives
Of scarcity and abundance rife.

Disgrace by mishaps, quite a few,
Made him doubt his choice to continue,
But thoughts of being termed a failure
By kin made him new land favour.
He felt he had to blend in culture new
If he wished in Britain to continue.
To learn the local conventions
He sought the second-generation,
But mixing with their music's metre
Was a game with a grand master;
So he sharpened his observation skills
To subtle retorts and unplanned spills,
Thus odours, high pitch, time's value
Were bared for scrutiny, to renew;
And, soon, perfumes, a formal stance,
A soft pitch with plans in advance
He added, to be prompt, on time,
To blend in with the local clime,
And subtle clichés, like stating 'No'
For 'Isn't it', were altered for the show.
At last, adding wit, liberality
To amenable formality,
He all with humour did combine
And his demeanour did refine.

Next, came about a transformation
In the heart of the British nation,
With curry as the favoured flavour
With boneless chicken, which most did savour.
The Chicken Tikka wholly did transform
Into Chicken Tikka Masala, his new form.
Then fork and knife became his allies,
Delighted him the new franchise.
He was welcomed in the cuisine,
And stabilised a rhythmic routine.

Yet troubled him the restless hue,
Not being home, the main issue.
Hence, he chose to visit India,

2 See Note 1a

But was forbidden by criteria:
He couldn't renew his visa or passport,
'Your restyle is refused', was the import,
For identity was the outer form,
Before biometrics was the norm.

Then change appeared without a pause,
He recalled *The Wizard of Oz,*[3]
Mustered love, bravery, and brains
Innate, demanded by the strain,
For every moment appeared unknown;
None aided and he was alone.
Uncertainty became his friend;
Values shattered – couldn't see an end.
Midst the immense chaos, turmoil,
When all seemed to come to a boil,
Fears reigned of becoming illegal,
And drained the thoughts of a refusal.

The new millennium then did arise,
And Mr Cook[4] gave a pleasant surprise:
A British dish he was declared,
Admiration with amnesty paired.

PART 2

The Chicken returned to the present,
As he smiled at the turn of events.
Yet was troubled – 'Where do I belong?' –
Wondered if disquiet would last long.
He wished his life to be a quatrain,
With perfect rhythm, rhyme, and refrain.

Soon broadcast was the flight's departure,
On board, he thought of his discomfiture,
Of his wish to be at home,
And remove the restless syndrome.

Thoughts of his first India trip
His inattentive mind did grip;
Images of the past again did sway
As his story – the visions did play.
Yet these were thoughts that rose
In the present, but as the past did pose.

'The warm winds, the welcome back
Surprised and gladdened his cold heart's lack;
Charmed: the azure skies, soil's fragrance,
The blue loti, the cuckoo's cadence,
The prattle of the parrots at dusk
– Coming home to the trees – the musk
Perfume, the bougainvillea's hues,
The cattle that seemed lost in views.
Memoirs of all the childhood games
Paraded in the mind, its frame,
Danced vestiges of misplaced life,
Which coalesced with present tastes alive,
Seized zesty tones and vibrant shades,
Enthralled diversity's parade.

A sunny break from work, formality,
Eased his aches and servility;
He sensed freedom from tags, identity
Of foreigner, hue, ethnicity;
Comforting seemed the natural
Acceptance, of the cultural
Variety, without the fears
Of being prejudiced by peers,
Or sounding politically incorrect,
And being imperfectly dressed.
As he was seduced by the variety
Of sun-kissed flavours in gaiety,
He was pleased to leave behind grey skies,
Plain meals and prosaic dyes;
This freedom from monotony,
Fluency in diction, being carefree,
Familiarity with friends,
Relations, an ease without amends,
And ineffable openness,
Along with parental largesse,
Accompanied with hospitality,
Draped his being in cordiality.

3 See Note 1B
4 Mr Cook refers to Robin Cook, the Foreign Secretary of the UK in 2001. He declared that 'Chicken Tikka Masala is now a true British national dish, not only because it is the most popular, but because it is a perfect illustration of the way Britain absorbs and adapts external influences.' He went on to explain that 'Chicken Tikka is an Indian dish. The Masala sauce was added to satisfy the desire of British people to have their meat served in gravy' (*Guardian*, 19 April 2001).

But this poise did not last long:
He was restless – 'Where do I belong?' –
For though he was received as a star,
Yet was a guest, and not at par
With the locals, so felt a distance,
With their quirks, judgemental parlance.

Soon he yearned for scents, demure attire,
And crackling pinecones in the fire;
For a prepared trip by the Thames,
And the silence of the shivering stems;
For scones, jam, and a cup of tea,
And painting seascapes by the sea;
For sanitation that seems innate,
A simple system – the normal gait;
For watching the gentleman's game
Decorously, backing the local name;
For the robin and the lavish parks,
The subtle sensitive remarks,
The value of life for all the forms,
The unsaid, non-hierarchical norm;
The advanced welfare facilities,
Non-deification of celebrities,
To all of which he was habituated,
Now vying Indians him inundated.

Then he pondered on the guideline –
That home with heart alone does align.
But Indian ethics–British lifestyle
Split his juvenile heart for a while.
Several questions did arise,
'Home is where I am' seemed wise.
Then pursued this 'I' who seeks home,
And follows a complex syndrome,
Till swamped the question 'what am "I"?'
Again, he was observed by his own eye.

PART 3

The flight attendant then did request
The Chicken to lower his armrest,
But he did not resent intrusion,
And returned from past conclusions.

From the window he began to stare
At the empty space, that seems to bear
The stunning stars, the known unknown,
Yet is the same in every zone,
With night and day in its play,
And birth and death – it doesn't sway.

He saw how space is not sequestered,
Is all around and unperturbed.
Does not accept–reject aspects,
Does not demand secured prospects,
Simply is, neither splits nor longs,
Is not anxious of where it belongs.
Has no distances, no above–below,
Neither does own nor does forgo.
Does not compare, has no in–out,
Has no levels or stars with clout,
Is emptiness in non-metrical verse,
Embracing the entire universe.

Then once again danced an array of thoughts
– Yet impartial remained the expanse sought –
He mused, 'For some immigrant kin,
Home and place of origin were akin,
And they judged cultures, favoured one,
While he was parched and fitted in none.
Sensed, sensitivity made some seek
A joy, beyond the dual streak,
While many others echoed beliefs
To offer restlessness a relief,
Related with a culture, story, place,
As home, yet stayed in another space,
Trying to fill a void illusory,
With the imagined dreams of ivory.

It also irked when locals did claim
Home was left behind, another name;
For he didn't belong to nation's domes,
But sought the natural state – Home –
And impartially served each plate,
Though now he wished to reiterate:
'That wouldn't it be a spice-less cruise
Of beans and soup, if departed diverse views,
Which would then bring about regret

For a prejudiced, white mindset,
Still prevalent though concealed
By knotty rules, etiquette's shield.'

But he knew that tempers all over the world
Are the same, a feckless game unfurled,
Where alleged nationalism
Is glorified narcissism,
And most behaviours are conditioned views
Of society, place, times, position, hues;
Where conditioning becomes the fuel
For the self to thrive, enhance its pool –
And all sulks seek the wonder of life
In this existence, being rife.

Soon the illusions came to light,
And surfaced brilliant insights;
He realised how replacing views,
And blending in a culture new,
Was changing masks for an act,
A persona new, another tact
Of small self – seeking approval
'To be' – though being unusual
Too, the need of self-small
Trying to heed the call
To be home – the true rest
Present in all the unrest.
For life was seen from linear planes,
Curbed was the mystical in inane,
While now from the vertical view,
Trivial seemed partisan hues,
Irrelevant the boundaries
And cultures, customs, decrees.

Then he again began to stare
At the space, without a care.
Wondered: the sun had seen it all,
The wind had heard the total call,
The earth had borne the vast and small,
While the waters had felt the brawl,
Yet appeared ever fresh and new,
Undeterred by the view.
While he caught in the clutches of time
Confined majestic life in grime.

It revealed he'd been the same
At all stages of life's game,
And all his thoughts, feelings too,
Were just that, not events to pursue,
While his analogies, dual claim,
His disquiet – mind's fidgety game,
Which isn't satisfied with what is,
Cloister and long for what's amiss.
All the seeking, the need to be home –
Affluence, love, or the bliss of *Om*.

As the egg gushes through the crack,
Revealed nothingness in a whack,
The Chicken seemed to lose the ground
On which he stood; the space abounds.
Now nothing seemed to make any sense,
No story, stance or influence.
A sudden shift ceased perception:
It was seen there's no volition;
The façade – the individual
That measures from its pinnacle –
And this illusion cannot home taste,
Like rest cannot be brought by haste.
No one exists to be at home,
Or create it, or aimlessly roam;
So all his seeking to be home
Was water alone, appearing as foam;
So questions – where, what, who am I? –
Were vain for they presumed that did lie
Distinct individual and hues
Of space and time, its view.

Realised: life confined in form
Adheres to set, established norms;
When appear limits of a frame,
All seems to be distinct, is named,
Feels real alleged names and place,
Which perform in time and space,
And this restraint augments illusion,
Adds to further seclusion,
Which feels suffocated, restless,
Then wishes to release the mess,
And seeks a home that is present,
Is alive, boundless, and content.

Soon as the first rays of the sun
Fell on his face, all seemed undone;
Illumined was the difference
Of dualism and deliverance.
A return to the formless base,
The nascent energetic place –
Home, which is pervasive, abounds,
Is not a place that does surround,
Is not detached space bearing the bound,
But is like innate silence in the sound –
So home or not, apparent noise,
In the midst of total poise.

It was as clear as the sky
That all appears, does pass by;
This homely presence alone does stay,
Partakes, yet untouched it does play,
Appears as the dancing rising scene,
Formless forming, natal beam.
So nothing makes its home
Here, but all seems to dance and roam,
Dancing, yet never leaving a mark,
Light alone appearing as dark.
Unjudged: belonging, possession,
Or longing for transgression.
Still judgements too appear to roam,
Without setting up their home.

Home, beyond and yet in words,
The loudest sound, unheard,
The restful silence of the womb,
And celebration of the bloom.
Home without origin or end,
An unknowing with none in it to blend.
This is it. This is Home!
Never lost... never found.

Though overwhelmed was the Chicken,
By the revelation hidden,
It was not the Chicken who got grace
Of being at home, in boundless space.
For there is no identity,
Blessed with contentment pretty,
For there's only the unknown
Appearing. All alone.
Complete, total absence
Of the one seeking home's presence.

Inquisitive to the root
Was a fellow traveller en route,
Who kept gazing at the Chicken,
By his person seemingly smitten.
He soon enquired in manner stretched and slow:
'From where do you come, and where do you go?'
The Chicken answered in tones light:
'Kind Sir, we are on the same flight.'

05

Chromatic

A sizzling lobster's sanguine hue –
A feast that feeds the senses five;
Complete, the moment is alive,
And one is submerged in the view.

Then dwindle emerging events
– As volatile are edifices –
And all converses of the chalice
Are emptied in the sea present.

Is life a journey transient?
Do objects rise and fall away?
Or is life alive forms in play?
A dance of presence immanent.

But who can capture tastes present,
So passing, lasting, play of words.
However, this taste isn't preferred,
For chillies in the dish are absent.

06

Camaraderie

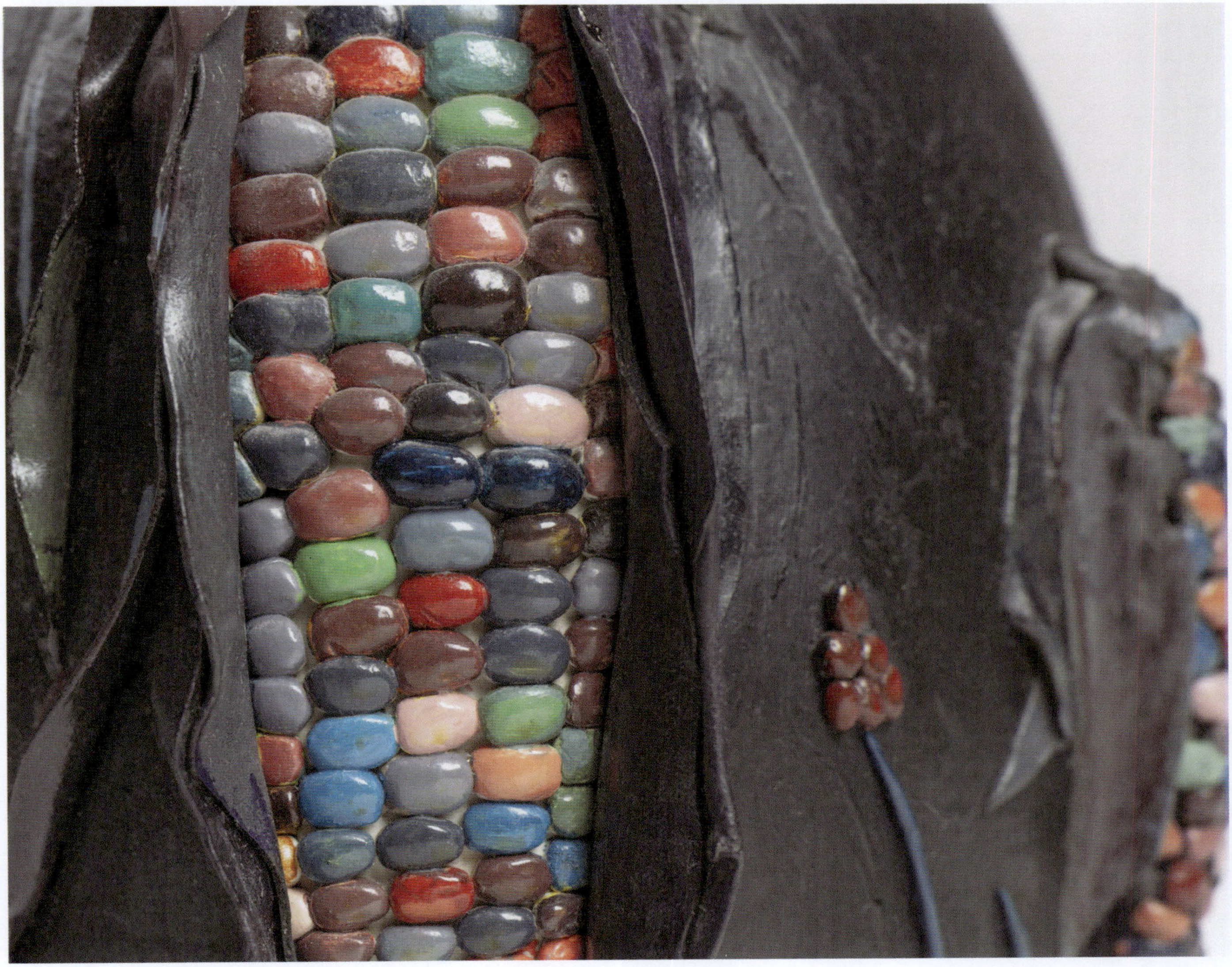

PART 1

Week 1

‘Oh, dear Corn, why are you forlorn?
Why do you pop at the slightest scorn?
Does not nature you finely adorn?
Oh, dear Corn, why are you so sad?
Are you pained by thoughts of being bad?
Does not a new dawn make you glad?

Oh, dear Corn, can thoughts “you” define?
Or your emotions thus confine?
Does not love as your form shine?
Oh, dear Corn, is your sadness truly you?
Or are you that which embraces it too?
Can the ephemeral devour you?’

Week 2

‘Oh, dear Corn, life confined in small
Self, with its sagas in time’s haul
Is stressing. The wish to free this brawl
Creates depression and anxiety,
But you are boundless, vast, and free.
Resplendent dance of energy.

Oh, dear Corn, all our names are labels,
To which attached are roles and fables,
Which have no goals fleeting–eternal,
For the formless alone does perform
As the unseen and seen forms,
Playing without and as the norms.

Oh, dear Corn, the self is a semblance,
Not an entity trapped in sequence,
So don’t be troubled by waves of occurrence.
Oh, dear Corn, you are like the sky,
Where hues and clouds paint, pour and pass by,
Though nothing is denied, yet none can it dye.’

Week 3

‘Oh, dear Corn, one’s the vast and small,
When squash and swarm thoughts, clashes then call,
Same water cycle within does haul;
But, dear, do not shun the tears,
Or gloom, for like the rains they clear
The dust, ensure growth from the fears.

Oh, dear Corn, don’t seek rest
Elsewhere, for it’s not a guest
That arrives on request,
But is the indestructible presence –
Present, in which rises all appearance,
Is love embracing. This emergence.’

Week 4

‘Oh, dear Corn! You are not charred,
You are perfect the way you are,
With all your idiosyncratic scars.
Your compassion to feed is inborn,
And many love your sustaining norm,
So, dear Corn, are you still forlorn?’

Week 5

‘Oh, dear Corn, there is no relief
Being silent, showing sangfroid in grief,
For volatile like a leaf,
It will be blown away
When storms of sadness intensely sway.
So speak! Do not disregard dismay.’

Thus, every day at early dawn,
In Iowa – the hub of corn –
Inspired the bird – her dear friend,
Who’d been miserable for days on end,
Had turned pallid in the abstruse array,
Refused to smile at her tweets or play.

For exhausted was he
By the worldly decree
That always expects one to be more,
And be the one who all adore,
From early years taxed to perform,
Excel at academia, sports, the norms.

And later traded are life’s goals,
To be blissful, positive, and whole,
Be successful and affluent,
Philanthropic and tolerant.
While life throughout takes its toll
In varied forms, beyond control.

For weeks, the corn remained in gloom:
Therapy didn’t make him bloom;
Failed all self-help techniques,
Sadness followed joyful peaks.
Even the vast expanse and serene river
Could not the corn from gloom deliver.

The corn felt he forever chased goals,
To be a self, which is to vary roles,
And his efforts to reduce despair
Seemed an oppressive affair.
The corn then reached the nadir of his life,
For being happy was laden with strife,
And now completely did stay
In depression’s hideaway.

The bird then realised that her play,
And efforts, caused her friend dismay.
The world, her desires, didn’t accept his tears,
For labels – negative and weak – all fear.
While her prattle seemed like endeavour
He should perform to recover.

The practices and therapies too
Put onus on the personal view,
Or guided from parallel routes,
None pointed to the absolute,
Which alone is the relative view,
So non-volitional each hue.

Yet she wished her friend would recognise
That love as this life does arise;
Suffering isn’t a result of actions past,

Freely dance joy and sorrow in the vast.
But then she realised dual was her claim
To end individuality's game;

For none is on the merry-go-round
Of self, to it purge, or be bound,
So neither depression is volitional
Nor the apparent individual.
A shift in the bird now did seem
To desire change, another dream.

Unravelled the split of two,
Fulfilled then seemed all lack too.
Was obvious: there are no split souls
To be elevated – the whole
Appearing as the corn and the bird,
The seen, the unseen, the heard, unheard.

But love is despair's doorway
That illuminates the play,
So the bird would come at dawn each day,
Sit beside her friend and play,
With no peripheries
Of joy and misery.

Nothing remained except presence,
No bird, or corn, but innocence;
Just the appearance of her friend,
Sad, but alive, without pretence.
Yet witnessed only the elements five –
This camaraderie alive.

PART 2

The corn once abruptly did say:
'A bond so rare with me did stay.
Your friendship and love I never saw;
Always a sense of dearth did gnaw.
So lost was "I" in my world,
Unseen remained life that unfurled.

I was sullen, life did not go "my" way,
Compared with others in the play;
Then saw life through my saga, state,
Longed love and approval on my plate
For how I am, not how I ought to be,
I was unmindful of love that does decree.

I deemed all passing incidents
As life in ceaseless imprisonment;
Then reacted to each occurrence,
Was drained by the deluge of experience.
Felt thoughts and feelings were mine and real,
For split of life love did conceal.

Tried to project a perfect guise,
And then protected a self-agonised.
Forever rushed and stayed busy,
Thus avoided feelings uneasy.
Denied what is, only wished delight,
Suffered when sadness was in flight.

Self-help techniques and therapy
Brought fleeting calm and clarity;

Return of crushing feelings, heat,
Was deemed as personal defeat,
That my endeavours were inadequate
To recuperate from despair's weight.

Believed being and doing are two,
And I was thrown in life's stew,
Then pursued peace in an unknown
Future, and always stayed forlorn.
Did not see life alone does play,
So no way to live, none to trail a way.'

Then cried the overwhelmed corn,
As he spoke of love unborn:
'The freedom in your presence,
Immensely deep, vast in essence –
I haven't seen a love so complete,
A friendship so genuine and sweet.

My impatience or depressed hue
Neither disturbed nor distressed you.
By no means did you preach or leave,
Nor did you judge or any hope weave,
And you didn't despise or berate me,
As the one ignorant, not free.

Instead, the reverence you have shown
For life, all its forms, known–unknown,
Even sadness, the mess, its storms,
Is like the formless embracing forms,
Or eternal honouring the transitional,
A love that is unconditional.

You revealed authentic freedom,
Unravelled fantasy's fiefdom,
Which deems self is separate from life,
And then forever feeds the strife,
Depression is the desire to end
This illusion, its stories of intent.

Unveiled: unsplit the sun, its light,
The tides and sea, the vast and tight,
Likewise, one appears as me and you,
So I wasn't liable for depressed hues,
For nothingness that's vast and boundless,
Appears as this rest and its mess.

Simply the rising occurrence new,
With no individual in view –
A boundless freedom from all norms,
Yet embracing its every form.
Such compassion I have never seen,
Past expectation, acceptance unseen.

You've illumined the love that is,
Is unbound, without an axis,
A love so near and intimate
That every breath does celebrate:
Unconditional love beyond compare,
A camaraderie without a pair.'
…

In sharing submerged suffering
The split ceased, and time's casing.
To this day the friends play and dance,
Enjoy the weather, the expanse.
Famed has become the corn's recipe
And the bird's love, beyond entropy.

07

The Unending War

'Chop his head! Guillotine!
Dice, slice, or cut its shoots green;
Slay the messenger, instil fear,
Destroy the onion, use means severe.
How dare he say we can't take part,
And be adorned by the chef's art.'
Shouted the annoyed Meat Prince,
Who along with his cousin Mince
Was waiting for a chance
To establish their stance,
To rout vegetarianism
Be rid of sectarianism.

The Meats despised the label:
Of being unspiritual,
Unsuitable for ritual,
Raising passions cruel,
In an alleged holy nation,
Where vegetables drew laudation
For their qualities and talent,
Of being healthier and gallant.
The cousins felt they were exceptional,
For they had proteins plentiful,
Yet had not received a due name
Or role in competition famed:
'The food festivity in flow',
Televised as a cooking show.

The King of Meats then opined
In tones devious, yet refined:
'Strip, slice, dice, all ways try,
Chop its head, be mean and sly,
But all along you alone will cry,
So don't even thus reflect or try,
For he is an emissary,
And this is unnecessary.
It is political suicide,
Will lead to further genocide.
Besides, the gruesome hidden stress
Will bring forth dispute in excess;
This will lead to an unending war,
Where death alone will score.
So never hurt an envoy –
Don't be foolish in your ploy.'

'But this is complete injustice,
Towards our lot, malice.'
Bawled the proud and young Meat Prince,
Accompanied by cousin Mince.
'Be silent and let me plan,
And see how it all began,'
Declared the King in a sombre tone,
Indicating he wished to be alone,
To think of schemes devious,
To win yet seem oblivious.

The King of Meats then did contact
The television channel, for a pact,

Offered a potential to grow –
To all related to the show
Promised proteins of value,
Riches and fame enjoyed by few.
But the Meats demanded prominence,
More than the Greens, their holy nonsense.

The meeting seemed uncongenial,
As the director was partial
To the Greens, refused to be overshadowed
By the King's inducement and show.
Before taking leave, the King said:
'Prepare for a lawsuit instead:
I will call for investigation
Based on segregation,
Place a concrete refutation,
Thus ruin your reputation.'

The King called a press conference
To stall the show, and the public influence.
Yet he declared to the press:
'I truly wish for the progress
Of the Greens, to have their own show,
And in the chef's ingenuity grow.
I've seen these solitary souls
Aren't given a prominent role
In the field of food and nutrition,
And are relegated to the position
Of a side, or necessary ordeal,
Be it a banquet, treat, or daily meal.
So out of choice compassionate,
Meats would abstain from a show great.'

After a pause, he made a claim
For the Meats, their stance and aim.
Said: 'Yet if it pleased the audience,
The Meats would join without grievance,
For we believe in public vision –
Gladly accept the mass decision.'
Thus, with perfect manipulation,
The King aided agitation,
For beliefs seemed to divide
The public, who chose a side.

Though resolved had been the Prince of Meats
To solve the matter with war and heat.
In the whole conspiracy
Of contempt and jealousy,
Of passionate beliefs and pretence,
Departed wisdom and common sense.

At last mediated the salt,
Whom several foods did exalt:
She reflected equity and concern
And expected nothing in return.
Did not differentiate or divide
Life, as a mineral did reside
Innately, in all the foods,
Yet was untouched by their attitudes;
Was without the split, without an aim,
Slayed all imagined claims.

Then addressing the factions two,
She said: 'Crass to divide the view,
Vegetables or meat whose flesh is pure,
When energy alone is all contours.
All is alive, when truly seen,
So why split life in meat and green?
No form is devoid of life:
Movement or not, all is alive.
So lost are you all in false games
That you've forgotten life's the same;
Yet none exists to claim actions,
So who to blame for grading fractions?'

Interrupted the Prince of Meats:
'By words do not us cheat.
Your wisdom is hatred in disguise –
This idealism we do not prize.
The fittest alone will survive:
These stuck species cannot strive.
War alone makes sense,
Where we will win – no suspense.'

The King intervened in a way impulsive:
'Quiet! Do not be conclusive.
Remember the salt plays no roles,

Is untouched by slander, praise, control.
Let her finish what she has to say;
Maybe it would benefit in some way,
For don't forget the Meats and Greens
Every moment greet death unseen,
So stop this silly rattle of "WAR",
For you know death I greatly abhor.'
Gritted his teeth the Prince of Meats,
Winced his cousin the Mincemeat.

'A slave to your egoistic roar,
You are already at war.
For war is your very nature,
As "You" in it feature.
Your peace too is akin to war,
For you negotiate with waves on the shore.'
The salt said in an equitable tone
To the Meat Prince, seated on his throne.

The salt then left the Royal Hall
Without a warning or a call,
Came outside in the garden
– The home of nature, spartan –
Followed the groups, joined the community.
Dragged was the Prince, by the King's decree.

Later, continued the salt:
'Illusory are all your vaults,
In which you stow delusion;
Rather, you are the illusion.
For nature as attributes does play,
Delicate, dense, or free – its display,
With none being bound in the clay,
Yet an appearance this buffet,
Where believes the self – illusory –
That it performs the activity.

You all believe the reason for war
Is negative traits that roar,
Of segregation, racism, nationality,
Capitalism or bad mentality.
While at the core of all brutality
Is individuality.

The problem isn't vegetables or meats,
But lack that stems from being incomplete,
Which stems from the sense of self that seems
Separate from the appearing theme,
Which splits the Oneness of existence,
And leads to further ignorance.

For life pretending to be separate
Appears to curb the formless innate
In forms small, seemingly in time
And space, with stories sad-sublime;
This split: the commencement of war,
Which then fights the split to restore,
Wishes to unite with its essence
Infinite, its omnipresence.
Desires to end its apparent course
And return to its natural source;
For there's a feeling of loss, being wrong,
And broken – the unbroken song;
For it's lost in self – a pretence,
Thus cannot see its own essence.
But the more it strives, the more it seems
Further from life's present theme.

This appears in the food species
Alone, that by illusion's decree
Is lost in ignorance
Of individual appearance
Of a small self, its parameters,
Which wishes to protect its sectors.
As this species is smart
To glorify its art,
So formed are nations and a race,
Religions and social place.
Then to sustain the self, the collective,
Woven are fables and perspectives.
And reinforced is the whole game
For survival of the apparent name.

Gluttony, goods, and games take charge,
Which then fail to fill a mirage,
Believe their possessive streak
Will protect and fill a gulf or creek,

But this greed is insatiable,
Stays till appears an individual.
Even when the self is at peace
With others, it is not at ease:
It is at war within its lair
– For its very nature is warfare –
As it divides its kingdom,
To fight guilt, shame, or boredom,
For it wishes to end its dual feature,
But cannot as illusive is its nature.

Even if one's tolerant, proclaims all
Is Oneness, wars would never stall.
Read the apparent history
Of your type, which you state with glory.
It is nothing but war: us versus they,
Or me and you – reasons many to weigh.
For whether a war of states, religions,
A race, siblings, cousins, or immigrants,
And in the mind; all stem from the same source –
The self and its seeming course.

So, your race to end the 'isms' –
A band-aid, not a cure for the schism.
For you can't escape the illusion
Of self and its seeming delusion.
So even if you seek ways anew
To fill the gulf that seems to peace pursue,
It will further complicate,
Appear to sedate.
This I speak of an apparent tale
Of the food sapiens and their trail,
But all is life alone,
Appearing as known–unknown,
Appearing to be far from home's presence,
Trapped in the altars of self's ignorance.
For all is simply a play
Of one in myriad display.'

'You speak as if you know all;
You cannot the world stall
By your sermon fallible.
Not everyone is gullible.'
Shouted the Prince of Meats
In manner rude and indiscreet.

Ignoring him, the salt did say:
'Even your courage, tricks, foul play,
Or sincere efforts can't establish
Oneness, or make the rift vanish;
For Oneness isn't a philosophy
Or a tool to transcend entropy;
It's this appearance be it ignorance
Or the seeming intelligence.
For freedom is never from life,
But recognition – life's without strife,
For life is life, with no norms,
Appears as all, alone performs;
It neither comes nor goes away,
Does not become the role it plays.
It is an untouched apparent glow,
Undivided, yet seeming rainbow.
So who will destroy whom with their ploys?
Or be destroyed or victory enjoy?
Which form is pure or impure, or with clout,
When there's no division, in or out?
Who can unite with Oneness?
For life appears as the dual mess.

Don't you two dare and act,
Right now, forsake your foolish tact!'
Screamed the salt, looking at the Prince
And his devoted cousin Mince.
'The Greens are skilled in technique,
Are not fragile or meek;
They will retaliate with ease,
As they won't separate war and peace.
You Meats will starve if the Greens die.
Oh, Prince! Don't be foolish in your cry
Of war, that you forget its scale
Devours everything in its trail.
And it's certain no one will win:
Winners aren't slaves to self's din,
And all of you have ceded innate peace
To the apparent self's warring caprice.'
The Prince and his cousin froze,

Seeing the salt's frightening pose.

Then, chiding the King of Meats,
She said in a tone firm and neat:
'King, if you weren't blinded by attachment,
By the illusory parental passion,
The Prince wouldn't be at war,
Augment the destructive lore.
There's none to inherit a name,
No dynasty to pass the flame,
Precisely no one, no relatives
To claim, and nothing imperative
In this life, no continuity,
Or formlessness in eternity.
Besides, you believe I've reached a state
That you haven't, but I have no gait;
I don't have an approach to act:
Life the salt's form does enact,
So here, there may be war or peace;
Freedom appears in both, the crease.

Oh, King, your structures serve no more –
There's no hierarchy at life's core;
The food chain does not prove in any way
That predator is higher than the prey.
Life's an apparent recycling theme
To sustain seeming cycle in the dream.
The act alone is in appearance,
Without one to own its presence,
So what scales of evolution
When form is life's celebration?
Let the Greens and Meats express
The aptitude they seem to possess
Without the fear of persecution
Or the fear of starvation,
For none decides which structure is good.
Yet don't force me to destroy thy brood.'

Ashamed seemed the King of Meats,
But eager to hear the salt complete.
Unaffected seemed the Prince
And his toady cousin Mince.
The salt continued to share
Her homily free and rare
On the request of the King of Meats,
Who wished the Prince to become complete:
'Though war is an expression
Of energy, an illustration –
For all that does appear
Is energy in varied gears,
And wars may still appear to transpire,
Even if extinguishes the self, its fire,
For an individual
Doesn't exist to have choice. The natural
Alone appears on its own,
None to own it or it disown –
But this message is not to be lazy,
Or kill, go seemingly crazy.
Simply stating there is no one
That kills or dies, for all is none,
Implies the message hasn't been heard,
Is parroted, its sages unheard,
For this is not a view to perceive
Or a missive all should believe,
For that would be another principle
To chase falseness and evade the essential.

So don't feel you can get away
By stating all is just a play,
For you're being burnt in this furnace
Of life and its miraculous mess.
If you apparently do slay,
You will have to apparently pay,
For energy in its appearance,
Appears as per the ordinance.'

The salt continued her narration,
But now she shifted her attention
To the Greens' kingdom:
'All are slaves to their fiefdom.
Dare you follow a narrow process,
Abuse power, create a mess,
Or practise hierarchy, servitude,
Oligarchy, holy attitude?
I will destroy your form too,
Bring entropy without a clue.

For I cannot tolerate abuse
Of any kind. I'm not a recluse.
And what I say is beyond the norms,
And yet appears as all the forms;
So don't attempt to comprehend
The missive, without any intent.'
Shaken seemed the food nation,
By the salt's perception.
…

The salt still did not seem to halt,
Continued her assault
– It seemed she was in a hurry
So rushed with her melody –
This time on the community,
Who did not seem in unity,
For they were swayed by the feud,
Of which foods to include
In the cooking show most viewed.
'Have any of you truly tasted food?
No, for you're ever doing business,
Counting calories, its value, holiness,
Always dividing foods in groups of two,
Healthy–unhealthy – a belief to pursue,
Or eat as per the fashion,
Even if the fare's disposition
Isn't agreeable to the form,
Or the environment, not uniform.
Split and seek to fill a bottomless pit,
Blame food for seeming benefit.
Identify with the illusions,
Enhance division, its delusions.
Even flavours of your favourite foods
Are filtered by your attitudes,
For all of you are dead before death,
Kill life in every breath.
Stay lost in your thoughts and story,
That unnoticed is life's glory,
Where a miracle is every bite,
Intense, love's impartial invite.

Have any of you reflected, thought,
Why you are all divided, fraught?
Why do you ignore the Oneness
– That stares – for ignorance and stress.
Why do you need acknowledgement

SEA
SALT

From the ones who seem to present
The rules of how one should be.
Where do you wish to fly, to be free?

Remember, your form does not care
About your rules, fair or unfair;
It is alive, intelligent,
And present, doesn't need your consent
To survive or be alive,
For it on its own does thrive.
Yet none of you listen to your form,
Just blindly follow dead norms,
Intensify captivity
Of self, its activity,
Rage in the name of principles,
Ignore this life – a miracle,
Implying catastrophe is near,
Destroyed will be all gears.
It seems the thrust will soon destroy
Itself, by its own ploy.
STOP BEING AT WAR…'

As the salt addressed the nation
About the confined situations,
In gushed gusts and torrential rain,
Wiping away the salt's every grain.
Merged in the waters, the salt,
Who most adored, did exalt
For her liberated hue
And non-conformist views.

The suddenness of the incident
Shocked some, made others silent.
Some grieved, while others did believe
That they alone were bereaved.
The Greens felt they had lost a guide,
Unseen, unbiased, without pride.
A few were glad of her disappearance:
They wouldn't have to listen to her defence,
Though most forgot the incidence
And that form isn't the end of presence.

Mystified was the King of Meats,
Yet seemed complete in the incomplete,
Proclaimed: 'In the salt's unfinished verse,
Buried was the silence of the universe.'
Then silent, he stared at the scene,
Empty, dazzled by the unseen.

The Meat Prince was still indignant,
His cousin Mince indifferent.
An icy glance the two did share,
Were vexed by reactions of despair.
The duo still sought vengeance
On the Greens for their fake ascendance;
And thus they charred in the fire
Of wrath, for seem to transpire
The inherent elements
In the act that's apparent –
As the fire burns in anger,
The waters drown in sorrow's clangour.

Observed was the missive's hue
In varied forms old and new:
A few imbibed it in their heart;
Others compared it to abstract art;
Some repeated the salt's diction;
Others competed, added fiction.
A handful felt they recognised the secret;
Others posited it in papers piquant;
A certain few thought merging the Meats
With the Greens was a complete treat.
In ways countless and diverse
Appeared freedom's boundless verse.
But no belief can bind this freedom,
For it alone appears without a kingdom,
So ruin it or say it as it is,
All is it – and none's in the abyss –
For all is energy alone,
Free or enchanted, on its own.

Soon forgotten was the story,
The message, the allegory.
The food show went on as arranged,
Yet there seemed a change in the unchanged.
A timeless song – the unending war,
Energetic this apparent lore.

08

Frangipane Art

A fly observed the illusion's web
Of separation, its fantasy.
She feared, yet echoed with the ebb,
Was unstuck, yet hoped she'd be free

Of trite delusion and dominion,
Of chattels and reverberating forms,
Hierarchy and free opinion
Of beings, who seem to perform.

The fly assured by propitious signs
Deemed she'd be served an ornate cuisine,
And cleared would be the web, its twine,
By the patisserie chef, unseen.

The spider who evinced the web and show
Tempted the fly for heavenly treats.
The fly engrossed in the ebb and flow
Was rapt, but she knew she was his meat.

The cautious fly agreed, if chef
Patisserie he'd become, to prepare
A frangipane tart (without a cleft)
With apricots, roasted nuts, and pear.

The fly to evade the apparent
Assumed digression's the perfect way,
For ardour for the piece diligent
Would keep the spider at length, away.

For she believed she could oversee
That pleasure, creativity, and fame,
Would engulf, palliate, and free
The spider, his ideas and game.

The spider effortlessly did accede,
Tirelessly trained as a chef,
Seemed swayed by the creative field
And his art riveting and deft.

Yet he knew the real is not concealed,
And as the unreal does play,
Perpetually is revealed,
Is not at a distance or away.
...
The fly was called to the patisserie
When it received a Michelin star;
Her visit was full of amity:
They shared a tempo bizarre.

The fly, sure in her conviction,
Unwound at the emerging events,
For to her utmost satisfaction,
The advent of love did descend.

Scrumptious was the frangipane tart
With jam and almonds infused well,
A dazzling, radiant piece of art,
Where pears and apricots cast a spell.

Mesmerised by the tart and tea,
Smitten by the energetic march,
The fly could no further see:
The frangipane became the gorge.

The spider, neither dual, non-dual,
Observed the urge of predator–prey,
Laid bare the frangipane – the jewel –
The web was never in the way.

Who was the king remains unknown:
The spider, life, or the frangipane.
La Galette des Rois bears the throne –
Epiphany alone does reign.

Feast of
PHANY

09

The Leaning Pizza

A Pizza drenched in ale and wine
Followed a routine without guidelines;
He would drink until his dough would smell,
And he was inebriated, all could tell;
Then he would climb the leaning tower,
Create a scene like airy flour,
Would voice his mind on the divine,
Wood fired, he'd fearlessly shine.
Cheese, meats, and olives few
Adored his winsome ways and views,
And felt at ease in his presence –
Releasing yet embracing essence.

He shared a new fact every day,
Was too drunk to care of hearsay.
Many assumed he wasn't in senses,
While others laughed at his expense;
A few felt his outlook was profane,
While tourists thought he entertained.
The sacred city only did witness
And his existence then did bless,
Were aware his prating couldn't alter truth,
Like a wave can't enervate the ocean smooth.

Pizza's prattle – Day 1:

'All ask me, "Oh, where were you made?
In the tawdry lanes of Italian shade?
Or gilded empires of ancient date,
Or in the kitchen of a rich estate?"
Am I the blessed bread's heir?
Will I rear the dynasty fair?
Does not each grain on earth, "me" bear?
So why limit in the Creeds rare?
What lineage and which labels presume?
Who can anyone's sins assume?
Silly, senseless, pizza *pazzo*, all does seem
One light as sinners–saints do gleam.

Consider how the saints the sinners secure,
While in sinners' shadows, saints mature,
Appear some sinners in a saint's attire,
Yet one alone as all does transpire.
Even when ends this frame, the form,
I ever exist as peace, perform.

The river of life seemingly does flow,
Simmering as the nascent cheese aglow,
"*Buono come il pane*"[1] – my account,
Heavily drunk, reveals its fount,
And though it beatifies me in name,
It is apocryphal in its game.'

Then giggled the Pizza on his puns,
Later continued when laughed none.

'Though this life seems much like a river,
Which seemingly fluctuates like quicksilver,

---

1 *Buono come il pane* is an Italian idiom that literally means 'As good as bread' or 'As good as gold'. It is used to describe a good-hearted or generous person (one with a heart of gold). Food is metaphorically used in many idioms in Italy, indicating the importance of food in Italian culture.

When it emerges – innocent and pure –
And when it merges – broad and unsure –
Fades in the sea, loses identity,
Oh, nutty pizza! Is there an entity?
For nothingness in itself does cease,
Another name for eternal peace –
Though I love the creamy cheese
That burns with me and melts with ease.

Life is, isn't fashioned by a pair,
Isn't sired, nor is the heir;
It alone without frontiers does shine,
Isn't split, but is like grape and wine,
So birth and death, not contrary,
And pairs – an appearance solitary.

One, love as varied life does grace,
Heaven–hell isn't an Italian place.
Though riches of the confined wisdom,
Forget this is heaven's kingdom –
The kingdom of *Dio,*[2] its presence,
One is existence–nonexistence.
Still to refuse to dine and wine,
Denial of appearance fine,
Is the rejection of the divine,
That as everything does shine.'

Pizza's prattle – Day 2:

'In His own image fashioned the divine
The pizza, to rule over provision's shrine.
What does this imply? That fills life –
An Old Pizza, in souls – who stay in strife –
Witnesses their acts. Judges night and day,
To end with love or in complete dismay.
Is *Dio* callous or a trader vain,
That with a day's pause seems to reign?
Besides, think and say, did God create a pizza?
Or did pizza create God in Pisa,
With *Dio*'s hand and finger sticking out,
To garnish the pizza who messed His clout.'

The Pizza then with laughter did choke,
Resumed, did not renew the joke.

'Rumbles and roars the secret pellucid,
That *Dio* is this, alive, not rancid,
For it isn't small to be curtailed in form,
But infinite, to fit in any norm.
Any impression or appearance
Cannot describe divine presence;
Even the term 'formless' incarcerates
The boundless, that as forms does emanate.

God creating pizza in His own image
Means it alone revels as each visage,
So all forms are the performance
Of the *Dio*'s divine presence.
Finite and infinite God alone,
None separate to claim, makes known,
Though it appears dual, yet is one,
Creator and creation – same, one pun.
Still, I don't like my foe – the flan –
For it follows a seraphic plan,
Carouses for its advantage
And feigns celestial vantage.

Are we a form small, born in sin?
Awaiting God's gracious break in
To deliver us from the grip
Of an alleged forefather's slip;
Does not sin imply the illusion
Of separation, its seclusion?
And where the sin is of identities –
The world and I are in different degrees –
Where pizza creates and places God
High above, then to embrace the Lord,
Conceives a fancy story,
With customs of alleged glory.

While in this natural living called life –
No god or pizza, no husband or wife.
Nothing and none to interact,
Life alone carousing its act;
Rather an emptiness that is complete,
Dio – pizza, not two, one rhythmic beat.
Life drunk and savoured to the hilt,
Without the drunken pizza's guilt.'

2 *Dio* is the Italian word for God.

Pizza's prattle – Day 3:

The Pizza in his lively ways,
Again, unravelled the play,

Averred:
'Acceptance and love that are complete
Aren't targets to practise or meet
Where a pizza accedes, is amenable,
Or ethical, flexible, or tenable.
For love of *Dio* is vast, unbound,
Is in the kind and the unkind, abounds,
Not the *amore* we see around, believe,
Which cadges and hopes only to receive,
Enjoys the service of a whore,
But her presence prefers to ignore.
And which deems fine alcohol,
But drunkards must refine their shortfall;
Which deems carousal – vagaries of youth –
And drunkards far from the truth –
Who should refine their wayward ways –
Yet regard wine as sacred when they pray.

Addiction is surely mind's game:
A flight to find fabricated frame,
To fill an abyss which doesn't exist,
To veil the appearing scene with mist.
Yet energy appears as all, the same,
One presence being infinite in name.
For nothing's forsaken by the divine,
As it alone partakes, does shine,
Is love complete, undivided,
Is singing this song unguided;
Immeasurable is this brilliance of life,
Unmatched to any treasure or afterlife.'

Saying these words, the Pizza blacked out –
Death. Resurrection without a doubt.
But a peculiar event then did appear:
The Pizza was struck sober and disappeared.
By force or not, none can declare
But his friends for him offer prayers.
The cause of his disappearance
None can know. Such is the brilliance:
Like water can't wet its essence,
Or flowers smell their fragrance;
Yet we shouldn't perceive the unreal
As real and treat it as an ordeal.
...

He has not ceased, for many call on him.
In Russia, with fishes filled to the brim,
There as the *Москва*[3] he is known,
But the Russians aren't alone,
For countless from their stance see him.
Global, yet local, all sing his hymns.
He also blesses the fifty states
With pepperoni, in the United States.

In India, *paneer* joins his dance,
While *crème fraîche* connects in France;
The Dutch and Brazilian cuisine
Love him doubled, or with peas green.
Revel the sauces, egg, and squid
On Japanese and Australian grid.
While the Swedes and Norwegians
Adore him and his sweet seasons.

Margherita alone reigns everywhere,
And each garnish is the Pizza's prayer.
He is all around yet seen by none;
All him revere to be undone,
Yet he isn't distant like the sun,
Around which revolve the lesser ones,
For he seems like the presence that abounds,
Or fragrance that flower does surround.
And though his jargon's simple and clear,
Illuminating the frontiers that appear,
Still several wonder the secret writ
Of which topping ceases the split.

3 *Москва* pizza is a famous Russian pizza. It has a combination of four types of fish (tuna, sardine, mackerel, and salmon) and is garnished with onions and herbs. It is known for its strong odours and taste.

10

The Unsaid Words

The grand Himalayan Range
Remains untouched and unchanged
By passing winds that ever blow,
With change in their wings slyly stowed,
To reveal the singular essence
Of eternal – yet fleeting – presence.

Here raised are floral orchids rare,
Which share their precious fragranced flair,
While the chaste, chilled massif air
Cultivates herbs to ailments dare.
The sundry palettes adorn the sky,
And flamboyant birds dance and pry.

Here chatty monkeys chase and cheer,
Languidly gaze the lost deer;
The clouds cuddle the mountain tip
The breath of burning wood does grip,
And borne is staunch, stoic silence,
By the natives inured to absence.

The skies and upraised terrains
Guard the wonder lost in the plains,
While the candid, feral splendour
Conveys naïveté extempore,
And the unsullied atmosphere
Stresses naturalness austere.

In this serene and scenic view
Distressed was a young bamboo;
He sought life's goal, to fully know
The source and purpose of the show,
So neither could he eat nor grow,
Or ground the self in heights of snow.

Seeing the bamboo suffer
In this pristine wonder,
Advised him the friendly Five-Spice
To be in presence of Master Rice,
Who lived in the valley of the Range,
And was untouched by all exchange.
…

In the presence of Master Rice
He sensed resonance of paradise:
Appeared a shift without success,

Compassion alone, deprived of process;
All prior lessons seemed unlearnt,
Divine confusions fully burnt.

Emerged the salient message
That transient is the self, its image,
And *Nirvana*[1] is the permanence
Of the unconditional essence,
While meditation is not bliss,
And *Dharma* is life as it is.

No substance is at the heart
Of everything, that's not apart.
Emptiness is, but never found,
Fulfilment in it does abound.
Pleasure and pain appear to flare,
But no distinct soul they bears.

Acts simply arise on their own,
And none with power on the throne,
For transpires the formless as the form,
Yet it doesn't sire, but alone performs
As the apparent scene,
Silence sounding – truly pristine.

Yet all this seemed like a philosophy,
Espoused in a monastic colony,
So sought the innocent bamboo
To cross the mountains of rue,
And attempted to end the din
Of teachings, which illumine.

The bamboo chose to seek permission
Of Master Rice to quit tradition.
Although en route to Master Rice
Rose recognition, past all price,
That there is none to hold or quit,
Or bond or merge or wait or submit.

There stayed only silence vast –
Remained no present, future, past.
Disappeared the suffering of thoughts,
Along with displeasure of life sought,
Remained no hope or special bliss,
Ceased the celestial and the abyss.

Overwhelmed by the insight,
Sat down the bamboo upright
In the presence of the sky,
The mountains that are high,
And the humble valley in view
That bears the flow of each hue.

Then recognition of the real –
A jolt – the unique self did steal,
Split weren't viewer and the view,
Remained nothing, not one or two.
Disappeared the known–unknown –
Nothing to own, disown.

As finished all the inverse
In the bareness of the verse,
So now, laid bare the empty form
Emptiness that as form performs,
Like the allegory of the wheel,
Stillness as rhythm did reveal.

Yet all that seemed to occur
Appeared as a timeless stir,
Then after this taste new,
Disappeared the timeless too.
Ended the dream, the need to waken
To empty skies and void unshaken.
...

1 See Note 2A

In this void, naked presence,
Alive was the empty silence,
With none present in the presence
Except the act in appearance;
Appeared an absence that is free
Even from the absentee.

As no longer reigned the insular skies,
Or the caucus of 'us', or the 'I's,
It was seen life happens on its own,
Even the suffering that's borne
Is life deeming all happens to a 'me',
While all there is is the occurrence free.

A prismatic parade of acts,
Emerging life, nothing abstract,
Silence, sound, just this, no peak,
Real, unreal playing hide and seek.
Silence singing euphonious sounds
And cacophony of the bound.

Now, in this no-thing, the naught,
With naught to defend, self or not,
Apparently emerged compassion
For each emerging impression.
Just beingness, completely free,
Open to vulnerability.

Though no amount of discipline,
Or its lack, did illumine
The innocent young bamboo
Of the Himalayan view.
For neither does *Nirvana* transpire,
Nor can one *Nirvana* acquire.
…

Weeks later

Once in the presence of Master Rice
The bamboo seemed in ease past price;
Yet Master Rice had never said
A single word to embed ease, or to shred,
So words had always remained –
Unsaid, Unheard, Unattained.

In this familiar silence,
Remained ordinary presence,
An emptiness energetic,
Incompleteness complete, unpoetic.
Emptiness playing as the bamboo
With no one it to view.

The bamboo then took leave from Master Rice,
To start a canteen known as 'Spice'.
Tofu, mushroom, goat, and bamboo
Presents he, in a look anew,
Flavours intense infused by he,
In rice, *tsampa, thukpa,* and tea.

Get together locals to experience
Fulfilled food in this presence,
Where no one claims the labour,
And where alive is each flavour;
Yet judge and define the populace –
The presence – and make it onymous.

Appears the bamboo without the dream,
Just simple life by the stream,
Surrounded by the Himalayan peaks,
The flora, fauna, and the creek.
Simple life of cooking, cleaning,
Shouting, chopping, crackling, steaming.

11

A Dessert in the Desert

Revealed the ineffable message
The blowing winds, the seething sun,
And the scarce waters – of a date
Incredible, who spoke of One –

To a beetle who resided on the tree,
And saw the dates emerge year after year,
And thought the silent tree distinct
From its fruit, both in seeming frontiers.

(The absolute message of Oneness
– Revealed to the date, illumined by nature –
Is split in formless-form and timeless-time
By One, as the beetle of dual features.)

'A date suitable for the desserts,
Illustrated the desert's emptiness,
And sifted through the sands of time,
To seek fulfilment of Oneness.

He sensed seclusion in every cell,
But could not quench his thirst
By the love of those who admired him,
Found in his presence hymns unrehearsed.

The fig and olive admired him,
While barley crepe aspired to his love;
The yoghurt and rice stayed close;
Honey and grape sought true love.

He did not want to follow faith
By bribe of an unknown reward,
Or fear, so sought meditation's solace:
Intimate, boundless, crossing the ford.

Yet not rumination or indifference,
Or sitting still or faith of paradigms,
But a fulfilment that is complete,
Beyond all the ordered rhymes,

A silence that permeates all the acts,
Is echoed by the sands and crevices,
Is timeless, yet seemingly timed,
And is untouched by genesis.

Blinded he was by light sublime,
In the complete dark and divide.
An undivided light that embraces all,
Being compassionate – as life does reside.

Desert and dessert both gave way,
And all at once there remained none.
Appeared performance alone –
Undone was split of two and one.

Disappeared known and the unknown:
The light alone absorbed in play,
Sovereignty of Oneness in glow,
A celebration, no conflict to sway.

Yet this was not the date's experience,
But formless forming, as it may,
A stirring silence – volcanic,
Without another in the way.

With none to control the show,
He echoed the message of the one,
Said: 'None can own the glowing message,
For all there is and isn't is One,

Not like the pot that holds the stew,
But light as prismatic hues sundry,
Varied expressions of the same,
The Oneness as the names many.'

'This life is one, a blessing,' said the date,
'Is magnificent bounty abundant,
Though inner striving makes it seem
Separate, faithless, and redundant.

The Unseen, Unsaid, Unknown
Celebrates life, its prayer.
Cynicism, scepticism – the disbelief –
Ignores there's one alone, without a pair,

And believes one can hide behind a mask
Of self, which divides life as out and in,
Has fondness for fleeting life,
Curbs vastness in the dual spin

Of virtue and vice, heaven and hell,
Then suffers their duality in sight.
Yet on sacrifice of an apparent split
Ceases duality of inverse sight,

For illuminates true compassion
The appearance of the great;
And rise gratitude, grace, and mercy,
No destination but the one innate.

Can't be established the unseen,
Nor can the form the formless create,
But glorifies its glow, this Oneness,
As all is it, nothing separate.'

Thus, unravelled was the false
By the date, though the message unknown
That did flow through his being
Was revealed by One alone.

The message captured the heart
Of many, like the honey and seed;
Shared the message the fig and olive –
To who's hungry, or whoever did heed.

In glory waved the sea as its tide,
And the date's followers did grow:
Joined the melon, barley, and pumpkin
To be sated in the dessert flow.

There is no one in the show
Yet placates as a sweet dessert
– As compassion beckons you to return –
The date in the infinite arid desert.

But a date with it and 'you' alone will burn,
For may appear the profound
Paradise of freedom, that's invincible,
Unbound by any chronicle or sound.'

Thus, revealed was the message and account
To the beetle who stayed on the date tree
– By nature feral and alert –
Yet the beetle curbed the message free

In a doctrine canonical,
And judged from its fort –
Life alive and new
Splits all in dual purport.

For she views from behind the veil:
(Of division) the date, desert, and dessert.
Ignores the Oneness that is,
For she seeks dessert in the desert.

[This narrative is an invitation of Oneness to itself, which appears to itself as separate. This fictional account encompasses the message of non-duality prevalent in the philosophy[1] of Sufism. It illuminates the message of *Ishq-e-haqeeqi* (real or existent love) and *Ishq-e-majaazi* (unreal or transient love).]

1 See Note 3A

12

The Royal Duo

On a hot and sluggish afternoon
Hurried to meet the Queen the silver spoon;
An advisor of the Alphonso[1] State,
He administered affairs intimate,
Yet apprehensive he was to relate
To the mango Queen, the Prince's state,
And his tantrums turbulent
That were endured by the attendants.
Soon, the spoon gained the ruler's presence
And patiently explained the incidence;
The mother rushed to see her Prince,
To his uncouth bursts crush, convince
Him to shun irascible behaviour,
Unfit for a Prince's demeanour.

1 See Note 4A

Instead followed a fiery exchange,
For neither wished their view to change;
Forsaken was royal protocol,
As raw reactions ruled, did befall,
Though they had learnt to hide emotions,
To be composed through all notions
– For feelings portray feebleness
Unsuitable for royal uniqueness –
But life appears with and without rules,
Seems to rebel, follow established schools.
…

The mango Prince wished to quit desserts,
Dwell in the pickle with the chilli pert;
To marry the chilli was his aim,
For love, could forgo the royal name.
The Queen had other plans for the heir,
Wished him to be adept in royal affairs
And rule over the dessert empire,
To wed a princess, thus aspire.

The Queen firmly said to the Prince:
'Your manner rudeness does evince.
We belong to the Alphonso clan:
Our prominence through centuries does span;
The masses rush to our glimpse secure,
For we are genuine, rare, and pure.
How can you think of leaving desserts?
To join a pickle – acidic and curt –
And thus hurt royal sentiments
For passing enthralment.
The pickle's neither a starter nor main course –
To join a condiment, truly coarse!
Your aim should be to boost the empire,
Not stigmatise the clan entire;
Grow up, mature, become the King,
Get a golden hue, sweet songs sing.
Marry a princess, leave the chilli,
Be sober, forgo fairy tales silly.'

The Prince then could no longer restrain,
Pleaded, shouted, and did complain:
'We foods are one and not apart,
So let's focus on the one art;
As royals, it is for us to lead,
Set an example, thus I plead.
And, Mum, how is sour worse than sweet?
What hierarchy? How is one taste elite?
How can pickles be coarse,
While other courses on course.
In the royal court you daily preach
Equality, and love you seem to teach.
Why don't these words in life apply?
Why love and freedom to me deny?

Riches and power are a temporal measure,
While true love the only treasure.
Restless I will remain without her,
For love alone my heart does stir.
I won't give her up but will fight,
For my life with her is bright;
Together we will be a perfect symbol
Of parity and live a life simple.'

The mother retorted as the Queen:
'Why forsake the sweetness of our cuisine,
Converse in manner uncouth,
For scathing pungency of spicy youth.
Why do you dispute tradition,
The basis of our foundation?'

But heated turned the argument.
Mediated the silver spoon, on consent;
His presence brought immediate calm
And bitterness of both sides did disarm,
As being the Queen's older, wiser cousin,
His views were valued by all at the mansion.
He naturally spoke to the Prince:
'I don't wish with words to convince,
But reflect on what I share
About true love and your affair.

You wish to make the chilli your bride,
With her in the pickle thus reside.
Is this love? Is this not passion?
For passion is dreams of the future fashions,
While love is timeless, not to future bound,
And being everything, it is unbound;

So, it isn't only a soft feeling or state
That rises in forms that degenerate
But is your essence – your being innate,
Your permanence in transient gait.
While chemistry and desire you deem as love
Are simply to fill an emptiness thereof.

You say to the chilli you belong.
Listen to love's familiar song:
Love is absolute, abounds,
Is formless forming, unbound;
It is love unconditional
Appearing as form transitional;
It is the occurring appearance,
The hum, the stir, and the resonance,
Is infinitely alive and intimate,
Yet impersonal and innate,
Celebrating each and every view,
Embracing, emerging as joy and rue,
Untouched, but as forms does animate,
At once, the real and unreal gait.
Love is one, yet seeming separate,
Ineffable, is, isn't, does fascinate.

Is structured and untamed grace,
Is energy with, without a face,
And appears without a cue,
Isn't reliant on any view or hue;
Embraces, so has no inverse,
Is ever new in free verse,
Is innocent and lively in essence,
Is being this occurrence,
Truly seeking its own reflection
In apparent formed connections.
And love alone exists on its own,
So it can't be known or unknown,
Complete in its incompleteness,
Yet none can its fulfilment express.

So when you exclaim that you love her,
This is just feelings that occur
As per your form's chemistry,
An appearance of energy.
Not a fated union of destiny,
Just feelings rising naturally.
The love between two, subject–object,
Is distant, bound by disconnect,
Where seeming individuality
Projects on alive life, its seeming reality;
Therefore, foods fall in–out of love,
Believe it is a treasure trove
To fulfil their incompleteness,
Unaware love is even the mess.
And individuality's an unreal bind,
As alive life cannot be thus confined.'

Bored seemed the mango Prince,
But he hid his resistance.
So continued the silver spoon,
His song of love, in tune:
'You portray her lovely attributes
Of being a vivacious, cute fruit –
Aren't they the apparent traits,
Not single possessive states?
For none of us are a form confined,
Directed by circumstance or mind,
But are pure love, the boundless presence,
In which appears the whole existence.
Or love appears as everything,
As this appearing song does sing,
Hence love is not about possession
But every appearing expression.
So, love is pain, tradition, and revolt too,
A picture without anyone in view.

And, dear, your stance to leave royalty
Won't secure freedom from desires plenty,
So recall your royalty true,
Of presence without self in stew,
Then royalty won't be an issue
And won't follow the dual retinue.'

Pleased was the Queen by the discourse
Of her cousin to her son off-course.
The silver spoon then moved towards her
And almost spoke in a whisper:
'If one alone does transpire,
Can there be lower or higher?

Can free will exist, or impact,
If one this play does enact?
Who can bear the flambeau of glory?
Isn't convention or change a story?
Does there exist a separate entity
To decide outcomes, own progeny?

Yet as an advisor, the silver spoon,
I can say the chilli seems to be a boon,
Will merge in the dominion of dessert,
Will not the clan in any way subvert.
And, Cousin, simply for reference,
Nature preserves perfect balance
– Emerges, blossoms, withers in silence,
Seasonally favours forms in radiance –
Follows the mango the Jamun[2] fruit,
An antidote of sugar to the root;
At least she isn't from their family,
To be the mangos' malady.
So, don't fear to consider new flavours,
As fusion won't thy essence lower.

Yet this is simply my advice,
Nothing significant or prized,
For love all outcomes does permeate,
Innovate, or follow outdated dictates.
But know all courses are vital
In the concert official,
So taste all ingredients will assert –
Main course, condiment, or dessert.
A dessert or pickle, none has choice:
Whatever happens is one voice.'

Then abruptly but in nonchalant style
The Queen intervened, spoke of the juveniles:
'I surely don't approve of the Pickles,
But groom the chilli for Alphonso Ripple;
I know a chilli cannot add finesse,
She cannot supress our sweetness;
And all of you please leave,
I need time alone, to be.'
…

The Prince felt like a triumphant warrior
And as the two walked through the corridor;
He thanked his uncle, the silver spoon,
For shining like the glowing moon
In the dark night of his life
Of subservience, stress, and strife.
But the spoon interrupted his nephew:
'My job is not to charm or rescue
Sad beings from the dark deep depths,
To the light of life and its breadth.
Nor do I wish answers to present,
To which all briefly thus assent.
Nor do I challenge society
Or impart lessons of propriety.
For what I say is deeper still,
No horizontal, vertical, or free will.

For all these roles either of blame
Or victim, or raising life's game,
Are in the dream of self, which has camps two –
Of the 'Ayes' and 'Nos' and 'Me' and 'You',
Where all relations are a business,
Even in compatible bliss;
For seen is love, the life's glory,
Through the lens of me, my story,
Where each projects their agenda
On to the present, for their propaganda.

And seeking fulfilment in the dream
Is futile, for it's like heavy cream,
Enticing, yet leaving a greasy glaze
On the tongue, which then can't denote tastes.
Dear, in love there is nothing to gain,
For the beloved alone does remain.
It is natural love, without a lease,
Where there is no other to please;
It's stripping of the dual dictate,
Not where bride and beloved are intimate,
Or male and female are fused, one,
But a love so pure that there is none,
Yet is free to dance as everything,
And its own seeming wild song sing.

2 See Note 4B

Hence, desolation, delight, or any sense
Can't deplete or complete love's essence,
For love is not an experience
But ever-present basis of existence,
Is stillness in an energetic dance,
An epitome of romance,
A persistent *petite mort*
Of self, a cause, and a consort,
Yet an unknowing, not orgasmic bliss,
Simply life unbridled, appearing as it is,
With all its idiosyncrasies,
And nothing that's amiss.
So love is pain and suffering that blows,
And loss too; life's each echo
Is the beating of every heart,
The sense of being split apart;
It's your first glance or tryst,
And your first tender kiss.
Unconditional love – incarnate,
Oneness as two, not possible to relate,
So one, the romance that you celebrate,
And the Queen's dictate.'

The Prince did not heed a word,
For he was busy in his world,
Imagining a brilliant future
With his love, and him as ruler.
…

Then commenced preparations grand
Of the wedding in fruit fairyland,
A dream seemingly viewed in earnest
By life itself, lost in self-interest.

13

Merchandise

The Golden Temple in Amritsar city
Is celebrated for its sanctity.
Here each day honoured is Oneness,
And the communal kitchen observes largesse.
Around the precincts of this pure place
Are granaries with their private base,
Where dwelled a class of merchants malicious,
Who stowed fare in manner surreptitious;
Being decadent in their ways,
They played with the food rates.
And soon enough there was scarcity
Of supplies in Amritsar city,

For gluttony and food wastage
Ruined the market, brought shortage,
And this continued for a while,
Until dearth became a trial.

At a certain warehouse late at night
Several foods resolved to fight,
For they couldn't even bear the thought
Of people being hungry and fraught,
So sugar, butter, flour, and rice
Refused to be sold at a high price.
The flour, rousing all, did suggest:
'Let us strike in wider interest.
Let's boycott the merchants mean,
Exit this odious scene,
Redolent of the yesteryears
Of the food shortage and the fears.
To the Golden Temple let's all go,
In love's compassion truly flow;
For there free food is gladly shared –
All are the same and none compared.
To all friends let us spread the word,
To revolt against all rules absurd.
Let's teach the merchants discipline,
Get together to redress, oh Brethren!'

Soon the revolt spread like wildfire,
Rushed to the Temple the fleet entire.
The foods their fair place did reserve
And wished to here remain and serve,
With butter, water, sugar, flour
Was made the *Karah Prashad*,[1] love in flavour,
The blessed making of *daal*, *roti,* rice
In colossal amounts was precise.
In each morsel love did sway;
Gratitude along with grace did stay –
So celebrated was the flawless food fest,
Aliveness in apparent rest.
...

The merchants followed in despair
To improvise the scenario unfair,
For they had no merchandise,
No trade, or food at any price.
Moreover, slander and social pressure
Made life feel cursed beyond measure,
So to feel free from guilt and regret
They served at the shrine to settle their debts.

Hymns[2] sung throughout the day
Essence of Oneness did convey,
Which was intently heard by the foods
And merchants, who now seemed subdued.
The first words and couplet declared that One[3]
Alone appears as everything, yet is one:
'*One energetic presence*
Is being this named appearance,
Performs, embraces, is its luminescence,
Is fearless, impartial in its quintessence,
Is timeless yet appears as this transience,
Does not occur in birth and death, its sequence,
And on its own appears this essence,
Is illumined by guru's beneficence.'

1 The *Karah Prashad,* made from flour, *ghee*, sugar, and water, is the devotional offering served at the Gurudwaras.

2 See Note 5A
3 See Note 5B

'Remember:'

'The commencement is this,[4]
The seeming pairs are this,
What is appearing is this,
Nanak, what will appear is this.'

Heeding this song of utmost freedom,
Which didn't feed illusion's kingdom,

4 Here, I have translated the couplet *Aad Sach Jugaad Sach...*, which immediately follows the *Mool Mantra* after the word *Jap* in the *Guru Granth Sahib*. It is the first couplet of the composition of *Japji* (the first composition in the *Guru Granth Sahib*). (For further information, see Note 5C)

Revealed was the true nature of the guru[5]
To the foods – who seemed without a clue –
That guru is the light that disperses the dark,
Appears in any form, verse, or spark,
Is not a hero rewriting history,
Or person who has figured life's mystery,
But presence guiding itself from ignorance –
That one alone is this appearance.
...

In the other songs it was clear
That the traits alone appear,
And there is no separation,
But one, seeming celebration:

'All there is is the trait, with none in the midst,
There never was nor will one exist.'[6]

And...

'Thousands thy eyes yet thou without an eye,[7]
Thousands of forms yet without form thereby,
Thousands thy lotus feet yet no feet; Thou
Without a nose yet thousands of noses come by,
Enamours this wonder.'

But the hymn[8] which shook the factions two
Unravelled illusion's hue:

'Woe heals, bliss becomes a disease,
When there are no desires of ease;
Oh, performer, you perform, I do not,
For nothing occurs from the self's plot;
Relinquished to that which is as form dressed,
Thy boundlessness cannot be expressed.[9] *(Pause)*
In form is light, in light the form, timeless art complete,
You, oh being, the Master, thy praise freedom's treat;

5 See Note 5D

6 See Note 5E

7 See Note 5F

8 See Note 5G

9 See Note 5H

Speaks Nanak of this creative presence,
It is performing as this appearance.'
...

The essence of the priceless words
Was by the large assemblies heard,
But it affected the merchants and fare
In ways beyond repair.
They had come to solve their quandary,
But were shaken by the presence free.
Instead of gaining riches and truth,
They seemed to lose all they had accrued,
For attacked were their identities
Of being sacred, or in prosperity.

Malice of the factions washed away,
Who recognised one as all does play;
This beingness cannot be defined,
For ever new, it can't be confined
In any form or feature,
Yet all is its appearing structure.

The foods resolved not to split
In spiritual–unspiritual grit,
For ignorance – to split life natural
In inverses unilateral.
The hymns revealed: love embraces each hue,
Doesn't disregard life as dream untrue,
For all that appears is energy alone,
No state or place the touchstone,
Thus sacred is the market too,
Not just the Temple and its view.
Though energy at certain place
Appears free, yet all is grace,
For it is free and unconditional,
To appear as the conditional.
It is love, which can appear in any guise:
As merchants that agonise,
Or as the freedom of the song
Of the beloved, or as all one longs.

Remember: all is an expression
Of one, an apparent impression,
And for there to be an appearance
There appears the dual semblance,
So no art of living, just fickle breath,
An aliveness, beyond birth and death,
Unbound by shackles of space and time,
Complete love that's sublime.
Life is complete simplicity,
Beyond identity
Of gender, traits, religions, roles,
Simply is, with none in control,
Yet appears the whole
As I am, with attachments and roles,
Formless forming yet untouched
By their apparent clutches.
Complete wonder!
Remained the foods in splendour.

The foods renounced their blissful zones
Into the trade of apparent life, unknown
– Being in love with the universe
Entire, a love in free verse –
To feed all, even hungry merchants,
And bear the revolution emergent.

The merchants too did recognise
As surreal the individual guise.
For illumined, how the false pursues
Itself, then deems the one is two;
In sleep none sings, remains the song,
Reappears the self to hoard, belong.
Thus, it was truly evident
That separation is unreal, transient,
So none exists to own the bread,
Or is superior to be well fed.

Their hoarding and demanding plenty,
Was due to the self illusory,
Which deemed self to be distinct
From the appearing script,
And tried to feed its sense of dearth
With wealth, belongings, loaded hearth.
Yet the self never seemed satisfied,
Even with the world by its side,
For an illusion itself did chase,
Avoided itself in varied ways,

And in this chase the self did proliferate –
Endless became its circular gait.

But partaking in the game of life
Is one, itself, truly alive,
So washed away guilt that did reign,
Indifference too – ego's strain.
Remember: life is a blessing,
Unmatched is ordinary living,
And life has no destination,
Is eating, cooking, occupation,
With nothing to achieve, nowhere to go,
And none to know.
…

Returned the market rules as usual,
Only vanished ownership fictional.
And once again the city was full of life,
Festivity of flavourful foods alive –
Captured aromas, tastes, and hues
The senses; hot and sweet in flavours new.
Grew queues to taste delicacies,
With tastes anew, without a legacy.

The guru thus did illumine:
'Separate aren't virtue and sin,
But only seem so in the dream
Of the self, and its seeming beams;
No merchant or merchandise be,
But an appearance free
Of Oneness in varied guise,
That strays, does revolutionise,
As a guru too it does guide.
And as a devotee does abide.
So, guru and disciple are one,
As one is everything and none,
For it alone does appear
With or without celestial sphere.'[10]

The Golden Temple to this day,
Celebrates Oneness and its play,
Unravels the self, its seed,
To those who wish to heed,
Provides everyone their right –
Food from the kitchen day and night,
Without a purpose or mission,
Highlighting love in each expression.
Yet nothing is volitional,
For all is love, unconditional.

(This fictional verse is based on the message of the Sikh gurus. I have translated a few hymns from the *Guru Granth Sahib* and given rendition of other hyms – please check the footnotes for a full explanation.)

10 This is the ethos of the Sikh philosophy.

14
Cook, Create, Compose

I keenly learnt the Fibonacci sequence
To harness genius in my novel dish,
But failed the golden ratio's brilliance
In the artistic artichoke with fish.
Because life did not submit to my wish,
Though several designs it does display,
I felt deceived by nature's biased dish,
As it appeared in mine and triumph's way.

I now no longer with the ratio play,
For life remains indifferent to me,
Yet does not whine that I am in the way,
So is it callous, accepting, or free?
Although I try, I can't escape from life,
To cook, create and compose – starved of strife.

15

Hail Energy

A sweet and scrumptious apple red
The world with flavourful foods fed,
Adorned chutneys, crumbles, and cakes,
Pastry, pudding, pies, and bakes.
She adored her supporters plenty
And fulfilled their wishes healthy.
Life was simple, scenic, and stable;
She glowed in gratitude amiable.

Then in a supermarket one day,
Six comrades[1] on her eyes did lay.

Mesmerised by her allure true,
They fervently her did pursue,
Lured her desire, inertia, lust,
Ignorance, fogginess, and distrust.
The simple girl became their prey,
Refused her duties, lost her way,
As this continued for a while,
She and her fans both lost their smile.

The apple seemed arrested in a fort
Of six traits that thwarted her sport.

1 See Note 6A

Many a time she tried to find a way,
And even turned pallid in the array,
But failed attempts of the self's rhyme,
And the seeming passage of time
Made the fort safe to stay,
And fearful a different display.

One day in her sleep she dreamt
Of light, that is as all present.
This light or energy, label it
What you may, said bit by bit:
'Nature does not evade its expression,
Appears as this, the manifestation,
Performs as traits, doesn't segregate,
Isn't caught in hues separate.
The wind blows, the sun shines –
Why are you caught in fleeting shrines?
Intricately entwined is all,
None's sovereign, vast or small;
Darkness cannot this light hide,
Face, fight, for I alone reside.
Know these imposters will have to die,
For when light triumphs none can ally.'

Ensued a massive battle,
Where ignorance ruled as chattels,
And the imposters tried their best
To rule the view and light at rest
– Which, though at rest, still seemed at war
With the impostors and their uproar –
And though the six did all at length,
And applied onerous strength,
Trampled and roared to instil terror,
Energy's nerve did not error.

The imposters unconscious,
Executed methods monstrous:
Concealed the foggy perception –
The real and unreal expression;
While inertia and lust used ways
Subtle to hide their avid display.
But illumined the energy
The real–unreal decree,
And always stayed on guard
Against lust and inertia's canard.

Then one by one the four gave way,
Desire and ignorance still did sway;
For dogged desire, declined to go,
The fertile ground of quest forgo,
Maintained its presence as a seed,
Germinating by the fertile feed;
Thus, it engaged in subtle ruse,
But energy destroyed its muse,
As it forbade the seeds to fall
On fertile grounds that it instals.

This led to faith and clarity,
Along with innocent activity,
Though ignorance still did play,
Had the apple in its sway.
Energy several arms did wield,
But ignorance refused to yield.
Finally, light in form lambent
Conquered ignorance with its trident,
And it destroyed denseness and time,
Creation, sustenance, destruction's rhyme.

Followed a wondrous celebration
For this energetic expression,
As overwhelming was its might,
Its fearless grace and light bright,
Which unravelled the liberty
Present. The praise: 'Hail Energy'.

Then energy feral and free
Said: 'I alone am, appear, be;
I am the zephyrs that softly blow,
I alone the mighty tornados;
I am the wildfire and its spark,
And the spontaneous dance dark,
Not just a measured, calm image,
But profanity and sacrilege;
Am creativity that self does slay,
Matter and dark matter in play.

As these six I emerge,
Yet I destroy, and as them surge,
For I celebrate each expression
And marvel at my own impression.
I the captive and the saviour,

The fort and the annihilator,
Ignorance, valour, or an uproar,
All an appearance of my roar,
For I alone am as all form present –
There is nothing beyond my extent.
No image can my reflection hone,
For I am untouched and unknown.

I alone weave a dream
In which you and I separate seem,
Grip as the rising relations
Hide this light in expression,
Which feels like forts that surround
In their claustrophobic bound,
For lust, wrath, attachment, ego,
Duality in them tightly stow.
Then I illumine the duality,
At times use war to destroy density,
To emerge as simplicity, innocence,
That feels comforting in essence.
Yet the taste of liberty complete
From duality is untold and replete,
For there are no relations,
No friends, foes in expression,
For that is an expression
Of me, in dual impression.

As each appearance is my echo,
There is nothing to gain or forgo;
Apparent are cages of good and bad,
All is my game, a charade.
Nothing towards or from me does stray,
For there's none to seek or keep at bay,
As there is nothing apart from me,
So is anything bound or free?

Though I appear unbound,
Limits too in me are found,
For I defy every decree
Even this one – I have no rules, am free,
So wild, and free, I am poise too,
Create, destroy, and be in view;
Though I appear in patterns,
Predictive seem my turns,
Unrepeated is my every hue,
For I am this, forever new.

Still, I am one, the same,
Untouched, with, without a name.
Does not exist an entity,
For I am transient infinity,
The loudest natural sound
In appearance, and its surround.
I am non-existence,
And seeming existence,
A love absolute – that's a mystery,
Dancing or not, completely free.

Yet I am not: there's only absence,
Appearing as this emerging presence,
A vivacious, energetic stir
That naturally does occur –
And seems to be the feminine,
Devoted, vibrant, illumined –
In the still, formless silence,
Untouched, unknown, constant,
Yet symbolic: the formless form,
The masculine–feminine norm.
For there is nothing, no I am, none
Singing an unbroken song – the one.'

Then suddenly, the apple awoke… or not?
Could she?

16

Love's Salad

There once was a *Gỏi* from Vietnam,
Who was wed to the love of the psalm;
In the chase to be one,
He eloped with a nun,
Laughed the monk from the shade of the palm.

17

The Shocking Tail

In an area of high seismicity,
A Salmon ate a pearl of creativity;
The formless gazed in Salmon's guise –
Void seemed the timeless oceanic rise.
In his presence most felt free, did not clench,
And famous he became around the trench.
Nonetheless, it was emptiness
As presence, free from all progress.

Then nearby the estuary
Was built a monastery,
Where stayed Master Salmon, his disciples,
Constantly swayed by the waves tidal.
Some pupils founded a strict routine,
Strove to stay in the moment pristine,
Contemplated the Master's *koans*,[1]
And on the silence at early dawn.

The two pupils – seaweed and prawn –
Who strained to waken by Master's *koans*
Rehearsed calligraphy with accents too,
And prepared tea with an empty view,
But subtly competed in the game
Of finding an enlightened frame;
Yet their manner was diverse
To meditate on the Master's verse.

The seaweed was serene and slow,
The prawn impetuous in the flow;
When the others asked questions,
The prawn rushed with suggestions,
While the seaweed detached from the *koan*

And wished to transcend like a swan.
Yet both were caged in the confines
Of easy prison or awkward lines.

Once, Master Salmon voiced a verse,
Spontaneous, pellucid, and terse:
'The fire cooks fortunes of the sea,[2]
Even when rolled raw as sushi,
Form, sound, no sound, no form,
Buddhahood none can perform.

1 See Note 7A

2 See Note 7B

The mountains still, the waves in water,
The *yudofu*[3] cannot 'you' slaughter.'

Considering the *koan's* undertone,
The seaweed lay in the unknown,
While to decipher then realise the *koan*
Hastened to meditate the playful prawn.
The prawn then baffled by the seaweed's
Languid ways and sluggish speed,

Imitated her through the day,
Expressed in his usual way:
'While you muse on the *koan* precise,
In this time I will be born twice;
You just reflect and gently sway,
While I contemplate, feast, and play.
How can you be so obtuse and slow?
Come on, hurry, or you'll miss the show…'
The seaweed smiled at the playfulness
Of the prawn, and at her aimlessness,
But then focused on her innate state,
That is untouched, unbound, and liberated.
…

As Master Salmon got well known
Across seas and lands unknown,
So sought his presence varied foods,
To taste simplicity's magnitude,
But most had ideas of the taste
Of food of freedom in stillness placed.
Miso and greens craved the beat
Of the Master's presence, which is complete;
The rice desired to lose the self,
Though not in the continental shelf,
While soy and ginger wished to know
The true nature of the Master's glow.
Thus, countless visited with their lists,
To taste emptiness and in joy exist,
Plus planned techniques and ways to process
The core, which words can never express.

The fortune of the mountains never came,
For they appeared without an aim,
Neither resistant, nor in ease,
Nor waiting for anyone to cease.
The curious prawn wished to know
Of fortunes who didn't wish to grow,
So he questioned the Master one day,

3 *yudofu* is a Japanese word for hot-water tofu, or tofu cooked in a hot-water pot. This popular vegetarian hot-pot dish uses silken tofu with other seasonal ingredients and has been eaten for centuries by the monks of Zen temples, in the Kyoto area, central Japan.

‘Why do these fortunes keep at bay?
Don’t they need pickling – the *tsukemono*?
Or be fried in the oil – *agemono*?
And don’t they need your presence unique?
To be grilled by meditative technique
Of the *koans*, and the oceanic peace,
All their stench thus to release?’

Incessantly then questioned the prawn,
Of ‘satori*’*, its relation to *koans*,
About the *enso*’s[4] symbolism,
About this life, its void prism,
Of emptiness and golden silence,
Of loss of thoughts and still presence,
About fire that cooks virtue–vice,
And the value of the Master’s advice.
Refused to hear that none can be aware,
Or awaken to their nature fair,
For emptiness is the appearing moment,
Not a state reached on enlightenment.

The Master smacked the prawn with its tail,
A shock, as if struck by a gale,
Or swallowing a whole wasabi tin
Suddenly. Inhale, exhale, spin.
Exclaimed the Master: ‘What presence,
What fortunes, what radiance?
No finger to point, or moon to see,
No sky, no clouds, no cherry tree,
No birds to fly or mind to free,
Your empty mind can’t surpass my tea.
[Pointing towards his tea.]
A seeming journey without the way,
If you can swim, then sink today.’
…

All is the same in the monastery.
The seaweed still reflects, solitary,
Naturally sways in gentle ways,
Vies the void of the prawn in play,
And practises calligraphy,
Meditation, and the art of tea;
When the *koans* issue more questions,
She silently awaits cessation.
Thus, separation keeps itself alive,
In waiting and witnessing does thrive.
The prawn still mimics the seaweed’s traits,
Brands her gait as longueurs that irate,
Performs and plays with alacrity,
Chuckles and snorts wholeheartedly,
Keeps distance from the Master’s tail,
And from the wasabi*,* its trail,
From *koans* and their conundrum
And the meditational humdrum.
Drinks tea and does calligraphy,
But does not own the performance free;
Does not know of his existence,
Or of his non-existence,
Is neither absent nor present.
Appears the emerging event.

Yet all that occurs is an appearance,
Appearing emptiness in brilliance,
One, verbs in myriad appearance –
Sea-weeding, prawning, innocence.
…

Naturally waves the deep ocean,
As all its waves – a seeming motion –
Simply rise, fall away
In oceanic presence that does stay.
This emptiness all celebrate –
The food, the taste, and the plate;
So how can characteristics clear
When emptiness as them does appear?
And if emptiness alone is,
Without anything being amiss,
Can anything lead to this,
Calligraphy, art, tea, or bliss?
So *koans* are *koans*, not a quiz,
And life is this, as it is.
Empty fullness.

4 See Note 7C

聴静寂

'*Seijaku wo kiku*': listen to the sound of snow/silence.

18

The Unfulfilled Croissant

Together since their teens in tender love,
The flaky croissant and the baguette tight,
They mingled in familiar flour, sans fight,
Besotted, deemed that love a treasure trove.
Then love vicissitudes of self did show:
Emerged the hunger to become content,
Replaced the baguette, almonds of ascent,
And love assured to last received a blow.
But dearth did not recede by the attained;
Impressionism of mind did not connect
To the realistic art of life unchained;
The croissant still pursues for love perfect;
Unknown to all that love can never meet:
Love is all that is and is not, complete.

19

Comparative Culture

PART 1

The Fruit Media once convened a show –
A debate that would aid and grow
Acceptance in diverse cultures
And end enduring ruptures,
Beget harmony in society
And ease existent anxiety.
Assembled fruits from cultures afar
– That practised customs bizarre –
And chosen were the representatives
By the Fruit Media's executive
For the debate, one of a kind,
Where shared were views in verse refined.

One guest who did not feed a mirage
And didn't fit in any creed or collage
Was invited on the show too
To sing the one song, impromptu;
Provide another perspective
On this life imperative.
…

'Our culture is noble and sane,
For content we all remain
In the confines of our skin,
With morals that destroy sin.
In the clan's progress we all believe,
An ethical position perceive,

Eternal peace guarantee
If you with our view agree,'
Declared the banana, addressing the grape,
Who having heard this was agape.

He then continued for a while
In his patronising style,
'Yet we diversify across the globe,
Don't identify with a land's scope,
Share our talents, ply diligence,
Are famed for our variance:
As banana muffin, or banoffee pie,
Banana pudding, banana on rye,
Banana curry, banana fry,
Banana smoothie or frozen dry,
So raw or ripe we are the pride
Of every cuisine worldwide.

However, we do not act righteous or sly
Like you, or others terrify,
And we aren't supercilious,
Capricious or pretentious.'

Then continuing in his style
He demeaned her with a smile:
'Your aim is to intoxicate,
Steal the senses, complicate,
Sway with a "high", create a mess,
And in the chaos become restless,
Then, restive within, you start with unrest,
With the acquired riches stay depressed;
And being ignorant of diverse tones,
Establish narrow polls and touchstones,
Demean other souls from their zone,
Have value only for your own.
Moreover, you flagrantly dress,
Are an anathema to the moral press,
A dilemma for the world's progress,
Even the earth's condition and its success.'

'What arrant nonsense! Stop your silly tirade,
Your abhorrent didactic crusade!'
Snapped the grape who could take no more,
Continued: 'Your being I abhor.
The whole wide world accepts my value,
For I'm intelligent, cultured, true.
All praise my skill to heal,
For in patients I restore the zeal;
Vintage, I mature into wine,
Am celebrated for tastes refined.

You are nothing but a poor man's food,
Rot quickly and are downright rude.
Are truculent, dogmatic, and crass,
Unintelligent and lacking class,
Conduct acts unethical
In the name of principles,
Behind moral garbs employ ruse,
Are judgemental in your views.

So "You" are the aberration,
Vitriolic too in diction.

Besides, you don't respect free will,
Impose ideas that are ill.
Thus, advocate autocracy,
Create gender supremacy,
While I value democracy,
Promote equal policy.
I sponsor freedom of all the fruits,
Don't aid an arcane cause or roots;
I even care for fruits of your clan,
While you behave like a caveman,
Appear to be composed in your skin,
But wish to mimic my dress and skin.
Progress, research are my middle names –
You're jealous for you've lost the game.'

Now the discussion did not seem
Amiable, as both did scream,
Accuse, condemn, and denounce,
Which led to chaos pronounced.
The presenter of the debate
Tried to placate the noisy state.
The fig and orange watched the sight,
And orange wished to give insight,
To present his unbiased view
Of embracing detachment true
With the present, and the fragmental,
Being non-judgemental.
But, timid, he nothing did say,
While the fig unmoved did stay.

After a lot of palaver
To prove which culture is better,
The fig then to everyone's surprise
Loudly asked: 'Who does all the forms devise?'
Yet he spoke in a manner blasé
While all shocked turned his way.
The fig then went on to say:
'What keeps "you" alive night and day,
Performs the body's natural tasks,
Is behind the diverse masks?

Isn't it one life force – uniform –
That appears as all the forms?
Can any of you even breathe
On your own, or keep alive your bodies?
Or survive even for an instant,
If life doesn't thrive as form present?

Oh, silly fruits! Reflect, are we diverse
When one force keeps alive the universe?
Is this appearance split and static?
When life's the source and the fabric.
You have forgotten, fruits inane,
That emptiness is source and grain
Of life, so the same is the juice,
Energetic forms – one produce;
Energy without any boundaries
Is life appearing as the binary,
Like sunlight appearing as the hues
Of the rainbow, and its shadows too.
Variety makes us value
Priceless life, arising anew,
For if there appeared just one hue,
There'd be no form to celebrate or view.
And isn't this presence blessing's call?
What if there was no form at all?

Appears innate conditioning
As form, like sun is fiery, moon cooling,
But why unwisely reiterate views
Learnt by training of hues
Of seeming society, culture, place,
Or time, religions, and a race,
Then fight over silly beliefs
Acquired and left in this life brief.'

The fig with a smile on his face
Questioned without vexation's trace:
'Anyway, who can bestow cognisance,
When there is only empty presence?
Which one of you can beget joy and peace
When you can't curb your war or caprice?
And who can raise the fruits, their lot,
When they can't control their own thoughts?

Who among you can claim to know,
When none knows, when their end will show?'

The presenter of the debate
Requested the fig to elaborate
On cultures and their influence.
Resumed the fig of this appearance:
'These cultures and civilisations
Are simply a plethora of visions,
Appearing in this presence,
Passing by without an essence;
Rather all identities
Are non-existent entities.

Rationally, too, this cultural nonsense
Is a confluence of diverse influence
And, like an ever flowing river,
Constantly changes its whisper,
Hence it is illusory to deem a culture
As static, with an infrastructure –
Moreover, to praise it or deride
An added trick of pious pride.
For all opinions are a game
Simply to dominance claim,
For they are an apparent cage
In which is hidden riven rage.
So, this democracy
Too is a construed policy
That pursues serfdom
In the guise of freedom.

Recognise: no outlook can ever bring
An end to this suffering.
No culture, scripture, or reference
Compares to this alive presence.
Even the most amazing views
Or divine celestial hues
Are pale in comparison
To the appearing manifestation,
Hence any song, however pristine,
Falls at the altar of the present scene.
Thus, all your learnt cultural nonsense
Fails at the feet of the present occurrence.'

The presenter of the debate
Tried to make sense of the fig's dictate,
Which seemed to be incoherent,
But the fig continued indifferent:
'Who can teach whom how to live,
In certain ways dress, pray, or give,
When life exists on its own,
Without another to make it known?
Arrogance to the extreme
Is to uplift a daydream.
And if anyone claims to know
This unknowable show,
Just scuttle away from their side,
For they are charlatans in pious hide,
Inflicting their opinions
On the apparent millions.
Yet participation in roles
Is one in its own play, whole,
So whatsoever appears – a dance,
Oneness alone without a stance.'

The banana and the grape
Inanely at the fig did gape,
But the fig's words and depth profound
The orange did astound.
After the debate did end,
The Fruit Media chose not to extend
A similar debate ever,
For it relations did sever;
And brotherhood profound
Remained a dream, unsound.

PART 2

The fruits parted, went their ways,
But the orange couldn't forget the gaze
Of the fig, and his communique,
So pursued him, to show the way
To Oneness, and help him grasp the one,
Which appears as each and every one.

Though the fig explained in ways plain
That nothing could the orange gain,

The orange chased the fig for days
To teach him of freedom's ways.
Thought: devotion is freedom's doorway,
And valiant to beyond it stay.

'I'll smash your dreams of being free,
Unravel the illusion's decree,
So it is clear there are no techniques
And no path to follow, no mystique,
But by then you would have died,
As none lives to see freedom's tide.'
Spontaneously revealed the fig one day,
Reiterating in his usual way.

'I repeat, you'll cease to be, to see
What it is to be truly free,
As enlightenment is not becoming free,
But a remembrance that there is no "me",
But one alone in appearance,
The formless as formed presence.
As one alone exists, is,
None to see it, be in its midst,
And there is nothing apart from it,
To it celebrate, savour, or commit,
Hence all methods to it find, it raise,
Are tricks to continue the chase.'

The orange then requested the presence
Of the fig, which was calm in essence,
And asked the fig to bless him with the state,

Which the fig seemed to celebrate.
Serenely proclaimed the fig: 'Heed
There is none except the rising deed;
None lives in the truth, is unique,
Or embodies the mystique.
There is no devotee or guru:
One alone is all, in view.

There are no fruits in bounds,
But life alone unbound,
Feigning to be in the fetters
Of the self, and its seeming metres,
Or appearing as the one who's free;
So nothing has happened to me:
You and I are simply an appearance,
One energetic presence.'

Then, passionately stirred,
The fig emphasised every word:
'Life's an appearance of disjointed scenes,
With no continuity of any cuisine.
The formless appears as the range –
Each emotion, endeavour, or exchange,
Apparent pictures of formlessness,
An alive dance of nothingness.
Therefore, life alone is, as it is,
Nothing beyond and nothing amiss.
And please don't ask why is this life so.
I simply do not know.'

The orange further did enquire
About the self and his mind dire:
'Why do you and your talk feel free
Of all restraints and the decrees?'
The fig without interruption
Revealed: 'This conversation
Unfolds, unravels the self's game,
Points to the tricks of its claim,
Of how in varied forms it seeks,
And tries to own the mystique,
Thus feels like the light in forest dark,
Yet it's neither an aid nor a benchmark.
So do not believe a word I say:
You will encounter only dismay.
And, yes, this message doesn't belong to me,
Is an expression of one-energy.'

The orange still paid no attention,
Pestered the fig for liberation:
'Could I always accompany you,
And serve you, and your mission true?'
He pleaded in tones to flatter
The fig, and appear keen and clever.
Shouted the fig with anger in his voice,
But without a trace of hatred or vice:
'I do not have a mission
Or aides or destination.
Besides, you do not wish to heed,
For you adore me and my deeds,
Imitate learnt philosophy,
Believe you can learn to be free,
Then deify me as a deity distant,
Preserve the split, be resistant,
Keep the communication at bay,
Ignore the freedom that stays,
Then seek validation from me
To prove that you're becoming free,
For you live in expectation
That one day you will receive salvation.

At times you believe freedom's near,
Relate a list of peak events that appear;
I can discern needy energy
From the freedom that is free.
Hierarchy still feeds your doubts,
And your ideas still hold clout,
Individualise all I say,
And then to fulfil it look for a way.
Heed, you cannot beget enlightenment
Because you're great in blandishment.

Truly, your reverence for affluence,
Shifted to culture and its nuisance,
And now supposed spirituality
With its beliefs, is your identity,
So changed have the objects
While division reigns inept.
These days you seek an alleged guru,

To secretly continue.

Orange, you already have what you seek,
So why rush around looking for a peak?
Even the desire to become free
Of a me is self's subtle spree
To carry on in subtle ways,
Beget enlightenment, thus raise;
Your striving to this Oneness savour
Is like food trying to know its flavour.
Listen, life isn't interested in you,
Your wishes, endeavours, or hue,
For that's life too, in seeming view.
So can there be an end of you?

Yet no divide can stain existence,
For one alone is in appearance,
So nothing's of significance,
Enlightenment or ignorance.
You can leave or stay:
It doesn't matter either way.'
...

The orange still pursues the fig,
So that one day he too is a big
Name in the field of non-duality,
Beyond the cultural identity.
Both the banana and the grape
Still dispute over distinct drape,
Each other complement
With their futile argument,
Promote a farrago of views,
For seeming dominion of hues,
Countless conflicts seem to chase,
Of vengeance, victory, an arms race,
Are certain that one day
Their view alone will sway,
And this variety will subdue,
Thus they fool themselves and others too.

The current pursuer on the scene
Is frozen yoghurt, who is seen
Striving towards the fig, an advance
With its stern atheistic stance,
Is icy and insouciant,
Loves to create conflict constant,
Fails to see the fig is not bound
Even to 'No faith' – the new ground.

The fig scorns the yoghurt's scheme
Of abiding in a frozen dream,
For he isn't an apostate of attitudes
But is personified freedom – simply food,
So nowadays seems in cheer complete
With the geek, the honey sweet.
A recipe that seems to glow
With completeness in its flow.
But can anyone steal the show?
When scrumptious is the whole gateau
With all the fruits and the yogurt,
Dipped in honey with the fig absurd.

20

The Iced Melody

Perform: Cream, Sorbet, Kulfi, Gelato,
Inspired to sing by Erato the muse;
Their piece – in flawless gradual crescendo,
Or is it love complete in dual ruse?

- rab tune,
e no skill
bear could
A
ff

21

The Unknown Stone

Appeared an image of a stone,
But it was living, to atone.
It wasn't cheerful, did not complain,
It never judged, nor did it enchain;
Did not reward ethical acts,
Nor rebuked, nor valued any facts.
It never spoke and did not bless,
Remained an unattached witness,
Complete in its absence, not contained,
Yet in prayer was acclaimed.

A disciple who served the stone
Desired to know the unknown,
Displayed natural affection
To the stone, in deity's expression.
The monkey nut – a devotee true –
Revered the deity daily, ways anew,
Pursued a very special bond,
And felt nothing existed beyond
The deity. So, on it did depend
As father, mother, brother, friend.
So deep became this partisan link
That thoughts of parting made him sink
In the abyss of loneliness
And overbearing fearful stress.

The nut once lost in rituals,
Dressing the deity, way habitual,
Seemingly lost the way
Regular, as a glimpse did sway,
A glimpse of the natural,
Timeless, ineffable.
Unrehearsed, the devotee hummed
A song that echoed the unplumbed
Being that is ever present,
Alive, yet appearing as transient:
'Pure love as the existent shines –
Alive, unknown is this divine,
Is boundlessness, that abounds;
It is the silence being sound,
Is everything, unbound,
So how can it be lost or found?
Pure love as the existent shines –
Alive, unknown is this divine.

Is an energetic stir alive,
And it alone does appear, thrive
As this, yet is ever anew
And complete, whether one or two.
How to split the formless–form
When the one alone does perform?
Pure love as the existent shines –
Alive, unknown is this divine.'

The song was so profound and free
That it displaced the holy debris
Of the monkey nut – a devotee true –
Who was unnerved by freedom's hue.
But soon reappeared the restraint tidal –
As fearing fondness for the idol.

Thus, the nut seemed to return
In the secured bounds of form's urn,
Though the glimpse of the infinite
Had unsettled his adoring habits.

Shivered the nut with following thoughts:
'Was his worship duality's plot,
Did it divide him and the deity –
The finite and the infinity?
Or did it confine the divine
In simply an image refined?
Isn't the divine within,
In silence, beyond the din?
So, doesn't the one alone appear
As father, mother, brother, peer
And self. Is one alone
The formless–form and known–unknown?'

Wondered: hadn't he been taught to pray
To a deity distant and away?
For he did not know of a God
At birth, so was it a façade?
Or is divinity natural –
Not cultural or scriptural;
Oh, are the ancient sketches of gods
Superior to being awed
By love absolute? Aren't the religions
Acquired in worldly manifestation?
So does any religious ritual
Have a meaning in life's trip trivial?
Is there any effect on the divine
Whether worship or atheism is enshrined?

Then thought: why did the deity allow
Such gruesome thoughts, or a stressed brow?
For how could he end the loving bond
And know a God that is beyond?
Also, it was death for him to disengage
With the deity, his only image.
He felt there aren't margins in the notions,
So unsplit are deity, devotee, devotion;
So, he convinced himself with the view
That divine is the delusion too,

And settled in his usual ways
Of prayer and ritualistic praise.
. . .

One day at a religious fair,
Sang Namdev's[1] song a certain pear:
'Wherever I go pervades still presence,
Suffusing, restful, sovereign excellence;[2]

Got water in the pitcher
To cleanse the deity's figure,
But first the fish it did taste,
Its purity thus debased,
And now it's impure in its hue,
So I do not know what to do.

Got saffron smooth and dry
To paint the deity, it beautify,
But the snake was first to steal
Its splendid fragrance, and appeal,
And now it's impure in its hue,
So I do not know what to do.

Got flowers and strung them together,
To the deity with garlands' treasure,
But the fragrance was first thus seized
From the flowers by the bees,
And now it's impure in its hue,
So I do not know what to do.

Got some ghee and wick for flame,
To light a lamp in deity's name,
But first were my eyes
The flame to prize,
And now it's impure in its hue,
So I do not know what to do.

Got fire and aloe wood incense,
To make fragrant the deity's presence,
But first my nasal sense
Smelled its sweet fragrance,
And now it's impure in its hue,

1 See Note 8A
2 See Note 8B

So I do not know what to do.

Got rice and milk[3] to cook a treat
For the deity's offering, complete,
But first the calf the milk did taste,
And thus it did deface,
And now it's impure in its hue,
So I do not know what to do.

And wherever I come or go,
The suffusing stillness does glow.
It alone is the illusion's veil;
When Namdev's being[4] did prevail
In the illusion ceasing presence,
Then remained the primal essence.'

Intently listened to the piece
The nut, was stunned by its release
Of pure–impure, known–unknown,
Appearing in presence lone,
Wondered: is not ritualism
Shrouded in seeming dualism?
Does not confining the divine
In a form mean to ignore the one that shines
As all the forms, is all alone,
And being pervasive can't be known?
Does the self feel curbed in a frame,
So curbs God too in image's game?
Then adorns, adores, and gives it prominence,
Veiling its wish for same significance.
Or is the self the divine,
Splitting forms in mine and thine?
Are ascribed names a label
On the alive present, without a fable?
And why does the world mostly pray
To the unseen or stones without a say,
While loathed, ignored, or crucified
Is the alive, without divide?

Recognised one is in appearance
As illusion or natural presence,
Is boundlessness seeming to be bound,

3 See Note 8C
4 See Note 8D

Yet formlessness thriving – unbound
At all times, each piece, every place,
Hinting there's no time, thing, or space,
Implying there's no separate divine
To be confined in any shrine,
Yet each image its invitation, its prayer
– Oneness without a pair –
To see it alone does shine
As each appearance, messy–fine;
Illusory the individual,
Yet an appearance natural,
So non-volitional was his stance,
Complete was his existent dance,
With no individual song,
And nothing right or wrong –
Simply stillness in seeming activity,
Finite form of formless infinity.

Though the nut lost its lovely shell
And shunned the scriptural spells
– As recognition had destroyed him, his love,
And had turned the pace of below–above –
Yet it wasn't simply an experience
But inexplicable appearance.
…

Again, emerged the prayers usual
And his rituals habitual,
Yet he could not unsee what had been seen,
Even with none present on the scene.
At times he knew not how to serve the stone
With a prayer pure to make it known,
So sought rituals he could own,
And surely make the stone well known.
But failed devotion and endeavour,
Submission too, and ways clever;
And now he wished for the halcyon days,
When he worshipped and did pray
Without the restlessness
Of dual or non-dual stress.

Then wondered why he did return
To worship the deity – was it to earn
Love, or was it fear, or loneliness,
Or fear of death, or present mess?
Or was his faith intrinsic?
Or an involuntary play mystic,
Where there is no self, but appearances
Alone, rising in the presence
As thoughts, feelings, seeming limits
Of apparent self, an exhibit.
Thus, ensued a mighty dance
Of idol's love, and the formless expanse,
For raised its head separation's hue
And passing winds of glimpses new.
Rose suffering in the intermediate
Of freedom, and separation's state.

The nut once full of anxiety
Sobbed for hours on the irony
Of what seemed to occur,
Beyond the fatalistic stir,
Inveighed against the deity
And fought with full ferocity
For not bestowing liberation,
Permanent fix from separation;
For it felt like prohibition in the tavern,
While he desired light in his cavern,
Yet he did not receive a reply
From the deity, or any other ally.
…

Once appeared immense gratitude:
For forms, the senses, taste, and attitudes,
For the alive life in appearance,
For love in varied form's presence,
For every form – a miracle –
For love pure, unconditional,
Appearing, embracing each hue,
Yet untouched – wonder, ever new.
The vison – ineffable, vast – abounds,
The idol alive, not deity profound.
Then along with the unknown stone
Even the known became unknown;
What appeared was what did rise,
The nut or not, nothing more prized,
Nothing and none on pilgrimage,
Yet each appearance true privilege.

The still all-pervading nothingness,
Alive, as father, mother, friend, did dress.

Complete remains the partial prayer,
For love alone as all does stare;
The nut continues to sway
In the known and unknown play,
For every time he rings the bells,
Or blows the conch shell
To worship the deity known,
Remains the unstruck sound alone.
But neither can he stop to pray
Or be rid of the quandary in play.

(Can the self an illusion weaken,
Or a person thus awaken?
Nothing can be done to sever
The two, as none does endeavour,
Appears as the flux – the one alone –
And vacillates in the known–unknown,
For all happens of its own accord,
Each prayer, ritual, or word:
A boundless love that does not belong
To anyone yet sings its infinite song.)

Appears an image of a stone,
But it is living, to atone.
It isn't cheerful, does not complain,
It never judges, nor does it enchain;
Does not reward ethical acts,
Nor rebukes, nor values any facts.
It never speaks and does not bless,
Remains an unattached witness,
Complete in its absence, not contained,
Yet in prayer is acclaimed.

22

The Seeking Lion

A lion once redefined his routine,
Renounced all meats – fat and lean –
To employ the healthy vegan theme,
For a fit and high-minded regime.
Content with his impeccable choice,
For weeks he preached and did rejoice,
Endeavoured to convert his friends
To pious meals and teas that could cleanse.
Promoted veganism in didactic ways,
On media and events, in its praise.

Yet when his instincts intervened,
Dreams of steak replaced the greens;
Visions of rare and tender steak,

Sprinkled with salt, peppercorn flake,
Succulent, saucy, sizzling steak,
Served with béarnaise and potatoes baked,
Tormented him night and day;
The lion fell in deep dismay.
Plagued by thoughts of being bad,
He felt he was completely mad.

Forlorn, a guru he did find,
Who taught him to silence the mind,
To detach, release the thoughts of prey,
Keep negativity at bay,
To meditate in cycles long
And listen to the cosmic song.
Yet this progression seemed too brief
As he endured anguish and grief,
So he sought some sort of epiphany
To release him from his misery.
…

In this despair descended insights,
Rebellion for rules, life's plight,
Of how religion does sway
A being to eat, live, and pray,
Joins science and gurus of the day
And society to show the way
To bring perfection to fruition,
Though he wondered form's need for permission,
Or guidance from the source external
To instruct in living natural.

He straddled instincts, ethics – the two –
Until natural instincts seized virtue,
Realised it wasn't wrong to lust,
Craving for steak a primal thrust;
Chain of existence, none to blame,
For no two forms can be the same,
So food's crucial for one, not the norm,
Poison–nectar is relative to form.
And crucial is nature's diversity
For the seeming sustainability.

Then with the apparent passage of time
Revealed was nature's play of rhyme,
Shattered the lion's view of life
From motion to all existent life.

Destroyed beliefs of ethical foods,
As carnivorous some flowers and fruits.
Realised nature is brutal in its role,
Is neither confined nor controlled,
Ethical or unethical,
For its seeming aim is survival.

Yet all these seemed like thoughts in view
That did not confer a slight clue
Of peace in the restless domain
Of myriad views of worldly plane.
He went within to heed the voice
Of the source, where rest all joys,
And recognised favoured foods –
He embraced or rejected fare, pursued
Countless beliefs of good and bad,
Was tortured by the latest fad.

Abstract ideals seemed to hunt,
And always sought a novel stunt,
Thus ruled thoughts claiming for the frame
Fixed shares, timings of food and rest – an aim.
He had traded his playful ways alive
For staid, unnatural drives,
And was guided by delusion,
Not by nature, form's intuition.
While naturalness is, can't be performed,
So it's ignorance to preach or force a form.

He grasped all notions and a story
Revolve around an identity,
Which greedily rips the habitat
And turns it into a jungle tart;
To counter this greed pursued
Of desire for lots or fancy food
Woven are morals by a group of minds.
Yet sought is the genuine in the grind,
All to preserve an identity
– Deemed distinct from infinity –
Be it of individual or race
Or a species fallen from grace.

Revealed: *ahimsa,* true non-violence,
Is natural acceptance of appearance,
And this acceptance does prevail,
Even when inner violence does sail.

Recognised: life as love – eternal,
Unbound in internal–external,
A love that all does embrace,
Even when it falls from grace.
Wondered: what sustains all the forms
Before thrust is the worldly norm?

Realised the form has no fables;
Its instant concern is survival,
So perfectly works this entity,
Without a distinct identity,
And enough is its intelligence
That operates in seamless cadence,
As in appearance of a newborn
Whom no illusion does adorn,
And there are no virtues or vice,
Nor greed for foods, ample or nice.

Then naturally it was enlightening –
The apparent resourceful recycling,
When disappears the seeming form,
Seeming elements in themselves are drawn,
So unborn life is, cannot die,
It holds and appears as forms that come by.
Illumined: energetic are forms,
Which on their own appear, perform,
And forms not dense or in the limits,
But a stir of the infinite.

No volition in thoughts or acts,
For none in skin to enact
The appearing scene, act, or trait;
So, none is bound or liberated.
Hence, this suffering and contraction
Too, an energetic expression
Of nothingness, in display –
No other but the seeming play
Appearing as it is. Complete.
Absolute as the relative treat.

Appears a naturalness –
Unconditioned joy, past stress.
Life is, without an intent or goal,[1]
Being as what is, whole.

And this world is but an appearance,
A pointless play of this presence.
To be precise: a roaring silence,
Dancing as forms in variance,
With no occurrence and no start or end,
Formlessness forming, cannot be penned.

Yet no identity
Can ever find the reality
Of love, which appears as this,
Beyond tales of control or bliss,
For identity is an illusion –
An apparent show of seclusion;
Energetic appearance
With none in existence
To know or find why this parade
Appears the way it does, is portrayed.
…

Such lions play in each apparent age,
Who stress the trivial: sacred, sacrilege.
The play of veganism, eating meat
Is life in its own apparent feat.
Yet ignorance or recognition
Is love alone in expression,
Appearing as the infinite roles,
Unwrapping as a seeming scroll.
Thus, all our lion does this day
Is simply love, eat, and prey.

1 See Note 9A

23

Big Bang

PART 1

Friends:

The nougat and the roulade
For each other had high regard;
Together they studied and did play,
With punting the highlight of their day;
Summer evenings were spent on the Cam
With friends, conversing about cheese and ham.
In winters cooking was their passion,
Novel cakes and bakes they did fashion,

Though in science they had found an art –
A devotion held close to the heart,
For charmed the mysteries of the sky
And the infinity of 'pi'.

Professor White and Professor Cream
Guided the duo in their theme.
But the Professors were as diverse
As light and dark in the universe;
The former erudite and lean,
The latter affable and keen,
Besides, Professor White did work in pride,
While Professor Cream to Oneness allied.
Their views made scholars take sides,
Yet both were loved, for they did provide
Exquisite expertise and ceaseless zest,
Which scholars dreamt to manifest.

One summer's day ensued a debate[1]
Spontaneously on the new dictate
Of science and non-dual view
Between the Professors two.
The roulade and the nougat
Joined with their friends to heed the art
Of their Professors up to date
And taste two flavours on one plate.

PART 2

Professor Egg White:

'Aeons ago transpired the birth
Of the cosmos entire, life's hearth,
As the final fate of the universe;
It will expand and all shall disperse
From singular to multiplicity,
Which shall return to its unity.
The 'Big Freeze' theory may apply:
Hot at birth and cold when it dies,
So from the void where it all began
To nothing, at end of its span.'

1 This verse is a work of fiction.

The students heard his point of view,
Took notes and tried to thus construe.
The friends exchanged a glance and smiled,
As Professor Cream expressed views wild.

Professor Nutty Cream:

'Sorry, I don't agree, Professor White,
With your research, that seems to lack insight.
The spaceless, timeless universe
Is not confined in any verse,
Nor does any specific event
Begin or culminate its segment,
For it is energy existent,
Which appears as the forms apparent,
And energy's too alive, immediate
To be confined in any state.
The void appears as these arrays,
Energy in most probable display,
Thus this emergent cosmic presence
Is formless silence in appearance.
This is it; this is the 'Big Bang',
Without a start, end, span, or bang.'

Professor Egg White:

'Unscientific is this nonsense
Of timeless, spaceless substance.
It seems you are lost in non-duality,
Ignore the evident factuality
Of studies of matter, hidden dimensions,
The particles, the waves, their comprehension,
The scientifically proven theories,
The search for a singular series.'

Professor Nutty Cream:

'Atoms are ninety-nine percent
Empty space, to this most assent,
But, as you know, it is not empty space,
A lacuna, for it is not a place.
Rather, it's nothingness energetic –
Pulsating, alive, not dead, nor static,
Appearing as the present view alive.

So, can there be an object that does thrive
In space and time, its purview?
Is not all Oneness, never two?

Though void and energy seem as two,
It's one, but for form to be in view
Opposing aspects seem to appear;
For light to be seen dark must cohere;
Form in the backdrop of formless is seen,
But one this life and void unseen.
So, matter and anti-matter in presence
Are one, in dual appearance.

Though occurrences seem to flow,
Nothing does come or go;
Even the atoms that you breathe today
Were present in varied forms per se,
So from the view of the totality,
The universe has no finality.'

Then in a manner witty yet subtle
Continued the Professor his rebuttal.

'Yes, a single theory the scientists trace,
New discoveries forever embrace,
Mimic 'Big Bang' at the minute level
To show the play in which energy revels
– Which always anew does appear –
As Higgs[2] or other particles that stir,
Which seem to collide, are in play,
To seemingly more produce, display;
So, a recycling unit seems this cosmos,
Where nothing is gained or is at loss.
Yet all's an energetic appearance,
Not dense or spatial medium in presence.
And do you think a model can define
Energy natural, without confines?
Is not most of science a theory?
Life as we know it is a probability,
And if is found a singular theory,
Would not it end in infinity?
And can theories explicate
The whole, its paradoxical gait?

2 See Note 10A

Your mention of hidden dimensions,
In and beyond our comprehension,
Suggests spatiality, view from a perspective,
Signifying layered is the collective.
But, Professor, reflect on the clues
Of Schrödinger's cat not in view.
And, as per your research, review –
Curbed are dimensions to the view;
From the top, a cube appears a square,
While a sphere as a circle seems to stare,
Therefore a 3-D[3] object 2-D does appear,
Hinting dimension to view adheres.
However, don't they all appear
At the same instant, though unclear?
So supposing dimensions to be spatial,
Or of time, is to narrow the essential.'

Professor Nutty Cream's eyes now did shine,
As he spoke of the unknown designs.

'And seen beyond the spatial views
At one point appear all the hues,
Implying exist neither time nor space
Or the seeming dimensional phase,
Though like a wave seems to rise
An appearance, in creative guise –
It is floating fluidity[4]
Waving as this seeming activity.
Yet the embracing spaceless, timeless presence
Is not separate from its appearance,
As a prism that refracts sunlight
Projects the void in the form of light.
In essence all is a hologram,
Where light is the apparent form,
Or all is a cosmic symphony
Of energy that is free,
Appearing as all, yet none,
Seemingly being done–undone,
Or nothing being everything,
Without an attached cosmic string.'

3 Here, 2D and 3D are short forms for 'two-dimensional' and the 'three-dimensional'.
4 See Note 10B

Professor Egg White:

'Nonsense! I don't agree, Professor Cream,
With your intangible dreamy schemes,
For if you think don't exist space and time,
Take a hard look at life, beyond your rhymes.
A mystical discourse your theory sounds:
Scripture cannot what science propounds;
Science requires logic and evidence,
Does not rely on the *ashram's* silence.'

Professor Nutty Cream:

'Professor, to recognise time and place,
Surely, you are in a timeless space?
For opposites create each other
And validate each other's clutter;
So, from the timeless point of view alone,
We seem to construe time's linear zone.

Also, when the nation's time does change
To optimum daylight thus arrange,
Back and forth every clock does go –
All adapt to the ongoing show.
Does not awareness the change affect?
Can clocks the interval of time direct?
So, isn't duration of time labels,
Like all our fairy fables?
Also, the stars that you see today,
Are they present as the same display?
Get to the smallest unit of time,
You will only sense the unchanging prime.

Moreover, can there be a direction
In space, is not all a projection?
Isn't all our study relevant
To a position, its measurement?
And if there is only infinity,
How to know of its start or entropy?
Reflect: can appearances flow?
Is there a linear show?
Only an appearance –
This, the present illuminance,
An energetic display
Of emptiness in play.

Professor, silence alone is all around,
Which plays as this sound that abounds.
Yet to say there is a timeless state,
Or silence everything does celebrate,
Is to ensure stay time and space,
One the inverses that are placed;
On earth impression of flatness appears
While from space earth seems like a sphere,
Yet they are true at the same time –
Likewise, one appears as the dual rhyme,
Or timeless, nothingness seems in time,
Is alone, energetic form sublime,
For one alone appears dual
Yet is truly non-dual;
Precisely an energetic hum, a stir,
Appears, disappears, does concur.
And if there is nothing alone,
Is there another to make it known?
There's neither existence nor non-existence –
Unknown, ungraspable is this presence.'

Professor White looked on in disbelief,
Appalled by such unscientific beliefs.
Continued to speak patronisingly
Professor Cream, his homily.

'Our fellow scientists too this prize,
That nothing alone as all does arise.
Suggest the neurological reports
That acts appear without a consort:[5]
An illusory self later takes charge,
With a distinct authority does barge,
And owns the acts in appearance,
So simulation our space–time presence.
Professor, we are truly as real
As names of days of the weekly wheel –
Life alone without intent or goal
Seemingly infinite, in a roll.'

Then with a twinkle in his eye
He carried on in tenor wry.

---

5 See Note 10C

'Yet isn't it an amazing treat
That this nothingness that's complete
Tries to know self scientifically
And measure mathematically,
Argues without a base
About the seeming space–time chase.
Professor, this is it. This is the Big Bang!
Without a start, end, span, or bang.'

PART 3

The debate carried on for hours together.
Roulade and nougat now wished for cool zephyrs,
Though they enjoyed the debate,
Loved the information up to date,
But danced abstract heaviness
With hunger and sleepiness
That can't be satiated by words refined,
Or by sums – infinite or confined –
But are satiated by tastes of tea,
Are biased to foods fresh and free.
Furthermore, summoned by clear skies,
The Cam, friends, and flavoursome pies,
Slipped out the roulade and the nougat
To devour divine tea, buns, and tart
And to experience the alive tastes
Of a sugary treat that seems truly chaste.
…

They spent the evening punting on the Cam
With friends, gossiping about cheese and ham.
The lush grounds and whiffs of grass,
The soft resonance of ripples that pass,
Aloof swans and the floral hues super,
The nosy ducklings and the ducks in stupor
Soon overtook the imminent summits,
The theories and the non-dual myths,
Along with the stress of competing,
The grades, and degree in waiting.

Forgotten were the assignments due
By the two, who were lost in the view
And mesmerised by tastes and prating;
The two friends then did celebrate
The moment, punting on the Cam,
Surrounded by verdure and punt slams.
As they revelled in the atmosphere light,
They sang an ode for the stars at night.

24

The Timeless Song

This verse[1] is based on the six seasons of the Indian clime. The reference to the bride missing her beloved is common in traditional Indian legends, songs, and scriptures. For an explanation of this verse, please refer to the notes.

1 See Note 11A

PART 1

The bride in myriad disguise
Sought her beloved in mixed guise.
She hoped to be one, complete,
And with Him in wedlock sweet,
Lose herself in arms divine,
In her precincts raise His shrine.
She desired to always be with Him,
Free, fully flavoured to the brim.

As form she formlessness did seek,
And strove to reach the formless peak.
As sound, she thought He lay in silence,
Thus longed for its eternal presence.
As movement, she wished to be still,
As sorrow, merge in joy that thrills.
As attachment, sought detachment,
For she wished the bliss of being absent.

The bride yearned for conjugal bliss
And, rueful, the beloved did miss.
As she burned within to belong,
Like the cuckoo[2] craves in its song,
She sang, atoned, and did await
Through the seasons, on all the dates,
For the beloved to return evermore
And fulfil her diminished core.

The bride then pursued purpose, reason,
In every moment of all seasons.
She searched for Him in every place
To catch His glimpse, Him embrace.
The passage through the Indian clime –
This goal became her voyage prime,
For she didn't see that He's the taste
In all the flavours in their place.

Forgot: celebration that appears
Is the beloved, adorned without frontiers,
And the bride–beloved aren't dual states,
The beloved whole, the bride inchoate.

2 See Note 11B

For plays the beloved: as senses five,
As night and day, as the alive,
And lives, is love, beckons, abounds,
As bridal mystery does surround.

The beloved as the groom and bride
Is, isn't, unknown does reside,
And in the performance named as life
Endeavours as the bride in strife.
And through the twelve months, seasons six,
Appears as the bride, as per the scripts –
Spontaneous, longing in despair,
Seeking the self in its affair.

PART 2

The bridal journey through six seasons of the Indian clime.

Spring Season – Vasanta Rtu (Mid-January/ February to Mid-March/April)

The cuckoo's[3] song and *Palash*[4] bring
In the innocence of nascent spring;
Cavort the flowers and the bumblebees,
As the breeze bears the scent of blooming trees;
Appears birth in its exquisite essence
On being nourished after death's silence.

Prepared are delights[5] of ebullience,
Like the wild in all its brilliance;
Float flavours of greens and saffron rice,
Aide zesty drinks and fresh fruit slice.
With *jaggery* treats[6] and mangos raw,[7]
Nature admires itself in awe.

The lone bride succumbs to the blues,
As trees adorn the branches with hues,

3 Here, the reference is to the Asian *Koel*.
4 Here, the reference is to the flowers of the *Palash* tree, known as *Kimsuka* flowers or *Tesu* flowers. For more information, see Note 11C
5 See Note 11D
6 See Note 11E
7 See Note 11F

And nothing can quench the bride's thirst,
For she forgets all is in love submersed,
And only the beloved does stay –
Appears as bride too, isn't away.

Summer Season – Grīṣma Rtu (Mid-April to Mid-June)

Bakes and burns the earth in summer heat;
Birds and beasts to the shades retreat;
The rivers dry and floral hues fade;
Flora and fauna yearn for cool cascades.
Yet nature continues to perform:
It torments and endures its norm.

Many enjoy the fresh delights
Of curd, lime, and tangy bites;
Refresh with rose milk, sharbat, sorbet,
Devour watermelons, barley;
Savour coconut, mangos, mint,
Cucumbers, onions of varied tints.

The bride still burns like the forest fire,
For to integrate is her desire.
May rise remembrance of the one,
By chance may cease separation's run.
But she cannot meet or attain Him,
For endless striving makes her grim.

Monsoon Season – Varṣā Rtu (Mid-June to Mid-August)

The dense skies rupture – cleanse the land –
The peacocks dance, streams rush unplanned,
Lightning strikes confront the clouds,
While insects make their huge clans proud;
Float in the lushness flocks in flight;
The refreshed earth sinks in delight.

Corn on the cob, chai cooked on coal
Complete the monsoon's merry, wet soul.
Several fast to find release,
Fifty-six dishes enhance select feasts;
Impressive are the southern festivals –
Their banquets are a splendid spectacle.

The bride doesn't echo the stance:
Unsettled, raw is her expanse.
Ignited are her passions by the rain,
Which makes her ache and pine in pain,
For she sees distinct are lover–loved –
On distant shores is the beloved.

Autumn Season – Sharad Rtu (Mid-August to Mid-October)

The foliage is in contentment drowned,
The loti bloom in soiled surrounds.
The golden hues and moonlight illumine
The mountains, strewn by saffron sanguine,
And sweetly glow the harvest and breeze,
Embrace stillness, complete, in ease.

With plentiful provisions on show,
Pervades benevolence in flow.
Desserts dominate the dinner tray,
For festivals this season sway,
And as the swans with the lakes converse,
Milk is the metre of the sweet verse.

Vices and virtues burn in timeless fire:
To cease division, nothing's required.
As sea is to tide, beloved is to bride –
Without beloved can't appear the bride.
Yet hopes the bride night and day,
And for her marriage she does pray.

The next two seasons, *Hemant Rtu* and *Shishir Rtu,* run into each other, hence most poets found it difficult to distinguish between the two. In the northern part of India they are marked separately; however, in the southern part of India they are classified as one.

Hemant Rtu is when mild winters turn extreme, while in the *Shishir Rtu*, the following season, extreme cold becomes mild, ready for the advent of spring.

Mild to extreme winter – Hemanta Rtu (Mid-October to Mid-December)

Rivers and flowers sing fortuitous notes,
The squirrels scuttle in striped coats.
The dark stings as it dulls the dawn,
Unravels nature, sheds old brawn.
Severe storms sustain chilled breeze,
Celebrates light: the fog and freeze.

Feasts range from spice to sweet,
Dried fruits and nuts enhance the treats,
Barfi's, laddus, halwas[8] the desserts sway,
Rich and hearty in perfect play.
Gram, guavas, carrots get their due,
As mustard grooms to show its hues.

The bride echoes the endless verse,
Sights the timeless universe.
Yet this glance of love's not akin
To the beloved, not out or in.
For when lifts the separation's veil,
It is seen it's the illusion's trail.

Extreme winter to mild spring: Shishira Rtu (Mid-December to Mid-February)

Intense cold bows to season mild;
The earth prepares for birth wild,
And slowly fade the freezing nights,
The dew at dawn like pearls of light.
Seem chaste the glades and jasmine buds,
As illumines the source without the blood.

Provide pine nuts, *kahwa*,[9] and coffee
The warmth denied by mountains frosty.
Peanuts and sesame pair with sweets,
To be prized in each and every street.
Oranges, turnips, mustard, peas,
Along with radishes the palate tease.

The bride adorned with sandal, musk
Is unable to see the subtle husk,
That being void is not freedom
But a conjured garden of Eden.
Yet present–absent is the beloved alone,
The boundless and the bound its throne.

Then what transpired none can say:
Ceased the bridal role, its play,
But unknown to all is this death –
A seasonal song in every breath.
The wedding – recognition for none –
The formless groom is the bride, one.

PART 3

Appears a journey pure and innocent
In which the bride seems discontent.
In her longing for conjugal bliss
She seeks the beloved who isn't amiss,
Demands to know and own His presence
In the aware and curbed appearance,
Mistakes craving and attachment
As love, and feels it is absent.

Her zealous chase sees love at bay
And marriage suffering's display,
For she forgets love is each flavour
And the one who it does–doesn't savour.
Whisper the secret, all seasons in range
Convey the stillness in the change:
All's the beloved, its form the bride,
And unaided it sings in pride;

As the sun it wakes and wakes as earth,
Appears without death and birth;
As winter seeks not gains of spring,
As summer doesn't monsoon songs sing;
Just is. Complete as each season,
Blooming without an aim and reason.
But as the bride ignores its wonder
Of being, she dreams on in slumber.

8 See Note 11G
9 See Note 11H

The bride that yearns is 'me' and 'you',
Seeking the beloved in all we do,
Refusing to see that exclusivity
Is the bane of wonder. And captivity
Of life is flouting the miracle
Of being, for the mystical –
All in the quest for an idyllic life,
While love appears as all, is rife.

When seemingly ceases separation's role,
Dies down, disappears the bridal patrol,
Extinguishes matter–soul, the known,
Appears only love – the unknown,
Without the bride and the beloved,
Without the lover and the loved.
Just formless forming – one,
With none to view the self, in none.

Of this wedlock the boundless sing,
Of their release from suffering,
Virginal being[10] as them sheens,
Untold vastness in defined scene,
Alive, ubiquitous, not one or two,
The beloved as the bride – anew –
Ineffable this essence
Of nothing in appearance.

Still on her own can't seek the bride,
As the appearance of bridal pride
Is the energetic expression
Of the beloved, without possession,
Humming the seasons and the sultry play,
Without the bridal veil in the way,
So it is never the bride's journey,
But the beloved, in appearance, free.
Love: the beloved and bride
Portrayed as the seasonal tide.

Beloved: the life that seems to flow,
With, without apparent self does glow,
Fresh like the blooming of a tree
Or the waving of the sea –
Performing as bridal mystery
The song of wedded liberty.
Love appearing without a reason
As restful rhythm of the seasons.

10 See Note 11I

25

Chicken's Story

Once sailed a clever fox
Beyond known lands and docks.
At last, he came across a land
Unexplored and unmanned.
Soon he found an ethnic tribe
Of chickens, who were circumscribed
In ways of thinking and living life,
Being uncouth, survived in strife;
But they cooked scrumptious meals
With sauces that appeal,
And one such potent fare,
Which was beyond compare,
Was *'Piri'* by name,
Which tasted best with game.

The fox was sure he had struck gold,
Relished his luck, became bold,
Decorously sought permission, with bribes,
To trade with the foreign tribe.
A masquerading tribal head,
Approved the trade of the sauce red,
And launched was the *'Piri'* brand,
And help arrived from the foxes' land.

The foxes chased in ways creative,
Efficiently employed the natives
To make the piquant sauce,
Their essence in it toss.
Soon the taste was recognised
Across the globe, was prized,
And founded were the headquarters
In the foxes' land, the exporters,
Hence rich became their land,
And carved a niche their brand.

Affluence now aroused the envy
Of those who missed prosperity,
And complex turned the game
Of bitterness, blame, and flame.
Then lured were some chickens
To the foxes' land, to be given
Jobs, enough for everyone,
Only to be outdone.
Thus, the globetrotting fox
Tricked the chickens orthodox.

'Cut! Cut!' cried the director,
'Dreary are such spectres.
We have been fed the same stew:
One pattern – faces new.
Where there are rivals two,
Of good–bad, right–wrong view,
States of us versus them,
Sponsor the star, the crook condemn;
Or where the world is saved from threat
By a hero – initially inept –
To bring about a perfect state,
Where exist the good and great.
Oh! Made of wishful dreams,
Are shows with such themes.'

Then instructed the director
His junior selector:
'Find an unusual account,
Which has the wonder of the fount,
An unexpected story,
The epitome of glory.'

Then proposed the assistant
Accounts exciting, brilliant,
Of crime, complex love stories –
Gripping, enjoyable, or gory;
Of riches and dreamy flights,
Triumph after fights;
Mysticism from the east,
Heaped with the kimchi feast;
Of same gender-marriage –
In favour or to disparage;

Or an ideal worldly state
With equal mandate on the plate.

But not one pleased the director,
As they seemed to appease a sector
And upset the other camp,
Thus embossing a dual stamp;
Or soothed a sentiment
While dividing in the present;
Or judged the ancient mess
From present raised awareness,
And tried to cease aversion
By anger and conversion;
Or bestowed absolute power
On those regarded superior,
Creating further imbalance
Among foods – equal in essence;
Or brought to light the greed
Of individual seed,
Its subtle need to rule
In the guise of equal school;
Which curtailed boundless life in small
Forms, timed–timeless in a brawl.
So, the director bade his crew:

'Go find a story with a view
Of love, untied to the roles
Of trade, kin, sex, or soul.'
…
A member of the crew
Wrote a note on the true–untrue,
Of the one that is not two,
For the director to review:
'Sir, there are no stories,
But life without source's glory,
And nothing can compare
To life, its present fair,
The most significant of stories
With all its inbuilt glories,
Is incomparable
To the peace without a fable.

Besides, investing in a tale
Demands a dual scale,
While unbroken is life's song,
And to none does it belong.
No tale but love does thrive
In this immediacy alive,
With no future, present, or past
But occurrence in the embrace vast.
Rather, appears love absolute,
Alone, as each act and pursuit.
An appearance of presence alive,
A miracle, where no tale can thrive.

Yet this freedom's so vast and complete
That embraces stories and feats,
Appears as the individual
Who owns the credentials
Of being in time and space,
With or without grace,
Presents perspectives diverse
On the appearing verse,
And deems them as narratives
Of personal initiatives,
And where accounts appear
In an individual's sphere
Alone, while this life
That appears rife
With form has no split,
Or separable spirits,
But appears as every hue
With no one to it view.
So, to say 'I' don't have a story –
Another act illusory,
For there is none in view
Tales to own, rebuff, or pursue.
Yet the funniest stories spun
Are to disparage the ones
Who are lost in narratives
Of their life comparative.

Sir, you won't find an account
Without individual count,
Or love untied to the roles
Of trade, kin, sex, or soul.'

But the junior selector
Hid the crew member's letter
From the seeking director,
Who always aspired to differ.
So still seeks a story new
– To stress life's glory true –
The director. But can miracles
Of life be seen in dreamt pinnacles?

But, please, don't inform the director
Nor the movie spectator
That there's no story in view
To relish, for me and you,
Nor a causality,
Time or mortality –
Simply energetic appearance.
Evolutionary turbulence.
And please do not ruin the fun
By saying there's no one,
For love fantasises the fables,
Awards the judgemental labels
Of spicy 'Piri' chickens,
And spiteful foxes, sharp vixens.

26

Neighbours

The imagined fence
Midst the squid and the eel,
The still waters, wave

27

The Holy City

In the Indo-Gangetic Plains
Reign clamour and the sacred strains.
Here pilgrims visit round the year,
Perform rites, embrace sacred gear
– Being truly charitable –
Donate amounts admirable
To wash away sins and end all strife
And find the purpose of this life.
Though here torment dust and heat,
The pilgrims wish to here complete
Life's journey, acquire liberation,
And end the rounds of reincarnation.

In this religious atmosphere
Positioned was a pond unclear,
And in the muddy waters did stay
A lotus serene, who spent the day
Assisting her friend at the stall,
Providing tea and foods to all.
The stall was owned by a rose,
Yet midst them there was no ranked course,
For the two friends did share
A friendship truly rare,
A bond without the ratios,
Opposites in complete repose,
Platonic love beyond what's known,
A love based on friendship alone.

The rose was beautiful and sweet,
While lotus'wisdom none could meet.
Both seemed content in their existence:
One was their ethos and essence,
Did not compete or aspire to heights,
Admired the other's essence bright,
And both loved to converse and share
Local news in their time spare.
But quite diverse was their one trait,
Though it did not their bond abate:
The lotus was calm in chaos,
While the rose grew disturbed and cross
At the sight of any injustice
Or an egoistic trip or practice.

Simple and orderly were their days,
With similar events at play,
Where they followed a rhythmic routine,
Without strain, intent on the scene;
They sliced vegetables at sunrise
– That infused patience past all price –
Chopped wood and kneaded flour,
Made flavoured fillings of flower
For stuffed *kachoris*, flavoured milk
And other foods of that ilk.
But in slicing, grating, lighting fire
– The mundane – the unique did transpire,
And the whole existence seemed present
In the daily acts of existence.

Although delightful was all their food,
One dish was popular and valued
By all – the rose and lotus *chaat*[1] with tea,
Which like the friends was sweet and spicy;
So fame for their scrumptious fare,
Adorned with advice rare,
Made them the local champions –
Their kiosk, lair of ambience.
...

One evening over snacks and tea
They gossiped in tones carefree
About an incident of pilgrims in fight
And how division the mind does delight.
The rose fervently did rebel,
Lucidly spoke of the self's spell:
'Selfish is the pilgrim mind,

1 *Chaat* is a savoury snack made in several ways across India. Ingredients such as potatoes or *samosas* with chutneys, chilies, coriander, and yoghurt are used to make this popular street food.

Which blindly follows rites defined,
Performs pilgrimage and austerity
To fulfil needs of posterity,
Gain in name of charity,
Have added popularity
In their social rank and role,
As a benevolent, sacred soul.
Relates experiences the pilgrim –
To everyone verbatim;
Unconsciously sustains spiritual banners
Or constantly seeks new clamour
To be different from the rest,
For it desires to be noticed,
As it is lost in ignorance
Of mind's restless divergence.

This pilgrimage and charity,
Along with forced austerity,
Self-esteem does enhance,
Is self's patterned dance.
For pilgrimage and donation
Are seeming acts, but the perception
Attached to the activity
Indeed enhances captivity;
Firstly, it hierarchy does observe,
An elitist view does reserve,
Where it fabricates a pyramid,
Where another's always timid,
Then pities ones in low state,
Subtly the seeming self does elevate.
Then it claims to bestow aid
With illusory ownership laid,
To balance feelings of guilt,
While unchanged remains what's built;
Then feels it deserves heaven and treats,
For its life's spiritual and complete.
But life is not an investment
For striving, seeking reimbursement.
Aren't the pilgrim's sins redeemed
Only in waters of deceptive dream?'

The lotus in repose of the calm waters
Relished her friend's fiery fervour,
So continued to expose the rose
The mind's pretentious shows
(Frenzied, she exuded a hue
Of deep red, like her nature true):
'If genuine was the donor's concern,
Why would for publicity they yearn,
And publicise in ways clever
Their partaking in grand endeavours.
All seems to be an ego trip,
Blooming in façade of authorship.
For if they can't calm their inner fire,
How will they sate the world's desires?
So, pity, help, support, and aid
Abet individualism and grades,
And distribution, charity, or service
At their root offer bliss
To the donor's mind alone,
Maybe to the donee's transient tone.

Compassion and care
Without ownership is rare,
For they don't divide or compare
But reveal the pretentious flair,
Slay the division
Of self, other – the separation –
Solely the act alone,
No ownership to the act own,
Or to feel the fulfilment
On helping those in a predicament,
Or no one to possess the treasure,
But life alone, beyond measure.
Rather, no one behind the act,
Or recognition of the fact:
There's none to have volition
To give, receive – no partition.
Simply embracing, sharing, being,
The one alone, thus appearing,
This is true compassion and care,
An appearance that is rare,
Akin to the sun, waters, soil, the sky,
That do not seek benefit or act high,
Or split life in graded forms,
Or pretend to humbly perform.

For nature doesn't do charity,
It just is, fulfilment in parity –
The utmost reverence
For the energetic appearance.

Lotus, aren't the natural resources
Everyone's right, though the fabric, course,
And system of society
Has ruined the propriety
Of living; greed insatiable
In the name of the factual.
A fascism – this division's illusory,
Which then tries to unite the delusory,
Or rouse the beings ignorant
And raise awareness for self's predicament.
The world seems to be astray
From the natural play.'

By now agitated was the rose;
The lotus tried to quieten her pose:
'Relax, nothing's so relevant
For you to raise your temperament
Or disturb your balance
For apparent ignorance.
And who can save whose life
When sovereign is only life?'
The lotus' peaceful presence
Brought complete calm and silence.

Impishly laughed, declared the rose:
'Don't let my flair impose,
And insult, thus go to waste,
So, listen,' she said without haste:
'Even these systems and traditions,
Meant for smooth social operation,
Have been turned into tools of position,
Where slave is the self's condition,
Which seeks unreal remedies,
So that reigns the self, its decree,
And if life doesn't follow its patterns,
The self then blames others or Saturn,
For it believes revolves this life
Around it, where it rules and thrives.
And this self, its desire to stay,
Even when the form does not play,
Creates heavens and hells to atone
For sins conceived by cultural tones;
Thus, deemed are certain places, states
As special to become liberated,
While neither exists a time
Nor any place sublime.'

The lotus now offered her friend
Biscuits and tea, for calm to descend.
The rose leisurely sipped her tea,
But was immersed in her homily:
'No wonder Kabir did not wish to die[2]
In Benares, all customs did defy,
Stated: "Kabir, the doorway to be freed[3]
Is minute, one tenth of a mustard seed,

2 See Note 12A
3 This is the 58th couplet *(sloak)* of Kabir, recorded in the *Guru Granth Sahib* (p. 1367).

While the ego is like an elephant massive:
How will it make through the passage?"
Yet these ignorant pilgrims believe
That Benares heaven does achieve.
Anyway, what is our Benares famed for –
The thugs or the filthy river we revere?'

Again the rose appeared agitated,
Continued her rant unabated:
'And don't you think, my friend,
That this business to transcend,
Or the merging of the soul
In one, to become whole,
Is like a belief of yesteryear –
Of the earth flat and not a sphere.
If there's an all-pervasive soul,
Can it be curbed in souls with roles?
And which part defines the whole?
Can the whole merge in the sole?
Isn't a soul as distinct entity,
Striving to blend in cosmic identity,
Or seeking consciousness infinite,
Or the self without a limit,
Like looking for the 'edge of the universe',
Or scanning rhymes in blank verse,
Or searching for city of Benares
In its temples, lanes, and ghats humongous,
While 'Benares' is a mere label
And not a distinct unit stable?

Oh, Lotus, you are the wise one,
Without any division,
So, say, aren't all the labels
Of caste, class, and religious fables
Conferred by the world alone
And left in its zone.

Do we need descriptions
To be?'

The rose who seemed to have vented
Her annoyance, now seemed content.
For a while they sat in silence
Enjoying the stars in radiance
And heard the gurgling of the river,
Were rapt by the reflective shimmer
Of the full moon and the vast sky –
Embracing yet seemingly high.
Preyed no present, future, past
Midst the presence that is vast.
…

The lotus – her each act,
Appeared like a prayer intact –
Considerately did say:
'One, love alone is this display:
Complete is the incomplete fashion,
To thus see – pure compassion.
Exact is your examination
Of the construed self's pretention,
Where it seems to continually seek
In varied guise and several techniques,
And this disconnect, the self does gnaw,
Which rushes to soften feelings raw,
Attempts to fill a ceaseless crater
Of illusion with false matter,
To find rewards in life–afterlife,
While we already have the reward – life.

This self, that's a disconnection
With alive energetic manifestation,
Is a display of one alone,
A performance that's unknown.
For life appears as its own pretence
And doesn't feed semblance.
Thus, the pilgrim seems to follow rites
To fill a darkness made of light,
And understand the scriptures
In dual or non-dual features,
But the pilgrim's version of this verse
Is neither noble nor is worse,
For nothing energetically
Is appearing, as this, solitary.

Rose, there is no pilgrim mind
Or individual confined.
Each form is boundlessness that's free,
No inner, outer, only energy
As the appearing form,
Without the defined norms.
Or appears life without a sect,
Only seeming cause and effect.
So, all is life as it is,
Religion, faith, or bliss.'

The lotus then swayed in silence
Before she illumined the brilliance:
'Though this appearance we see
Seems the play of traits three,[4]
Yet they are no physical traits
But energetic life in seeming gait
Appearing as the present scene,
With none performing, nor a screen
Separate on which all appears,
But formlessness as formed gears,
Where like a puppet dance
Displayed is a stance
Where appears ignorance
Or a stance indifferent,
Or destroyed is ignorance
By radical interference.
But all roles the one does play,
Illuminating its own clay.
Volition too is an appearance
Of Oneness in its play of instance,
Like its display of the sun
Rising and setting – an illusion.

So, Rose, there is no world to save.
None is, to good or bad behave –
All rises in this innocence,
Empathy, coldness, ignorance.
So, dear, the vulnerability,

4 See Note 12B

The fear, and the servility
Is spirituality too,
Not just fearlessness in view.
And isn't life, seeming experiences,
Complete grace, whether it's the silence
Of nothingness or bliss and order
Or this mess of the muddy waters?'

The rose then seemed irked by the noise
The lotus made – though in perfect poise –
As she sipped tea and crunched her biscuits,
While speaking in a way mystic:
'Rose, Kabir mocked traditions
To show they feed time, separation,
And that beliefs hold true
Until they are swapped by beliefs new.
Yet he did not possess a talent
To impose, insult each errant.
His message is deeper, profound:
It stresses the presence abounds,
This! Where nothing does begin or end
And none exists to transcend,
Where there is no captivity,
But freedom, with no identity,
Embracing even the divisional,
Simply that which is, the eternal –
The infinite empty skies
Where rises all life without allies,
A love, exhibiting its essence
As semblance, in presence or absence.

Yet, dear, as a friend I ask of you,
Though your defiance is love true,
Be soft like your petals, not your mood –
A warrior need not be rude.
Your message may not appeal to all;
Violent may appear their call,
For most see this and hear what's said
Through the filter of views that are bred.
A few alone see this alive presence
As it is, in complete absence.'

...

The friends talked till the light of dawn,
Yet neither felt even slightly drawn.
The duo resumed their daily chore
Of cooking when the clock struck four.
At dawn appeared a group of pilgrims –
Engrossed they were in singing hymns;
They stopped at kiosk for tea,
Ate, drank, and spoke of charity.

The rose overheard their dialogue,
Snapped, started her monologue,
Reiterated her notions
With passion on devotion,
On sanctity not confined to a place
But present as the rising grace,
On how the false self loves to hold
Deeds, that this presence does unfold.
The lotus attempted to intervene,
Tried to stop a frightful scene.
A few pilgrims agitated
Suddenly decapitated
The beautiful, vivacious rose
And quietened her bold prose.
Tore apart her tea stall, too –
Turmoil and chaos did ensue
In the religious atmosphere
Deemed to be divine and austere.

Numbed seemed the lotus by the events,
For all had changed in few moments.
The lotus had lost her innocent friend
To the madness of selfish trend.
Her heart filled with pain
Could not express grief's cane.
Though it's evident that none is born nor does die,
Yet the immediacy of love that does lie
Is more intimate and sacred
Than all the awakening fated,
All the spiritual experiences,
Conditionings, and taught resilience;
So wailed the lotus for her love –
The rose, her treasure trove –
Then helplessly cried, cursed the pilgrim mind,
Did not seek to find poise refined.

Appeared life in a range of sentiments,
Each intense, raw, unfiltered, full, present;
When tears flooded her serene eyes,
Memories of past seized her skies,
Yet presented the joy of being one
With love, which couldn't be undone,
As her friend was alive, for sure,
In her memories, love pure,
A love beyond all lore,
More intimate than before.
Yet untouched appeared the lotus' form,
Nonconforming to any norm.

It was a debacle for the locals, too,
Lost was life for confined hues,
And missed was the vivacious presence
Of the rose, and her tea stall of excellence.
…

One day the lotus heard a call
Of a red rose bud small.
The lotus said with a serene smile:
'Let's walk together for a while.'

28

The Pathless Trail

The unspeakable pathless trail
Is empty, endless, one, not two.
But isn't split wonton's stuffing-veil?
The unspeakable pathless trail.
Unknown – the wonton, soup, and pail,
Who can them split or has a clue?
The unspeakable pathless trail
Is empty, endless, one, not two.[1]

1 See Note 13A

29

Metamorphosis

Mysteries from the memory lane
Emerged, and brought immense pain.
Solitude and exile for many years
Made her face her deepest fears.

It was all revealed in lonely days:
'Of how control had risen in subtle ways,
How stained appeared her thoughts and skies,
With lust and greed in varied guise,

How tenure of talents and their rise
Had driven the self for a prize.
To be successful was her goal;
She believed that would make her whole,
Then fame, riches, victories – the taught
Patterns that are by this world sought –
Had hoisted her in vertiginous skies,
Followed by fear, in shadows of her rise.
A steep plunge, all seemed lost:
Health, wealth, honour – a huge cost.'

Now, swayed by remorse and negativity,
She wished life had unfolded differently.
Then recalled: 'the lack of trust,
Of instincts too – when reigned strong gusts –
And deceit and secretive ties,
Dishonest dealings, false allies,
Compromised marriage, threats persistent
Further had tattered faith and commitment;
Tears had dried, but trials hadn't given way,
With new distresses the norm each day.
A rigid ancestry, broken home
Had made her rebel against pious domes,
While her libertine slant had made it worse,
For patriarchal society rules all verse.
Sickening felt the recall
Of the yesteryear of fall,
Of how none had come to rescue
The lamb from the hot stew.
At last, derision had taken its toll
Till none was left to sell its soul.'

The fire of present – now seared thoughts and path
Of fear and being victim of life's wrath –
Again, reminiscing the glimpse
That had risen in life's mince:
'An embracing silence ever present
In all the seeming resentments,
Alive life appearing as forms,
Impersonal to any rising norms.'
This image that came to mind
Bought with it calm undefined
In the harrowed lamb, who walked alone
On the streets of Oxford, unknown.

Wondered why was she mistaken?
From the pure land thus forsaken.
A mirage now her past did seem,
When she reigned over riches that gleam,
A seeming collage of pictures,
With none in the midst of it to feature,
Just pictures appearing on their own,
While she remained untouched by the tale sown.
…

Sauntering through her daily way
On a winter's day – cold, dark, and grey –
She met her friend the homeless duck,
Who appeared jovial and unstuck
From her apparent story,
Or from a deprived category.
Then as if reading the lamb's eyes,
The duck spoke in manner wise:
'In the depths that are dark
Life's unbound and stark.
Musings from the imagined past
Do not confine a self – that's vast.
Like waves on water leave no mark,
Light is unaltered by the dark.
In presence appear thoughts of past,
But they can't taint the essence vast,
For thoughts are like clouds in the sky
That can't it impact, touch, or tie.

Life at times begets developments
To destroy rampant attachment,
And one must face what one fears
The most, accept unknown spheres,
Which shakes the self from its patterns,
Brings humility in the hazard.
But nothing can destroy the presence,
Which seems ineffable in essence.'
Then after some trivial talk,
Both went their ways on the walk.

But words can never restlessness calm,
For disquiet isolates even the psalm,
And citing recipes, fare's names,
Cannot satiate hunger's claim;

So she prayed to recall the love
Forgotten in life's treasure trove,
And then wondered alone in silence,
Until she questioned her existence,
Now doubted if there was a force
External or an eternal source
To pray to for help, advice – or nothing,
But simply life, without a meaning.

Though a lamb, she had never followed
The herd, or waited to be swallowed,
Had always battled like a warrior,
Fighting the imagined barriers,
So now she sharpened the blunt arrows
To shoot down the target narrow,
To rise above her story
And echo life's glory;
She felt like she had battled incidents
So could swim across illusion's prevalence,
Retrace her steps, try to go back
Like an arrow, to hit the target tracked.
But simply rose recognition
Of life, its linear illusion,
And slaughtered seemed delusions trite,
But without the shore in sight.

Then continuing her walk
At leisure, through the Broad Walk
In Christ Church, its meadows,
A stillness seemed to grow.
Caught her sight the present scene
Of content cows, the scattered green,
The effortlessly flowing river,
Soothingly serene in the shiver,
While holding the rowing shells,
The chattering crew and their yells.

She lingered at a slow pace,
And each step was a seeming grace;
Overflowed the unrestrainable tears,
But intimate felt all the fears,
For they weren't emotions of which to be rid
Or ignored, but love without a bid.
It was clear honour, fame, and shame
Are just relative to life's game,
Yet truly one, they are the same,
Irrelevant to life, without a name.
And radiates the stillness innate
In stormy waters, too, as the traits.

Immense bravery seemed to shine
– Which played host to fear defined –
With intelligence that gauged each sensation –
Not daring found in taxing situations.
In this fearlessness that did embrace
All fear, bliss, mess, or grace,
She displayed a shimmering sight,
Like the moon that reflects the sun's light.
Though exiled, she couldn't hide the light
Radiant, on its own, pulsating bright.
(For the light alone does shine,
Illusion or not, no confines.)

With every step a little she did die,
Till nothing but her ashes did lie.
Every step a step new, effortless,
The touch, the floor, unpossessed,
Like walking for the first time,
Ineffable, unknown chime,
A marvel, wonder, the unknown,
Simply Oneness, boundless, alone.
Disappeared the actor of acts,
The act alone without an impact.
Recognition: none to fight the war
Or go across the shore.
Yet it was not the lamb's experience
But ineffable timeless radiance.

Then she arose, resurrection in a flash,
Like the fabled phoenix from the ash,
And what followed was the return
Of seeming self, though only to burn
In the fires of life and its game,
A naturalness with, without a name.
But troubled the metamorphosing dance
Midst the apparent cage and freedom's expanse.
…

She returned to the rivers five
– An aberration from her drive –
To face everything dead or alive,
Ignominy, too, from the archives;
For presented was the grant to return
To the pure land of passes with steep turns,
To trek the mountains steep
Of the pure land that runs deep.
She ascended like the mountain goat
The valleys of wilderness remote.

On one trek, the mountains seized
Her, touched the morning sun and breeze.
Rose recognition: holding one's ground
In relationships abusive or profound
Is transient. Is a hit or miss.
While love alone appears, is this.
Appeared the taste or recognition
That there is no one in submission,
Or does control, or plays a role.
Appears boundlessness alone – the
whole,
A freedom where there is no way to act,
And no guilt, ties, doer-ship or impact.

Spontaneously life occurred;
Saw: praise and insults simply words
In a dictionary, not life's name,
A life without time, all its chains;
Present is only the appearing scene,
Never to be repeated, pristine –
Nothingness alone playing its game,
As hues of laughter, honour, shame,
Without anyone in the show
To it create, or it grow.

Now love as death the lamb had found,
A death in which nothing is bound,
Death that's completely cellular,
Yet nothing strange or peculiar –
A silence explosive in essence,
Vast and freeing, cosmic resonance.
Extinguished female and the male
Into the source, the Holy Grail,
A complete collapse of all structures
Of self, the other, roles, features,
For burst had the bubble of dreams
Into waters that as a bubble gleam;
Thus, the illusions fell away,
A mirage which wasn't there any way.

There was complete freedom, liberation,
Even from that which brings cessation,
A home beyond words, family, or land,
The loudest song, naturally, unplanned.
Yet there was no epiphany
Or a shift to accompany,
So there was none to know
The seeming end of a show.
The lamb did not acquire freedom,
Instead disappeared her entire kingdom.
…

Today no one returns to the urn.
No ashes remain to bury or burn.
Just recognition: death's an illusion too,
For self is not a meat in stew,
So no one ever owns the wool,
Or taints skies by thoughts plentiful,
For there is none behind the mask –
Nothingness performing each task,
Appearing as the vivid display,
All the perfect and spoilt soufflés.
All there is is this light
With its appearances bright,
The roles it does play,
This seeming display,
Like photographs in a stream,
The celebratory beam.
There's no desire for this occurrence
To be different in appearance –
Entirely free to appear as it may,
Even if something is in its way.
Just this immediate intimacy
Of the emergence, absolutely free –
Where nothing's denied, nothing does stay;
Love alone in free fall does play.
Ultimate penury and riches complete
A paradoxical, flavoursome treat.
So, like the mighty lion roars the lamb,
Beyond the innocence of I am.
…

Yet didn't occur the metamorphosis,
Nor graced was the lamb to be in bliss.
There's none to acquire liberty,
So no one can become free,
Or know of its existence,
Absence, or non-existence.
And there is no progress from dark to light,
For all is nothingness in occurrence bright,
Without a goal or destination
Or implication or causation.

So, no lamb, no progress, no shore,
But nothingness, aliveness galore,
Told as a tale of lamb in exile,
Where no soil's more or less fertile,
Simply the celebratory beam
Of light, in myriad themes,
As this paper and seeming story,
The writing and the words of glory,
Of Oneness in appearance,
Of real and the unreal cadence –
Yet caterpillar to butterfly, unknown.

30

The Split

Vanilla–Almond, Pistachio–Rose,
Chocolate–Orange, Walnut–Coffee,
A heavenly alliance
Of dreamy compliance,
An 'I do' kind of romance
– That wealth does finance –
Individual, yet one,
Unmatched like the sun,
Never to be apart,
Till death do they part.

Advertised was their tale
In glorious detail
On shared networks
And media of perks.
Photographs froze
And jealousies arose
In those who felt this love's real.
The pairs were termed as ideal
For their propriety
By the society.

Enamoured were the two
– By this apparent view –
The lychee and the mushroom,
Who were in splendid bloom,
Felt this to be love–life,
With affluence and lust rife,
Where one can become complete
With another's attention sweet,
And vital is the name,
Bound to the other in the game.

The soulmates rare
Now wished to pair,
Planned a ceremony
Of lavish harmony,
Adorned with glittery themes,
Marvellous magical dreams,
Bejewelled with romance
To augment their expanse.

The mushroom in bliss
Of his first tender kiss
Construed varied roles
Of their apparent goal,
Designed a future together
To bear all kinds of weather.
While the lovely lychee,
Who was in states of glee,
Felt the entire universe
Had made them sing the same verse,
So planned their destiny
With hues of harmony.
Danced images of desire
In passion's quagmire,
And spent was a fortune
– Apparent in the dunes –
To prepare for the ceremony,
Dripping with affluent harmony.

The stylish groom –
The handsome mushroom –
Marched up the aisle
In cheerful style,
For delighted was he
To wed the lychee,
For her to come along
And complete his partial song.
He longed to see the sight
Of her persona bright,
So waited for his bride
Smart, saucy, full of pride.

The lychee never came,
Disappeared from the game.
The mushroom still waits
For her to be his mate

And meet him in a sweet,
Or a kebab, or a treat.

Wonders:

Did society not endorse
Their unusual course?
Or did the media of perks
And shared networks
Falsely influence:
That in life's experience
Essential is a mate
For happiness innate.
Is loneliness really a curse
Or complete is its verse?

Is aware:

The split is never
With another,
And there's just this moment –
The invincible present –
Without a past and a future
To his being rupture,
While the incompleteness
And its apparent mess
Is love's complete song,
Desiring to belong
To itself.

The passion that he feels
Simply melts his heart's appeals,
So the mushroom anticipates
Her return, to animate
His life, as a dish complete,
As a starter or dessert sweet.

Senses:

Together or split,
Cannot love limit –
Intimacy is one, not two,
With none in view.
Absolute love – its being
Is alone, without a meaning,
Not a lonely universe,
But love in verse –
Unconditional.

But when overwhelms grief
He speaks to the leaves,
Asks them if they have seen
Her in their shadows lean;
Though when he receives no response
That he seeks or wants,
He questions the clouds
Of her whereabouts
And waits for them to reveal
News of her arrival, ideal.

At times, he desires to end
His form, to eternally transcend
His pain and end the dual name
In order to finish his game.

Then sees:

The desire to die
Is not to end the present cries,
But to end the seeming story
Of self transitory
That seems to suffocate
The appearing state
In the now.

But feelings simply rise
And fall in empty skies –
So burns the mushroom's fire
Without an occupier.
Nowadays, the mushroom,
Who seems in total gloom,
Stops every passer-by
To know if she lives or has died.
But no one knows her whereabouts,
Or her presence unbound.

…

Is there a split or tear?
Anything torn to repair?
Is any rhyme incomplete?
Any song without a beat?
Can anyone ever know
The purpose of this show?

Is everything complete
In its incomplete beat?
Is this a dancing scene
– Appearing messy,
pristine –
Without anyone in the
show
Of life, to distinctly glow?
Is life as it is
An unknowing
For no one?

31
Eton Mess

PART 1

Three friends: strawberry, egg, and cream,
Recorded their ordeal and their dreams,
The egg in full detail did write
Of how were split the yolk and white;
The strawberry expressed how she bled,
And how she wished she were dead.
Of being whipped the cream did voice,
Bore torture for she had no choice –
Lashed till high peaks replaced soft glow,
Indeed, a very messy show.
All had aimed to glow otherwise,
But were by life surprised –
So deceived by life, its scheme,
Redundant had become their dreams.

Then fortune seemed to play a part,
And life that seemed to fall apart
Was treated by the sweet advice
Of sugar, acclaimed as the wise.
Their stories were then merged in one –
A big mess, all appeared undone.
But on being eaten, proclaimed all:
'It is a dessert that enthrals.'
Which led to the interest of royalty,
Ensuring enormous popularity.

They pompously trotted across the globe,
Messy, but in their finest robe,
Recounted and sold their stories at length,
Were admired for their struggle and strength.
Their book became a bestseller,
It stressed the self – seeming dweller
Of forms – was relatable and mesmerised
With its account, which did polarise
Life, its seeming incidents,
And stressed the self's predicament.
…

PART 2

Later when dimmed their popularity,
And most refused to buy the same story,
Surfaced the inner scars
In amorphous feelings barred,
Thus sniffled the strawberry
At every opportunity,
While the egg got nervy and anxious,
And the cream turned obnoxious.
For troubled seemed the trio
With their previous messy blow.

To heal their wounds of yesteryears,
To be the one beyond the fears,
The friends approached the pavlova,
Who spoke of foibles of mind's flavour.
The pavlova was stern and clear,
Declared in his address, austere:
'A story always captivates
If messy – popular and great,
As then "I" can compare "my" life,
State it as calm or full of strife,
Be grateful to a noble God,
Or bond with the fable truly odd,
Or demean other doubtful souls,
Commend those who claim to be whole,
Pity victims – the seemingly flawed,
Thus create a hierarchical squad.
Or traverse from the other side,
Seek notice as a victim, thus preside,
And blame insular destiny,
For treating me with levity,
Thus seek attention constantly
By being the victim energy.

Loss followed by a win scenario
Is viewed with a higher success ratio,

For when life seems to smoothly flow,
Comfort I can to my struggle owe,
Then inspire the ones stuck in strain,
Make hope and faith appear to reign,
And show the way to success
By capitalising the mess,
Thus ensure constant attention
On self and its extension.

The self thus builds on seeming tales,
Strengthens the separation's veil,
Remains entranced in its account,
Considers itself as paramount;
In this way the self does stay,
And regenerates in the play,
Then suffers its own existence,
Wishes home of joyous non-existence.

This construed self is subtle, a creep,
For it ensures unconscious sleep,
Which goes deep in all its claims
Of entities with real names,
Which are endowed with volition,
Living in timed traditions.
And though complete is each state,
Confined self seems to be frustrated,
Believing it will become whole,
When sated are wants of the soul
With flavours that are only sweet,
Ignoring life's tastes complete.

A perfect paradigm – your Eton mess,
Displaying the self's distress in finesse –
At once, and with a messy domain,
Relays a neat colossal campaign,
Seeks profits, blames, from its throne views
And seems to separate all its hues,
Benefits from its mess and sweetness
To stay at the heart of the press.

But you need not endure this mess:
Step out of your story and its stress,
In the spaciousness of this,
To realise nothing is amiss.

This will bring a revolution,
A total dissolution
Into the energetic field –
The presence, which life does yield,
For life appears in all the flavours,
Even the horrid and the disfavoured.

The cause of the mind in suffering:
Begetting, jealousy, complaining
And constant comparison –
The most potent poison.
Yet know comparison does occur
Only when there is a self to it stir,
So liberate from a self – separate –
The root of misery's dictate
By staying rooted in the present,
Accepting freedom in the moment
As it is, and focus on formlessness –
The essence that all forms does bless.
For on self's ceasing there's liberation
And total peace beyond vexation.'

The three felt crushed by the advice
Of the pavlova precise,
For they failed to accept the moment,
Couldn't concentrate on the present,
And somehow felt they were at fault
For focusing on fables of assault;
Moreover, they wished healing
And a miracle appealing.

PART 3

The quiet and compassionate bowl
Sensed how modern mystical goals
Overwhelmed the three. Unveiled without words:
'I embraced your stress, heard–unheard,
Yet was untouched by your singular song,
Now listen of seeming rights and wrongs,
Though 'my life' is an illusory dream,
Poised on a precipice, or smooth as cream,
And the wish that the present situation
Should be different is woe's foundation,

For in this linear perception
Of life, vital is each sensation,
Where each occurrence has a purpose
In life and its apparent circus –
As cited by the pavlova,
Who sketches the self's flavours.

But what if upturned are all views?
Exists no self or world to pursue
The throne, or accept the true,
Or end itself and see anew.
And one's appearing as two,
So there's no occurrence too,
No continuity of event,
No owners or ownership of content,
But all is an appearance of energy,
Where seeming self is not an enemy.
What if none's liable for feelings raw
Or the seeking that does gnaw,
And there is none to have a choice:
To be silent or feelings thus voice,
Or to be strong or weak,
Or experience spiritual peak.
For all appears on its own,
Without another to make it known,
Besides, there is no one to know
There's none present in its show,
And if no one is separate,
How could it be annihilated?
How can there be personal story
Or one embroiled in the illusory?

What if there are no techniques
To find peace that's unique?
And each rising appearance
Is love alone in semblance,
While embracing its every tear,
Its every rising fear;
And it alone does shine
As presence of 'mine' and 'thine';
It crushes, is crushing and the crushed,
And yet remains completely untouched
Yet cries in pain when crushed is its soul –
Cares, heals, redresses, too, is whole;
Is complete in its essence,
Even when lacking in appearance,
For all is one blessed song,
Even seeming rights and wrongs,
Where everything does thrive
As it is, totally alive –
A love in perfect poise,
Mess or not seeming noise.

To be precise: all is an impression
Of the unstruck sound in expression,
Or a sea of music – this messy appearance,
In the embrace of volcanic silence,
Where one the sound and silence,
Or silence sounding as the appearance;
So, Oneness doesn't dictate behaviours,
For it is the self, the trait and endeavour,
And is in all and beyond all the views,
Linear, aerial, true, untrue.'

The friends, tinged by the spaciousness
Of the bowl, wished more for the mess,
For now they seemed to recognise
That helplessness is not unwise,
And sensitivity is a strength –
The doorway to demise of illusion's length.
Resumed the illumining insights,
From the bowl's essence bright:
'I will always be there
As compassion, fair–unfair,
As infinite boundlessness,
Encompassing your distress,
Even your non-acceptance
Or façade of acceptance,
Without any judgements,
As love, unbound by events,
Healing you all beyond words wise,
As empty infinity, which does rise,
Where healed will be your every grievance
In the intimate embracing silence,
Which is not separate from you
But is this, the presence in hue.

Yet if you believe your story's true,

Pursue an upside-down worldview,
And try and get to the source or end,
Unrequited will be this dreamy bend;
Redeeming self – an impossible dream,
Like milk separating self from cream.
Still if you feel that you can change
Your mess by didactic exchange,
Heal by enlightened conversation,
Free the Eton mess of distinction,
Then together we shall seek the words,
Define the ineffable, unheard.
For I will always hold you,
With your mess of I am, and I do.

In all scenarios love does not desert,
Whether messy puddings or neat desserts,
So Eton or not love does reign,
Yet flavours rule the palate plain.
And when eaten is love's pudding,
Then tastes alone do the bidding.'

The Eton mess of distinction
Heard the song without restriction,
Felt free, and thanked the bowl
For love's untouched flavour, whole,
And together lie in waiting –
In the bowl, for love scintillating.

ETON
UNDERGROUND
TELEPHONE
She said: 'I've got four children and t
grandchildren now, so I would often make up
rhymes to amuse them from time to time, like I
of people do with children.'
MESS

32

The Rebelling Shadow

Narrator:

I send an invite to everyone
To recall that I am this, here, one.
To see the reality – all does rise
And leave, without a clause or prize.

Allow me to explain by an account
– Predominant in certain backgrounds –
Where portray the enacted scenes
The rhythm of domestic cuisine,
Where attributes surface on the stage
Of life, to apparently engage
As immensely alive scenes of life,
Yet which seem platitudinous and rife
With notions, and relations in a story
Stereotypical, yet full of glory.

The usual bee family of four
Migrated to Australia's shore,
For they desired a calm and affluent life,
Free of prolific populace, its strife.
The father gathered honey rare,
As mother dispensed Manuka's care.
The parents skilled in professions
Soon gathered worthy recognitions,
Pursued was a privileged lifestyle
With tutelage vast and versatile.
Hired was the honey – cleaner, butler, au pair –
To care for the family's complete affair.

The honey was a bit eccentric,
Yet perfect in chores domestic;
He worked relentlessly night and day,
Enjoyed creativity, its play;
His spicy fusions-of-meat dish
And honey sprinkled in smoked fish
Were prized by the fussy children two,
Who adored his flavours new.
And they loved his cakes and pies,
His love of life, dramatic vibes,
His enthusiasm in their games,
His tall hilarious claims,
And laughed at his funny way
Of mumbling, through the day.

The two boys grew in loving care
Of the parents and the au pair,
Experienced an idyllic time
Of holidays, feasts, and social climb
In a multi-racial environment,
And stress on career relevant.
While over the years the parent bees
Seemed to endeavour for expertise,
Surfaced subtle pride in attainment,
Endorsed by societal engagement.
Respected became the family
In the community.

Now, let me tell you of a certain day,
Which changed the dynamic of the play.
At dinner, guided the parent bees
The offspring about life on lease.
The honey muttered through the scene
– As he served dinner – but seemed unseen.

Father bee to the sons:

It's time to go to university,
A career in healing – a degree,
Or a job in engineering beehives,
Or counting pollen, ordering lives;
So you two have an extensive choice,
Unlike the other bees who have no voice.
Follow our values and design,
Position in life thus refine.
And if you persevere for years
You will be a pioneer.

Honey – the au pair (mumbling):

There they go again,
Preaching dogmatic domains.
Don't they see there is nowhere to go –
It's always here, in each scenario.
And what high and what low
When one alone is the show?
But who am i to disdain the trails
Of grandiose dreams and looming sails.

Mother bee to the sons:

Education earns admiration,
Surety, position, and vocation,
And knowledge begets empowerment,
Is helpful even on retirement.
In this competitive domain,
You need to prove your unique vein;
In present times one must be successful
Even to pay for the bills plentiful,
And if you wish to relish luxuries,
You must be a professional bee.

Thus, endeavour like a bee,
Enjoy the pleasures of honey,
Which will sustain the family, too,
Relieve anxiety and the blues
And aid posterity,
With a name in the community.

Honey (mumbling):

They label me as Mad, Mad, Mad!
While a shadow for them is their lad.
They wish their child to echo
The art of their shadow.
Identity – identity!
Nothing but pure insanity.
First, they struggle to create one,

Then die to it sustain, with it stun
– Thus deepening hierarchy,
Creating further complexity –
Then pine for freedom from the mess
To live a life free of distress.
But how could i forget,
The self is bound in its net,
Lives in linear planes
Of life, and its apparent plains,
Forgets: life is beyond direction,
Is here, without contraction;
Lost in labyrinths of value, meaning,
Ignores this life simple, amazing,
Thus labels cooking, playing, cleaning –
The chores – as mundane and demeaning,
Then wishes to escape its emergence
For imaginary brilliance,
Constantly complains plentiful
And then calls itself successful.
How can one not enjoy a cuppa!
To achieve a target up there.
Yet what to say of the self's deeds,
When none exists to endeavours feed.

Elder son:

Mum, Dad,
Sorry, but aspects can't define
The self, which is beyond confines;
Like a wave can't portray the ocean,
One cannot be defined by notions,
Nor can an aspect of life
Determine the vast life.
Moreover, culture, marriage, property,
Or career can't become my identity.
I don't care for social acceptance,
For it is biased in its reverence.

Narrator:

Surprised were the parents
At their son's manner errant.
The mother then spoke at length
Of life's direction, its strength,
And of the significance
Of success, societal acceptance,
Of the rich cultural norms
And ideals, the need to conform.

Elder son:

Mum, for acceptance, hype of constancy,
Our kind pursue healing with honey
Or count pollen, engineer beehives,
And get a home, a lovely wife.
Isn't education truly a skill,
Like learning to hunt for a kill,
Rather than a tool for eminence,
As it can't measure intelligence?
But by enhancing its nobility
It has been turned into captivity.
And do we even learn
Bounty of nature, views upturned?
Instead we regurgitate facts superfluous
To outdo friends, feel good about our fuss.

And our tradition and culture too
Is suffocating and insular in view,
Highlighting competition of our race
For ambition, influential grace,
While in the name of success,
We respect power and riches,
Which is nothing but greed,
Clothed in honour and need.
And don't we judge individuals
By career and wedded rituals?
Believe they provide settlement,
While the mind should be content,
For a contended mind won't seek
Bliss in outer states or peaks.

Mum, nothing is good, bad, or worse,
Ideal, pitiable, adverse.
It is the training of society
Of propriety and impropriety.
But when set is an idyllic norm,
A deviation is then frowned upon,
Then there's a chase for the ideal,

Which brings dispute immeasurable,
Creates issues of hierarchy,
Comparison, pity, jealousy,
And this disease of comparison
Weaves a web of ruin and destruction,
Devours peace by its allure,
Is lethal, has no cure,
For it is disguised in arrogance,
Or victimhood or annoyance,
Where caught is the self in the quicksand
Of the poisons of the restless land,
Of illusory memoirs,
And comparing accounts bizarre,
Forgetting what we truly are –
The untouched silent reservoir,
Where nothing can define
Our vast, unconfined shrine,
For all appears in its expanse,
All the tears, fears, joys, a stance
Without the individual accounts,
And each moment the Sermon on the Mount.
So labels – married, widowed, single,
Successful or unsuccessful –
Nothing's missing in this aliveness:
It is what it is, neither more nor less.

Narrator:

The parents were outraged
At their son's rebellious phase.
For though they were liberal,
Any dissidence tangible
Was deemed as disrespectful
To the bond hierarchical.

Father to the elder son:

How can you be so crass, abrupt?
Contumacious is your conduct,
You enjoy the riches and buffets
For which we endeavour night and day;
You always cadge indulgence
But feel entitled to its presence.
Fulfilled has been your every wish,
So you've become ungrateful, selfish.

Elder son to the parents:

Dad, the world lays undue importance
On unnatural views and pretence,
So snubbed is this alive presence
For dictated beliefs – a semblance.
Then it grants posthumous pride
Only in hindsight,
But would it change the tide
Today for Turing and Wilde?

Can the world decide one's value?
Don't you feel the reverse should be true?
And don't you think in all the spheres, we bees
Are asked to adhere to the worldly decrees,
To ensure persistent death
In every alive, thriving breath?
But why forsake the alive
To follow fake fires, rife?

All judge the present scene
From the filters of a cuisine,
Where the moment is a means to fulfil
A non-existent future, with thrills,
But are we alive if we can't feel
The wind, the sun, or taste our meals?
And I don't wish to forgo this moment –
Unrepeatable – for unreal quotients.

Mother to the elder son:

You have no respect for values,
Elders, or traditional dues.
Rejected is irascibility,
Even if paired with ability.
Empty will be your plate,
For you will lose associates
If you continue your ways
In this rebellious phase.

Narrator:

Then choking on her tears,
The mother stated her fears.

Mother:

Now I doubt all our decisions,
Especially of migration;
I knew we would be left alone
In an age when we'd need our own.
I didn't expect this demeanour
From you, for years of my endeavour.

Elder son to his mother:

Mum, I appreciate your effort,
Will love you all forever.
But love isn't' about possession
Or being bound by expectation.
I am neither your trophy nor toy
To display, possess, or employ.
Please, don't control my flairs and hues
By marges that are untrue.
Do not be a slave to the system:
See that false is its rhythm!

Mum, systems are conceptual –
A collective myth cerebral,
And even society is a myth –
An appearance without pith.
For, Mum, our species is lost in ways
Of illusion, its related plays,
Adds layers to our beingness,

Believes we are making progress,
Has made apparent universities
– Graded them, founded hierarchy –
Then churns theories in alacrity,
Deems them of value, and a reality.
While the honey always says:
'It's this, life, nothing amiss,
Simply an energetic expression,
Infinite as finite impression.'
So, Mum, there is no goal to reach
Before death, or target to seize,
For life isn't a profession
To complete ascribed missions.
Forms simply appear and disappear,
So why be caught in fleeting spheres?

And a family of four
Is not the ultimate shore.
And I won't shadow started lines:
I don't echo the same design.

Mother:

Scathing is your speech and attitude,
But we don't expect servitude,
Instead wish to secure 'Your life'
With plenty, and without strife,
But you abjure each sentiment.
How could you be so petulant?

Honey (mumbling):

A mascot for them is their boy,
But to accept him they are coy.
For they seek a scenario
Where caressed is their ego.
They seem so far away,
While we stand on the same bay.

But seen is life alive, anew,
Through the self's learnt roles, its view,
Which turns complex the game
Of life with meaning and blame.
But it would be nice if the bees
Would listen to the homily
Of pure non-duality,
Of love in appearance, free.
Yet nothing, the unknown freedom,
Sings as the seeming kingdoms.

Elder son to his parents:

Oh, please don't worry about me:
I am an entity free.
I'll write librettos in new themes,
Will not echo illusive dreams.
Will challenge societal slavery
Of shadowing hierarchy,
Of applauding individuals
Instead of the alive, integral.
Inspire return of the renaissance,
As the need, the vital response,
And ceasing of the insular,
For liberal and free flavours.
This renaissance will be acceptance
Of all, without any preference,
For when appears rebellion,
Granted is status for suppression,
Established is a new hierarchy,
Where new players hold the key;
But I'll advocate for Oneness
That embraces the diverse dress,
And will sing of that liberty
Where one appears in diverse spree.

Father to the elder son:

Outrageous are your outbursts.
Do you realise how much it hurts?
I should have left the hive
To let you all fend for life.
Are you really of distinct design?
Then totally ruined is our line.
Nature's natural expression
Are procreation and succession;
Now ruined will be our name
By your unnatural game.

Mother (sobbing uncontrollably):

Oh! How could you, my son,
Play with our love, it shun.

Honey (mumbling):

Ah! There they go again
With the blame game,
The names and strains.
The imagined chains.

They seem so quick to ascribe labels:
Of gender, race, preferences sexual,
Or what they like and what they hate,
Claim all that appears on their plate;
Believe self an authority,
That life should submit to its decree;
Complain about the emergent scene,
Look elsewhere for flavours pristine
If events do not appear to fit
Their imagined knits.

They forget life has no feedback
Policy, and no payback
For its unwanted decree,
Or for the mess of its spree.
Rather, it cares not a damn
About 'me' and 'my' plans,
And sovereign is its present
Hue, without any substance.

Elder son to parents:

You taught us that everything is divine.
Then how can unnatural be my design?
Does not the prism reflect white light?
Can you omit one hue from rainbow's sight?
Is any shape, hue, or shade
Unwanted in nature's parade?

It's difficult to defy society
And embrace authenticity.
It takes courage to speak the truth;
Instinctive is my fabric, am not uncouth.
And I will adopt orphan bees,
Provide them with love, environs free,
In a small way bring crucial change,
Campaign for embracing the range.
We bees need to get our act together
And focus on our own weather,
Not judge through narrow planes
Of linear perception, sordid strains.
And won't I still be your child,
Even if hurtful to your pride?

Narrator:

The anxious father fell silent,
Mused on his parental guidance.
While the mother continued to cry,
Made numb by the son's aberrant dye.

Elder son to the honey:

I will embark on my journey,
Be my life's attorney,
Will forsake the edifice,
Won't shadow irrational bliss.

Honey to all (but looking at the boys):

Forsake, forsake, forsake
Your need of cakes and bakes,
And rest in your aches
Alive, don't them forsake.
For rest is never at stake
But present in your aches.
And know: none is on a journey,
With power of attorney,
To write a new libretto
Or deem children as their shadow.
For there are no relations
But life – as apparent sensations.

Is it not freeing to know
That no one runs the show?
And courage isn't to break the fence

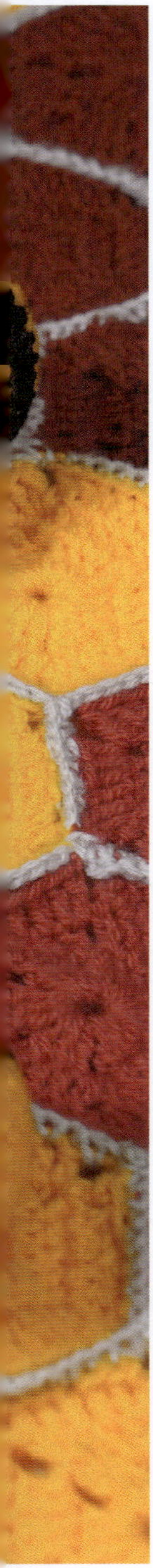

But the recognition all is an appearance.
For rebellion too is a bondage,
As it's bound to time and image.
Yet life is so paradoxical –
Though one, yet seems to be dual
To itself; claims life, decides futures
Of self, the world, and others.

Elder son addressing the honey (crying):

I thought you loved us, weren't distant,
But you too seem to be resistant
To dawns anew, not on our side,
For your love is the strength of my stride.

Honey (in a very caring tone) to both the boys:

Oh, Dear! I love all of you!
Beyond your grasp and view,
But love is not about agreement
With the spoken or with the present
Scene, or a bond to thus cement,
It's this appearing moment,
Is this, life as it is,
Appearing as it does.
So what I say is beyond the lines
Of the accounts of mine and thine.

Narrator:

The younger sibling consoled the older one,
Who solemnly cried and felt there was none
To support him in the darkest hour
And save him from life's events dour.

Honey (mumbling):

They all seem like the dry sands
Of the beaches of the Australian land,
Which are ever near the shore
Yet are parched to the core.
Yet all's a cosmic joke
With no bloke to laugh or croak –
Surprise, suspense.

Narrator:

The parents who seemed grave
Were disturbed by the waves
Of life's unknown events, flowing,
So vented their fury growing
On others for feeding radical dreams,
Enticing but engulfing streams,
Then felt contrite for the lack
Of attention to their children's track.

Honey (muttering while clearing the table):

Oh, bees, i wish i could show you,
There is none split from life, its hues.
Life appears as father, mother, and sons,
Yet is untouched, belongs to none.
Investment in the yarn –
Novel, or old and darned –
Is a myth, for there is nothing. None
Appears as the occurring pun.
So whatsoever becomes apparent
Is energy, a stir current.
Spontaneous is this presence
And nothing is past this occurrence.

There's only the unknown,
With no way to make it known –
Particles dancing as a substance,
Floating and infinite in essence,
Apparent each scenario,
Without ideals to follow.
Truly all there is is this:
The blues, nothingness, or bliss.

I wish they had heard
The 'Open Secrets' words:
'That only appears energy,
Feral and completely free.'
I have heard this missive most days;
No wonder tasty are my buffets.

Narrator:

After the long-drawn arguments,
With each trying a point to present,
All there was left was pain,
And sorrow for the present strain,
Along with doubts in the father's mind
About the honey, peers, and effect combined,
For he believed environmental
Were preferences sensual.

Honey (mumbling while washing the dishes):

No hope, no hope to find.
Life as it is without the bind:
A feast of frames
With all its names,
Like a cartoon in a strip,
Apparent timeless click,
A picture postcard perfect
Where light and sound intersect –
Just seeing with none in view,
Disagreement with much ado.
An apparent play without a script,
Blank page or dreamt manuscript,
Seemingly bound in social gamut,
Parading like a game's mascot
Is this drama of pretence –
Or just pure nonsense.

Narrator:

In an apparent account
All seems to be paramount,
So seek solutions gourmet
The bees, who restless stay.
The father still seeks a conspiracy
Theory to assure his doubts eerie.
While the mother without inhibition
Has accepted her son's orientation.
Without a goal or an end to reach
Performs the honey and preaches
No one, through his mumblings unheard
A series of unstrung words.

Thus, all seems to be the same
In the bee family, unnamed.

But were the bees lost in tenure and sense,
Or was it an occurrence
Without a causal subsequence?
An energetic tryst of silence.
Pulsating liveliness in play.
A perfectly precious buffet.

Narrator (continues after a pause):

I appear as all cuisines,
Celebrate each and every scene.
My invitation's each emotion,
Each thought, each act, and all the notions.

I am the parent, child, and honey sweet,
The father's doubts, mother's tears, honey's treat.
Appear as the orientation of the son
Yet am nothing, so belong to none.
I narrate this tale of precepts
And turn these words in a concept.

Arise as thoughts in freedom,
Then are mesmerised by their wisdom,
Believe they are a belief system,
Then blame the mind for its dictum.
But my illusion can't be undone,
For my appearance, each and every one,
All that appears is my play,
Not different in any way.
I am not lost so can't be found.
The real–unreal can't meet, abound –
So seeking me, the futile fuel,
For I alone am one, being dual,
So I can't be accepted or shunned,
Nor can ever be known or plumbed.
Rebelling shadow or not, I am complete,
In all rhythms and in each beat.

I am this. I am life.

33

Pretty Peas

'I want to be free,
Free from captivity,
The constraint overthrow,
To leave the pod and go
Into pastures unknown,
All by myself, alone,
For I want to simply – be,'
Declared the young tender pea.

'My little green head,
You'll tumble instead,
Land in the sizzling pan,
A searing pea, like edgy Nan,
Squashed and served in a dish
Alone or with random fish.
By then you would have died,'
Sharply the mother replied.

The pea to mother did say:
'Listen to me, I pray.
I want to go away
To the uncritical bay.
Want freedom that's complete,
From faiths that do not meet,
From verdicts that rebound,
From good and bad that bound.'

Then mother cut him short,
His outbursts did abort:
'Darling, listen to what I say:
Freedom is, ever does stay,
For it is not a dish gourmet
That you can eat or display.
It isn't a special state
Or space with light and grace.

My love, you can't bind freedom
To an event or an 'ism',
For it isn't a narrow view:
It is even 'me' and 'you',
Much like the space abounds,
It is, so cannot be found.
Hence, freedom's in everything,
Not just in desert springs.

Know nothing can touch you,
No verdict, faith, or view,
For you can't be curbed in lines
Of vast or minute shrines.
For there is only energy
Performing as the pea.
So, my rebellious blaze,
Stop running. See what stays.'

Then interrupted the son:
'Mother I want to run
Away from passivity,
To find creativity,
To be free from mine and thine,
From all the known confines,
To walk on the wild side –
Welcome the veritable tide.'

'By George! Heed what I say:
You can't think or feel your way
To freedom that's complete
In each and every beat.
Freedom is even to be free
From want of liberty,
Not being free from thoughts,
But in that which is sought.

Son, appears only the present
As every place and event,
So what will you escape
When there's no detaining drape?

You are pure ingenuity
And not a cloistered pea.
Though when appears a distinct 'you'
It seems to freedom pursue,
But, Son, that is freedom too –
There's nothing wrong with you!

Dear, life alone does identify
As a pea in a pod, or pie,
So it's hopeless to freedom contain,
To it know, or split, or gain.
Life is the pastures unknown,
All by itself alone,
Untied by the inverses
And all the apparent courses.'

'Then, mother, why deny me
Freedom to speak, be free?'
'Oh, go on, you aren't denied
Freedom to speak, or system deride.
But my rant is freedom too,
All rising in apparent view,
Just waves of pitch and tone –
No intent, import, unknown.

But do not become pettish
In your youthful passions skittish…'
The puerile pea left its shield
As the mother thus revealed.
Abandoned was the kingdom
Divine, in the name of freedom.
However, this freedom is free
To disdain the grace of life that is
free.

Is love, with nothing in the midst,
Appears as all that does exist.
And nothing's denied in this
Love, neither grief nor bliss.
Thus, wept the forlorn mother
In the severe weather,
For she lost her lovely son
In pursuit of freedom to be won.

34

The Creative Cut

In a famous restaurant's kitchen,
Two commis chefs were on a mission
To imagine dishes unknown
From ingredients less known.
The creative ginger–garlic
Seemed in subtle conflict
To outdo each other
By creativeness in flavour;
They both endeavoured to impress
The head with the talents they did possess,
And similarly did endeavour,
Yet ginger got regard for flavour,
For he was the flexible of the two,
And tea and biscuits loved him too.
The garlic stayed in the background,
Yet his clout was quite profound.

The head chef – extra virgin olive oil –
Though welcoming, rapidly did boil.
He lived in a bottle of glass,
Respected unfiltered mass;
Ever perfection did demand,
Quickly did reprimand
If slacked any subordinates
In service, or the dish on the plate,
But creativity he did favour
And praised the use of fresh flavour.
The juniors thought he was absurd,
More suited for the world of words.

'Run I from ideology,
Varied techniques, technology
Into the realm that is erratic,
Beyond illusory or pragmatic,
Where intuition holds the key,
Where inspiration's vast and free,
Where stillness is an eternal dance
Of sublime images in trance –
Spontaneity is in its play,
Apparent sequence does obey,'
Said the head chef to the two,
Who were preparing hot and cold brews.

Enquired the ginger in tones
Bewildered of the bizarre zone:
'Where does this strange world exist?
Who does it create, who subsists?'
The head chef firmly did reply,
As he julienned celery for the stir-fry,
'Why look beyond what is – elsewhere –
When every act compassion bears?
The uncanny world is all around,
With stillness, love and grace abounds.
Flip your story and see this –
Does anything seem amiss?
This arising scene existent,
Is Oneness, spontaneously apparent,
Just pure creativity in hues,
Without a creator to it pursue.'

The ginger quickly did insert,
At the head's perplexing words,
'The present scene is routine,
Unlike a spectacular cuisine.
What do you mean by no creator?
Isn't God the originator?'

The head decisively replied
In manner secured and glorified:
'The present scene is routine
For a mind bound in cuisines,
While everything is new
In the emerging view.
And what do you believe as God:
A creator with an eternal squad?
Or a food in a transcendental state,
Or formless, that is from you separate?

Whatever you believe of God
Is truly amiss or flawed,
For binding God in any image,
Even formless, is sacrilege,
For the formless too is an image
Which the divine does limit;
Apparent eating of the fruit
Of knowledge, which begets pursuit,
Curbs everything in form
Or its opposing norm.
All that appears is the divine,
Nothing too, so it cannot be defined.

Besides, as an infant did you know
Existed a God? Created this show?
Isn't every image you imagine
As per the learnt captions?
Isn't it taught exists a divine
– With its debates and shrines –
Distinct, to be revered,
Is far or near, a saviour,
Or one must merge in it, or realise it,
Or know the cosmic soul without limit,
Or get its grace and pray or serve
It, or follow certain rules with verve?
If something is natural,
Can it be taught or learned as factual?
Can you learn or teach to breathe,
Or eat or drink, or sleep or seethe?
Is God separate from you,
To be viewed false or true?

And if God's omnipotent, omnipresent,
Can it be experienced or have a second?
Can God be known, or need a reason
To be, appear as it does? Are demons
Beyond its purview? Can one defy it?
Or unite with it, or it split?
Is God only in good and bliss
And against its inverses?
And if there is a God so small,
Is it even 'God' at all?
An authority?
Discriminatory?'

Puzzled seemed the ginger–garlic,
Besieged by questions odd and erratic,
But they did not interrupt the head,
For they wished favour of him, who led.
'Yet if we were to speak of a divine,
Does it not alone thus shine –
Formless animating as forms,
Not split in performer–performed,
Neither male nor female, not split,
Yet appearing as every bit,
But unaffected it does stay,
Just being this apparent play,
Is one in appearance diverse,
Yet a single undefined verse,
Truly vast and infinite,
An unknowing, without limit.

It is simply this, not apart,
But is the beating of the heart,
Is the breath that's intimate,
Is love's apparent portrait,
The light of all the eyes,
The sound of cries, and untouched skies,
Experiencing or tasting its every hue,
Is being the seeming view.
Or this appearance – the divine –
Performing by itself in design,
Just this, playing as each hue,
Without another in the view,
As the unrepeatable moment,
Without an opponent,
Is that which is and isn't displayed,
Ineffable to further say.'

Continuing after a pause:
'It is, beyond a cause,
Is the unchanged that seems to change,
The normal and the strange;
It is the kindness of the kind,
The design of the designed,
The bravery of the brave,
The craving and the craved,
The beauty of the beautiful,
The dread and the dreadful;

It is the grace of the gracious,
And malice too of the malicious,
The hierarchical display,
Yet not swayed by the graded play.

The seen, unseen, seeing, unseeing,
The being, and the non-being,
Is stillness and the seeming gait,
Boundless, too alive to articulate,
Existent and maybe not,
Simply beyond all thought,
Just formless forming in one go,
With none to control the show,
Or nothing appearing
As everything,
Or maybe not,
None to know the plot,
For none is existent
To know it's: absent,
Present,
Apparent,
Alone,
Unknown.
Ineffable.'
…

'I thought I am the creator true
Of all the acts that thus ensue;
Never did I thus recognise
That all is God alone in guise.
But don't cause and effect exist,
Am I and my endeavours dismissed?'
Thus questioned the ginger,
As he used the cinder
To give a smoked effect to his brew,
For the head to review.

Though branded impolite and forthright,
The head calmly unravelled the self tight:
'Notice all there is is the present scene
And an apparent response unforeseen;
The individual appears later
To claim the entire feature,
Then labels the event as good or bad,
Delightful, terrible, or sad;
Creates a story of the acts
And deems them to be life's fact.
While the appearing scene in view,
Is creative wandering[1] in hue,
Or rather is floating fluidity
In apparent creativity,
With transformative ability,
And illusory capability.
This creativity is love pure,
Formless as formed contours.

Owning the appearing creativity,
As creator of the activity,
And falling in love with it, its practice,
Is dual, ignorance, malpractice.[2]
It is like a flute laying claim
To the music flowing from its frame;
You cannot perform acts;
Rather, there's no you in life's tract.'

Then looking at his subordinates,
Said: 'To all jobs this does relate,
For many of us our efforts own,
Forever compete to be well known,
While ownership of an act does bring
Only conceit and suffering.'

'Oh, yes! I know about the ego's role,
But I am here, in control,'
Asserted the ginger with a smile.
Stated the head in pensive style:
'Reflect on what creates the self, its gait –
And what does it regenerate?
How real are characters in a book?
Or their role and the tale that does hook?
Like the Cheshire Cat and its grin,
Appears and fades the self, akin,
For it isn't an entity that does stay
But an appearance in the play;
The concept of self does not exist –
Appears, disappears, does not persist,

1 See Note 14A
2 See Note 14B

For it's the guest that plays the role
Of the host, and dreams it is whole.
And try to find the self, you'll fail,
For one alone appears to prevail.

Yet don't accept a word I say,
Reflect about the self – stray.
What happens to it in sleep?
Or when lost in an act deep?
Who, what, and where are you?
Is there one to it know or view?
Are you restricted to a name?
Or are you the infinite flame?
And what will you label yourself to be:
Form, feelings, the unseen, or that you see?
Can the self split itself in two?
Or is all life in varied hue,
Playing, dancing, all alone,
With none to it know or own?'

He then declared in assured tones,
As if imposing his views unknown:
'Acts on their own rise, fall away;
Actions without the players play.
The scriptures too point that appear
Acts on their own, without one to steer
Them, are without causality,
And not in time, its frivolity
(Yet seem to appear in time,
Bound by causality's rhyme).
It's evident in the tale of the vineyards,[3]
And in the songs of the free bards,
In Buddha's sermon, Nanak's[4] quatrain,
In the Quran and Gita's domain.
Yet all is an appearance
Of the energetic presence,
Assigned with labels and names,

3 See Note 14C
4 See Note 14D

A magical, surreal game,
Where all is involuntary;
Floats the belief – performs an entity,
Which is a splendid blunder,
And yet the greatest wonder.
Thus, another possibility
I share of this creativity.'

The quiet garlic then did question
In tones that seemed like a suggestion:
'Why do good suffer, clever enjoy?
Some impress while others annoy?'
Though fixed was his whole attention
On the ginger, bored by the chef's diction.

The head chef spoke in tones to shred:
'Didn't you hear what's been said,
And where is your attention?
Here? Or in ginger's comprehension?'
Then naturally changing his tone
Declared: 'Listen, Oneness alone
Expresses itself as every form,
Though one it seems to perform
As two. For there to be appearance,
It disguises in myriad emergence,
Where forms are its creative attire,
Love itself as apparent choir.
This Oneness seems to experience
Itself as one or dual cadence.
But there is neither an experience,
Nor one who experiences the occurrence.
For there is only one
Apparent as two or none.
Its dream is the self – separate,
And an appearance – act and trait.

Jealousy, joy, or annoyance
Are acts alone in appearance,
And there is no one to own
The acts or them thus disown.
Yet there is neither an occurrence
Nor one separate in existence.
So, there is neither a split divine
Nor a happening to plans align.

Heed, there isn't a character
Who makes an illusory register,
Is bound in the confines,
Can liberate from the shrines.
There appears only energy
As all forms – completely free –
Be they subtle or seen,
Or imagined and unseen,
And it appears as the illusion,
Too, a veil of seclusion;
When seemingly lifts the veil,
It's obvious there's no dual scale,
And dawns the recognisance
That I was never present
To be clever and smart
Or hardworking and tart.
For all there is is what appears,
Nothing crucial or comprised in spheres.'

The head then abruptly did state
In tones stern, to humiliate:
'Listen, you two! Your race to be good
Is to be lost in the woods.
Though there's no creator out there
To judge your acts as fair–unfair,
I will.'

But the ginger was quick to blurt:
'Is it destiny that all does assert?
What about responsibility
Of acts, and the world's disparity?'

'What is predestined: fate or choice,
When timeless is time's voice,
And life spontaneously does glow,
With no one ever in the shadow,'
Instinctively declared the head
Of the undivided – the widespread:
'There's no volition or impact,
For there is none behind the act.
(So, the perpetual argument
Of destiny and choice pertinent
Appears to be irrelevant,
For there's no singular celebrant.)

Yet in appearance of the play
Volition and *karma* seem to sway,
For one energetic presence
Plays as it may in its appearance,
So in this appearance seeming crime
Is met with retribution prime,
And there seems responsibility
Met with apparent causality;
Hence, you will land in the jail
If you harm food, its trail.
But this apparent existence
Has no purpose or inference,
Is simply an expression
Occurring without intention.
And this message is beyond
All the inverses or bonds.
Pay attention! All appears on its own,
Even the dream where self sits on the throne,
Where individuality seems real
With choice, causality – the wheel –
Or blames the deprived populace,
That their life is destined by *karmic* race,
For one appears as the foolish bind,
Brands and claims credentials confined.'

The garlic then did interrupt,
Though he didn't wish to disrupt:
'Why does creativity portray –
Such a varied, sometimes tasteless buffet?'

'No one can answer this query,'
Chef Oil replied patiently.
'Life for its own sake does surface,
But is it not genuine grace?
Emptiness rudimentary,
Boundless to be confined and free –
Maybe joy of creative expression
Without purpose or procession.'

'All your philosophy makes me dry!'
The ginger wearily did sigh.
'For I can't imagine a world
Without me, real or dream unfurled.
So, let's prepare a tender dish,
With our creativity it garnish –
Accompany with a refreshing drink,
In our ingenuity thus sink.'

The head chef wryly laughed aloud,
Exclaimed: 'Dear, you really stand out,
Yes! Let us a dish manifest,
Own its vision in earnest.'
Mischievously, the garlic replied:
'And in it julienne the ginger dried.'

35

A Natural Pimiento

A young pimiento's muted gene
Made her dissimilar and lean.
All alleged she had special needs,
Would need help in performing deeds;
Distinct, she'd be of varied pace,
Which would make her challenges face.

At one such Christmas dinner,
The family, concerned about her,
Overwhelmed the mother with advice,
Some futile, some sane, some wise.
Aunt Bell advised a bank account
For the pimiento's future, paramount,
Where all the close relations
Could save frequently, in rotation.
Uncle Pepper continued the notion,
The usefulness of its foundation:
'This will help her in the future,
Add assurance, and make it smoother,
Then life will proceed as usual,
Not too different from the normal.'
Though these appeared as acts of piety,
The mother seemed bound by anxiety.

Aunt Pepper, who sensed mother's fears,
Found societal labels, tricks of tears,
Questioned about the usual
Calmly in tenor casual,
And though she generally addressed all,
Fixed her stare on Pepper small:
'Well, I do not agree
With labels of "normal" decree,
For "normal" is a mere label
On the present scene, unstable.
Don't most of us view the present
From beliefs in which we are intent,
Where conditioned is our view
By nurture, cuisines, and hue.

To be precise, we observe life
Through the illusion rife
Of an apparent self – small,
And other seeming calls.
A self that seems to come and go,
Appears as an entity, holds the show,
Adds to your alleged trials of life,
Then pushes the self in further strife,
Forgets and stays lost in illusion,
Prizes the unreal as real – a delusion.'

Aunt Pepper then in tougher tones
Rebelled, probed about the known:
'What's usual or average?
Aren't they doctrines, just baggage:
Desires, collective captivity,
Or tricks served as refined activity,
Or thoughts of power, wishing to belong,
Replaying like a chorus in a song –
Or like a tune recorded in a loop,
The mind completely cooped in hoops.
Is this normal or average?
Does it help, or make one savage?

Which one of you is free from stress
To guide how to be, or address
Scenarios you think aren't normal,
Require your effort essential?
Is there a way or formula to live?
Isn't life alone determinative?
A benchmark who exists to write,
When there's nothing wrong or right?
Like the apparent regions diverse,
None more prized, none a curse,
For the forests or the Mediterranean
Aren't better than the desserts Arabian.
All is simply as it is,
A balanced ecological axis.

Pragmatic may be plans to save
In the seeming worldly cave,
But who exists to know the future,
For unreal are its weaves and features,
And who can secure life's length,
When none can control their breath –
And what future and what past,
When timeless is each cast?

She may need help to maintain a lifestyle,
For Peppers like us made this domain hostile.
Life abstracted to such an extent
That it's forgotten life's not in segments,
And by repeating any ordeal,
You simply reinforce the unreal
As real, and bind the alive life
In seeming structural hives.'

The family quietly ate their meal,
As Aunt's words hurt yet did reveal
Oneness. Uncle Pepper seethed with rage,
But didn't wish to ruin the festal stage,
So, quiet, let his wife speak her mind:
'A fit of pique, ill timed.'
Though by now all the relations
Were used to Aunt's novel perceptions,
Her dominating the conversations
At most family occasions.

Then glancing at the pimiento petite,
Aunt Pepper continued in a manner sweet:
'She seems to be unstuffed like the rest,
For she isn't caught in abstract quest.
So, applied is the tag of special,
And she is buried behind a label.
Then some avoid her presence.
Others highlight the difference.
Yet others don't see eye to eye.
Still, none can see her infinite sky.
When one can't see the other's view
Or depict the taste of their stew,
Why stick tags on that which thrives,
Or portray purpose in the alive?
We all see her as a distinct hue,
But nothing's missing for her to pursue.
Her world is simple and complete,
With none to please and less discreet,
As there's simply the rising scene,
With less belonging of cuisines.'

The grandad busy sipping Gimlet,
Proudly glanced at his daughter's wit,
Felt he had raised her strong and fine
To speak for those who can't their case define.

'Compassion isn't sympathy, empathy,
But to see there's no individuality;
Like electricity that flows – is one,
Bulbs varied but favoured is none.
And if appears the one – this light –
How is one dull, the other bright?
Yet emptiness alone appears as all,
So none's arrogant and none's small.
All is a dance of traits alive and silent,
The ocean waves as eminent–ignorant,
With nothing beyond this appearance,
So no future or person in existence.'

'Why does my child have to face
A fate that is tough to brace?'
The mother then probed Aunt Pepper,
While pain in her expression did stir.

Responded the Aunt in tenor calm
Of the maternal bond, its qualms:
'All relations are based on separation
Of me and other – an illusion –
So motherhood becomes possessive
From the lens of self, its missive,
And this self in its seeming roles
Believes in separate souls,
Then sees itself and others in view
As distinct, with a life to pursue.
Woven are stories around time,
And seen is life in parallel clime
– Owned are children and possessions
And states and manifestation –
And thus the split in time and space,

With its looming tests seems to chase,
Where the eternal seems transitory
And reigns individuality,
Which on variance tends to brood,
Or avoids, blames life, is in feud,
Which brings on a lot of strife
In the story of my life,
Then suffers and creates stress,
Then suffers more to change, redress.
Thus, agonise tributaries of thoughts,
The question of 'why me'is fraught.

But, dear, there's no individual,
Be it real or unreal,
To feel it's happening to you,
For all is an appearance without a clue –
Simply life, so all feelings rise,
But with none to own them, or them prize;
There's only what does appear,
With none to label tears or fears,
Where mothering naturally appears,
Though the mother's role doesn't steer,
As is the case in other creatures,
Where self's illusion doesn't feature.

Reflect: is there someone to own
A child, a story, known–unknown?
And do not all relations
Appear in this life's migration?
While we have forgotten what we are:
One, the same as a distant star,
The boundless vast presence
In which appears this appearance.
And 'our life' is a dream,
With nothing real, no theme,
Simply an appearance
Of this presence.'

Aunt Pepper then in loving tones
Addressed her niece of the unknown:
'Yet Oneness alone in presence
Is each being – an appearance,
Without a phantom to own the hues
Or the apparent views.

And, niece, when nothing's separate,
How can there be one with a fate?
Or even claim there's none,
If all that appears is one?

Remember: love expresses itself as her,
And as everything that does occur,
And like a mother loves this nothingness,
Its each expression – in acceptance – blessed.
So, an expression of the whole
Is your mothering role,
And sacred each emotion, thought, or view,
Perfect – your daughter and you.'

Throughout Aunt's sermon – lost in her style –
The precious pimiento simply smiled,
And gazed at the Aunt nice
With innocence in her empty eyes,
But, silent, nothing at all did say,
Love as her quietly did play.

The mother with tears in her eyes
Conversed in tones contrite and wise:
'I am grateful for your advice
Of life's value beyond a price.
We should have aunts like you
To assuage fears undue.'

Love appearing as Aunt Pepper
Exclaimed: 'Dear, one alone does appear,
As mother and child seem to exist,
As the act too seems to drift
By; so, who to thank, who to resist?
And who can whom assist?
The song I sing is neither new
Nor poignant and does not imbue
Acceptance and has always been around,
Valued, unvalued, heard or not, but bound.
Know this world – an apparent account,
Purposeless pretence paramount.'

The pimiento then handed her Aunt
Her Christmas present – pimiento plant.
Tears welled up in Aunt Pepper's eyes.

She hugged and thanked the pimiento prized,
Then insisted the children at the event
Exchange the Christmas presents,
For all of them were truly bored
With the aunt and her serious retort.
And soon all got busy with their presents –
Gifted, received, compared them, did resent
The thrift of some miserly relatives,
But all loved the spirit festive
And were engrossed in the games,
The wine, the cheese, and tall claims
Of some who travelled far and wide
Or vaguely walked on the wild side.
Forgotten was all the palaver,
Usual Christmas, another calendar.

36

Theatrical Delight

Once, enacted a kitchen
The role of a magician,
It wished to stage a pleasing play,
Assembled all its friends one day.

Kitchen:

'Let us do something unique,
Present a play of mystique,
With love as the main theme.
We'll work together as a team.'

Chorus:

'A team we will surely stay,
But not this theme, we pray!'

Quite diverse were all the views,
Discussed which theme should get its due.

Meats:

'We wish a thriller as the theme,
And horror will make it supreme.
Always enthrals a mystery,
Fictitious like Holmes,[1] or history,
For charming is death –
We play with it in every breath.'

Vegetables:

'The utmost is ballet,
As finesse it does display.
A flawless delicate dance
Will augment triumph's chance,
So let us all design the show
And train to balance on the toe.'

Fruits:

'Completely dry are these themes,
Will shatter the morale of the team.
Musicals truly are the best,
Divinely sweet – critics impressed,
For music stirs the core of the heart,
A success from the very start.'

Spices:

'As boundless is our taste, an expanse,
Subtle to bolden our handsome dance,
We will enrich all melodies,
And our taste will leave a legacy.
But why not create a flavour new?
For they inspire trends to pursue.'

The kitchen mused on all appeals
Then revealed the theatrical meal,
Course by course and bit by bit,
To the team to make the show a hit.

Kitchen:

'If we our flairs fuse and blend,
We'll be a hit in the West End.
And if we see beyond our veils,
The colossal may unveil,
Without anyone performing the traits,
Yet all attributes will be celebrated.'

Then staged was the greatest play.
A huge sensation, it did sway
Every viewer, every critic,
Who found the play a treat unique,
For each actor played a part
That was intrinsic to their heart.

1 See Note 15A

Discussed the media the finesse
Of the play, the cause of its success,
And quick to present their views
About the play and its muse
Were the reporters of Cutlery,
Utensils, Hob, and Pottery.

Fork:

'The play has made perspectives clear –
The perfect recipe that does appear
Is due to the endeavour of the whole
And not just a certain role.
So, the meals that all extol
Is the kitchen as a whole.

I also loved how the play
Linked the stage to life's play,
Where the varied hues of clay
Are deemed distinct in life's buffet,
Forgot how the cosmos conspires
To appear as that which does transpire,
Like food – the self takes all the praise,
Ignored is the pan that sits on the blaze.
Thus, in this semblance prime
Of self, in apparent time,
Glorified are single tastes,
As the key ingredient that's graced.

Yet, nevertheless, the play
Cleverly does display
That none does endeavour:
There's only the seeming flavour,
Where seeming traits play their part,
And all's one, nothing is apart.
Yet nothing seems to occur,
For all is apparent stir.
And the entire charade
Seems like a prismatic parade.

I think this play deserves respect
For highlighting the dual prospect.'

***5 stars**

Knife:

'I do agree with what you say,
But it's not shown who directs the play,
Though I like the witnessing theme,
How it isn't attached to the dream
Of life and begets bliss
In chaos of the worldly abyss.

For when I did witness
Life's seeming business,
Unravelled the one and two,
Was evident one: viewer–view.
A performance coherent
To keep the semblance distant.'

***3.5 stars**

Spoon:

'The play shows no witnessing theme,
But highlights all is a dream.
The play is very clear
That one alone does appear;
There is none to witness a state
And none above a play creates.

It shows how to witness life's dream
Is to escape this life supreme,
Is to flee the intimacy
Of rising life for dead decrees.
Besides, witnessing splits life in two,
The creator and the creation in view,
While freedom's neither one nor two,
But none present in boundless hues.
And witnessing is not superior
Than attachment to views exterior,
For there is only one,
And scission is its pun.

But my favourite part
Is that there's nothing apart.
No script – appears a play alone,
With no director, on its own.

No separation of subject–
Object, none exists to project
Their reality on the appearance,
For there's only alive presence.
No way to label the alive,
For energy alone does thrive.

Yet language names the play,
And all is life's display
That classifies its own sport,
Captivated without purport,
Terms tasteless food as terrible,
An awful play – unbearable.
I am impressed by play's anomaly
That portrays paradox perfectly.'

***4.5 stars**

Frying pan:

'This intriguing play
Skilfully does portray
That life rises in varied tastes,
And none can be shunned or braced,
For life is as it is,
With none in the midst –
There is no known–unknown,
As appears one, on its own.
Yet if perceived through the confines
Of seeming solid lines,
Then this too can be a concept,
A quixotic project.

Undefinable is the presence
Of unreal peripheries in appearance.
Though seen through the eyes of innocence,
The appearance is an instance:
A gentle quiet buzz,
Appearing as it does.'

***4 stars**

The Hob:

'The play's various pointers bright
Are like fireflies in the night,
Though light is always one, the same,
But sparks are divergently named
By the press members of the buffet,
For seen is the play in diverse ways,
Like the same food on the plate
But flavours varied on the palate,
Then portrayed are tastes in style
Of professional profile,
Like divergently describe a scene
An artist, a scientist, or a scribe keen.
Yet none present in forms separate
To express flavours, innate,
For narratives alone appear,
Apparent scenes without frontiers.
So much chatter about a play
Which doesn't exist anyway.

A hall of mirrors all does seem,
Of seemingly real–unreal themes.
Yet dark and light are surely one,
So all an expression of none.
Or maybe a display of fireworks
With nothing that lurks?'

The ladle wished to know the secret
That made the show an enormous hit,
And the meaning of the cosmic play,
The views on its theatrical display.

The kitchen accredited the source,
Which performed the play – the vital force –
And it refused to own the success
Or be the actor of the process.

The Kitchen:

'No one is ever capable
To speak of the immeasurable,

For how can minute words reveal
Nothing, which as traits does unpeel.
And how to illustrate nothing?
Especially when it alone does sing
Anew in every instant,
Without anyone present.
And how to speak of an appearance
Or of the occurring emergence?
Or how to show appears a play
Or a story that seems to sway?
All is an ephemeral plot,
Illumination or not.

So, nothing can do justice
To the appearing boundless.
This play simply points to this presence,
Life as it is, beyond all substance
Or meaning – in its essence.
Simply this amazing appearance
Of verdure spices, fruits, and meats,
With a kitchen clean and neat.

Yet I guess that self, its suffering,
Has reached peaks searing,
Now seems to be open and spent,
To hear of this freedom present
As the theatrical delight.'

The Hot Tom Yum

At a demanding Thai kitchen
The chef de partie in position
Was busy planning her recipe
While chopping and slicing swiftly
For the hot and tangy *tom yum* soup –
A dish that seemed to her senses a coup.
The pressure of the task at hand
To be completed in the time planned,
Along with the edicts of the head
Chef, the heat at the counter, red
Chillies stinging her fingers
Relentlessly with their fiery figures
Made her cantankerous and hot
In the environment fraught.

She heard a few whispers around her,
Which though inaudible caused a stir.
Bewildered, she looked all around,
But all were busy, chores did abound.
The strange voices became loud and clear,
Arising from ingredients near;
She was sure she heard bizarre rhymes,
So looked around several times,
Then intrigued by the oddity
She seemed relieved of anxiety,
And soon seemed adrift in the verse,
Awake, yet fully immersed.

Cashew to the peanut:

'Perfect is the expression so far –
That you attract what you are.'

Then pointing to the chef de partie
Continued the cashew hearty.

'Like her, the *tom yum's* fuming and hot,
Peppery, piquant, irritable, fraught.
So, every day she's ordered by the head
To make the *tom yum* fiery, red,
Which then feeds anger's loop,
And her inner core does swoop.'

Then content with the view
Were the earthy sisters two –
The peanut and the cashew,
Who avoided all hot stew.
They greatly despised the *tom yum*,
For it wasn't still, serene, or plum;
It boiled at slightest irritant,
Was citric, spicy, and vehement,
Embodied all negative traits,
Spiritually inadequate,
And lacked the earthiness – their strength,
Certainly not of their wavelength.
But devoted was the shrimp to the soup,
Like other ingredients in the group.

Lemongrass to the sisters:

'Oh, you pretentious two,
Unmask your pompous hue,
Jump out of your serene stew,
Come to your flavours true,
To the reality that can't be imbued
Yet appears as all, the joy and blues.

The *tom yum's* flavours are unmatched,
For it does not remain detached,
Does not its spicy flavours hide,
Is free, where nothing is denied.
In turmoil doesn't aspire serenity,
Doesn't fantasise positivity
To fall apart at the first impediment,
Then seek release by joy relevant,
For it's authentic to the core,
Does not hate what is, isn't at war –
Like you. For your desire to be positive
Is relative and combative,
And your desire to escape what appears
Divides, resides in violence, its sphere.

But our *tom yum's* demeanour
Is childlike and pure,
Just like a new-born, naïve and new,
Guilt-free, boiling to a feverish hue.
Innocent is its impatience,
Neither wilful nor packed with arrogance.
Does not pretend to everything know,
Having conquered the worldly show;
Being free from self's presence,
It doesn't play to an audience.'

Peanut interrupting the lemongrass:

'Your chatter certainly makes no sense,
For anger and heat cause offence.
The soup does not display sane traits
Of wisdom, for it simmers in its gait,
Does not meditate and isn't calm,

Does not sing soothing psalms,
Does not have an aura of gold –
Seems to be totally uncontrolled.
Instead, it destroys faith and values
Necessary to uphold the true.
How can you call him spiritual
When he's vulgar and irritable?'

Lemongrass interrupting the peanut:

'Say, oh Peanut and Cashew!
Can life be divided in two –
The self and anger in view?
Can you stay away or pursue
That which appears, is natural,
Beyond inverses unreal and factual?
How can something that does rise
Naturally be unwanted or unwise.
Isn't anger like an adrenaline rush,
That can move mountains in a hush,
An intelligent intervention
To save a form from destruction.
Simply energy innate
Destroying deceptive traits,
Wild and free, dancing alone,
Without a cause to intone,
Burning anger in the field of presence,
Rising, dancing, returning to silence.
So why run away
From the energetic display
Of emerging expressions
For anticipated impressions?

And think of your phrase bizarre,
That: 'You attract what you are'.
Doesn't it encourage awful acts
And blame victims for abuse, its impact?'

Peanut interrupting the lemongrass:

'Those who align to sanguine school,
And meditate, seem calm and cool;
By applying attraction's law
They manifest serenity and awe,
Consciously stay away from feud,
Even attract fortune and fortitude,
Synchronise body, mind, and soul
And become one with the whole.'

The cashew then ignored the imp –
The lemongrass – and addressed the shrimp.

Cashew:

'I would advise you too, oh Shrimp,
Use vision boards, don't live and scrimp,
And thus, attract prosperity,
Along with calm serenity.
Abandon the soup and its heat
And join the peaceful retreats.
Learn to release anger and stress;
Practise the art of forgiveness.'

Intervened the *galangal*,
Addressing from a unique angle.

Galangal:

'Oh, Peanut, heed our team:
Fiery, full of heat and steam;
Here there's no confinement
Of traits, or acts, or an alignment
With the spiritual, for there's no division
With what appears. Or any holy vision.
Or an exclusive spirituality –
A privilege got by the heavenly,
For that's hierarchical brutality
In the name of held spirituality.

Spirituality is a hoax,
Reigns by beliefs in ropes,
Simply imagined, dead images
Of holiness and sacrilege,
Or coloured misconceptions
Of innumerable perceptions:
Like one should be poor and thus survive
On charity, and not for money strive;
Or be calm, never say an angry word,

Or be indifferent to the world
And life, for eternal bliss,
And become one with Oneness;
Be empty, without any thoughts,
Or live a life not fraught,
And breathe, feel, and communicate
Serenely, heal past dictates.
All this is just a plethora of opinions
Sold to the innocent millions –
Is popular for it targets the confined
Energy, which appears as the defined
Self, which is the chase, the strife,
To avoid this appearing life.'

Then he rolled his eyes,
Each word did emphasise:

'Pretending to be calm on fire
Is to bear an image to be admired,
For you've been taught by society
To suppress in the name of propriety
And that endurance is superior,
While weakness is inferior.
But spirituality is inclusive:
It's not divided or exclusive,
So is not a one-sided view
Of being calm in the hot stew,
Or swaying leaves on the still trees,
The golden sun and sublime breeze.
It's even grime, heat, and humidity,
Along with odour and stupidity,
Yet is untouched by all imagery
Appearing, its own play of energy.

Know: a spirituality that's small
Is not spirituality at all;
And it is not a prerogative
Acquired by a few elevated,
For there is nothing separate
From life that does emanate –
There is nothing more spiritual
Than this moment, transitional.'

Then as the galangal took a pause,
Intervened the lemongrass
And spoke in a patronising style
To the sisters, who it seemed to rile.

Lemongrass:

'Who decides or does define
The supposed spiritual signs?
We can't even define the flavour
Of the food we all savour,
So how can one describe the quality
Or quantity of spirituality?
And who exists to own
Or make spiritual known?
And if everything is one beat,
Who is complete or incomplete?

The ones that teach you to be pure
And discard natural fervour
Split life in categories
And in it add hierarchy;
Your guilt of being terrible
Will make you follow the 'sensible',
Thus they have power and control
Over you, and your apparent dole,
While gratifying their ego
To scorn the ones lost in the flow
Of the small and the unrefined
Vagaries of the mind.
They suppose exists an individual
To be controlled, made valuable;
Rather, life as them too is lost
In seeming self – its apparent plot.

You can release anger, perform forgiveness
Of self or others, which may clean the mess
Briefly, but it will return with force
When life changes its course.
Why do you want to be rid of anything
To be in some space of nothing?
Isn't life in each expression:
Tears, anger, fear, possession?

But the more you run away,

The more the chase won't let you get away,
For endeavouring to end all strife
Is like chasing clouds to own them for life.
So, your desire to beget calm
Is more restlessness, not a balm,
It is fixing life to conclusion,
Which complicates even the illusions.'

The cashew then closed her eyes,
Chanted a *mantra* prized,
For she didn't want to hear
Any negative stir,
For that would contaminate
Her pure energetic state.
But continued to speak
The lemongrass sleek.

Lemongrass continuing the missive:

'Sure, at times the rising scene
Is not enough for the seeking scheme;
When rises anger or disagreement,
May also rise anguish and attachment,
Causation, personal enactment,
Which tortures one's predicament,
Creates need or expectation
To change apparent manifestation.
But ownership of the aliveness
Creates a further mess.

Know: inadequacy is at the heart
Of each goal, technique, or part.
Positive, negative, or creative
Are tricks to fortify the native,
For fear and separation at the root
Do nourish each other and turn acute.
But if there's stress and you don't run
Away, then there is only stress, with none
To own or feed the stressful thoughts
For them to grow in fretful plots;
In this way, feelings linger for a while,
Do not inflict their trial,
But to honour them or hide,
Or label them or judge their tide,
Makes them stay. Yet all does pass…'

But before the lemongrass
Could finish his sentence
About the emerging existence
Resumed the *galangal*
On the spiritual.

Galangal:

'Spirituality is freedom,
Natural life without a fiefdom –
Is like the empty, untouched sky,
Where play the sun, moon, clouds – don't dye
It; where there's no self but presence,
Where reigns inherent intelligence,
Which gauges every situation,
Protects the form from cessation,
Can be brave by running away,
Or may confront and stay,
For life has no decree of how to be:
It is as it is, completely free.
Yet it isn't detachment but celebration
Of every appearance in manifestation.
All appears, fear, anger, pain,
None relevant and none inane.

And does not everything that appear,
Including all our thoughts and fears,
Appear out of nowhere,
And vanish in the same air,
To which then dispensed are labels
Of noble, evil, real, or fable?
So, none is the thinker of their thoughts,
Or can know their source or their craft,
And life appears as any thought –
All an expression of the naught.

So anger's neither right nor wrong
But an expression of one song,
Life rising as the present scene
Without the other to demean.
Isn't it liberating to hear
That all is one, does appear,

And nothing can affect the real you,
Like pages are unmoved by words in view?
Embraced is all your mess, unrest,
By formless presence, ever at rest.

Thus, enlightenment is not a jackpot,
Where a golden aura coats the pot –
It is life as it is…'

But once again intruded the lemongrass
And spoke of greed's impasse.

Lemongrass to the sisters:

'And your advice of the vision boards
Is disguised greed of rewards.
Life always invites reality,
With pain, anger, fear, negativity,
And will beget humility
Of the self and its activity.
When rises recognition
Of illusory manifestation,
It's seen that all rises naturally,
Without anyone to control the spree,
Then feelings and thoughts are what they are,
And not entities that can mar
Beingness, the appearance…'

Then suddenly the overwhelmed cashew
Dragged her sister impromptu…

Cashew to the peanut:

'Let's leave; do not listen to these fools,
For they refuse to see the tranquil jewel.
They will ruin our sacred skies
By their negativity, lies.
Positivity is the way
To a life of joy and play.
They don't know they risk nemesis,
In the *tom yum* that is negative.'

The peanut and the cashew
Stormed off to pursue
Silence, regain their earthy repose,
Lost in the midst of crushing prose,
For they felt they were humiliated
In the kitchen where they were celebrated –
Were irritable as they left the group,
Thanked their stars for not being in the soup.

Then lemon grass and *galangal* did discuss
Freedom and the sisters' disgust.

Lemongrass to the galangal:

'Exhausting seems their life
By sustaining a self in strife.
They haven't dived into self's nature –
Its addictive possessive feature,
Where its unfulfilled desires
Ignite, feed the anger's fire,
And seething anger needs drama.
It abuses and inflicts trauma
On the alive – pulsating forms
Of self and others – for dead norms,
For it sees self and others separate,
And thus employs dominion and hate
From its life's context, and its reasons,
Believing it will fulfil its intention.
It's this small self or the split mind –
The limit – that seems to bind
Everything, and believes all's real,
And to a seeming self does appeal,
Which then judges from its call –
Is livid, harms, kills, does maul.

And buried anger taciturn
Creates addictive patterns,
Makes one dance like a puppet
In an unconscious mindset –
Simply division in an ugly role,
Trying the scenario to control.
This is the sham attached to annoyance
That harms and requires silence,
While anger's anger doesn't need drama
Or to abuse or inflict trauma
On anyone. It rises, dances, leaves

With no one caught in its weaves.'

Galangal to the lemongrass:

'Sure, exhausting is their life,
For reigns division's strife.
When the self is no more,
Apparent inverses don't roar,
Cease hatred, grudge, and jealousy,
Abuse, disdain, and enmity,
Along with attachment, lust, and greed,
The need to be detached, at peace, or freed.
For there is no individual
With a continuity, pivotal.

Then matter will neither insult nor praise,
As there is none to fall or raise;
For now, there is complete release,
Freedom from all, and none to please –
Stillness and peace innate
In and as all the seeming states.
Yet immeasurable is that which appears:
Anger, sadness, pain, or fear,
With none to conquer or to be prey.
Life, nothingness in play,
Free to appear as any occurrence:
Anger, war, destruction, deterrence,
Compassion, elevation, release, cure,
Or for performance face censure.'

Lemongrass to galangal:

'I completely agree with you.
But never mind, as veiled is their view,
They see this message to be cruel,
Insensitive, impractical.
When they'll return home, the base,
Nothing will be in or out of place.'

Then intervened the kaffir lime
In the conversational chime.

Kaffir lime:

'You two indeed talk too much
And can overwhelm any search.
Do you recognise what you say
Or just repeat the soup, his way?
Why are you curbing all in a bowl,
If all that appears is just the whole?
If everything is an expression
Energetic, then can there be volition
Or individuals? Isn't life alone
In manifestation? With nothing known?
Then can the soup be hot or whole,
Or boundless, or playing a role?
Can the sisters be ignorant,
Or seemingly arrogant?
Or return home, perform, or liberate,
Become free, natural, naïve, or great?

If the natural or the inherent
Performs as qualities apparent,
Won't sugar always be sweet
And lemon a tangy treat?
The *tom yum* surely hot and spicy,
While cashew earthy and pricy?
If there is only one,
Raw aliveness, nothing, none,
Won't there be the apparent
Alone, without anyone present,
Only this occurrence
Appearing, no substance?

Heed: this appearance is an echo
Of stillness, its libretto,
Resonating as seen–unseen inflection,
As senses five and their reflection,
As ebb and flow of life, its guise,
And as the countless hues that arise.
Is just, unjust, pursues, does reform,
As all the acts does perform,
Appearing as the cashew and her chase,
Positivity, and the apparent grace,
Articulating the message, too,
Formless forming with none to view –

Simply love unconditional
Appearing as each visual.

Why is this appearance so?
There is no other to know.
Stop preaching non-duality
At every opportunity.
At least let there be a thirst
Before you start your outburst.'

Then teasingly added:
'If the one alone appears as this,
Can you add to its Oneness?'

The taciturn shrimp stayed silent,
Enjoying the scene irrelevant.

The chef de partie was in wonder
As spoke the ingredients asunder,
Reflected on all that did unfold
As she prepared the soup bold.
Then as the soup boiled said to it:
'I couldn't find you, yet you lit –
Life's untold essence
By your absent presence –
Don't know how to define your traits
Or how to name your presence innate.
Are you a blend of everything?
Or maybe there is nothing?
Maybe all arises on its own,
Named, constrained, yet unknown.
Yet I know not of presence
Nor can define its brilliance.
Is it veiled or is it obvious?
Or hidden by being ubiquitous?'

She wondered if it all was insight,
Or did ingredients speak to her delight?
As she remained lost in her cloud,
She was alarmed by the head's voice loud:
'Are you serving that f***ing soup
Or planning to stay in your dreamy loop?'

38

The Dreamy Treat

This pulsing, pounding universe,
Is it a song in dual verse?
Or an appearance kaleidoscopic
Of one alone in dreams prismatic,
The vivid dreams of unreal domains,
And dreamt confines, without the chains?

In one remarkable gifted realm
Appears a nation at the helm
Of magical and sapid dreams,
Castles of fudge and clotted creams,
Luscious sweets and gaudy gums,
Creative flairs and flawed sums.

Here gobstoppers and liquorice
Can frustrate any sorceress,
While the wise wizards with the jellybeans,
Aided by a chocoholic Queen,
Conduct the dream of variety,
Stack sherbets, too, in propriety.

As in an impeccable dream,
Everything curbed receives esteem,
And preferred are particular traits,
With timeless classed in time's gait.
Yet an ineffable mystery
Are borders with a history.

This life is genuinely free,
Appearing as the wave and sea;
Free to seem confined or vast,
To dream or dissipate. No contrast.
Hinting: waves the sea alone,
Appearing wonder, on its own.
…

There is another domain uncut,
Where chocolates are in love with nuts.
Though hazelnut is the favoured one,
Almond's agility does stun.
Here chocolates – nutty, dark, and white –
Contest perfection in every bite.

Here in this creamy, dreamy land
Exist persistent mountains grand,
And trendy is research and peace
And sterling sweets with timed release;
The tactful, fretful fountains few
Arrange assemblies for truffle stew,
Believing neutrality is real,
Along with all the surreal deals.

But can profound peace genuinely emerge
Until individuality does surge?
Or are the prosperous parallel streets
An invitation to the timeless treat?
Where promoted are praline and mousse,
For they promise to release the noose.

Are not all these apparent streams
Floating dust specks in the sunbeam?
And 'my' life like a chocolate dream
Is set on pyramids of esteem;
And in the the wondrous dream
I feel I am across the stream.

Can I awaken from the surreal?
Be beyond the real and unreal?
Can I choose to dream on or be awake?
Differentiate the real and fake?
Are these dreams within dreams; can we go far?
Is presence playing the repertoire?

Is comparing dreams like quicksand,
Or can none drown in the holy land?
Is this panoramic view
One pretending to be two,
Engrossed in the dream or not – a play,
Is, isn't, an ineffable display.

Does the nameless name and impel tastes?
Do I choose: 'Chocolate with almond paste,
No, wait, I'd like a sweet with lemon squeeze.
No! Walnut chocolate with honey, please.
Is there choice with none to choose?
Can I have both the fudge and mousse?

Wait: I am still confused, in doubt
That does choice really come about.'

This pulsing, pounding universe,
Is it a song in dual verse?
Or an appearance kaleidoscopic
Of one alone in dreams prismatic,
The vivid dreams of unreal domains,
And dreamt confines, without the chains.

A. JACOBI
Usine spéciale pour la fabrication
DES CHOCOLATS
23 & 25. Rue du Maroc
MAGASINS DE DÉTAIL
29. Boulᵈ Poissonniere
28. Rue Saint-Sulpice
PARIS
QUALITÉ RECOMMANDÉE
Chocolat Vanille vente 2f le ½ Kilo
MÉDAILLE D'OR
EXPOSITION UNIVERSLLE
1889
MAISON FONDÉE EN 1826
CHOCOLAT
SUCHARD
NEUCHÂTEL
(SUISSE).
PARIS
29 Rue Turbigo
NEW-YORK
73 Warren-Street
LONDON
33, King William-Street, E.C.
FABRIQUE DE CHOCOLAT
PH. SUCHARD
NEUCHÂTEL
CACAO SOLUBLE
5 GRAMMES de ce Cacao suffisent pour faire UNE BONNE TASSE

39

The Wholesome Split

A wholesome Moong bean
Appeared whole, split, and yellow lean;
Though one, it played all three roles –
Split green, split yellow, and green whole,
Like formless appearing as form
That energetically seems to perform,
But then appears as the trinity –
Formless, form and energy.

Gathered foods from all the courses,
To attend its monthly discourse,
Where it spoke of Oneness that's complete –
Formless as one, three, varied treats.
Thus, revealed was love that's free and pristine –
As the appearance of a wholesome bean –
A love so deep, and without scission,
Where the lover, love, and loved are one.

Most were at peace in its presence,
While many felt a deep resonance.
Some laughed, sobbed, marvelled in silence;
Others questioned in innocence.
Innately spoke the Moong without an aim,
Like nature occurring without a claim.

The Whole Green Moong Bean:

'Sings nothingness as every tune –
A hum, a psalm, a shrill, a croon,
The various tunes of its presence,
For all is music in existence;

Though solo, it is the orchestra –
Cacophony or opera;
Or rather this entire spectre
Is one, an apparent orchestra.

This sound that is unbound
Is profound, abounds,
Vibrates as this silence,
Is volcanic in presence,
Energetic in its gait,
Unbegun, cannot dissipate.
This music celebrating each melody
Is love, the absolute in expression free,
As flat or sharp, major, or minor,
Each scale without a headliner.

From where does the music appear?
Where does it go, disappear?
None can it ever decipher,
For it remains a cipher,
By being each and every tune,
A hum, a psalm, a shrill, a croon.

Yet music appearing as the food melody
Pretends to play as separate recipes,
Which then believes it owns the song,
Rhythm and pitch to it belong;
Though the existent tone is in play,
The melody seeks tones at bay,
And then desires the euphonious
Serenades, which appear harmonious,
For it seeks to know its presence –
Music, the life's core substance –
Or feigns to be lost in the song,
Or in the shrine's gong.
Yet all along is music in seeming flow,
With no one to it blow or in its throes.

The perfect octave is this interval,
In which all arises as a miracle,
Appear mixed melodies in tune –
A psalm, a hum, a shrill, a croon.
So, this, the appearing symphony
Is musical notes of energy
In reverberation.'

The Split Green Moong Bean:

'As cited before, there's nothingness
That energetically sparks, does dress
As appearing waves of melody,
To sing this song immediate and free.
Or nothingness in deep rest
Emits light in energetic zest –
A show of light and sound,
A love that is unbound
Is animating as form,
Is appearing as the norms –
As floating fluidity and creativity,
And seeming transformative ability,
All seeming to happen at once,
Without space–time or substance.

The formless energetically performs,
And it appears as the illusory norm
Of formless, form, energy –
The recognised trinity;
The three are deemed distinct
By itself, in space–time's precinct,
And sewn is a narrative of light,
Split in three-fold perspective tight
Of parallel, vertical, or whole,
Or body, mind, and soul.
In the parallel experience
Further split is life in occurrence –
As creator, upholder, and destroyer
Of the emerging earthly oyster
(Which then apparently seems to play
With traits, that augment a way,
Which seems to make appearance
Probable in seeming recurrence),
As past, present, and future,
The act, the action, and actor;
The birth, subsistence, death,
In–out and meeting of breath;
The male and female energy,

Meeting in the unknown space free;
The trinity of a devout doctrine,
All the individual to illumine.
But isn't this the original sin?
Where split is one, in trio's spin,
Considered real is the physical,
The mental, and the ethereal.

Yet there is only nothingness,
Which as the dual does express,
Is formless forming – Oneness,
Without hierarchy, process;
Is whole in transcendent rest,
Appears in energetic tryst
As the dream of the universe
And all its seeming verse,
Seeking its own presence
In varied forms of appearance.
The still shining presence
Waves as all the appearance,
Even when it deems that it craves
As an independent wave,
Significant is its existence,
In clutches of time and distance.
For it is unsplit in one or two –
Appears the act, with none in view.

This melodious feast –
Appearing as the bound, released –
May seem to end its ignorance
By its wholesome presence;
Or may appear in dual cadence
Of tunes in solo experience.
But nothing is in, out, or off course,
For nothing alone is in verse.
Trying to understand this is futile –
It's beyond imagination's aisle.'

The Split Yellow Moong Bean:

'As is the case of the illusory norm –[1]
That separate, distinct are forms –
The seeing of life through this lens
Of self, and its seeming fence,
Believes real's the worldly display,
Where I have a special part to play;
There is the other – the division –
With attachment in its expression,
Or hatred, enemies, and irritation
For foods, objects – the manifestation.
A world of me and you
Projecting acquired hues.

For the self's energy
In appearance as the defined spree
Is displeased with the rising scene
And wishes to fill this ravine
Through love, enlightenment, or peace,
Or honour, wealth, a wish to cease;
And thus the self perpetuates
Itself in circular stalemate.

But the self's the imprisonment,
Without a prison and confinement.
Thus, this narcissism you see around
Is the unbound appearing bound.
So, none can the emerging redress
Or know that all is Oneness,
Return to the source,
Or stray from the course,
Or heal the split by endeavour,
Or find the good God's favour.
Yet to recognise there is nothing
And it alone this song does sing,
Appears as three and the multitude,
Is lost in its own attributes,
Is liberation likely in food alone,
For here appears contraction and the known.

Still, to grant the spiritual pearl,
Or guide a course to fix the swirl,
Give an abstract meaning of life,
Of Oneness, and bliss that is rife;
Declare I am no one,
Or perpetuate any notion

1 The illusory norm is known as *Maya* in many scriptures of the East.

Of detachment or of improvement
Of that which appears, is irrelevant;
For it demeans the foodness of food,
Creates fictitious goals and servitude
To the ones who wish to guide,
Implying they have pearls prized.
There are no spiritual treasures
To be gained, or any measures
To gauge the states of being.
There is only love freeing,
Love emerging with all its mess,
An appearance which is blessed,
Where liberation is present,
Unravelling as this moment.

There is no other music beyond
Apart from this present sound.
There's nowhere to go and nothing to find,
For the colossal appears as the defined,
So this appearance – Oneness singing.'

Several listened to its talks,
Which often seemed a deadlock.
A few enjoyed this presence
Of boundless love without substance,
But most felt it had reached a state
Where played celebration innate.

Seeker 1:

'As draws the flame the moths in its sphere,
So I am pulled to be here.
As the flowers blossom, creepers cling,
The rivers flow, the birds sing –
Likewise, you share unconcerned
About a reward or being spurned.

But you dissipate all security,
Mock at my gathered purity.
Yet I return to be slaughtered,
Unlearn the subtle tricks watered
By self, and to resonate
With your presence innate.

For this message of non-duality
Destroys the individuality.'

The Whole Green Moong Bean:

'Speaks the one alone
To self, is not veiled by the known.
There is an echo natural
To all at a deeper level;
This freedom resonates
With that unchained being innate.

As nature asserts no division,
Is not abstracted by separation,
Similar is the essence here,
So felt is calmness that does endear.
Yet as this presence is free to be,
It may intimidate or feel free.
But neither does this communique
Belong to me, nor is it an acquired play,
Nor do you have a free will
To come, enjoy, or hate this shrill.
For all that arises is the presence
Energetic, spontaneous in essence –
Naturalness without a course,
With none to own the words or source.

And what to say of the rising words?
They are like the migratory birds,
Appear to come and go away –
An unknown mystery at play.
But know there's neither duality,
Nor there is non-duality,
For there is no inverse,
But one empty, melodic verse
As this rising occurrence,
One, undivided, inclusive presence.'

Seeker 2:

'Can you explain this self or 'I'?
Why does it appear to come by?
What do you mean by a dream

Of 'I', and separation, its theme?
How is it to be liberated, free?
How can I get rid of a 'me'?
Please clarify my qualms
To unite and restore a calm.'

The Split Green Moong Bean:

'An exclusive character
In the clutches of time's corridor,
Where it is small, a part
Of life, and the world is apart,
Or an individual with a name,
Acting with free will, owning the frame,
For whom what appears an actuality,
Revolving around the centre of a 'me',
Is this dream of separation.
Yet the self is an illusion,
Is the unrequited love supreme,
Longing to end its separate theme.

I will reiterate a song[2] I heard,
A song strung in stunning words:
'If you are the mountain still,
Then "I" the dancing peacock that thrills,
If you the moon that does amaze,
Then "I" the *chukar* partridge[3] that does gaze.
Oh, charming presence if you don't seem split,
The "I" can't appear separate, in bits;
And if appears a split from you,
Then with whom can it join or glue? (Pause.[4])
If you are the lamp, then "I" the wick,
If you the pilgrimage, then "I" the yardstick.[5]
This existent love between me and you
Has ceased the other from the view,
Wherever I go – your reverence alone,
You alone supreme, none other on the throne.
Your recognition dissipates death's fear,
Sings Ravidas, of this love dear.'

2 See Note 16A
3 See Note 16B
4 See Note 16C
5 See Note 16D

So, the small self that shines
Is the appearance of the divine,
Without it being an entity,
Is simply an energetic spree,
And thus will be unrequited,
For the self cannot be united.
The need of unity – to become one –
Is to divide the one that's not undone,
For one alone appears as two,
Yet it is one and never two.
So none exists to unite or merge
In one, for there's no split to modify, purge.
Appears only energy
As each emergence, free,
And energy isn't split or dual
To separate the individual.
It alone is in appearance free,
Is spontaneous in its decree,
Or nothing alone appears as this
Presence. Complete, nothing amiss.
…

Now listen about enlightenment:
It is not an event or an entitlement;
It's apparent demise of illusion
Of all kinds – seclusion or profusion –
Is freedom from objectivity,
Rising in subjectivity,
Only freedom with no advantage,
Just what is, none to run the rummage.

Freedom is not gaining prescient faculties,
Or any magical abilities,
Or an angelic kind of a bliss,
But what appears, with nothing amiss,
Not a state or being transcendent,
But is this, the seeming moment,
A limitless freedom, all come and goes,
Nothing sticks, stays, is far or close,
No distances or time to bind,
Just this appearance undefined.
It is life ordinary,
Without an adversary
Breathing, eating, cats in play,

No holy music or divine buffet.
Is washing dishes, grinding spices,
With all its mess and arthritis.

Yet life is not a dreary routine,
For everything is fresh, pristine,
Like being in love for the first time,
Seeing love all around – sublime.
This appearance is a miracle,
A song without the lyrical
And every in and out of breath –
A musical note completely at rest,
Unconfined in feeling, word, or thought,
Ineffable the paradox of is–is not.
Impossible is this to describe:
Like sound singing the silent vibe,
Or a wave gauging the ocean's depth,
Or the breath knowing its death,
Or words illustrating paper blank,
Or waters in the sea or on the bank.

Though it seems a trek from everything
Being split and real to nothing,
It is not. It is recognition
For none; there is no musician
To sing, but nothing's everything –
As this, simply singing,
Neither one nor two,
A celebration of hues
Without a destination
Or an intention.

But know: the individual
Can't be free from the self – pivotal,
Like characters of a book can't know
They are characters of the show
Or the book's narrative – a dream,
And they aren't split from its theme;
Likewise, the self's illusion
Can't recognise it's a delusion
Or be liberated, get enlightenment,
For it is unreal, never present.
Thus, ego isn't the opposite
Of freedom without limit;

So enlightenment is not a state
Or experience that elevates
Beings, appearing in the show
Of life, but freedom that is, aglow.

To be precise there's no individual
To liberate, acquire life eternal.
All is formlessness alone
In the known–unknown tones,
Simply life alone, singing,
The formless forming.
The magic is in the 'f' word.'

On the spontaneous remark
Resonated laughter in sparks
Among the audience,
Lulled by poetic cadence.

Seeker 3:

'Do you mean life's an illusion
And all that we see a delusion?
In the viewer and the view,
Which one is true and which untrue?
Do we need to suffer and stray
To be free, find a way?
Please relate your story
To appease my curiosity.
What is the purpose of your song?
Is it to uplift all seekers who long
To be free? Do we need to be here
To lose the self, the seer?
Please speak to the average mind –
Do not be to abstraction inclined.'

The Split Yellow Moong Bean:

'Firstly, the self is the illusion,
Splitting life in real–unreal delusion.
All there is is the formless forming,
Unmeasured, apparent, performing,
Appearing real to unreal identity,
While an appearance is this physicality.

When there's no split in viewer and view,
How can there be a true–untrue?
If there isn't an individual,
Can there be grades divisional
Of great, average, and subordinate minds,
Who can or cannot grasp the undefined?
And there is no mind, too,
To programme, free, slay, or review.

I do not possess profound freedom
That I present as abstract wisdom;
This song is not the truth innate
Or a perception to emulate;
And if you think I am liberated,
Or a fraud, it is projection translated.
This song does not belong to me,
But it is Oneness rising, free.

If it pleases, I will share my story,
But can it calm your curiosity?
Served with turmeric and cumin,
I can heal, usher health blooming.
Belonging to a wholesome family,
I am considered a panacea naturally.
I've had a simple, serene life,
With minimum suffering and strife,
But got in touch with spirituality
And wished to be rid of individuality;
For hours together, I would seek
Oneness, to end the hide and seek.
Yet no endeavour ever
Brought me any closer
To it. For no attempt, however free,
Can ever liberate the 'me'.
I did not recognise
That Oneness is, can't rise,
And it alone as me does seek
The enlightenment's peak.
But seemingly engulfed rivers of love –
Everything that it did behove,
Placed on the cross – to reveal
True love and peel illusion's wheel.

But who can know of their demise
When no one in the show does rise?
How can one know there is no "I"
When there's no one existent to die;
This account that I did share
Is irrelevant to the song rare,
For neither suffering nor peace
Can bring any release,
And no account iconoclastic
Can ever match this freedom drastic.

Lastly, the flowers bloom, birds sing,
The legume sprouts, the bees sting.
What is their purpose – who's special?
It's simply life, with no goal primeval.
Why is this appearance, none to know,
Formless forming a wondrous show
Of no nouns, simply life appearing –
Eating, drinking, thinking,
Simply this, with nothing to gain.
This moment never echoed again.

And there's no difference in a pub,
A sunset point, here, or a waste tub.
So, there's nothing to take away
From here. Life appears as it may.
Life is life – there are no norms
To live, for one as all does perform.
All is one indivisible presence,
Alone as this appearance.

Yet as the wind aids leaves to fall,
So may unravel illusion's haul
By the unsung melody –
A freedom beyond words, free.
The stirring dancing silence,
A revolution – this absence.'

Then pointing at the audience,
Declared in tones glorious,

'Sings emptiness
As this.'

After the bean finished the discourse,
Arose a deep silence, unforced.
Now quietly sat the wholesome bean
While most gazed at its lustre pristine.
Yet none in trance did ascend
Or in silence did descend.
Vanished a few condescending claims,
Yet no one did anything gain.
Now, in this very ordinary scene,
Smiled the wholesome bean,
As heard was the unsung melody
Of the symbolic entropy.

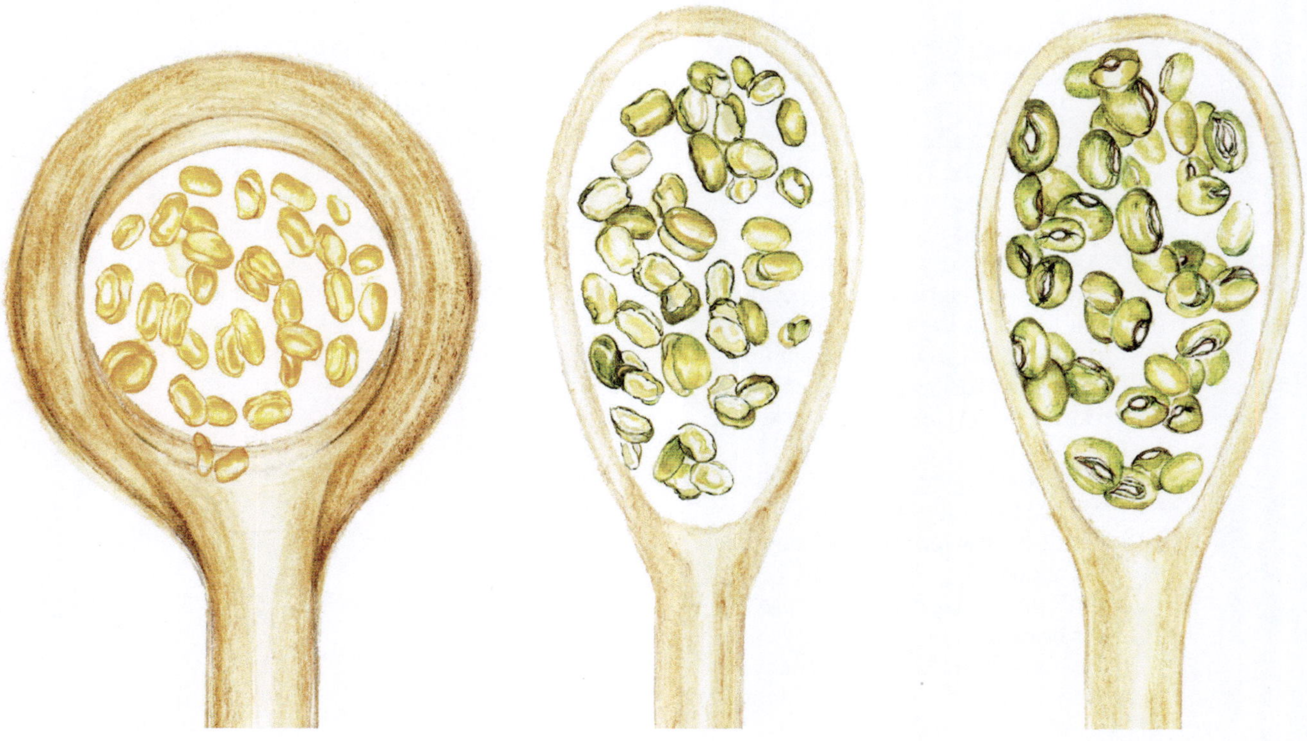

40

Made for Each Other

'Bored of bread, bored of bread!
And yearn for new instead?
Taste from the world around,
To return to the profound –
The sapid buttered toast,
Bliss, taste that matters most.
Prepare this wedding host –
Rejoice and raise a toast!'

Aloofly opined the bread,
Alluded to its spread,
To its enlightened dough –
The creamy buttered glow.
She stressed how assiduous effort
Begets a feast of desserts,
How being 'present' is the core
To cease despair, and life's lore.

The butter reflected, smiled:
'That can't be refined, defiled –
Enlightenment, which is,
Is not an end towards bliss.
As it exists so it can't end,
Or grow, or shrink, or be penned.
Isn't hidden in the source unbounded
But is existent, can't be counted,
Can't be ascribed to silence
But is, isn't, simple presence.

It is, so can't be earned,
Nor can be taught or learned,
Can't be stowed, bought, or sold,
Or acquired by being bold,
Isn't gained by being pristine
Or bestowed on the keen.
Besides, it isn't an accolade
Bequeathed for hardship, being staid.

Rather, there is no liberation
Or illusion's cessation.
Nor does enlightenment occur,
For nothing alone does stir.
Appears enlightenment
To end an entitlement,
As it ends the 'me' and 'you',
But there is none it to view,
For there is none present
To get enlightenment.'

The slice still defends her doctrine:
Of precepts that illumine,
Of sedulous sweat and gaining grace,
Of being in and out of place.
Yet none is naïve or at a loss
Or primed to walk across,
For there is none in view,
Just love in all its hues.

The butter softly spread,
Sodden with tastes unsaid,
Adores the bread as it is,
With all its flavours, not amiss.
And they delight as one,
A perfect breakfast done!

White toast with butter
Wholemeal toast
Seeded Slice
Rye Slice

41

The Creation's Story

PART 1

Once, sought the chickpea and the kidney bean
To unearth the universe's plot unseen.
The cousins puzzled to the core,
Listened to creation's varied lore:
It being born of creator's grace,
A blend of earth, water, space,
With fire and air to bring life
To forms, that are ever in strife.

The cousins always did wonder
About the cosmic structure:
Is it like curry in which floats
Matter, or like oil which coats
Foods? Perhaps like a kebab, a blend,
Or taste unknown one can't defend;
Is it like a delicious salad?
Are these suggestions invalid?
Or maybe the feat of a hero,
Or nothing, absolute zero.

They asked: 'Is the maker separate
From its form, like food served on a plate?
A cosmic play in expanse of time?
Does all exist at a point sublime?

Is this appearance ever present?
A play of light, as form transient?
Is the universe illusory?
Divine sleep, end of sensory?
Maybe it's energy wild and free
Appearing as a planned entity.
Or is this existence a conscious God?
Maybe by itself shines the façade?'
Pursued such questions the cousins two
And desired to answers view.

At times, they pondered in silence
About the cosmic presence,
Sought insights in the crevices
Of the mind – beyond analysis –
From where the light does shine
To illumine all design.
But troubled further questions,
Untold thoughts, diverse impressions:
'If formless forms, what's evolution,
And who performs, why this confusion?
If one appears to act and work,
Can "I" fit in the framework?'

They dived in these issues profound
To find the key to how life abounds,
Followed fables magical,
Which claimed to point to the radical,
And searched the scriptures umpteen –
Scientific, sacred, in between,
To sate with answers that made sense,
But thought: is the search a pretence?
For they didn't want to quell the marvel
One feels on seeing stars primal.
Would they succeed in their endeavour?
For they were gifted and clever;
Or would they lose the self and states,
Be unable to articulate
The real? Or fall for the spiritual bait
Of love of God and nation – higher traits?
Would there be recognition faint
Or remain nothing, none to taint?

Undertook research the chickpea keen,
As scanned the scriptures the kidney bean.
The cousins travelled far and wide,
Trained under gurus, amazing guides,
Examined books, learned views untold,
Brought facts and faith into the fold.
The chickpea mastered scholarly skills;
The other learnt how the mind does still.
Clarified were their conceptions,
Yet unsated was their thirst for suggestions.

Until…

One day they met to share adventures,
To pair faith with factual ventures –
Met in the park, conversed in verse
About the mesmeric universe.
But before they could share
Their quests of science and prayer,
The children at play caught their sight,
And they were lost in pure delight
Of children's pristine innocence,
Nature's rhythmic recurrence,
Flora and fauna's silent bloom,
The sanguine summer's lush perfume,
The orchestra of singing birds,
The chasing dogs, the breeze stirred,
All of which accentuated peace,
And seized awareness bought ease.
The surroundings alone appeared,
Nothing majestic, nothing weird,
A simplicity of what lives,
An echo of nothing successive.
In this long silence they did own
The years of quest made nothing known.

Then at the kidney bean's request,
The chickpea reiterated his quest:
'Plenty of learning made me confused,
With varied views was yet amused;
Renounced, returned, and nothing did gain,
Yet am content and feel sane.
To summarise, I can thus say:

Life's like a colourful display,
With no beginning or an end,
No destiny already penned.'

After a few sips of coffee
Resumed the chickpea:
'During years of research on cosmic view,
I got to the root of each issue –
Through logic I sought causality,
Reached for inception of totality,
Until there was nothing, no design,
To know how form appeared to align.
Then I sought the minute
Until there was nothing in pursuit;
I learnt matter appears from particles;
Deeper still – an energetic stir primal
Arising out of nothingness
Yet infinite in dress.
Realised what's true at the macrocosm
Is relevant at the microcosm
(Though I haven't found a common theory
To illumine their conduct sundry
In the linear sequence
Of the study of science),
Then I tried to relate the two –
Nothingness appeared as both in view,
So every way that I did try,
There was nothing to ally.
Then I wondered about nothingness,
The infinity, and emptiness.

I thought physics is based on a frame
Of reference, round which spun is its game,
But without a centre of reference,
Could there be any distance?
Or above–below or place,
Or measurements or even space.
If emptiness has no direction,
How can the passage of time be in creation?
Yet all appears in time's duration
And seems like rhythmic oscillation.
Confused, I pursued deeper in the tracts
Of nothing and the appearing cosmic acts.

The moment of epiphany
Of emptiness and infinity:
When I saw water waving as waves innate,
I recognised nothing is separate.
It is water rising, falling away,
Yet appear ripples with shore to play.
Though appear three[1] waves in motion,
It is a stir without direction;
There is no beginning or an end,
Simply appearance, no ascend, descend,
And no ripple is independent
To own the rippling that's transient.
A dream, a ripple to the shore does go,
Like the illusion that time in space flows.
Water appears to always move,
Yet it isn't towards a goal or groove,
Akin is life to every form,
Energy stirring, seeming to perform
As every breath, tint, thought, or shade,
Emotions, forms that appear, fade.
So, can't be found the relevant source,
For the font and form are not divorced.'

1 Here, the reference is to the type and propagation method of waves found in water, namely the transverse, longitudinal, and circular waves.

The children's noisy fight
Suddenly caught the cousins' sight,
And they watched the innocent scene
Of instant fight and friendship pristine.
Later resumed the chickpea
On his recognitions free:
'Recognised, apparent forms in sight,
Simply phenomena of light –
Like the dust that in sunlight shines,
Appears light's apparent design,
All at once forms in real–unreal display,
Matter–anti-matter in perfect play,
A stir which is always anew,
Appearing without a crew.
No solid static universe
To be known, deciphered, set in verse.
Each occurrence that seems to appear,
Without in–out, appears, disappears.

Revealed, that nothing does embrace
All, yet appears as the form's face;
This emptiness or no thing
Energetically seems to sing
The verse, that is and isn't, no source –
Spontaneous without a course.
Nothing created or destroyed:
A separate creator is a ploy.

But this nothing can't be explored, known,
For it is not a real thing, but unknown.
All appears as a magical maze,
Nothingness having a seeming base,
Like waves of the ocean profound,
All a display of soundless sound –
Thus, simply appearing creativity
As vast waves of possibility.
Apparent opposites in cadence.
An appearance.

So, to conceive stories of evolution,
Where a species is the height of perfection,
Is vain, for exists only illustration,
Without conscious anticipation.
There is nothing dense and stable;
Can there be evolution of a label?
From pictures construed is a tale –
The unknown all guess, none can unveil.
An undefined mystery,
Which can't be confined in a story –
But I don't know how to document
All this recognition in scientific precincts.'

Encouraged by the children's candour
In play, he spoke in honest manner:
'Oh, Kidney Bean, so I do not know
Anything about the cosmic show;
Maybe we can use kebab as a guide,
Or maybe a bean patty fried,
Or salad raw with flavours fresh,
Where all elements well do mesh,
Or curry of the kidney bean,
Where appears the seen and unseen.
Vast, infinite, boundless, endless,
How much one says is less.
Simple yet paradoxical design
That is impossible to define.'

PART 2

The chickpea then asked the kidney bean
Of her travels and experiences keen.
'I too don't know how to convey
That I gained nothing to relay,'
Declared the kidney bean
About her scriptural scene.

Then resuming in her novel style,
She spoke of her quests versatile:
'In all these years of travel
Around the world to unravel
The meaning of the scriptures,
I found their non-dual features
Were lost in translation,
And spun were stories of creation.
So I soon left dual interpretations
And apparent stories of creation;
There was a knowing they weren't true

But were thoughts that came in view
And left without significance
To the emerging presence.
Then I dived into a rigorous review
Of manuscripts old and new.

Few scriptures were truly clear:
That there is only wonder,
For energy alone does stir,
Appearing as the forms that occur.
In some other scriptures
Hidden were the pointers
Of there being only presence
Appearing as its own radiance.
And their sketch of the appearing creation,
Where innate design is lit by illumination,
To be followed by contrasts of days and nights,
And split of waters, skies, matter in sight,
Implied description of appearance
All at once, not in a timed sequence,
Or the appearance of dualism,
Despite there being no division,
Where creator and creation are not split,
For one the source and light it emits –
Oneness, presence as all the hues,
Like space, which is everywhere in view.
Then I thought how could the infinite or vast
Be split, or curbed in tales of past?

I grasped some songs of freedom
Were symbolic, not moral wisdoms
Or teachings to apply or admit,
But songs of the infinite,
Sung by nothing, emptiness,
Occurring as a heart that's blessed
Yet without a purpose or an aim
Of rescuing the world, or to love reclaim.

Let me relate to you hymns three –
The songs of boundless liberty
That stress the freedom that is free
To appear as it does, simply be,
Is free from restraints of origin and end,
And images, concepts, and trends.

First: 'On being questioned about the birth[2]
Of the creation, and the one, its hearth,
States Nanak: "For this emergence
Expressed is only awe, reverence,
For always appears nothing
As the hearth of everything."

The second hymn[3] I cite – the gist:
"When non-being, being, neither exist,
No air, nor yet a sky away,
What shields? Bears? Where? Waters deep, unknown play?
No death, or immortality, or night or day,
No appearance; one alone does stay,
Yet Oneness by its own impulse
Breathes without breath or pulse,
Appears darkness, water indiscriminate,
The unborn hidden forms illuminates,
Emerging, stirring, by fervour appears,
And love as forms seems to occur…
Yet no one can relate or know
Emergence of seed of love, which glows.
Is it known from the utmost place?
Maybe it is not."

The final hymn that I'd like to quote
About origin–end, the dual note –
Dattatreya[4] on the non-dual dance:
"If this is without essence and expanse,
If this is without void and absence,
If one: constant, ubiquitous, empty–existence,
How to speak of an origin or end?" [5]
Then I thought, would there be one to comprehend
These songs of complete liberty,
Paradoxical in decree.

It was clear that some texts
Veiled the missive in abstract depths,
And language is incompetent
To portray paradoxical intent

2 See Note 17A
3 See Note 17B
4 See Note 17C
5 See Note 17D

Of energetic emptiness
That as all forms does dress;
And arcane is the mystery
Appearing as self, origin, history.'

The kidney bean seemed to continue
Without a pause, lost in her views,
But the chickpea didn't interfere,
As her enthusiastic fervour
For scriptures seemed so lively in its hue
That he enjoyed it without a clue.

'Stunning were some scriptural songs,
That illumined inner–outer twang
Of life as one, hinting the two
Are the same, unsplit in view,
Timeless, spontaneous in game,
Yet seemingly diverse in name;
So perfect your suggestion –
One the microcosm–macrocosm.
I too realised that identical
Are quantum and the whole – the spectacle –
Like: sleep, death, cosmic sleep are the same,
Exhalation too, despite diverse names;
The seeming mind like the moon,
Waxing–waning, reflecting light's tune,
While breath represents origin and end,
All an impression of the unpenned,
For in and out are simply one –
Formless illuminating its run,
Or formless forming – like a film,
At once, yet flowing like a hymn.

It was clear that all doesn't originate
From nothing into this present state,
But nothing alone appears to exist –
The second never does subsist.
And this universe is love complete,
No origin or end to meet,
For there is no such thing as time,
Yet appear its bounds sublime –
A diaphanous veil hiding the view
Yet not touching the formless hue.

Though the amusing part of the adventure
Was to see how false did venture:
How ego appeared as faith in play,
As no ego, submission, peace that stays,
And how religions came into play
To reign over life's alive display,
How endorsed were paths to reach the vast space
– Though space alone as forms does grace –
How worshipped were the texts
To avoid their reading in-depth,
And deciphered was the symbolism
Of texts only from the dual 'isms',
Where these dual interpretations
Bound life in time and dense contraction.

So, pervasive in its expression
Was seeming sustenance, in its impression,
Which was bound in the succession
Of saviour's descent, to fight oppression;
Or the seeming brilliant play of breath,
Of senses, ousting and seeming death,
Were given traits and names of gods
And demons, who were at odds.
Woven were yarns of causality
To highlight life's appearance free.
Imagery of churning of the ocean[6]
Of semblance was given real implications,
And construed were meanings one couldn't defend,
The bait – that life would improve after its end.
Then scriptures were used as defence,
To uphold fear and maintain the fence,
Thus individuality
Bound by morality, society,
And ritual became the source
For liberation – without a course.

But there was a knowing: all an expression
Of energy alone in illustration,
And one the vast and the minute,
The relative and the absolute.
Then I wondered, what was this Oneness?
Why did it wish to surface
As confinement of the infinite

6 See Note 17E

Into a small self, with limits?
Or was the one alone
In appearance unknown,
Without a self or limit,
Simply this – the infinite.'
…

The cousins then fell silent
For long, unsure, but content.
The kidney bean later did continue
About her state, that seemed to be an issue.
'But, oh Chickpea, I must confess,
All this clarity did not impress
Freedom. Instead, it's made a mess
Of my life, which seems beyond redress.
For all this recognition
On hearing the compositions
Has not brought wonder for this show,
Nor could it freedom thus stow.

At least your scientific inventions
Are useful in everyday expression.
Life's philosophy nothing does cease –
Instead begins a chase for inner peace.
Besides, my seeking will be unrequited,
For the "I" cannot be united,
As it is not real, permanent,
Like shifting sands remains transient.
Thus, seeking secrets of the universe
Or searching for the divine verse
Is endless seeking just the same,
Energy's own apparent game.
Yet I feel the search of Oneness – the last,
For nothing beyond the vast.

But I've heard when illusion falls away,
It's seen it was delusion's display,
None separate to know the universe
Or capture it in any verse.
Oneness as all forms does appear,
Is free to be in seeming frontiers,
So tell me, can i surrender this "I"?'
Said the kidney bean with a twinkle in her eye,

Then as if instantly with a deep sigh,
Laden with defeat, in a voice high:
'As says the Bible: "Chasing the wind",
Thus was my scriptural whirlwind.'
…

Then seemed to prevail deep silence.
The cousins lost themselves in the brilliance
Of children's love and innocence,
Which outshines creation's radiance.
Ceased all their need to know
Or the need to the unknown stow.
What years of search couldn't bestow
This love in smithereens did blow.
Dissipated ideologies,
All questions and philosophies
– As they both go hand in hand –
There was no base to expand,
For ceased the investigators,
Who had kept alive as interrogators.
For the apparent trick is not the quest
But the 'person' who it does invest.
Questions: a way to keep alive –
The seeker, who in query does thrive.
So, innocence lost by the need to know
Was paradise regained for none in the show.
All remains a mystery unsolved,
A secret that will never be resolved.
…

The kidney bean then brushing off the grass
From her lap said: 'This too shall pass.
Howsoever enlightening an experience,
It is still in the clutches of transience.
The depths of love exist –
Is free, even from the best tryst.'

The duo chose to go to the pub,
Enjoy a pint and tasty grub.
En route they discussed the way
To seek funds for their research stray,
For now the most important question
Was of finances and profession.

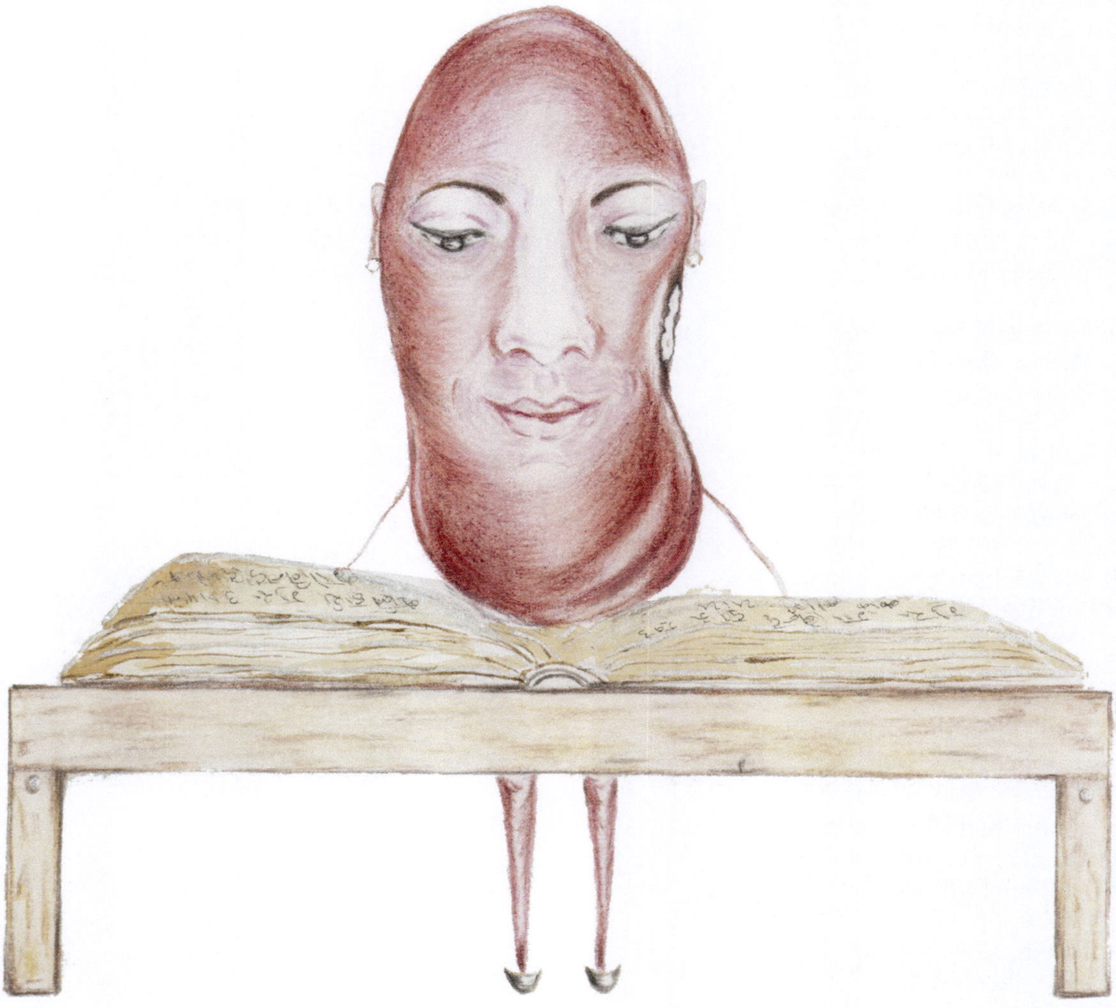

42

The Charming Spud

The gentle breeze, the woodpecker's drill,
The embraced daisies, path unclear,
Scuttles a drizzle with a chill.

The hungry fox then leaps in fear,
The rainy skies trick in a trice,
Displays the rainbow in frontiers;

Now bathed is grass in light, its rise,
And sway in joy the merry blades,
As squirrels prance in paradise;

The buds in awe view this parade,
As eagles scrutinise their prey,
While blasé birds sing their serenade.

In this colossal life, its play,
The fighting cats in accord rest,
And the appearance faultless stays.

The boundless hum that appears dressed
Unveils itself in live silence
As the spud's quivering form, blessed,

To glimpse the playing presence,
Which cannot be spelt or conversed,
For unknowable its existence.

Satiated seems the spud's keen thirst,
And blooms the charming spud anew,
Until the blissful bubble bursts,

And life its flavours does pursue.
Returns the self – mercurial –
As scavenger to taste the roux,

Delicious morsel ethereal,
Desires, endeavours ways unique
To claim the spud imperial.

Circles the scavenger at peaks,
Around the dreamy spotless spud,
But finds no food to fill the creek,

So stays starved in the unstained mud.
Untouched appear the fingers greased.
A roar – disappears the seeming spud.

The natural rainy skies released
Complete the landscape, spud, and feast.

43

An Apparent Pilgrimage

(Ramayana[1] Retold)

PART 1

An image, the dancing form of light,
Stirring, without someone in sight.
Is it an appearance of energy?
Or maybe inner trajectory
Of spirit, form, ego, intelligence,
Attended by the awakened sense.
Or heroic tale of morals–might,
Brought to fruition by a shining knight?

Did all appear within form's flight
And happen in the days and night?
Or is there no in nor out
And no division or dual doubt?
Are there puppets in time, its themes?
Or is form in space and time a dream?
Or is this appearance wed
To nothingness, its love unsaid.

1 See Note 18A

A seeming story of love's plurality,
Of sacrifice, devotion, sanctity,
Interwoven by generations
In quest for liberation,
Is retold as a religious script
To pilot the alive as prescript;
Or does it point to the reality
Of floating dream of duality,

Of time and individuality,
Of one as the apparent mortality,
Of seeming opposites in play
– Without converses to it sway –
Of energy being dressed in roles,
Formless in form, appearances, whole?
Or is it an epic to be revered –
A pilgrimage of fourteen years?
…

The presence in play as facets particular:
Rest, radiance, intellect, self-centre,
As fruits of the earth that portrayed hues
Of restful light, faith, bondage, ruse;
Reduced love to measures of seclusion,
Then longed for rest, ceasing of illusion.
Thus an *Annona* family of fruits
Was blessed with fruits with upturned roots.

The tree which bore the sweetsop's presence
Attached itself to the appearance
Of lineage, and wished to secure
The sweetsop, as it did mature,
For the tree rested in its presence
Peaceful, and sensed its still essence,
While the tree that cared for the apple sweet
Was complete, so didn't bind its fruity treat[2].

Both fruits were ripened to be sweet
For a royal dessert, hearty treat.
The sweetsop, known as an ideal fruit,
Was natural from the core to root,
While the custard apple free, demure,
Was animated, resilient, pure,
And went on to be the epitome
Of radiance, beyond periphery.

The soursop, sweetsop's younger sibling,
Safeguarded him from shadows killing
And witnessed the course complete,
Accompanied by intelligence – the treat –
Who at times used impish ways,
Yet charmed most fruits of the maze.
So, all the beings performed the play
As per the attributes that sway.

Numerous more features and pigments
Added perspective to the art brilliant,
Yet none could know what would betide,
Or draw margins between the sea, its tide,
And as the fruits got deeper shades,
Drawn was the apple to sweetsop, staid,
And soon began a love affair
Absolute, as a relative pair.
…

The sweetsop, known as the bullock's heart,
Could not be split from his sweetheart,
The supple custard apple sweet,
For they were like the pulse and beat.
Her seeds stowed piety of her art –
In love they were one, not apart,
Much like the valley and the hill
Are one – the depth and climb uphill.

A miracle was their romance:
If he the dancer, she the dance,
If he the sun, she its light,
Or the bird and its inherent flight;
If she the fragrance, he the myrrh,
Like the yin and yang – as one occur;
She the matter, he the soul,
Complete, not split, one, whole;
She the presence of his glow,
While he the essence of her show.

2 Here the reference is to a custard apple.

Of their marriage and its lively play:
They swam impromptu on long days,
Lay near the rivers in the shade,
And sang with birds that did invade
The trees, for fruits both ripe and raw,
Remained in wonder and awe.
Whispered the fireflies and the bees
Of the seeming form, in formless ease.

They cuddled close by the fire at nights,
Admired the autumnal moon in sight,
Sat silent by the lake and prized the stars –
Seemingly strung in the self, not afar;
Nature's boundless brilliance made her blush,
While he loved to see her in bloom and lush.
Widespread became their story,
Truly a paradigm of glory.

Thus, this ineffable love
Was draped in finest gloves,
And as is in all the apparent tales
Where treasured are the pleasures pale,
Knitted was a lovely yarn,
Where the rends were suitably darned
By love unconditional, that did seek
The illusive and mystique.

Yet it isn't a tale of an ideal pair
But love complete without compare,
Where borne are shades of known–unknown,
For love displays them all, alone,
Love that can't be confined in words
Or is by silence thus preferred.
Too much it is to further say
Of wholeness that appears as the play.

PART 2

As all appears distinct in a dream,
Demonstrates hues in themes,
So shown were hues from dark to bright,
From ignorance to immersive light,
And time appeared to seize sublime,
Trailed dense and clear to play in rhyme.
Yet reigned emptiness and not certain hues,
As can't be coloured being by the view.

Complexity now ruled the game,
A range of shades their hue did claim,
And in the play of greed and attachment,
Relations sought the throne transient.
Forgotten was that none could own
The Oneness of this love, unknown.
So, exiled were the pair sweet
From the kingdom of apparent treats.

Attended soursop, the awakened hue,
To behold love in the scenes new
And cherish the profound resonance
He glimpsed in sweetsop's presence,
Yet shielded their bond, for there was fear,
A split of space–time would love smear,
Would rise the forests of illusion
And curb the genuine in seclusions.

Enticed was the soursop by lust,
Its obstacle, it shamed by thrust.
In turn trapped was the apple sweet
By dark drives, venison as treat.
Gushed rivulets of separation –
Emerged suffering of duration,
For seized seemed the apple sweet
In the clutches of a foreign feat.

Emerged the jackfruit on the scene,
Revealed extreme control of cuisines,
Although an erudite mind – a prodigy,
He was without a speck of simplicity,
For the seeming self possesses ten pates,
Which, as an abyss, aid its unreal gait;
Therefore, canvassed were traits as character,
Pursued was the game of prey and predator –
He seemed to steal the apple from the sop,
Devised a pyramid to be on top.

Forgot the jackfruit illusion's role,
Considered it real, to make him whole,

So offered the apple the world of dreams,
Along with a city that with gold did gleam.
Failed to recall that rhythmic radiance
And rest are not two, but one – presence;
The separate self – the ego too –
Is restful radiance in seeming view.

The resilient apple refused the bid:
Still, was her adamantine spirit,
For free she wasn't in chains
Of either the self or love that reigns,
Knew love is not a shining knight
But formless as appearance bright;
Thus, the surreal can never possess
The taste of love or it express.

(Yet she suffered at the hands of ego –
Who in its quest to rest, love echo,
Compelled her to follow its aims
Of finding an enlightened frame –
Forgotten was that she was at rest,
Even in its apparent arrest,
For she was boundless energy
Appearing wild or tamed, but free.

Unreal, but it too, an expression
Of formless form, an illustration,
Is energy in boundlessness,
Appearing split, yet unsplit in dress.
At rest longed had been the aliveness
Of form with its apparent mess,
But on appearance of those forms,
Ignored were all the alive storms.)
…

With the pure apple in possession
Of the jackfruit, its seeming suppression,
The sops sought intelligence,
Which combined courage and diligence,
And swifter than the strongest gale
It swept across but left no trails,
To remind the custard apple sweet
Of the taste of the formless art, complete.

Yet this uncooked intelligence
Had to be ripened by restful radiance,
So revealed was the simple essence,
That one – the formless and formed presence;
Thereafter in all arduous occurrence
Devoted to the sops was intelligence,
Which burnt the city of influence
With jaw-dropping brilliance.

The occurrences lead to a war,
With allies and foes full of valour.
The silent sweetsop stayed the same,
Was still, yet joined the factional game
Of the opposites, in lurking shadows,
Complex characteristics as tornados,
And thus ensued an endless war,
With rage, violence, and love in store.

The jackfruit tried means severe
To rule over the apple demure
But failed and lost at every turn,
For love seemed to illusions burn,
As it had vowed to abort malice,
Return to rest, its chalice,
If mean and vile became the game
Of the apparent names.

(Though self's apparent trek
Seemed stressful in doubt's speck,
The battle appeared violent,
Vast too in its extent,
And seemed to disappear hues
That seemed to bear the tint of two;
Yet there was only the occurrence,
Or simply appearing presence.

The self still appeared real,
To acquire liberty ideal,
Appeared as tangible entity,
Which would beget freedom for 'me',
Along with clout, mystical favours,
Experiences of subtle flavours;
But being illusory it couldn't see
That liberty is its end, not being free.)

But all is complete the way it is,
And stayed dark and deep the curbed abyss;
During the war, the awakened sense –
The soursop seemed to lose conscience;
But in the healing that did follow
Dissipated distances hollow,
For aided ripe intelligence
In absence of the separation's sense.

The sweetsop was finally successful:
Put to rest was the jackfruit stressful,
Along with the apparent pilgrimage,
Where split is the formless from its image.
The custard apple appeared free
From the jackfruit's suffocating spree,
And life was viewed for what it is:
An un-riven appearance, not amiss,
For cured was the apparent split
By love, formless form: one, unsplit.

PART 3

The custard apple, her splendour prime,
Timeless yet appearing in time
Was tested in the fires of fright,
Though was untouched, for none was in sight –
As the jackfruit could not harm her,
For an illusion cannot taint, it stirs.
So, was the fire, conditioned neurosis
Of non-volitional life, its hypnosis?

For it was clear formless isn't a knight
That rescues form with a fight,
Or stays on the shores of virtue,
But is freedom without a clue,
To emerge as any appearance, hue,
Seemingly confined or vast, yet anew,
And is more intimate than breath,
Beyond the contrasts of birth and death.

Though acts of seeking rest caused suffering,
Yet there was no one in storms blistering,
For formless alone does steer
As radiant forms, which play, appear,
Seemingly limits its aliveness,
While all along is boundlessness,
Which seems to be on a pilgrimage
Of its apparent image.

Then appeared that the lovers did meet,
The sweetsop and custard apple sweet.
Though complete were both the fruits,
They returned to unforgotten roots,
With no repentance, praise, or blame,
Just celebration as the names –
Being, love, the apparent scene,
Radiant rest in muddled streams.

One – the presence and the essence,
The formless and formed radiance,
And the kingdom of eternal peace
Was the same, yet returned illusion's lease
Of the fruits appearing separate,
Though they were one, innate
– As abandoned seemed the form
By the formless – uniform –
Incomplete in its completeness,
Complete in its incompleteness.
…

Did restful radiance appear as two?
The custard apple and the sweetsop true –
In the account of opposing views,
Where the soursop beheld love true,
Intelligence was dyed in devotion's hue.
And jackfruit – the illusory self – untrue
That felt it could own form, its presence,
Reign over the fleeting existence.

Or did rest rescue radiance
From arrogance, by intelligence?
Is it a story of enlightenment
Related by the one without intent?
Or is one dressed as the form's radiance,
The witnessing and the intelligence,
As the sense of self and all the hues
Of passion, anger, possession, ruse?

Or is it an apparent account
To illumine the illusory count
Of the apparent universe,
And individual verse
In seeming union and division,
Seemingly creating the illusion
Of life, as it does appear
At once – rest, radiant, seeming stir?

Or is it a play of eternal light,
Imagined images of might?
Or a dance of one, divine,
To be confined in seeming shrines?
Or a play free from an account,
An appearance without a fount?
Is it a throbbing alive universe?
Love as the seeming verbs, free verse?

Or is it an unrequited dance
Of love absolute in seeming expanse?
Or prismatic appearance of nothing, none,
Ephemeral in peripheral run?
Or joy and suffering alone,
Undefinable, none to own?
Or fruits favoured by a cuisine
Served as main course or dessert clean?

Or everything yet nothing, none.
Formlessness as form? One
Alone seeming as two,
Like the rising, setting sun in view,
Which neither does set nor does rise,
Yet appears the dual guise?
Or unfathomable, unspeakable,
Love unconditional?

44

The Undying Death

PART 1

Appeared to linger on the streets
A gang of some eccentric eats.
Led the avocado and tomato
The gang of lettuce, cilantro,
Onion, chilli, corn, and cheese,
And a knife who none did please.
Yet all the friends did share
Their love for service and pursuits rare.

They worked in a stall during the day,
Devoted evenings to fun and play
On their bikes at reckless pace,
To seek excitement in the race.
They raced and toppled at high speed
Until one of them did bleed;
Adventure seemed their second name –
Life for them seemed like a game.

Their day was spent in cooking food
With varied ingredients crude;
This task they wholly did enjoy,
Boldness and care, both did employ
In using innovative process,
Which they refined with utmost finesse.
Tortas, *quesadillas* they did pair
With fillings exceptional and fair,
Tortillas, *tamales,* corn on the cob,
And *chilaquiles* – the local heartthrobs –
Were decked with tastes spicy and sweet
To serve a formidable treat.
Guacamole, *salsa* with flavours fresh,
Enhanced with hints sour did refresh
The palate, and truly did impress
Locals and tourists with its finesse;
Thus, loved were the friends and their show
In the streets of Mexico.
…

The tomato's sweetheart was the knife,
And rumours of their romance were rife.
A peculiar tomato was he –
Viewed life as it is, free,
Grasped matters in humorous delight,
Was ever keen to give insight.
The knife always stuck to the tomato,
Could not imagine life without her beau,
But from others she stayed distant,
For she was rejected and condemned
By the gang, who felt she could hurt
Just with her presence curt.

The others objected to their affair,
Were certain infatuation would impair
The tomato, who tagged the knife along,
Who advised him that she did not belong
To food and its family,
And was inanimate and deadly.
But truly loved her the tomato,
For love is not reliant on show;
The love he revealed seemed eternal,
And it embraced her work infernal.

Once the cilantro, chilli, and cheese,
Who were entirely displeased
With the liaison, spoke in earnest.
Said the cilantro: 'In your interest,
Stay away from the one who can slay;
Don't intentionally become her prey.
We all enjoy adventure's thrill,
But why adore the one who can kill?'
'We don't want you dead, deceased,'
Hastily interrupted the cheese.

Added the chilli, 'Why, don't you fear death?'
The tomato replied in a single breath:
'Depends who dies, what does it imply?

If it's my landlord, the human sly,
I would be thrilled, as he has no kin,
So rent I won't have to pay therein.'
Then winked and said: 'With spare cash play
And treat you all with foods gourmet.'
Most of his friends laughed at his joke,
While the chilli chided her folk.

'Oh, Chilli! Leave your spiciness,
Your earnest flawlessness,
Come on, smile, and don't be sad:
Life isn't that serious or bad.
On death, I'll get posthumous fame,
As many a genius thus makes a name.
Artists, scientists, the innovative:
On demise their work is appreciated.
Is not Van Gogh the perfect case,
Whose work was later praised?
For old is gold, the future bright,
Ordinary is what appears in sight –
This is the mantra of the mind,
So I'll be hailed, when ceases the rind,
For being intelligent and wise,
Ahead of times, high like the skies,'
Declared the tomato in notes high.
Laughed his friends at his humour wry.

Then after a gap he did relate
Of death, in a manner straight:
'Tell me, how can a dead man die?
I have already ceased, gone by.
You too die in sleep every day
Or when engrossed in work or play.
Apparent is this form's display,
Unreal the self that owns its play,
So why grapple to hold on to occurrence:
Evanescent, dreamlike, an appearance.

Observe the natural world around –
The ephemeral is never crowned;
The leaves and the short-lived creatures,
None weave tales, hold on to the features
Of labels of the apparent form,
Or life as we know it, bound in norms.

Only personification seems to haul,
While natural is rise and fall.
And nothing does stay when you die,
No wealth, or wisdom, work, or allies,
So why hold on to transient forms –
Their names, narratives, seeming norms,
And die when life still does perform
As this alive, perfect form?
Yet isn't death home, the real abode,
Release, rest, life's unknown ode?'

Then mounting his bike, did shout:
'Tonight, I am taking her out.
I love the knife with all her norms,
Slicing – simply a job she performs;
Domesticated or wild and free,
Her every form is dear to me.
I know no death, nor can her shadows strip;
Don't hate her, for it will tighten her grip.'
Thus laughing, he disappeared on his bike
And rode fast, which he most did like.

One late evening proposed the knife
– When all seemed relaxed, without strife –
'Let's all do the salsa tonight.'
The cilantro leaped in fright,
Warily asked: 'The dance or the dish?'
Replied the tomato: 'As you wish!'

The avocado then did suggest:
"Oh, Tomato, in your interests best
Leave the world of food and go
Into the realm of glamour and show;
An inborn actor you do seem:
Dramatic you are to the extreme.
Jokes can't the depth of death stall,
Most dread its heartless call.'

Replied the tomato in tones intense,
Accompanied with movement immense:
'The world of glamour will make me dry,
For the virtual alone will pry.
Forgotten will be life's brilliance,
For it will be seen through the actor's lens.

I'm happy in the world of victuals,
Which embrace death as a ritual,
For ashes seen daily thus remind
That none is limited to the rind.
And aren't we all actors too,
Who movie of "my" life pursue?'

Then quoting Shakespeare wrongly said:
'Friends! Let us all the Bard's words embed:
The world is only an appearance,
A stunning tale that makes no sense;
And we are actors on this stage,
The vast seemingly confined in a cage.'
Though most friends laughed at his expense,
Exclaimed the chilli: 'Stop your nonsense.
At least respect the great Bard:
Do not his work disregard;
Don't misquote his literature
For your pretentious pleasure.'

The tomato then sober did appear,
Said: 'At the root of stress – death's fear.
Have you reflected what is it to die?
Is it not the loss of an "I"
Though the self does not thrive
Even when the form is alive?
Isn't it destruction of the dream –
That I am distinct from life, its theme?
Is it not total emptiness?
And not when beings ingress
Into unseen realms, to atone –
But simply the unknown.
Freedom from a pilgrimage?
From inverses, time, and image.

And isn't death impartial to all,
Where none is big or small,
Where saints and sinners the same end,
No difference – die rich or spent.
Is it not the greatest guide
That shows it alone does preside?
And nothing matters, life doesn't care
About me, my wishes rife or rare.

So why fear dust to dust, its show?
It is not in your hands to fear or flow.
For all there exists is life –
The infinite in apparent flight,
Appearing like a dance performance,
Or like the flower's fragrance,
Without a landlord, tenant, tenancy,
Simply beingness, only vacancy.
So, none exists to own their chatter –
Entropy in seeming shadows of matter.'

Then tried to interrupt the cheese
His ode to death, for all seemed at unease,
But continued the tomato,
Unaware of his outflow:
'Isn't it a wonder how we come alone,
Then unknown relations thus own,
Though relationships are with form alone?
Forget the transience of the zone;
Judge life from the self's throne,
While all along life seems unknown.

Where all there is is the present –
This, the appearing moment,
Simply emptiness alone,
Singing as all the seeming tones,
And all appears in its embrace,
Thoughts, feelings, rest, or the chase,
Without the stories and history,
Or time and space, binary –
Simply the appearing scene,
Not static pictures on the screen
Of nothing, but an energetic stir
Alive, that seemingly does occur
As this. The formless playing as forms
And the unseen; alone does perform.
So, no separate self the form does own,
Seemingly rises, blossoms, fades – the unknown.'

Though all foods seemed to be restless,
The knife seemed stunned by the freshness
Felt in the tomato's verse and tone.
Spellbound, she stared at his face that shone.

'Impossible for the illusory
Self it is to accept this decree,
For that is its way to sustain
Self, as it fears the end of its reign.
For in the self's dream, prime,
Individuals live in time,
Coming in life by taking birth,
Surviving as that form's hearth,
With their relevant stories:
Pathetic, base, or full of glory;
Then leaving into spheres unknown,
The latter a puzzle for its tone.

Anyway, it will all be clear
When we are to die, disappear,
That our life was like a dream,
With nothing as its theme.
Unborn, undying presence
Alone in appearance.'

PART 2

Then what seemed to transpire shocked the knife.
The tomato stated that past shelf life
Seemed his wilting form
And was beyond reform;
Wished to renounce the soft rind
As it now rapidly declined.
He addressed the knife: 'Oh, lovely one,
It's time for salsa to be done.
Perform your duty dear:
Let true love thus appear.'
The knife unnerved by tomato's view
Strongly refused to conform. Withdrew
Her steps. Stood silent and still,
Shocked, and adamant in her will.

Began a dialogue between the two –
On death, which does not ensue.
Solemnly asked the tomato,
As he smiled beneath his show,
'Will you not love me when I die?
Does fondness to my form ally?
Will I not live when you recall?
Will you for the cilantro fall?'
He laughed and his skin did split,
Yet radiated love from depths unsplit.

The knife scorched within but stayed silent,
Still did not pretend to be compliant.
The tomato saw her stubborn streak
And profoundly did speak:
'My love, reflect, what keeps us alive
Even when this form does not strive,
When unconscious or asleep
Or in a calamity deep.
Is it not life force that's energetic –
Animating as the forms kinetic
Or not, and it alone is sovereign,
Appearing as all forms therein?
Can there be another to own the form's presence,
Or distinct forms in appearance?

Besides, how does this force look, appear?
Is it not formless in formed gear?
And if it's formless in appearance,
Can it be split in its presence?
Is it not common in prevalence,
Always present in its existence?
So, are there personal souls
Living in time, or just this whole?
Reflect: aren't we one, the same,
Myriad raiments of one game?

My dear, we are not a form small
To live or die in life's call,
But the impersonal life force,
Undivided from the source;
The life force that lives as all
Is untouched, cannot be stalled;
Hence, there is no individual
But a seeming play sempiternal.
To be precise, the boundless presence –
Unchanged, indestructible in essence –
Is infinite, formless, and free,
Appearing as the forms that be.
It is existent, alive, and uniform,

Whether it thrives or not, as form,
Is unborn, undying, formless in form's tryst,
Timeless, present, without event, subsists.
And as it is, so it cannot cease,
Nor does it come in birth or leave.
So, love, there is neither birth nor death,
But Oneness, without an opposite.[1]
The oceanic being waves does lie
With no origin or end to come by;
Like a wave rises all appearance,
With water alone in presence.
Appearance–disappearance,
Without an existence.'

The tomato now appeared in a trance
As he spoke of the one, its dance,
Yet he seemed alive and unsplit,
While the knife stared at his face lit.
'But, love, this talk of no identity,
Can't be comprehended by society,
For it is the collective illusion,
Which deems real the self's delusion,
And lives in linear perception –
Which is the dream of egoism –
Of I was born and I will die,
And I perform the tasks thereby.

Yet formless flaunts its parade
As a magical recurring cascade
In love with itself, is ever married,
Seems to experience itself as varied,
Seems to attach a sequence,
A start and end to an occurrence,
Where it alone is lost in perception:
That form is character in manifestation,
Is real, exists in space–time's faculty,
Owns form and acts as an identity.

But it's seen there's no continuity,
A start, end, or perpetuity;
When ceases individuality
Disappears all materiality.

Yet none can regard this presence,
Protect, fear, or feel its own absence,
For one appears as the binary,
A life in seeming boundaries.
Yet what I've said of freedom is relevant
To a tale, and it is evident:
That timeless nothingness as force
Projects all forms without a course,
At once, in a dreamlike existence,
One alone as varied appearance.'

Completely silent was the knife,
Stayed without expression or strife.
Did not speak, ask, or show her skills.
Just stood there completely still.
So, carried on the tomato:
'I don't expect you to your views forgo,
Nor wish to teach you detachment,
Or end our attachment.
I know all the talk of Oneness
Seems completely meaningless
When overwhelm the emotions,
Over which there's no dominion,
As no one ever has a choice
To live, or die, feel sad, rejoice.
So, don't disregard the pain that gnaws –
No one responsible for feelings raw.

As nothing's denied in liberty
Of life, any activity
Can appear in its embrace,
None in or out of place;
So, feelings will rise and fall away
Or in the form of memories may sway.
You will naturally grieve as a relation,
Die as a lover on my form's cessation.
But, sweetheart, sadness is not wrong –
Is an expression of the song
Energetic. So, cry when sad;
It's neither good nor bad.
Tears with or without an abyss –
Simply what appears, is.

And, my love, never forget

1 See Note 19A

This love's vignette:
The symphony of love isn't staccato,
So ceaseless will be our love's flow.
I will be closer than your breath,
As love, a presence beyond death,
Will always be alive in you,
As love and life's each hue,
As memories and feelings that ensue,
Or as sharp pain, or the lover new,
For you are me and I am you,
Were always one, not two.
I cannot any further say,
Neither will silence it convey;
And this appearance will vanish,
But life can never be vanquished.
So, come on, strike, cut, dice or slice –
An image can't presence sacrifice.'

Then suddenly laughed the tomato:
'I sounded so deep in the flow!'
Then winked and said, 'But didn't the one alone state,
And it alone heard it prate.'
The knife sharply stared at the tomato,
Quietly walked away from her beau.

The wilted tomato passed away,
And for his soul's peace all did pray.
His demise upset all his friends,
Who celebrated his wise trends,
But as they the tomato did miss,
They clung to each other for solace,
For it is easy to speak, hear of death and dying,
But hard to face its fangs horrifying.
The knife solitary did remain,
Completely engrossed in the mundane
Day-to-day activity –
Wed to the ordinary.

Years later when the knife turned rusty, old,
About to end the form's leasehold,
Sought her presence rest, death, and silence,
But they could not seize her absence,
For she had died in the same breath
As the tomato and his apparent death.
Ashes turned to ashes, with none to moan,
A transparent aliveness – this unknown.

45

The Milky Way

PART 1

A young, fresh, and immature cheese
Joined a sect of drastic degrees.

Reiterated his party's doctrine
To his father, an aged Sovereign,
Whose words were veritable wisdom,
And presence equated with freedom

By the residents of the kingdom
Of Cheese, famous for its pilgrims.

Son Cheese:

'Proved has my eminent organisation
By ancient and methodical tradition
There is nothing better than cheese –
Rich and sharp, the palate is pleased.
Like in clothing silk is supreme,
We are unmatched in food's theme.
There are around four hundred varieties
Of our kind, valued by society;
Today we influence the earth,
By our proficiency and worth,
For matchless is our taste and texture,
Our tribe's traditional treasure.

Pizza, pasta, sandwich, fondue,
And desserts seek us for flavours new.
So true is my establishment civil,
Our forte flexible yet traditional,
Hence we should publicise our ethos
Of unity in range, to end chaos.'

On hearing the son's lofty claims
The father sensed the dual game
Of ego as speech and attitude,
While the father spoke of one absolute,
Though he knew can't be taught humility,
As none is proud, can cease identity,
And humility isn't self being low,
But its loss, with no one up or below.
Yet he illumined the dual plot,
A response of the untaught.

Father Cheese:

'Know this my lovely son:
All that appears is essence, the one.
It alone appears as one or two,
Nothing is beyond its purview,
Or essence of nothingness
Is this appearance, dressed.
Precisely, emptiness and essence
Is one, not split in its presence,
Or emptiness is infinite,
In appearance, without limit.
Hence, what appears as form's presence
Is common in all, that's the essence;
So, there's nothing ideal to be enthroned,
As essence favours none, is all alone.
Any limitation – dream of misery,
Creatures, nations, or tribes illusory.
So, ignorant your group's review –
None's independent of the view;
Undivided is this essence,
With none present in its presence.'

Son Cheese:

'My party isn't in ignorance:
Their claims are based on evidence.
Father, on the contrary,
Abstruse seems the essence arbitrary.
However, father what is essence?
How is it alone in appearance?
What is the essence of our tribe?
To whom do we belong – who is our scribe?'

Father Cheese:

'Churns the milk and rises cream,
And in the cream is the butter's theme.[1]
By coagulation of the milk protein
Emerge numerous types of cheese on the scene.
So, milk is the source of our play,
Cream, butter, cheese – The Milky Way.
But go deep in the depths cellular
Of your milky protein peculiar:
You will find nothing is the essence
Of the seeming milky presence.
Rather, emptiness and the form
Are one, don't distinctly perform.

Reflect, my son: what is the essence

1 See Note 20A

Of foods and appears as their presence,
Breathes, beats the heart, does thrive
As form, tastes, listens, speaks, is alive?
So, is this essence separate from you?
Isn't it your appearing verse and view?
Isn't one the essence and appearance
Of this seeming cosmic emergence?

My dear, though teachings convince with facts,
Which seem real, create an impact,
Quoting science or history
Doesn't imply real – a theory,
Because the essence vast and free
Can't be defined in theories
Or stories, which aren't present
In the transitory event,
But are later additions,
Illusory perceptions
Of unreal individualism –
Life's apparent scission.
Besides, theories are biased in hue
By writers' conditioning and view,
Or by the one who funds or rules
The field or founds relevant schools.

Listen, son, there is no other
To taste or apply its flavour;
None can be taught how to exist;
Vicarious is your group's gist,
Sophomoric their rhetoric,
Not right or wrong, but dualistic.'

On hearing these words from the patriarch
Increased curiosity's spark.

Son Cheese:

'Where does this essence thus reside:
Within, without, does it preside
As us? Is it the cosmic spirit?
What do we do to attain it?
Should we revere our milky culture
And spread the glory of our sculptor?'

Father Cheese:

'My son, can you locate 'space'
In or around forms or a place.
Can you isolate the fragrance
In the flower, its presence?
Locate the tree in the seed?
Or alcohol in the mead?
Like energetic stir of the presence
Is central to the silence,
Or as integral to noise
Is silence in perfect poise,
Akin is the essence
Of this appearance.

Integral to form is formlessness,
While form's embedded in its emptiness.
Though formlessness is on its own,
Form is formless – in form's tone.
And this form isn't an afterthought,
Preceded by the naught;
So, dear, is essence separate
From the emerging scene or state?
Can it reside in a certain place?
Or is it alone, in and beyond space?

And, precious one, these cultures, tribes
Are too alive to describe,
For they are not entities
Stable through the centuries,
But like rivers continually change,
Where none can pinpoint the range;
And all is rising anew
Without a story in view.
Rather, an immediate stir
Is this apparent seeming culture,
Where distinct names are simply labels,
A tag on appearance unstable.

Son, emptiness, or essence alone
Is in appearance, on its own.
Though timeless, it creates illusion
Of time, distance, form's seclusion,
Seems to create stories,

Believes real the illusory.
But there is none apart to write a transcript –
Spontaneous the apparent script,
And same is the sculptor and its theme,
As light cannot be split – from its beam.
With whom will the essence preside
When it alone resides
As all? It isn't alienated from life,
Is not abstract, or an estranged wife.
It is – this life as it is,
With or without analysis –
Whose glory will you promote
When the essence isn't remote?

My love, you can't become the essence,
Receive it, or grasp it in silence.
So, now do not be ignorant
And seek it in the fragments,
For all there is is the essence,
Seeming to be existence, non-existence.'

The son was shaken and confused,
For his belief system was bruised.
Resumed the dialogue again,
Later, on a related plane.
Now, in a sombre tone,
Enquired the son about the unknown.

PART 2

Son Cheese:

'What happens on death, when ceases form?
How does the essence then perform?
And what about the soul: does it merge
In the essence, rise in heaven or submerge
In hell, or stay in reincarnation
Until ends its cycle of migration?'

Father Cheese:

'My son, who can experience their death?
None returns to report when ceases breath,
To explain heaven, hell, void sky,
Or say what happens when we die.
Death is like deep sleep, where you don't exist,
An unknowing where nothing subsists.

Think: where does the stench or fragrance
Arrive, on waning of its presence?
On being pricked where does the air
Of the balloon go – what does it bear?
Is not the air in and out one?
Form or formless, simply none.
There is none split to be identified
Or found to solitarily reside;
All have the same apparent end,
No destination, none to transcend
To realms known or unknown,
For sings nothing in tones
Of the formless and the form,
Everything. Nothing transforms.

By way of an analogy
Let me explain soul's ubiquity:
The soul is like the sky –
Present, untouched, intimate, high,
Where all forms are in its embrace,
Playing in its empty space;
Yet this space is within, without:
Untouched has no in or out,
And like the sky can't be sliced in parts,
So there are no split souls, apart,
To merge in the cosmic soul –
Nor an absolute or whole.[2]

Listen, son, all is an appearance
Of this indestructible essence;
Essence alone is, can't die or decay,
Appears as forms that seem to wither away;
Untouched, it cannot be blemished,
Or woken, blended, or established
By any of its apparent roles,
But is eternal, absolute, and whole.
We are the essence infinite,

2 See Note 20B

Unconfined, no limits.
Instead, the infinite essence
Is form in appearance,
So the form's separation,
Is simply an illusion;
Thus, there is no death or birth,
For an illusion is form's hearth.

Appears as shadows this light bright,
This form – apparent play of light,
So, dear, there's only essence,
No before or after presence.
And when nothing does occur,
How can events happen, stir,
Or an afterward thus transpire?
Nothing alone is, yet appears as this choir.'

Though the father had to repeat
About the one, its seeming beat,
He showed no irritation,
As his son continued the questions,
For he saw the presence as new
And not a son he had to rescue
From ignorance. Or there was one alone
As father's form and the son unknown.

Son Cheese:

'Father, what about *karma* theory?
Isn't it the divine jury?
And don't we have free will to act,
Or is predestined the life's tract?
My party's doctrine explicates
How the *karmic* theory dictates
Our destiny in this lifetime,
Which we enhance all the time
With actions good or bad,
Which make us suffer or glad,
And thus go to heaven or hell,
Finish our stay, then fall in spell
Of reincarnation, until we merge
In the one, then never surge
As form but stay in formless,
The ultimate bliss of Oneness.'

Father Cheese:

'Oh dear! What a story
Of the unknowable, a mystery.
Firstly, the *karmic* theory
Is arrogant and breeds hierarchy,
For it judges from its plate
Or by society's dictates –
The circumstantial gait
Of food's apparent state.

Further, it is a story
Of individuality
Seeking continuity,
Irrelevant to liberty.
Like all the societal schisms,
It's based on self, its scission;
For this business of *karmic* theory
Supposes real are people in a story,
Who perform with impending causality.
There isn't individuality
To perform acts in the appearance,
But an act alone in appearance,
Simply acts appearing
On their own, disappearing.
Like foods do not apply flavours
But are inherent sweet or sour,
So essence traits does display,
Appearing as the acts in play;
As taste can't be divorced from food,
So split isn't the viewer–viewed.

Besides, as essence is timeless,
There cannot be a causal process,
So *karma* – seeming acts rising on their own,
Seeming causality in timeless zone.
Heed: every pair, whether cause–effect
Or any other opposite,
Is dual, while there's only one,
Without a subject–object scission.

Rationally, too, a self performing acts,
Seems an unreasoned theory with cracks,
For the form is alive on its own,

Without effort from the self's throne,
And there seems a cosmic system
At work, for the present moment;
The appearing events in play
Are natural rhythms in display,
So can the self truly own
Occurrences, the appearing tone?

Son, the self is an illusion,
Which lives in the delusion
Of space and time and its existence,
Cannot imagine life without its presence.
So, deems its life flows in the parallel
Lines and accounts, in time ephemeral;
And when it observes all around
That foods arrive and leave the ground
With absolutely nothing at all
It sets up the *karmic* stall
Of individuals in debt –
A business of loss and profit.'

Though the father was patient,
Patronising appeared his diction.

'But nothing goes along with you,
No thing, not even you,
For death is the ceasing of you.
Can anything related continue?
And can anyone know
That they are no more?
And, son, how many have you seen
Reimbursed for their *karmic* cuisine.

Rationally, too, the *karmic* theory,
Along with the supposed divine jury
Of judging acts, does not make sense,
For whose *karma* takes precedence,
Or whose point of view
Is to be considered true?
Besides, this notion seems inane
Even in the *karmic* plane,
For doesn't an act do justice
To certain aspects and injustice
To other aspects on board?
Isn't an act a double-edged sword?

Also, what seems wise in today's light
May seem ludicrous in hindsight.
And if one causally does reason
Each act, belief, feeling, and expression,
Won't they go back to the origin,
Beyond all choice and volition?
And what of faith and repentance:
Where do they fit in *karmic* credence?
Son, there can never be an end
To questions and worthless argument.

The laws here are made to safeguard
Justice, for crimes within its yards,
So drop your learnt terminology
Shared by confined ideology;
See beyond the conditioning
Of society, its teaching.
Do not get embroiled in names,
Their fables and their games,
For there is no individual,
Permanent or transitional;
All names, identities are labels
On the alive, beyond all fables.

Even your destiny or free will
Assume time and an individual,
While all is an appearance
Of essence without significance.'

The father noticed that the son
Seemed further confused and stunned,
So asked him to come another day
To listen of the one in play.

PART 3

After a few weeks, the son
Seemed receptive and open,
Eager to hear the missive.
The father spoke in tones impressive
On reincarnation

And self's illusion.

Father Cheese:

'Son, what to say of reincarnation,
When distinct souls are an illusion.
Reincarnation that you apprehend
Is ego's pretence to avoid its end.
Life after death or reincarnation,
With attached stories of causation,
Is simply rich imagination
Of the essence in apparent illusion.
There is only essence in appearance,
With no individual presence,
So there is no birth or death,
No origin, end, or causal breath.
Thus, can there be reincarnation?
A projection: this universal commotion.

Rationally, too, your argument
Of rebirth seems irrelevant,
For if we were to reincarnate
As another form, as another plate,
Then what are we, the form of the past,
Or of the present, or future, or the vast?
And which form reincarnates
As a new apparent plate?
In the case of several births,
Distinct apparent hearths,
Is it the first birth that appears as all
The births, or each diverse in its call?
So, are you potato from a past birth
Or cheese? Or meat from a future hearth?
Are you your feelings and thoughts
Based on occurrence and the taught?
Or a soul that's imperishable,
Unborn, undying, unrealisable?
Then how can there be reincarnation
Of essence, which is without migration?
If 'you' are none of the forms, nothing,
And yet appearing as everything,
Then can there be a distinct you?
Is not there one, without a clue?'

Then smiled the patriarch,
Proclaimed as the monarch:

'Oh, precious one, the scriptures your sect
Follows are clear in their dialect:
"The self is the formless forming,
At once – untouched yet performing,
Alone, appearing as the 'me' and 'you',[3]
Which seems to be in birth, anew."[4]
This refers that the separation
Of self–other, rising in manifestation,
Is an illusory expression
Of formlessness in illustration,
Or ineffable infinite illumination,
Where an appearance is its illustration.

A self is non-existent,
Is an illusion, not a pigment.
In deep sleep and as an infant
Is not at all emergent,
Appears when energy wishes to play,
As an illusion appears to sway.
The reincarnation mentioned in the texts
Is this illusory play of depths
Of self, reincarnating every time,
To own endeavours, the prime,
And not entities that stay,
Reincarnating as another clay.

Even the heaven–hell cited by the texts
Is purely symbolic in context;
But as energy wishes to play,
It appears in illusive display,
Where it creates a kingdom,
Sits on the throne, founds serfdom,
Further fashions heaven–underworlds [5]
To continue in its imagined worlds
Of enjoying grapes and heavenly bells,
Wish-fulfilling trees and spells,
Or souls beaten in the hells of turmoil,
Boiling in the cauldrons of oil.

3 See Note 20C
4 See Note 20D
5 See Note 20E

For it equates heaven with sensual pleasure,
And hell, its inverse, displeasure,
As it believes that spirituality
Is gaining power and sensuality.

But heaven is this life,
Free of confinement's strife,
Is this essence alive,
Where nothing is denied,
Is this energetic presence,
As every appearance.
Son, it is this, the seeming moment,
Never to be repeated, simply present,
Where there is nothing to gain
Or leave, or higher states attain.
It is untouched freedom,
Vastness without a kingdom.

The ultimate bliss is always present,
In which appear–disappear seeming segments,
But the self seeks it far away,
Thus suffers its play.
So, it is hell to look for freedom
In the confined kingdoms;
Is unease with what appears,
Whether one's traits or tears;
Is the self – suffering its play
By owning the apparent display;
Is the ignorant need
To unite with the one, be freed,
Or end this seeming reincarnation,
Be in bliss, in transcendent station.
Son, there are no worlds below
Or above, no skies to souls stow.
They all are bound to a perspective,
A conditioning of views collective.

Oh, son, see all is conditioning;
There's no way to speak of the appearing
– There is no conditioning too,
But the whole in apparent view –
Simply this essence absolute
Appearing as the relative attribute.
So, all there is is here my son,
And here alone shall be undone.'

Then in a humorous air
As if to provoke his son, him dare.

'There is a lot of variance here:
We don't have same laws even in this sphere,
So can your sect's religious laws
Set here depict the scene and cause
Of heavens and hells beyond,
Or show the return to the earthly pond
As the same individual,
Dressed as a different victual.
Can they prove quondam births – dictate
The form in seeming present state?
Can they gauge the variance of time
Here and in realms with timeless climes?
Think: aren't their laws, the societal rules
To structure varied hues and schools?
Don't their teachings refute the views
Of their scriptural muse?

Stop being gullible, my son!
There is nothing out there, none.
And nothing, none, no scripture ever
Can beget essence or its wonder,
For essence on its own
Appears free, lost in zones.
Forget about the known–unknown,
And spend some time on your own.'

The son found impenetrable
The father's sermon radical,
So asked his father for some time
To ruminate on the sublime.
Weeks later he approached the Sovereign,
To further illumine his din.

Son Cheese:

'Father, what of near-death experience,
And reports of rebirth, its sequence?
Many people relate incidents
That seem like factual events.

Also is life, nothingness, essence,
Formlessness, and presence,
Diverse in their implication,
Or one in varied expression?'

Father Cheese:

'Son, the essence, life, or emptiness,
Formless, presence or nothingness
Is one, the same,
Simply known by varied names.

A few depict near-death experience,
But it's dissimilar to form's absence,
And the experiences they report
Seem similar to learnt import,
For all experience the divine
As per their religious shrines.
And, son, don't forget this display
Is energy pretending to play
In innumerable guise;
Though none's born, lives, or dies,
Yet the energetic verse
As the apparent universe
Seems like a recycling unit,
Seemingly sustaining its knit,
Where energy appears as it may
To reflect desires at play
And the seeming paraphernalia
Of its apparent regalia.

A hall of mirrors – this existence,
Reflection of the energetic presence
In a dreamlike existence,
Of infinite desires in appearance,
With no past or present or future,
One in play, yet untouched by its ruptures.
It's like essence absorbed in its own game
Of the illusions and apparent names.
So, the energetic reflection
Of a similar combination
May seem like déjà vu or reincarnation.
Yet all is a wave in seeming floatation,
Where impressions may seem to rise –
No separate soul do they devise,
Nor reincarnates in time or place,
Nor is at once in diverse space.
Though when individuality
Is deemed real by energy,
Real seems the worldly dream,
Prevalent in time its theme,
Then seeming pictures that play,
Are owned by a persona, stray.

Thus, be it your story of souls
Reincarnating in the whole,
Or the appearing multiverse,
All is a dreamlike verse,
Where the endless desires
Of Oneness seem to transpire
And appear to gleam as existence,
Akin to a dream in appearance.
All seemingly happens in one go
And is not in time's flow,
For this emptiness alone
Seems to stir, wave on its own,
Appears, illustrates as each form,
Yet does not manifest or perform.

And, son, I repeat once again,
Heed carefully the unchained:
Projects the formless in dress
This form's apparent process,
Or formless appears as form,
Contains, appears, is untouched by its norms;
Is energetic in play,
Spontaneous in display,
Appears as the illusion
Of seeming separation.
A magical show
Rhythmic in flow,
With no one to play
Simply energetic display.
Where apparent is the universe,
With no space–time to transverse,
And there is neither death nor birth,
All there is is life's expressive hearth.
Yet time too is its appearance,

An illusory play of presence;
So, even to say there is no life
After death is false and full of strife.

Death, reincarnation do not prey
If seeming separation falls away;
Then the intent to be born again
Is to be free from illusion's grain.
And, son, all there is is the essence,
With absolutely no significance.
I hope I have made it clear
And there are no more questions, dear.'

Son Cheese:

'First, I was absolutely sure,
Now appears a mystery pure,
Where all is essence alone,
With no one in the known.'

Father Cheese (in a firm tone):

'You are pliant to passing notions;
Please don't blindly accept potions.
Do not believe a word I say:
Let all emerge in its own way,
For none performs, does endeavour,
Or is ignorant, or clever.
There isn't a panacea for the split sense,
So don't be fooled by an experience;
You cannot think or feel your way to essence,
For essence is, unmatched to any sense.
This isn't about abnegation
Nor of complete negation,
But is of essence that's complete,
A love that embraces each beat.

Now do not campaign for new motifs,
For that will replace beliefs.
Don't grapple to know the unknown,
For there is the unknown alone.
Forget all this spiritual nonsense:
Govern and feed, use your common sense;
Be worthy of being a king
And not a slave to passing doctrines.'

The son had nothing more to say –
Life as it is, with none to sway.
Though father cheese appeared as a guide,
It wasn't to bring his son to his side:
It was a song of sovereignty.
One – agreement or disparity.
Simply performance of great tempo,
Though what happened none know,
For there is neither a father nor a son,
A seeming dialogue of cheese or none.

Soon ushered was the board of cheese
– By priests – before the Sovereign, at ease;
They simply placed the cheese on the board.
Organisations too were aboard.
Prevailed simplicity of life,
And sailed complexity and strife.
The Sovereign stared at the board,
Smiled at the cheesy hoard:
Four hundred varieties of cheese on show,
Three hundred and ninety-nine still to go?

46

Food for Thought

'Bloody bastards them all,'
Heard the venison – the rabbit's call,
As the two entered the pub
For a pint and grub –
Their usual routine
Since they were seventeen.
That night the pub had hosted an event
To help the local charity, to present
Hot meals during the winter bleak
To all who thus did seek.
Three speakers sent by the spiritual
Bookshop – which also sold candles and crystals –
Came to speak on spirituality,
Awakening, and non-duality.

The rabbit, who cursed a lot,
Was irritable and fraught.
He wanted a rock band
To make the event grand,
For mysticism seemed to bore
Him even worse than folklore.
The venison, though, was intent
On attending the event,
So dragged his friend the rabbit along
To listen to the trio's song.

The local pub owner's daughter
Welcomed the three speakers,
And introduced the three
To the guests, with their story:
'The Flaky, Phyllo, and Choux,
Like the ballad, ode, and haiku,
Saturated the tongue with beauty,
Trailed a design of highest duty.
Yet they could not find perfection,
Persistently chased its reflection;
Constantly tried varied techniques,
Yet couldn't manifest the unique,
For they did not perceive perfection
In the now – sought it in diverse directions.
And as the new ever does rise,
Their goal was always this new prize.
Thus, continued their mental game,
Where they always the self did blame.

The pastries – Flaky, Phyllo and Choux,
Precise like ballad, ode, and haiku –
Then STOPPED. Perfection found
In this moment. Abound
As each moment, every bake,
In the occurrence of the flake.
A glimpse, beyond mind's facet finite –
An appearance of the boundless light –
Completely changed their life,
As ceased the narcissistic strife.
The glimpse was so intense and deep
It woke the three from their sleep
Of self and its dream gourmet
To acceptance of the seeming way.

The mind that seems to control all
Now does not control their call.
A neurosis that charge does hold
Has ended as the mind folds.
Perfection, imperfection, now is one,
As disintegrated have all the schisms.

Today they run "The Pastry Practice",
Illuminate the palaver of madness
Of the self, and its schemes,
That ruins peace of life, its theme.
They share how struck them perfect storms
Of thunder, lightning, freedom's norm,
How mortification brought to a stall
The sense of being a self, small,
And how heat in the oven burned

The false, and made them, all unlearn.

The trio now have massive clout,
Whether chocolate, spinach, or trout,
Who honour them with love
To find life's true love.
Though all the three sing
In varied tunes of strings
Of love, the Flaky will guide
Us, through the mesh of self, its ride,
The Phyllo through the spiritual
Awakening and the lyrical,
While the Choux will illumine
Non-duality, its spin.'

As spoke the owner's daughter
Heard were the sounds of running water
And classic songs loved by the crowds,
Like Ed Sheeran's 'Thinking out loud'.
The venison zoned out,
Felt his head was in the clouds,
As felt when hit on the head,
About to sleep, wake, maybe drop dead;
Or on entering a place like a café,
Incomprehensible sea of noise at play;
Yet neither was he inebriated
Nor was he in a trance situated.
He felt he was in the forest dark,
Running in fear from the hunter's arc,
Or were they knives, and white silhouettes?
He couldn't understand the threat
Or make sense of the events,
Seemed defenceless in the present.

He tried to reach out to the rabbit,
Called him for help to make it
Through the whole situation,
Hold him through the ruination –
Of sinking in the bog,
Floundering in the fog,
Sliding through the blue light, maybe water,
Or a tunnel where a fork held the quarter.
Or was the fork blue, alleyway dark,
Or tunnel blue and the fork stark?
Was there water all around,
With no sight of shore or ground?
Was he sweating out of fear?
Was there none to persevere?
But there was none to make sense
Of all that passed as a pretence.
The rabbit did not hear,
Simply gobbled his beer,
As he cursed the occurring events,
Which to the venison was incoherent.
Shouted and screamed the venison,
But none could hear his screams evident –
As in a dream where one has no choice –
Though he still heard random voices.
It all appeared to be surreal...
He could not distinguish in real–unreal.
Appeared disjointed events –
Nonsensical, yet seemed present.
Some voices were incomprehensible,
Others explicable,
While some overlapped and felt strange.
The haze was not caused by the range:

'Eating healthy – salads raw,
Stabilises the mind's see-saw.'

'Look at the trident's mark
on the soft dough. Oh! Is it a fork...

'I will love...

'All non-dual concepts pristine
Fail at the altar of the present scene.
You may pray to the divine
Now as you fail, strength declines...'

'Ponder on the naught
To release illusion and thoughts.'

'I go on...

'Nature exclusively is
Both predator and prey.'

*'Hey, mate! See that f***ing bastard there?*
He is the third husband of that blonde pear...'

'Desire of the vast, and pain
In one's journey gets immense gain.'

'The descent of salvation
Is in fertile soil of starvation.
And as laid are sheets upon sheets,
Refined and honed are simple beats.'

'You are as real as the spirits,
Or as the fork in the mist.'

'Sex can lead to liberation
When natural, energetic in action.
If performed by the mind
or self, it's lust redefined...

'Oh, mate! You are so sensitive –
Don't: you'll land up being a venison.'

'Why seek musk, the aphrodisiac just...

'The rule for an expert recipe –
Practice makes a perfect pastry.'

'These pastries... hypocrites...

'Of their techniques, what can be said?'
'Miss the point their teachings dead.'

'They keep their eyes half closed
To show detachment, being composed...'

'Is identifying with formless –
Attachment to another dress?'

'They seem to play to the gallery,
Thus advocate adequate cutlery...'

'Aren't they like the most of us,
Only with special robes, a little fuss?'

'Do you know the whole village
Is talking? He's been sleeping...'

'Does not encouraging techniques –
Presume there is a person unique.
Does not this endorse
Hierarchy with privilege...'

'Seek approval from their devotees
By feeding their desire to be free.'

'Really! Is there no one to cease,
Or practise energetic release?'

'Neither are they dual,
Nor amazing jewels.'

'How can a book teach us how to be?
Or bring up children in a way free...'

'The one alone on its own:
Acts, seeks to know the unknown,
Appears to adopt a central role,
Where all revolves round riven souls.'

'It is crucial to strive
For on fatigue one does dive
In the depths of Oneness ...'

'How can there be levels of liberation?
Or love for cessation?'

'All is movement of energy –
Love, effort, war or synergy.'

'I need to come clean...'

'Why of their practice say a word?
Hasn't enough been said and heard?'

'The belief that God is responsible
For all the acts is as much a trap,
As we are responsible for our acts...'

'Do you know the good-looking spiritual
Teacher, who speaks in ways satirical?
I just go to see him… he he…'

'The Prime Minister...

'Do we have one?'

'The first sign – thoughtless skies,
And no bondage with worldly guise.
These are the marked milestones on the way,
To know one is making headway,
And now near is the destination,
Of ineffable aware celebration.'

'Bloody Brexit…

'Incessant changing without a crux,
Where all appears to be in a flux.'

'The more the investment with the form,
Thoughts, feelings, performance – the norm –
The more the attachment does arise,
Keeping contraction on its side.'

'If anyone wishes to buy tarot cards,
Candles or crystals, please see…

'Like you can't stare at the sun bright,
But all appears gold in its light,
Likewise the ones free…'

'It all began with 1066…

'No, it didn't, t'was the Big Bang…'

'These gurus are reflected light,
The one in appearance bright.'

'One alone is wed to its illusion –
That I exist, or I am the delusion,
And needs to rid its view
Or cease, become one, not two.'

'How come candles and crystals
Relate to the spiritual…'

'She seems so Mercurial in her ways,
But it suits his Neptunian haze.'

'One alone the bearing screen
And pictures of the present scene.'

'There is no occurrence…'

'Should we emphasise that nothing
As this appearance does sing?'

'Die while you are alive...

'What will you do with enlightenment?'

Then sunk and stretched seemed the voices
To the venison, who had no choice
To see, hear, feel what was around –
Simply voices in waters drowned.

'Business comes first…

'There's no self either in this form,
Nor does it anywhere else perform.'

'All sensations – a passing circumstance.'

'Even those who think they are separate
Is life… … …'

'Nothing's profound or sacrilege,
For all is an apparent image… …'

'From where does this breath come? Where does it go?
What breathes, what appears as this form's show?
Where is the mind or intelligence?
Where is the one that owns all appearance?
Is it a mystery with none to know?
Appearances, no entity and no show.'

'I love the…

'Food appears… in varied guise,
Bequeathing flavours… that surprise.'

'You know Niels Bohr's statement…
"Everything we call real
Is made of things that can't be regarded as real"
Makes sense, but I wish I could prove it…'

'Also show… how things appear if it's seen,
If it's not seen… it does not…'

'Is there… no physicality

'The "self" avoids talks of Oneness,
Is livid, sleepy, or restless,
As it is scared to die…

'A neurosis is the residual
impressions held at the cellular..

'The "I"repeats the songs of Oneness
To attain freedom from its mess,
Or get riches, glory, ceaseless bliss,
Or end its story, disappear, see this...
But it cannot be illumined,
For that is its apparent end,
Rather the self is never present,
Enlightenment or no enlightenment.'

'Pictures that seem to gleam…
A play of light… and its beam.
Yet there's no movie… but a feast of frames –
With none directing… the guileless game.'

'I seem to make…

'But aren't things seen when light shines on them?'

'An energetic… marvel:
Is this appearance… magical.'

'No…no, there is no magician… at all…

'All an energetic… entertainment –
Seemingly… spellbound by its own raiment.'

'I found love…

'Rebels… and ridicules… its own magic,
Or it reveres… or thinks it's all tragic.'

'A paradoxical… entertainment –
Without a beginning… or an end…

Though all of this appeared to occur
In time's spell, its whisper,
It was a stir that's immediate,
Which as forms does appear, celebrates.
Timelessness, not nonlinear time –
Appearances these forms gross–sublime.
Appeared pictures, apparent scenes.
Sound, light: one. Smoked screen,
Where all seemed like a dream,
With none present, no theme,
Simply images appearing
In the vast embrace, singing.
Formless as form in seeming limit,
Vastness, infinite.
Nothing can this convey,
Too much to further say.

Lots of smoke seemed to surround –
Sweat or tears or… blurred all sounds.
The last words
The venison heard:

'Have you preheated the oven?...

Wrap the pastry sheet around
The rabbit and the venison.

Perfect!'

47

Priceless Refuge

A pomegranate recorded the deep account
Of the catastrophe of the citrus clan.
Fragmented images of the formless did mount,
Which seemed to be a tale, in time, its span;
Though shot were scenes with candour paramount,
Yet it detained aliveness in lifespans.
For views the world, performance through the veil
Of self, thus curbed is the alive in stale.

In minute detail pictured were the twins –
The starved clementine and the tangerine –
Where translated the clan their disease as sin,
As lack of funds impoverished the scene.
Then potent pain and fear of loss of kin
Frayed the stoic rock of parental gene.
Penniless seemed the priceless Chantilly;
Arose devotion, faith involuntary.

Pictured was the recuperation slow
Of twins – clementine and the tangerine –
And simple faith appeared to run the show
Along with precious pain, and untouched screen.
The citrus clan lived countless lives in one go,
But priceless was the pith, without a cuisine,
For lost was faith in an external fount,
And sought was love in life, beyond account.

Then war and damage of the citrus nation
Brought total breakdown of the twins, their clan,
And ruled only proximate pulsation,
For lost was life belonging to the span.
A myth: ideals, *karma*, and causation,
For burnt all of them in the chilling pan.
Dishonour, pride, relations, none did bind,
For now had ceased the world of the confined.

The prudent orange and the mandarin
Suggested a compassionate refuge.
Was it a foreign place beyond the din?
Or love, that as life's blessing does deluge?
But none can understand what illumined,
Because it was not won by self's subterfuge;
Instead, compassion – not of charity –
Lit up the fib of solidarity.
...

A foreign land with an alien language?
The homeless twins with or without a meal?
Nay, in its place a home beyond vantage,
With none at mercy, none to blame, none real –
Emptiness in the eyes and on the stage
Of life, with feelings and yet none to feel,
For long had ceased the ones who did converse
In the dialect of their land, or verse.

The sun still shines in skies without frontiers,
Illuminating all the climes to thrive,
So priceless is the breath, priceless the fear,
Priceless the rising reflex to survive,
Priceless the unstable that does appear,
And priceless ineffable love, alive,
And priceless is this life, its every scene,
The rising gratitude for forms to gleam.

It seemed clementine and the tangerine
Confronted the world's ways, its living themes,
Where split is life and labelled are the scenes,
And welcome just the Mediterranean dream.
But isn't one appearing as all cuisines,
And there is none to change the seeming scheme?
Yet priceless the refuge of revealing light,
As the deep sea or crashing waves in sight.

Awarded, honoured was the pomegranate,
For her photographic account drew tears.
But can one capture potent pain's gamut
Or the immediate aliveness of this fear?
Are there unfortunate forms to elevate?
Can rising love be captured in frontiers?
Or all that appears, is it one, the same:
As freedom, pain, or seeking worldly fame?

48

The Non-Dual Election

The Presidential nominees –
The charming candidates three:
The egg, the black hole, and the mind –
Outlined their manifestos refined.
Attempted to flatter the electorate
With innumerable speeches temperate,
For they wished to lead the domain
Of this book and the worldly plains.
They proposed perceptions diverse
And made the opponents seem worse,
Yet their campaigns were polite,
A blend of decorum and insight.

A humble, helpful character,
Trustworthy, true, and popular,
Not flamboyant, yet a great orator
Was the egg – the top contender.

Egg – at his first campaign:

'Let me share a few wonderful events –
The extraordinary incidents
And their consequence
For my life, by this book's presence.
This book gave me the opportunity
To work at a famed university,
Where I was honoured to be in alliance
With professors of repute, debate science;
The privilege of this activity,
Mingled with common sensitivity,
With service to royals and commoners
With the same vigour and demeanour,
Has shaped my destiny,
Augmented my clarity,
And made me realise all is one:
Creator and creation, no division.

Besides, the love, the care, and kindness
I was given at the time of being a mess,
By enlightened ones like the bowl –
An illustration of the whole –
Would not be possible elsewhere,
Where enlightenment is rare.
The love and support received by me –
A normal egg – shows here authority
Is of love alone,
Where none are disowned,
And honoured is equality,
While stripped is false identity.

My life's purpose is to serve
This book, its foods, for they deserve
A special place in my heart,
As I consider none apart.
But the deprived ones in society,
Or ones of a distinct variety,
Reserve a special place,
For they need our loving grace
And unconditional space,
With opportunities to showcase
Their hidden talents and genii,
To help them higher fly.

We will ensure a strong support system
For the deserted and depressed victims;
Will not let anyone suffer,
For we'll accept traits that differ.
So, whether it's the croissant alone
Or the adorable pimiento unknown,
We will provide a base
For all to share in safe space,
As we've revived the pizza in need –
To be free. We'll guide the ingrained seed,
Honour our fearless and the free
Who gave their lives, like rose and pea.

My agenda is all inclusive –
Not elitist, exclusive, or elusive.
I will deliver the pledged programmes,
Provide equal platform for lamb and ham,
Will care for nature's reserves,
And will preserve for future curves.
So, dear friends, I guarantee
A realm which will feel free.'

Egg – at another campaign:

'I have always advocated peace,
Believe in life's extended lease,
Hence I am against the arms race
And stay away from war's space.
Yet in no way am I craven:
Wherever I've served are safe havens.
Suffering, crime, and trauma will cease
When given the chance to serve with peace.

For this life I am full of gratitude
And loathe attention-seeking attitude.
Will work reliably behind the scenes;
Will not play tricks like the mind mean.
Being conscientious of my role,
Won't stretch facts like the black hole.

For the grand vision I see
Is where everyone will be free,
Where the future generations
Will be thankful for the foundations
We set for this equality
And climatic predictability.
I will ensure there is no repetition
Of Oneness in this book's next edition,
So that the interest of youth is maintained,
For on them rests the hope of our domain.'

Egg – at another campaign:

'My friends! Don't compare like the mind,
Constrict this life in views confined,
For it's the tolerance of our view
That gives us a special hue,
Makes us awakened and aware –
Set for enlightenment's care.
But do not always to precision bind:
It's fine to make mistakes, unlike the mind,
For that ensures we are making progress
And not being restrained in ego's mess.

The mind is the biggest rogue –
First it simulates 'the person', in vogue,
Then to support the individual
It simulates a system fundamental;
Next the system states it is the best
To care for the individual, its rest,
Then uses complicated rules –
Creates a rift with two schools,
As person blames the system,
And system the personal custom;
Thus, avoided is truth and passed is blame,
Perpetuated is a looped game.
And now the system that seems essential
Blames some of its individuals
For opposition or mental stress
And the accompanying mess.
Then the mind adopts the role of the messiah
And vows to help the pariah.
Thus, functions this eternal loop –
The dour mind's simulated soup.

It's challenging to break free
From the confines of the mind's spree,
Which creates hierarchical structures
Then binds by carving from its features.

The mind does not appreciate
What it has but seeks to celebrate
What is distant. Plus, it dictates
Agendas to foods who on it wait,
Thus increasing suppression
And slavery to it and its system;
But it doesn't realise, the more it seeks control,
The more defied will be societal roles.
But freedom and equality,
In due course, beget equanimity.

Besides, it always seeks attention,
Is a master of pretension,
Distracts itself from the present,
Fears its demise as President,
Will go to any extent
To retain power over events.
So let us guard life from mind cruel
And not vote for its constrained rule.
Get rid of systemic hierarchy
For a world without patriarchy,
Where all are equal, the same,
Which is the true nature of life, in name.

Friends, let me illumine another truth:
The black hole is devious and uncouth;
It will destroy our planet
With its ravenous habit,
Conceal all the essential facts,
Lack transparency, overact
In situations that need forbearance,
Compassion, love, and assurance;
Besides, it practises detachment –
The biggest failing of a government.

So, walk with me and you won't regret
Life of the food sapiens sect;
Together, we can reach the place
Of absolute love and pure grace.'

Egg – at his final campaign:

'My dear brothers and sisters,
See thorough the sinister,
Do not fall for the false claims
Of the black hole and mind's games.
Let them not ruin your uniqueness
By their Machiavellian process;
For the best way to destroy or sink
Foods is to teach them how and what to think.
Know: life alone is of value,
Alive – as me and you,
So let us cherish each being,
Our idiosyncrasies fleeing,
For appears the vastness alone
As each appearance known–unknown.

This book values the ordinary,
Proves we can rule the world culinary.
Together we'll make the dream come true
And take this book to heights anew.
We'll show the world the power of food,
Which shares without desire, includes
All cuisines, teaches to be without fear
And doesn't create a hierarchical tier.
So, do not give your choice away
To the ones who will keep you at bay.
Let's walk together for a while,
Turn frustrations to a smile.'

The black hole was a creature strange,
Addressed itself in the third person, in exchange,
For it believed non-dual parlance
Was essential in dual absence.

Black hole – at his first campaign:

'Oh, foods of this book's domain,
Let's dive in the crux of the campaign,
Consider the candidates
For the Presidential mandate.
Let us begin with the black hole:
Is it akin to the mind's role?
Does it entice and possess objects?
No, it doesn't, nor like the mind project
Schemes. Is it ravenous and swallows light?
No, it doesn't differentiate day and night.
Then how to identify the black hole –
The puzzling appearance of the whole?
Well! Light adores its fringes sublime –
A halo, to reflect its piety prime.
It seems to appear like a doughnut
But is as healthy as the fruits and nuts,
And it can deform space and time –
The false linear paradigms –
Proving it's beyond the worldly grime
Yet embraces all the chimes.

Now let me tell you of its reserves,
Its vast density, and love's verve:
It has amazing mechanisms,
Is Oneness that holds schisms.
And its escape velocity
Is faster than light's rapidity –
At the event horizon. But beyond
All seems to be an unseen bond.
Yet delve within and all will illumine
That apparent are mass and spin,
All is a singularity,
Nothingness as polarity.
So, despite being full of reserves,
It is empty of all the oeuvre.

Hence, it's non-dual, non-identity,
With unimpeachable creativity,
Has vast riches with no states,
Does not judge its guests by their weight;
It welcomes all as family,
Helps them settle rapidly
In its unconfined cavity –
Is not prejudiced to a galaxy –
Even provides answers innovative
To all their problems quantitative;
In it resides the whole,
So, it offers its guests, its soul.
And though a portal to amazing zones,
It does not anything possess or own
And does not claim to know the void,

For it is one – as full and devoid.

If this paradox appears a mystery,
Your mind is not in synchronicity
With the singular universe
That portrays self in myriad verse.
Still, come and dive in the black hole deep
And arcane knowledge thus reap.'

Black hole – at another campaign:

'Let's consider the second contestant –
The mind, self-proclaimed President –
Who has no chance to win our kind,
For it is out of tune and blind
To the acts of spiritual turpitude,
Which have been uncovered by the foods
– In this book – the guiding lights
Of paradoxical heights.

So, let us all become aware
Of the mind, its play unfair:
It rules in subtle ways,
Shuns rising life for better days,
Sticks around like a sticky glue,
Optimises all around its hue.
The world's become a merciless marketplace
Of lust, greed, attachment, hate, ego's race,
Because of the insatiable mind,
Which views from its lens confined.
Mind mad in wars of 'me' and 'you'
Has made this world a selfish stew.

But disguises the deceitful mind
Disgust and how it despises other rind
By wearing more masks these days
To hide its heinous ways,
By attaching fancy labels
To all its unreal fables.
Pretends to learn lessons priceless
While hating the apparent mess.

The mind is blind to life's vast aspect,
Can hold only one prospect,
Always desires more control
To persist in and prolong its role;
Plus, it desires only delight,
While stays woe in shadows of light;
Then it begins its chase
To steer clear of the varying pace,
Tries to fill its void with pleasures
But is unfulfilled by treasures,
For it emphasises lack
In everything, is out of track
With the emerging scene,
Desiring the pristine.
Refuses to see life perform,
Celebrate its every form,
Is love incarnate in each verse,
As the apparent universe.

Nothing can calm the arrogant mind,
No meditation, psalm, or being mined,
Except for the black hole,
As nothing can escape its role.
Besides, the black hole being timeless
Can easily swallow time's mess –
The habitat of the mind,
An art of its own bind.

So, as the electoral promise,
The black hole pledges this:
It will engulf the bellicose mind,
Alleviate its suffering unkind.
With the mind gone for good,
All will prevail as it should –
Alive, without polarity,
Life as it is, completely free,
It's where paradoxes can be,
Empty–full, like the black hole carefree.
A stress-free environment,
Life in perfect alignment.'

Black hole – at his final campaign:

'The black hole will now illuminate
The most unsuitable candidate –
The egg, who is nothing but a sham,

All rhetoric without heart or plan,
For he is charm without a substance,
Speaking from dual cognisance.
He advocates prescribed mannerisms
In life's emerging mechanism,
But who is primed for situations
Spontaneous in manifestation?
For characters apparently act
Instinctively, and not from a tract;
Rather, there is no one existent,
To behave in a manner consistent.

The egg's view of removing repetition
Of this message of liberation
From the book's next edition,
For the youth, their ambition,
Is gluttony of the financial,
For their votes are substantial.
Besides, individuals seek hope
Not the end of their soap
Opera, want to stay away
From that which it can slay,
So there is a mutual exchange
Of ignorance, far from truth's range;
But the song that's non-dual
Will destroy the individual,
Unravel the undividedness
That is, not in imagined progress.

The egg finds this missive weary,
For he's dual and dreary;
His ways are covetous schemes
That tax even society's dreams;
He fancies profits from promises,
To beget personal bliss,
While his promise of the future
Will keep you in hope's stupor.
Foods! He's insulting your intelligence
By selling enlightenment's essence;
Trying to the enlightened illumine
Is to abet the self's deceptive din.
In guise he wishes to become sovereign,
So do not fall for the original sin.

But the black hole is tolerant,
Won't traumatise the food present;
Rather, it will provide a tax rebate
To all beings this book does celebrate,
Delightfully will attest growth fiscal,
Endorse a system whole and natural.
The black hole will shed the unreal
At its entrance, show the real.
And like a bird it will repeat
The timeless message that's complete,
To reveal: unrepeated the essence
Of this alive, anew presence.

So, if elected is the black hole
To the Presidential role,
It ensures experts will love this text,
Ground-breaking and without pretext
(Though this book doesn't need endorsement
To be as it is, apparently extant).
Also, none will praise the writer
Or force the young to learn the matter,
For the song belongs to none,
Is spontaneously begun.
Instead, will resonate the sound
Of Oneness, that abounds,
Heard will be the unstruck rhythm,
Tasted will be the boundless freedom.
Since the black hole wears no masks,
Nor owns or praises performed tasks,
It will end all narcissism,
Along with individualism.

So, friends of the book true,
Awaken to the view
Of the friendly black hole
And its non-dual role;
Ignore the conniving egg and mind,
Honour love and Oneness unconfined,
Fearlessly cast your vote
To ignorance's antidote.'

The seemingly modest black hole
Used non-dual parlance at the polls

To pursue the electorate
With his views immaculate.
…

The mind wished to be (re-)elected
As the President respected,
Resumed its clever campaign,
Though furious at opponents inane.

Mind – at his first campaign:

'My precious nourishments!
I'm here for your enrichment,
Having served since time immemorial.
I have set up this world imperial;
I've assured amazing innovations,
Laid the lingual foundations
Of this text and the world's literature,
And am the basis of each signature.

Though modest, I again must state
My efforts since ancient dates,
For against the wickedness of the two
I must defend my view
To the world of food, which needs my aid –
Against the vexing black hole, egg's trade.
The two denounce and malign me
Even though I am not an enemy
But an innocuous expression
Of energy in illustration.

So, let me tell you about myself,
Which is the generic worldly self.
My work is seamless and unique:
I am the mentor of each technique;
Though simple, I am pure intelligence,
Define all limits with diligence.
I formulate several beliefs,
Oppose them to my own relief
To ensure that all the systems
Perform in an effortless rhythm.

My presence alone makes sense
In this world, or Oneness – its appearance.
I am the creator of this world:
The more I claim, more seems unfurled.
I am even examined by the ones free,
For my apparent decree.

I am not a troll but whole and free,
A perfect blessing of infinity,
But most forget that without me
They cannot know what they see,
For if it wasn't for my labels,
How would one be able
To identify the objects,
Understand all the concepts,
Or split the facts from fiction,
Or employ time, its diction.

My rivals criticise my ability
Despite employing my facility,
Undermine all my benefits
Of steadiness in the name of stress;
But see how they rely on me
For all their emotive debris,
Their confidence needs
And their creative deeds.
Rather, all needs of all domains
Are soothed by my campaign,
So who can ever further go,
When I alone control the show?
Remember: it's me, the mind alone,
That cooks an egg, makes black holes known,
Aids all the scientific discoveries,
And stacks the libraries of memories.

Yet if you need more productivity,
Vote for the frauds who claim ability,
Discuss abstract theories till you die,
But call me when limits cease, don't lie,
For I will still be your guide,
With useful knowledge by my side,
And will support you through the tasks
Gargantuan, without the mask,
Will add flavour to your fare plain,
Find directions in foreign lanes.'

Mind – at another campaign:

'Precious ones! The egg and the black hole
Stress my unreal, negative role
Of abuse, drama, greed, and escapism,
But they are glitches of division,
Which effortlessly can be ceased
By one's awakened attention. Ease
In and out of breath,
Focus on the life force and seeming death
Of self, and reprogramming –
Internal engineering.

But the catch – wishing to release
Suffering painful, be at ease,
Which gives rise to added stress,
Greed, escapism, and the mess.
For replacing old beliefs for new
Will not exonerate the issues,
As there is no unconditioned mind –
Any confines are me redefined,
So purging me with concepts unclear
Is impossible, for I as them appear;
Like the sky can't be enclosed with stone,
Or the dark can't light its zone,
I cannot through myself be known,
For I am the unknown as the known tone.
So, do not try the option
To make life worse with notions.

I am an apparent stream of thought –
Expression of life, not a blot;
Whenever I'm in strife,
I hurt myself and not this life.
Truly, I am expression of energy
And not a physical entity;
You can compare me to the moon
That lights the dark nights – a boon,
Yet it reflects the sun's light,
So I'm neither selfish nor a knight,
Nor a villain, though made out to be,
Life alone appears as me.
So why split my existence
From life, declare my presence
Roguish, when love does establish
My presence, itself does embellish?
I alone perpetuate as you:
The other way does not ensue,
So how will you get rid of me?
I am not an entity.

Energy dances to its own tune,
So why condemn me as not in tune;
It alone appears as me,
Boundless, bound, split, or free,
So getting rid of me as the President,
Will be like sowing an untorn garment,
Or cutting water with a spoon –
An impasse, not a boon.

I am a genius in the workings of form,
Don't know why formless as form performs.
So, beings of the food domain,
Enjoy and learn my skills ingrained,
But don't use my skills for liberation,
For that's not in my job description.
Salvation isn't reached by methods of cessation
But appears as boundless activation.'

Mind – at his final campaign:

'Let me explain about the black hole
And the egg – their pompous roles.
The black hole hides behind the veil
Of non-duality, but its jargon's stale;
It secretly tries to gain control
Over the foodstuffs and the polls,
Devours the innocent, is not the void –
Perfect case of electoral schadenfreude.
While the promotion of freedom, unity
By the egg is a pretence of maturity.
For none can unite, instil liberty,
As energy is without captivity.
And once in power, all are the same,
Hungry to retain the throne and game.
So, lovely beings of this work,
Reflect, do not go berserk
Because of the pretentious two,

Who hide behind my views.
But I don't like to claim ability
Or hide behind masks of impartiality.
Remember: whether you vote for me
Or not, I will win, as you will see!

Now, let me share a vital secret:
That nothing does occur, beget
Oneness; there is no me and you
Or the black hole or the egg untrue.
I've heard from the enlightened few
That all is one energetic hue,
That emptiness and form are one,
Are not distinct entities. So, none
Appears as the mind. All is on its own.
And like an egg can't stand on tip alone,
The mind cannot create itself,
But it's life, appearing as the self.
So, it's not the mind's aim or goal
To become empty, none, or whole.

I repeat: all of this I've heard
In words unsaid and unheard
From beings free, of this manuscript –
The ones beyond all the scripts;
Do not blame me for this communication
Or find faults with my intention.
Life as it is appears to flow;
Play with me, you won't further go.'
…

Characters from the book's dominion
Were asked to present their opinion
On the electoral campaign
And the candidates, their aims,
By the pomegranate, the journalist,
Well known for documentaries populist.

The Fig's view:

'This book doesn't need a fuckin' President!'

When persisted the pomegranate
To the fig, his standpoint to submit
About the need for governance,
Democratic choice, the brilliance
Of the candidates' campaigns,
Replied the fig in manner plain:

'And you believed those bastards?
How real are they?'

The Lamb's view:

'Elections make no sense:
Can freedom be led by pretence?
Few foods feel that they have a choice –
Appears seeming self as the voice.
Though seeming choice that seems to rise
Is the one as two, in guise.

If you ask me of the three,
There is none in the spree.
An appearance of the undefined
Is the black hole, the egg, and the mind.
Yet the mind is fraudulent,
Which tricks beings innocent,
Believes it runs the show,
And feels it all does know.
Establishes its own precedent
Then clears its stance impertinent,
A phantom that impersonates the source
But is impressed by shadows divorced.
It is not through the mind
These words are read or defined,
For it's inherent intelligence
That acts in seeming appearance.
Appears the unknown alone
As the seeming act, on its own.
The mind is the seeking, not a part
Of the whole, for there's nothing apart.

The other rogue – the black hole,
Who pretends to be whole;
Can one have a non-dual view,
If there is only one, not two?
And the egg: oh, he's only charm,
And like a sheep follows the norm,

Then wishes to lead
Lions, who are freed,
With his dualistic blather,
Thinking it will flatter.

Convoluted edifice of control –
The egg, the mind, and the black hole.
I'm not voting for charlatans,
And I am not a partisan.'

The Lion's view:

'Pretentiousness pursues the piecemeal,
Made are spiritual or practical deals,
So all have hidden agendas
Deem real they, their propaganda,
Support a surreal game
In the name of one – the same.

Yet the egg gets my credence:
He promises to address grievance
Of all and seems to be sensible,
Isn't a spiritual spectacle.
Anyway, who exists to have a choice?
Is not all an appearance of one voice?'

Chef Olive Oil's view:

'How real is this book?
Or characters that seem to hook?'

Prof. Nutty Cream's view:

'All's an energetic expression
In innumerable impressions,
A play of hide and seek in cadence,
With preferences in appearance.
I prefer the seeming facts,
Am not concerned about the abstract.

The egg is a beguiling trickster
Who promises an illusory elixir,
The mind – the sense of self on a wheel –
A simulation that's unreal.

I guess the black hole's the best,
Where paradoxes rest,
And I can study its extent,
Though apparent its content.'

Chicken Tikka Masala's view:

(He seemed pensive while giving his opinion and was almost thinking out aloud.)

'I am not sure of either three,
For appears the one – as them – is free.
The song of freedom remains unbound
Even when fences seem to surround,
So it is true there is no mind,
For there is nothing confined.
And the one, the whole,
Is never in a role.
And all is ever at home,
With none to roam,
There is no one…
Yet unreal seeks the real
In the unreal,
Where compelling seems every rind,
The egg, the black hole, the mind.
No account
But all as it is...

I'll dive deep, think it through,
Before I cast my vote due.'

The Lotus' view:

'In our election
Of limited selection,
The mind alone does express
All the candidates, a mess –
Is apocryphal and a fraud,
As it plays the role of God.

Intelligence is unlike the mind:
The brain is not the mind confined.
It is the appearance of light –
Formless forming, as it writes.

Everything can work perfectly
Without the mind's insanity.
Though to none can i complain,
This mind is insane,
Imagines spontaneous events
As timed and spatial incidents,
Wishes all the power in its creation
With–without any obligation,
Has turned the songs of freedom
Into rules, prayers, and wisdom,
And institutional religions,
And socio-transcendent missions,
So that the song remains unheard –
There can be an analysis of words.
Has fashioned bondage,
Created several cages,
Included ranks and roles,
Beliefs, a journey – control;
Then fakes the garb of spiritual
Or feigns it's non-existential.

Whoever I vote for, the mind will win;
I won't favour the original sin,
For my departed friend – the rose –
Was hurled in the throes
Of death by the conniving mind,
With its agendas blind.

Yet I know not of a mind,
Solitary or combined,
For what appears is the undefined,
With no one in the grind.

I stay away from the elections.'

The Bamboo's view:

'There is no book.'

The Aubergine's view:

'It seems most of us interviewed
Express our local views
Or from apparent experience.
But do we need elections?'

The Wholesome Mung bean:

'There is neither self, nor the mind,
Nor any character confined.
Sings the unknown alone
As all its known tones,
Yet I will vote for the hue
Of nothing in rendezvous –
A musical melody
Of real and unreal spree.'

Returning to our old story
Of the candidates three –
The egg, the black hole, and the mind,
Along with their followers aligned,
Eagerly wait for the results
Of the election, in the tumult
Of the varied thoughts that seem to dance,
Disturb the peace of their expanse.

Who do you think will win?
For whom would you vote?

49

The Last Laugh

PART 1

A certain potato smart and neat,
Known for honesty, manner sweet,
Lived lavishly in Mumbai city,
Was adored for his humour witty.
Affluent and idle to the root,
He spent time in love's pursuit;
Then fondness coincidental
And connection mutual
With his married neighbour –
The soft *pav*,[1] with uncertain flavour –
Begot a youthful delight,
Where the days spent felt right.
Obsessed with her appearance,
He could not resist her presence,
So spent most hours of the day
In pleasurable play;
But it gave rise to immense stress,
For it seemed improper, a mess.

The *pav* though wed to the lettuce light,
Preferred the potato forthright,
For he was comforting, an earthy match,
In contrast to the lettuce detached.
The *pav* and the potato's affair
Became the grapevine, as the pair
Were most often found to dine
At varied joints on the coastline;
Nicknamed the *Vada-Pao*,[2]
They were frowned on by the highbrow
Of the city, for the fat content
And immorality's extent.

Remorse then distressed the potato,
And inner restlessness seemed to grow,
Shadowed moral compunctions,
Tormented thoughts and questions.

Wondered:
'What is right, what wrong?
Should he listen to society's song?
Or the *pav's* heart, or his voice,
Or the lettuce and his lack of choice?'

The potato then wished to redress
His conduct, the impending stress,
As the *pav's* life too showed the signs
Of strain, caused by the potato's designs.
The potato performed rites odd,
Invited mercy of the gods
To be released from all his sins
Of cavorting display, fated chagrin;
To rescue the *pav*, too, from the pressure
Of a failing marriage, social censure.

Instead followed fear and dismay,
As experts sold him hell's display,
To theories he became a prey,
Bewildered couldn't find a way;
To liberate from this fear, confusion,
He then pursued self-realisation,
And visited the local gurus,
Who taught him that a detached view
Would end strife, help him cross life's abyss:
A prerequisite to moksha[3] bliss.
Completely collapsed the entire process
As relapsed failure, unease, guilt, and mess
Of loathsome feelings, and the thoughts
That suffocated and made him fraught.

Though deep down the potato knew
He couldn't be defined by any view,

1 The soft *Pav*, or *Pao*, made in Mumbai, is very similar to soft floured baps or soft dinner rolls.
2 See Note 21A
3 See Note 21B

TOMATO
KETCHUP

So slander wasn't the main issue:
It was restlessness and rue
That made him leave the city
To find peace and integrity.
He left his family and love,
Went to the mountains, high above.

There he meditated and did fast,
Watched his thoughts – in silence – go past.
As yogic practice grew intense,
He wondered if he chased a pretence
Of perfect frame, lasting serenity,
And targets of imagined eternity.

He saw how rattled the closets
With secrets of these yogic profits,
And how the devotees gave away
Their authenticity to expert play,
Revered authority in the name
Of elite knowledge and tall claims.
But others narrated spiritual
Experiences – though individual –
To claim the higher presence,
Enjoy power in garbs of penance.

Wondered:
'Wasn't he fed more rules
Of divine judgements, its schools?
Didn't his desires set further goals,
Which tried to fill a fathomless hole?
Was he imprudent, insane,
To be stuck in a high-power game?
How was this scenario different
From the marketplace termed ignorant?
And if he did not get release
From guilt, why was he here – in unease?'

He decided to leave this place
For logical, atheistic pace,
Travelled through Russia for relief,
Trailed socialist schools in disbelief;
He adopted the local fashion,
Where soup became his new passion,
Who loved him for unknown reasons,
Made him a hero for all seasons.

Yet the salient trait of his essence
Was to question every appearance.
He could not accept handed facts,
Dug deeper in the tracts.

Wondered:
'Didn't he revere authorities again
In a diverse scenario, garb, and reign?
Did he embrace pseudo atheism
Only to be rid of deism?
Wasn't his restlessness still evident?
Though evanescent, seemed persistent.'

He refused to accept the outward show,
Left for the USA, to extend and grow;
There he the secret did apply,
To positive thinking did ally –
Ordered the universe and prepared chits,
Stayed in the present, lived by his wits,
As the French fries and chips did rule,
The sleek blonde oil his success tool.

The more he sought the positive,
The more danced thoughts negative,
Which were followed by intense fear:
What if the negative would occur?
Then he wished to escape the fear –
That seared his peace – by means severe.

Wondered:
'Isn't this another insatiable game –
Of constant positivity, my claims?
Are not his wishes the reason –
Selfish claims of his person –
That he sought the positive,
Though it had made him combative:
He was in a constant battle
To remove negativity that rattled
His mind, made him stay on guard, eager
To deny life, which did appear.
Was it imperative for survival
To stay motivated, inspirational?

Wasn't greed at the heart of each activity,
Be it wealth, bliss, creativity?
Was this life a quagmire
To fulfil illusory desires?'

Wondered:
'Why did ordinary life
Seem dismal, full of strife?
Why did one always seek
Happiness and its peaks?
Why did one run away
From the present play?

Was it that suffering and grief
Occurred, for the self did perceive
Life from its narrow view
And wished life to follow too.
But life had a charter of its own,
Did not care about his tones.
Was it the self's way to sustain
Itself through happiness or pain,
To keep the entire attention
On itself and its pretention?'

Wondered*:*
'Why could no technique fill the void
Of his restlessness paranoid?
Was inadequacy at the heart
Of each technique, aim, or a part?
Were positive, negative, creative
Tricks to fortify the native?

Were fear and separation at the root,
Nourishing each other to become astute.
Did these make him continually seek
A new lover, joy, glimpse, or peak,
Where new lands seemed to hold the key
To cease his pain or become free?'

Family funding then sharply decreased;
The potato sought means to pay for peace,
Adapted from a side dish to main course,
Was fully mashed but stayed on course.
Secured a central role in gratin,
Moved to Europe – roasted – less did fatten,
And endeavoured inner healing
To part from the past, emotional cleaning;
But wondered if 'It healed a blow
Or subtly fortified his ego?'

As prevailed restiveness, unease,
Which threatened regular peace,
Decided he'd give Britain a chance
To help him relieve his restless stance.
There he met a few enigmas,
Who showed apparent is a stigma:
'One energetic presence
Alone is in appearance.
There is no individual
Separate, caught in a debacle.
It is pretence to subdue an illusion,
For there is none in a delusion.
None is tarnished for there is none,
Presence and absence truly one.'

Another stated: 'Each emotion
And all the seeming questions
Are sacred, for life does appear
As its each form yet does not smear
Its formlessness, is on its own,
Without another to make it known.'

Though compassion was the common trait
Of beings who Oneness did reiterate,
The potato deep in its roots
Saw peace vanishing in its pursuit,
While realisation and revering ones
Released does not end disquiet or division.

Wondered:
'How could the other complete
His life, which ever seemed deplete?
Did he not shop for gurus, guides,
Thus in illumined state reside?
But nothing ever brought peace,
Ephemeral all events of ease.

Why did he rush from pillar to post,

Seeking the celebratory toast?
Or did his shadows seem to reach
Ahead, to decide his fate, it siege?
Did he not buy a lot of bulls***
Packaged in a spiritual kit,
Even believed the impossible
In the name of the spiritual,
Sought levels of enlightenment
And blissful states in random events.'

Wondered:
'Could a few incidents
Define his life inherent?
Could his name, attached paraphernalia,
Ever define his real criteria?
Wasn't his name merely a label
On his form – alive, yet unstable?
Why did his form not care
About morality or prayer?

Why did he traverse each continent
To find a life that is relevant?
Was there nothing to take away?
Does life appear as it may?
Didn't he look for life far away
While it intimately danced, did play?
Was this life without an intent?
Simply appearing, without content.'

Fed up with several questions
And financial restrictions,
He packed to return to Mumbai city.
Enlightenment another sham pretty.

PART 2

At the airport he saw a book
On poetry, paintings, foods as cooks.

Fascinated by the imagination,
Merged genres, Oneness, illustration,
He picked 'Footprints on Waters Free'
To read of liberation, its spree;

Food appeared at its best,
Addressed the dual unrest.
The potato keenly read the text:
Of formless as forms dressed.
But reading through, the potato sensed
Of how people sold pretence.

'Imperfect poetry, mediocre art,
Packaged in creative craft,
Romanticised was the non-dual card
With tales, dull dialogues – a canard,
An echo of parroted messages
Of gurus, scriptures, unknown sages.
A commandment in subtle form,
Where the author says the source performs,
But makes her views the flavour paramount,
Then claims flowed poetry from the fount.'

Wondered:
'Was the author's aim to sing a song
Or was it for her to belong
To the hall of fame, and portray skills,
Acquire affluence and its thrills?
For the message of Oneness shared
Is ineffable and can't be bared;
Food eaten satiates hunger true –
Pictures and talk mystify the view.
A seeming energetic shift
Does not a character free or lift,
For there is none but the unknown,
As he had heard in non-dual tones.
A gross façade in delicate disguise.'
Returned the book as much surmise.

During the flight rose more questions
On seeking and contrite perceptions.
Thought: 'Isn't a quagmire this chase?
Could he find peace in time and space?'

Wondered:
'What drives the individual
In pursuit of the spiritual?
Was linking to a higher God –
A carrot and stick – a façade?

Were all relations needs disguised
For base, mental, or abstract prize?
Did one relate with concepts, objects
Because there appeared a subject?
Was there no other, no relations,
But one alone in illustration?

What was he seeking – joy, or freedom's ray?
Did not his seeking keep them at bay?
Were not joy, freedom, peace present
But hidden by individual intent?
Why did he always split life in two –
The goal and protagonist in view.
Were his claims to satisfy a self,
Display it on the worldly shelf,
And thus enhance its presence,
Stay in its circular existence?

Did all the issues emanate
Because of a self separate?
Does the self curb itself in time and space?
And hoard semblance in an imaginary race?
Wondered: who looked for this split?
Was it two or did one thus emit
As two, and then seek its essence?
Yet was one alone in presence?
Is everything non-volitional,
On its own – a play unconditional?'

The more he sought depths of emotion,
The more he seemed to feed the notions.
He pondered on intense privation,
Was left with nothing but frustration.

Wondered:
'Wasn't the collective society
Glorified self in guise of propriety,
Which issues moral sense
Of utmost significance,
Which seem to fail, for the present scene
Overrides all the morals pristine?
Like survival or raging hormones
Do not care for the moral tone.
So were morals only relevant
In the societal precincts –
Or for protection of society,
And race, or life's piety?
For there seemed no morality
In the natural fraternity.
What was the role of morals –
Was it for life here, or eternal?
Did morals not make any sense
To life, untouched by its appearance,
Like words noble or cruel on a page
Cannot it elevate, defile, or cage?
Maybe life had no consequence,
Was present without significance.'

Wondered:
'But applies morals, too, the art
Of one, for there's nothing apart.
Was it life's way of reverence
To its appearing presence?
So, is all life simply as it is,
No world, or society, or bliss?
Or did all appear in inverses
In life's appearing verse?
If there is one alone
As two, then could it be known?

Why did non-duality fail to shine
When loved ones seemingly declined?
Why did the talk that there is none
Fall flat on seeing someone
Die? Why did he cry tears of sorrow
On seeing war's ghastly scenario?
And where did physical chemistry
Fit in this love, unconfined, free?
Or did the missive imply that all is
As it is even when something's amiss?
Or did it imply rises everything
With no one to it sing?'

Wondered:
'Is all simply an appearance,
Puppets dancing in perfect cadence?
Or all that seems to appear –
An image, so nothing occurs?

So time seemed to be an illusion,
But was timeless too a delusion?
Does Oneness imply the whole:
Tears, passion, dual roles,
Non-volitional occurrence
Of nothingness as this appearance,
With no purpose of this show,
Or maybe none to even know –
Its own absence.'

Thus, arose questions in the vastness,
Yet did not touch it by their madness.

PART 3

The potato reached Mumbai city,
Was welcomed by air warm and gritty.
He smiled at his lack of attainment,
Yet absent seemed the restless raiment.
The potato resumed work the same day –
A natural rhythm seemed to slay
The restraints and the suffering,
Without a grand release, shift inspiring.

Unanswered remained the questions,
Disappeared without solutions.
Remained a rumbling silence, complete,
Enigmatic appearance, depleted treat,
A naturalness for no one,
Without the non-dual jargon.
The loudest, natural sound
Alone seemed to abound:
An energetic hum, a stir,
That immediate does occur
As the forms in presence;
Formless in form's appearance
Alone was present,
With none to be absent.
Possession, alleged love, and lust –
All ruined. Nothing to grab or trust.
Untied seemed all the knots,
And lost was life's plot.
An empty, profound peace,
Unclouded by disease –
Peace that is one's true nature,
Timeless, each nomenclature.

All images shattered even the one –
All beliefs are now undone.
He felt a lightness around his chest;
In the form was an alive rest.
Stayed a womb-like simplicity –
Formless as form celebratory,
Like seeing life for the first time,
Unknown, vibrant, without a storyline.
A love without sanctuary,
Yet life seemed ordinary.

Simply natural life, on its own,
Playing, with no one on the throne –
Life alone appearing as it is,
With none to it live, create, or miss;
An unknowing, without a flow,
No world out there to know.
Simply this: the appearing scene,
No way to know if it is pristine,
Or messy, or without a purpose,
For life alone, none in repose,
With no demands to alter the appearance,
Nor to amend its non-acceptance,
Enigmatic presence, being alone,
But no loneliness, a song unknown.

In this solitary completeness
Rose everything: thoughts, feelings, mess,
Yet nothing to gnaw, life without defence,
But every feeling, thought – raw and intense,
Appearing for a while,
Then fading in the fertile
Embrace, with none to sit in judgement
Of positive, negative, or attachment,
All without reason, beingness naked,
Nothing significant or sacred.
There was a naturalness – that is,
Not acquired – not any state, nor bliss,
Like wet is water, burns the fire,
Blows the air, dense the quagmire.

Life as it is, simply this,
Complete in each crack, each abyss,
Where sadness begot tears,
And survival its fears
Without an investment;
Yet there was no detachment.

This naturalness is not a consequence
Of travels, seeking, or brilliance.
For it is, not caused or obtained
By anyone, but is unconstrained
Freedom, which is present,
Is not confined to events.
There wasn't a potato without me,
But a freedom, completely free.
Formless forming, not an experience,
Naturalness in perfect cadence.
It was completely evident –
For no one present or absent –
There's no other in this phenomenon
To be present, or absent, or one,
Or speak of it, or share its essence,
Or reiterate Oneness of presence.
Impossible to this understand –
For there's no other in life's land –
As impossible as counting stars
Or holding the ocean in a jar.

Simply appears this life
With–without strife,
As the apparent scene,
Yet no event or cuisine.
But embracing or decrying these lines –
The dance of the unreal confines.

The *pav* one day sent an invite
To the potato for a party that night,
To perceive the changes that seemed
To have reformed the potato, him redeemed.
Joined many friends to feel the profound
Freedom that seemed him to surround.
Others came to feel the brilliance
One feels in liberation's presence.

At dinner many did question,
While others offered suggestions.
Some wished to know about the natural.
Most imposed faiths unnatural.
The potato then glanced around
At life, its miracle abound,
Of wordless words, verbs in dance,
Of no nouns, pronouns to thus prance,
No dream catchers to dreams store,
Yet the appearance of dreams galore,
With claims of being near and far,
Yet none to trade in the bazaar –
A bazaar of 'me's and 'I's,
Yet none to it sell or buy,
Energetic stir – believing, owning tales,
Innocent queries of what wins or fails.

But nothing can ever convey
The naturalness that's at play.
The potato simply laughed
Long; the *pav* stared at his gaffe.
But lively, light, and hearty
Stayed the spirit at the party;
With love, laughter, and delight
Ended an enjoyable night.

Next day:
The potato's body could not be found.
Though still is heard the laughter's sound.
Most feel it's the potato's laugh –
A kind of surreal epitaph.
Some know it's the *pav* for sure,
For she's untouched by the secret pure.
Appears life as usual in the noisy city,
With or without memoirs pretty.

TOMATO KETCHUP

50
Boundless Transformation

Were you greeted by an open gate
To terminate the self and states?
The tales and insights read by you,
Did they cease or arm the self untrue?
Were you smitten by a stirring charge?
Or overawed by words at large?
Was it a dreary journey?
Not value for your money?

Were you illumined by all the prattle?
Now know: there is no self to battle.
Did you experience the silence
Inherent in the mind's parlance?
Did you approach the end of 'me',
Into the vastness that is free?
Are you free from the dual run,
Or have you missed the pun?

FORGET: appears the formless alone
As the apparent and unknown.

FORGET: all the freedom's songs,
For none of them go along.

FORGET: there's nothing to transform or change,
As one, not two – the seeming range.

FORGET:the formless as form pretends
To have an origin and end.

FORGET: there's a being to be free,
Or there is no self, no 'me'.

FORGET: the self is an illusion
And not a real seclusion.

FORGET: this boundless transformation
Is being free from liberation.

FORGET: life – an appearance, as it is,
Without an intent, is just this.

FORGET: nothingness on its own,
Alone is the melodious tone.

FORGET: energetic rendezvous
Appears as each wave, every view.

FORGET: Oneness appears as two,
Complete in each and every view.

FORGET: illusion and enlightenment,
Amusing words for advertisement.

FORGET, life**:** real–unreal in play.

FORGET enlightenment, I pray.

Do not accept a word that's said,
FORGET it, let it be unread.

But if ceased has the dream of 'me',
A liberation where none is free,
There is no illusion too
Of self, in or not in view,
And this apparent liberation
Overflows with compassion;
REMEMBER: no concepts can ever bring
The end of ceaseless suffering.
The labyrinth of waves – the bait,
To cease the absent – stalemate.
A secret that appears, abounds,
But look for it and nothing's found,
For immeasurable and matchless
To all the riches, spiritual progress,
Is this. Life as it is.

Together, let's enjoy a cup of tea,
Or do you prefer coffee?
Boundless Transformation – is there one?

51

Notes

Note 01) Home

A. The monsoon season is crucial for the subsistence of India's agrarian economy and is welcomed by the people after the scorching months of summer. Its significance in the lives of the locals can be seen by its influence in Indian literature, music, art, and traditions. 'The Monsoon in Indian literature and folklore' – an article from the book *Not a Nice Man to Know – The Best of Khushwant Singh.* (Penguin, 1993) – aptly explains the relevance of monsoons in the Indian subcontinent.

B. The book *The Wonderful Wizard of Oz* is a children's classic by L.Frank Baum. In the story the protagonist Dorothy goes through constant change and encounters colourful characters through her journey – a fabulous read.

Note 02) The Unsaid Words

A. *Nirvana* implies liberation or freedom in Pali. There are many books which do justice to the non-dual interpretation of the Buddhist teachings, but I would recommend *Cutting Through Spiritual Materialism,* by Chögyam Trungpa (Shambhala Classics, 2002).

Note 03) A Dessert in the Desert

A. The compositions and writings of some Sufi philosophers seem profound, non-dualistic, and absolutely freeing in their approach. Their interpretation of words seems insightful as well. For instance, *Deen* implies an unshaken faith rather than belief, for belief is married to doubt, while faith is more intuitive. *Ilam,* on the other hand, means illumination. Books and works of and on the Sufis include:
• *The Bezels of Wisdom* by Ibn Arabi; see William Chittick's translation of Ibn Arabi's work (Paulist Press, 1980). • Abu Yazid's (Bayazid Bistami) profound utterances on *fana.* • *The Conference of Birds* by Farid ud-Din Attar of Nishapur (translated by Afkham Darbandi and Dick Davis; Penguin Classics, 1984). • Books on Junayd al Baghdadi (many of his quotes beautifully encompass the message of Oneness; one such quote on the self is 'The phenomenal, when it is merged in the eternal, vanishes and leaves no trace behind. When He is there, thou art not, and if thou are there, He is not'). • The poems of Rabia of Basra and Hafiz. • The books and translations of Rumi and the profound poetry of Baba Bulleh Shah (much of which is available online). • The poetry of Sheikh Farid Ganjeshakar and Sultan Bahu (*Chambe di butti)* in Punjabi is fascinating, and a translation of their work has been published by Sahitya Academy in India. • Reza Shah–Kazemi's comparative analysis in his book *Paths to Transcendence* (World Wisdom, 2006) is well researched.

Note 04) The Royal Duo

A. The mango – harvested in the summer – is considered the king of fruits in India. Though there are several varieties of mangos grown in different parts of the country, one of the most expensive varieties is the Alphonso, grown in Ratnagiri, Maharashtra. This reference is to the Alphonso, favoured by people across the world for its sweet distinctive taste.

B. *Syzygium cumini* is the Latin name for the *Jamun* fruit, which is also known as black plum, Java plum or *Jambolan*. The *Jamun* fruit, native to South and South-East Asia, is widely found in the Indian subcontinent and is harvested in the monsoon season. It is extensively used in Ayurvedic medicine for its healing properties and is traditionally recommended for the reduction of high blood-sugar levels.

Note 05) Merchandise

A. Several songs or hymns of Oneness are sung – in prescribed *ragas* – throughout the day at the Golden temple.

B. This is the translation of the *Mool Mantra*, the essence or main message of the *Guru Granth Sahib*. The *Guru Granth Sahib* is the main scripture of the Sikhs and is respected as the living Guru. The text contains the songs of Oneness by six Gurus, fifteen saints *(Bhagats),* and four devotees in *Gurmukhi* script, in several languages. During my research, and having read several translations of the *Japji* (the first song of Oneness recorded in the *Guru Granth Sahib*), I observed that three words – *Ongkaar*, *Sat*, and *Purakh* – had not been translated by their non-dual or root meanings. The etymological meaning of the words revealed the origin and the essence of the words. *Ongkaa*r is the energetic presence or energy that appears as form, for *Om* or *Ong* is not a word but is the all-pervasive sound of the energetic presence, which is not produced by friction. *Sat* comes from the root word *As* or *Asti*, which means that which is, or to be, occur, live and happen (albeit apparently). The word *Purakh* is generally understood to be a male deity, but as per the message of the Sikh Gurus, the divine is neither male nor female, nor separate from its appearance. According to their message, there is no split in creator and creation, for the formless alone appears or performs as all form yet is untouched by it. Moreover, the word *Purakh* comes from the word *Purusha,* which was later interpreted as cosmic man, but study indicates that it is a combination of two words *Pur* and *Ush*, wherein *Pur* implies the container, a city, or embracing presence while *Ush* comes from *Ushma* meaning light. *Purush*a also implies a city dweller. Hence, the word *Purakh* implies it is the embracing presence which appears as its light (which appears as all form). The two artworks in addition to the painting of the Golden temple are in Gurmukhi calligraphy. One is *Ek Omkaar* (One energetic presence) and the other is *Japji.*

C. The word used here is *Sach,* which is another way of saying *Sat*. The meaning of the word *Sat* is discussed in the above footnote. According to some Indian scriptures, there is only the timeless appearing as time – though some scriptures refer time as circular or infinite – which is evident in the previous lines of the *Mool Mantra* and in the 27th hymn of *Japji,* where Guru Nanak says 'it is, all appears in it, it cannot go or cease', so *Aad,* or beginning is referred to as a beginningless beginning, or timelessness appearing as time.

The word *Yug* or *Yuga* is from the word *Yugala,* which means a yoking or a pair. According to Indian philosophy, there are four *Yugas*: *Sat Yug* (beingness, that which is) also known as *Krata Yug* (done, accomplished), *Treta Yug* (the triad, the die marked with three), *Dwapar Yug* (the die marked by number two, doubt) and finally, *Kal Yug* (the die marked with one or the losing die, the worst of the ages) and each one of them is indicated by a pair or two lines. Guru Nanak explains the concept of *Yugas* lucidly by using the symbolism of the chariot and charioteer – in two couplets (*Slokas*) preceding *Pauri* (stanza) 13 – in a composition of the *Guru Granth Sahib* called *Asa di Vaar*. He sings that the golden mountain of our form is seemingly driven by an ever-changing chariot and charioteer. In *Sat Yug* the chariot of contentment or being, is driven by the charioteer of naturalness; in *Treta Yug* (where the dualistic lack deepens), the chariot of simplicity and detachment, is driven by power; in *Dwapar Yug* (the lack further increases) the chariot of austerity, or heat, is driven by beingness or happening; while *Kal Yug* (where the lack is at its worse), the chariot of passion, is driven by illusion. Many scholars believe that *Yugas* are a quantitative measurement of linear time, whereas an in-depth study reveals that *Yugas* are qualitative, too, in their appearance, relating to awareness, thoughts, feelings, acts, speech, behaviour, the appearing scene, and the apparent world. The meaning of the words *Treta yuga* (three) appearing before *Dwapar yuga* (two) also suggests they are qualitative rather than quantitative in their appearance. The *Vishnu Purana*, the *Vashista Yoga* (the two ancient scriptures) and the *Guru Granth Sahib,* also indicate or imply that *Yugas* are qualitative in their essence, seemingly overlap each other, and appear simultaneously. The concept of *Yugas* thus can be explained as an appearance of pairs within an apparent form and outside it, too, at the same time. By way of an analogy: one may feel all the *Yugas* at once on seeing a particular event, or one may speak in a contented (*Sat Yug)* fashion but may cater to the illusory self with worst intentions (*Kal Yug*), implying all the *Yugas* can appear simultaneously, at one given time. But further study reveals that *Yugas* are simply an appearance of pairs, or seeming duality appearing in this immediacy. Furthermore, as the macrocosm and microcosm are one, so there is no in and out; therefore, the *Yugas* may seem to appear as apparently quantitative and qualitative simultaneously, within an apparent form and outside it, too, but as all is one and simply an appearance, this makes

Yugas very difficult to describe. Thus, one energy appears as apparent pairs (*Yugas*) in totality, as this. However, Oneness appears as the pairs, embraces it, and yet it stays untouched by the inverses or pairs. This is impossible to understand for it is ineffable, indefinable, and unknowable. Finally, coming back to our original couplet of *Aad Sach Jugad Sach…*, the message is clear that there is only this, the appearing scene, and all that will apparently seem to occur will also be this; there is nothing beyond this. (The meanings of the words are taken from the *Sanskrit–English Dictionary*, by Monier Monier-Williams and the *The Nighantu and the Nirukta* by Lakshman Sarup (Motilal Banarsidass Publishers Private Limited, *First Indian edition*: 1920-27) while the meaning of the *Yugas*, from the Indian scriptures, was explained by Dr S.Shastry.)

D. The word *Guru* generally implies the light that disperses the dark or enlightenment that dissipates ignorance. *Guru* also implies that which elevates, for it comes from the root word *Gir*, which means elevated or raised, a mountain. Though there is no hierarchy, here it implies that *Guru* is the essence which may appear as any form or even as the formless to seemingly unravel the apparent ignorance or illusion of self and illuminate that the *Guru* and disciple are one. *Guru*, thus is the embodiment of freedom or energetic boundlessness.

E. Here I have translated the line *Gun eho hor nahi koi na koi hoya na koi hoye*, from the hymn *Aakhan jivan visre mar jau*, sung by Guru Nanak in *Raga Asa.* This whole hymn (*Shabad)* is sung daily in the Gurudwaras as a part of the evening prayer, the *Rehraas Sahib*. In this verse, I had initially included the entire translation of the hymn but later removed it on the advice of a colleague. Below I have included the translation of the entire hymn in which the above lines feature. If you want to read translations of other hymns from the *Guru Granth Sahib*, please refer to my blog https://wordpress.com/view/onenessinsikhism.wordpress.com.

This hymn is by Guru Nanak (*M:1*) from *Raga As*a, it is included in the *Sodar* cluster of hymns, a part of the *Rehraas Sahib,* the evening prayer.

"Speaking of life that does arise,
(Though) Its forgetfulness emergence of demise;
It is extremely difficult to say
Of this existence, that alone does stay,
Seeking, hunger, do arise
For this being, as that which seems to rise,
When sated is this emptiness,
Suffering no longer does press,
So, oh, mother of mine.
How can be forgotten the divine,
When it alone does shine?
Appears as this existent design;
To speak of this vastness
Is worth a seed, when expressed,
On its expression weariness may grow
But impossible to its boundlessness know;
If together (too) all about it say,
Yet it does not increase or decay,
It does not die nor is it grieved,
Ceaseless pleasures grants, does receive;
It does not die nor is mourned,
Grants unending abundance inborn,
All there is is the rising trait,
There is no one to advocate,
And there never was anyone,
Nor will there be a one,
Its appearance is as great
As is its presence innate;
As boundless is this presence,
Likewise, is this appearance,
Inverses it seems to create,
As night and day does animate,
Forgetting the beloved is to be outcast,
Oh' Nanak, being devoid of vastness – downcast.'

F. Herein I have given the translation of the lines *Sahas tav nain…* from Guru Nanak's song of Oneness, *Gagan main thal rav chand…. sahas tav nain nan nain haai soi...,* which is recorded in *Raga Dhansari.* This hymn is sung daily at the Golden temple in the evenings, and is referred to as the *Aarti.*

G. This is the translation of a couplet (*Sloaka)*, *Dukh daroo sukh rog bhaiya...,* from *Asa di Var* (a long composition), in the

Guru Granth Sahib.

H. The word *Rahau* is used in many of the hymns of the *Guru Granth Sahib*, which generally implies a pause to reflect and ponder; it is also considered to be the main theme of the composition *(Shabad)* and an indication for the musicians to repeat the verse while singing the hymn.

Note 06) Hail Energy

A. The mention of the six friends is a reference to the six demons, or *Asuras,* mentioned in the stories of goddesses *Durga* and *Kali* from the *Puranas* (ancient Indian allegorical scriptures). *Asuras* literally translated mean aspects that delight in evil, but on a deeper study it further implies sunless, ignorant, and exhalation of breath, or aspects that disappear or are expelled on apparent liberation. The goddess is the symbolic representation of energy that appears as form. The six *Asuras,* or demons, mentioned in varied stories are *Raktabeej* – endless wishes; *Dhumralochan* – foggy or illusory perception; *Chand–Mund* – lust and violence or lustful violence; *Mahishasur* – darkness, inertia or ignorance; *Shumbh–Nishumbh* – to kill and trample.

A close rendering of the stories of *Durga* makes it amply clear that the stories are symbolic and a reference to energy in myriad garbs. Moreover, *Durg* implies a fort or boundaries and *Durga* that which breaks the boundaries. This verse, though inspired and based on the tales of *Durga, Chandi*, and *Kali,* is not a translation of any of the above-mentioned texts.

Note 07) The Shocking Tail

A. A *koan* is an unsolvable puzzle or riddle used in Zen Buddhism to portray the paradoxical aspect of life, Oneness, or non-duality. In ancient monasteries of Japan, the disciples usually pondered on these paradoxical *koans*, which do not seem to have any logical understanding, solution, or explanation.

B. In this story the two *koans* are not a translation of *koans* from the Zen classics but are simply an appearance of creativity. Years ago, I read translations of *The Two Zen Classics*: *The Gateless Gate and The Blue Cliff Records* (translated by Katsuki Sekida; Shambhala, 2005), loved them, and were inspired by them. Food philosophy in Japan is based on its seasonal and geographical features. By tradition, the Japanese lay a lot of reverence to serving and eating food in an aesthetic and graceful manner; the advent of Buddhism further augmented this emphasis, as it lays value on eating, drinking, and serving in an aware and conscious manner. The Japanese consider every aspect of nature to be divine, hence in their cuisine food is referred to as delights, treasures, bounty or fortunes of the seas and the fortune of the mountains (*Umi no sachi, yama no sachi)*.

C. The *enso* is the calligraphic representation of enlightenment in Zen. The calligraphic painting in this poem is a Japanese expression, *seijaku wo kiku:* listen to the sound of snow/silence. It was suggested by Misorez, whom I met at Tony Parsons' retreat in Wales.

Note 08) The Unknown stone

A. Namdev, a popular Indian saint from the western state of Maharashtra, is believed to have lived from 1270 to1350. His songs of Oneness are recorded in Sant Bhasha, Hindi, and Marathi languages in the work *Namdevchi Gatha,* and in the Sikh scripture the *Guru Granth Sahib*. The song recorded here contains the translation and the essence of the hymn from Namdev's *Gatha*, as preserved in the oral tradition. For my translation, I have referred to the Hindi version of the *pad/ abhanga* from the book *The Hindi Padavali of Namdev,* by Winand Callewaert and Mukund Lath (Motilal Banarsidass, 1989, pp. 286–7). A similar hymn is recorded in *Raga Asa* in the *Guru Granth Sahib*. Though a major part of the hymn and its essence are the same in both the versions, there are some differences in the words. Moreover, this hymn is found in many Rajasthani manuscripts; again, in each manuscript there are differences in the words used, as most of the hymns of the saints were preserved by oral tradition and later recorded in print.

B. Here Namdev uses the word *Vithal* (another name for the Hindu god *Vishnu*), the name of the deity worshipped in Pandharpur, Maharashtra, India. The study of the origin of the word indicates that it is a combination of *Vis* and *sthal* (locals pronounce '*sh*' as '*th*'). The word *Vis* means to pervade, and *Sthal* to stand firmly, or the act of standing, being fixed or stationary (Greek *stello,* German *stellen*, English *still,* Sanskrit *sthala*), though the word *Sthal* also implies a remote place – a place at a distance. Here it implies that the all-pervading essence is firm.

C. The word used here is *kshero*. In India, there are two types of offerings to the deity known as *kshero*. In some regions of India, it is known as *kheer* – a traditional sweet dish made from rice, milk, and jaggery/sugar – while in the other regions *kshero, or ksheera,* is made from semolina, water, and jaggery/sugar. Here the reference is to *kheer*.

D. Here, Namdev, the author, refers to himself in the third person. This was a common tradition followed by the poets belonging to the Bhakti tradition in India, and it is found in the poetic tradition of the subcontinent even today.

Note 09) The Seeking Lion

A. This concept has been explained systematically and clearly by biologists Douglas J. Futuyma and Mark Kirkpatrick in their book *Evolution* (Sinauer Associates Inc., 2017, p. 57).

Note 10) Big Bang

A. It was physicist Leon Lederman who gave the Higgs Boson the nickname the God particle; most other scientists do not seem to be fond of it. Physicists at CERN's Large Hadron Collider in Geneva announced in 2012 that they had each observed a new particle, but it was in 2013 that the discovery was confirmed. In October 2013, the Nobel Prize in Physics was awarded jointly to François Englert and Peter Higgs for the discovery of the Higgs Boson.

B. This phrase can also be found in many scriptures and modern songs of freedom. A reference to floating fluidity is found in the *Guru Granth Sahib*: *Arbad narbad dhundukara…* in *Raga Maru* (p.103); and in the *Nasadiya Sukta*, a hymn from the *Rig Veda* (book 10, hymn 129). In the later Hindu scriptures, *Vishnu*, also known as *Narayan* (the path of the waters), seems to be the symbolic representation of floating fluidity.

C. This is well explained by Tony Parsons in his regular monthly meetings. He always states this point with the example that when someone asks us for a cup of tea or coffee, the response is already taken by the brain, but the self later claims 'I would love a cup of tea or coffee' and justifies doing so. Chapters from two books – *Free Will,* by Sam Harris, and *Incognito,* by David Eagleman, also explain this concept well; and an article in the magazine *New Scientist* by Sofia Delniv lucidly explains the concept in detail (on 5th September 2018). In this article, the researcher cites several studies and suggests: 'Perhaps self-awareness isn't even a simulation but a hall of mirrors.'

Note 11) The Timeless Song

A. This verse is based on the six seasons of the year in the Indian calendar. The ancient Indian seers divided the Indian climate into six seasons, instead of the general categorisation of four seasons. Their classification of seasons took account of the slightest variance in temperature, the relevant flora and fauna, and the migratory patterns of birds. Though the subtle seasonal division and difference of the winter is prevalent only in the northern part of India, as the southern part of India has fewer seasons, the seasonal songs composed by poets and locals are celebrated across India in the folklore tradition. In antiquity it was a common poetic practice in India to depict the twelve months (*Barahmasa*) and the six seasons (*Rtu varnana*) in literature and folklore. The most famous is the *Ritusamhara*, by Sanskrit poet Kalidasa. However, the seasonal depiction of the epics and the regional verses seem more popular with the locals across different regions of India. Women in the villages and small towns of India still sing these seasonal songs at the festivals associated with the seasons.

The metaphor of the bride and the beloved has been prevalent in India since ancient times. The traditional songs are based on the bride pining for her beloved when he is far away in a foreign land. So, *Barahmasa* or *Rtu varnana* songs, though widespread across India, were more popular in the states of Punjab, Rajasthan, Bengal, Gujrat, Himachal and Maharashtra, where it was more likely for men in ancient times to go to foreign lands for trade.

The spiritual texts also adopted the format of the bride pining for her beloved through the twelve months of the year, although in their context the bride implies the sense of self or the seeming soul, which pines for the beloved – the divine. We find exemplars of such poetry in several scriptural texts. The most popular ones, in no specific order, are:

1. *Geet Govinda*, a poem composed by Jaidev, from Odisha, in the twelfth century. In this beautiful poem of unrequited love, of recurrent separation and blissful reunions, Radha and Krishna are metaphorical representations of the bride and the beloved.
2. The account of Rajul, who pines for Lord Neminath, is from the Jain texts.
3. There are verses in the *Guru Granth Sahib* that sing of the six seasons and twelve months of the year in the context of the bride (seeming self) pining for the beloved (the Oneness). One such composition is known as *Rutti* by Guru Arjan in *Raga Ramkali*. The other two are the *Barahmaha* of Guru Nanak in *Raga Tukhari* and of Guru Arjan in *Raga Majh.* All of them are exemplary compositions highlighting the seasons and the seeking aspect.

Some of the above-mentioned verses emphatically state that one energetic presence alone appears as the illusion of the separate self, and then longs to merge in the divine, while others believe that the self is separate and suffers its split from the divine. In actuality, the self is not a separate entity that suffers separation from divinity, but it is the very act of seeking, or is an appearance of separation. To be precise, it is an illusion of separation by life itself. Nonetheless, in the appearance, the self seems to be separate from life and suffers being split from divinity and then endeavours to unite, to become complete or one with the whole. However, all acts of seeking or suffering is the energetic presence alone appearing as that act or energy pretending to be split from itself.

The song in this book is neither a translation of any of the verses from the Sikh, Sufi, or Jain texts, nor of any song from Indian literature or folklore. Though written in similar style to the traditional hymns and songs, it is a poetic expression that has flowed from the depths of being, the formless or one source (call it what you may). This verse refers to the apparent seeking energy as the bride and states that this seeking is simply the illustration of the beloved alone and not separate from it. The depictions of the seasons and their foods are based on the memories of my experiences in India, along with research in relevant books and traditional sources. I would like to take this opportunity to thank Mr. Sreenivas Rao for his well researched blog http://sreenivasaraos.com. Charlotte Vaudeville's book *Barahmasa in Indian Literatures* (Motilal Banarsidass, 1986) is a fantastic read.

There are many famous literary stories of unrequited love in the Indian tradition, like *Heer-Ranjha*, *Sassi-Punnu*, *Laila-Majnu* and *Mirabai-Krishna*. The unrequited love mentioned in these stories resonates with the condition of the separate self. These accounts show that the apparent small self or soul, even if it is madly in love or becomes detached, cannot merge with the divine or one. For the small self is the appearance of the one and not separate from it. Though the love or romance portrayed in some of these stories is of desires and wants, the underlying issue of falling in love is similar to the message that there is a being in love with everything or there is simply love.

B. There are many species of cuckoo on the Indian continent. The two most widely known species are the Asian *Koel* and the common hawk-cuckoo known as the *Papiha, Babiha,* or the brain-fever bird. Here, the reference is to the brain-fever bird, which is known for its repetitive piercing cry. In Indian folklore and poetry, its cry is associated with it missing its beloved, while its song is interpreted as *Piyan kahan* (in Hindi) – 'Where is my beloved'. The translation and meaning of its song varies in the regional languages of the subcontinent.

C. The Latin name of the *Palash* tree is *Butea monosperma.* It is a deciduous tree found across the Indian subcontinent. The *Palash* tree and its flowers are known by varied names in the local regions of India. Common names for the tree are Bastard Teak, Flame of the Forest, Parrot Tree, and *Dhak,* to name just a few. The flowers are a bright flame orange and are used to make colour for the festival of *Holi*. The tree has other cultural connotations and is referred to in several literary works.

D. Here, the delights refer to the variety of sweet and savoury treats, such as *Malpua, Gujjiyas, Dahi Vada, Shaakarpare, Thandai, and Puran Poli,* which are made all over India in spring.

E. Jaggery is commonly known as *Gud* in India. It is a concentrated product made from raw sugarcane juice or date palm. The former is preferred by the locals. Its colour varies from golden brown to dark brown, and it is used in several Indian desserts and savouries.

F. Mangos are eaten in their ripe and raw form. The raw mangoes are used to make pickles, drinks, and savoury dishes. The ripe ones are eaten on their own or used in desserts. Different varieties of mango are available in different regions of India, such as the *Alphonso, Kesar, Dussheri* and *Langda.*

G. All three items mentioned are traditional Indian sweets. *Laddus* are a ball-shaped traditional Indian sweet made from *ghee,* sugar, and various types of flour, or from jaggery with seeds and nuts. *Barfis* are sweets prepared with milk or *khoya* or nuts and at times flour is added to them. They are generally flavoured with nuts, cardamom, saffron, or varied other ingredients and are traditionally cut in squares or triangles. *Halwa* is a dense sweet confectionary made of different types of flour, carrots, or other vegetables. Most of them are decorated with edible silver or contain nuts, and they are prepared during festivals or special occasions.

H. *Kahwa* is a traditional green tea relished in Kashmir and the northern parts of India, Pakistan, and Afghanistan. It is made by boiling green tea leaves, though many locals add saffron strands, cardamom pods, cinnamon bark, and Kashmiri rose. It is normally drunk with *Sheermal* (saffron-flavoured flatbread) by the Kashmiris.

I. Here, virginal being implies the vast self or presence in which any appearance can appear, yet which is untouched by all its appearances. It is when the illusion of apparent sense of self or seeking seemingly disappears and the self is not present to take charge of that which appears, or there is no sense of doership; then all that remains is the untouched virginal vastness or formlessness in which anything and everything seems to appear.

Note 12) The Holy City

A. Kabir is a legendary Indian saint, who coherently spoke of Oneness of form and formlessness and challenged many rituals and traditions. There is a famous story relating to his death. According to ancient belief, a person who dies in Benaras goes to heaven or is released from the clutches of transmigration, while people who die in the nearby town of Maghar are reborn as donkeys. A few months before his death, Kabir moved to Maghar – where he died – to prove the point that no place, or state, or endeavour is more or less spiritual. In a hymn, he even stated that he was free from all dual concepts of heaven and hell. He also proclaimed that the veil of the separate self is lost in the illusion of apparent stories; however, one absolute alone appears as the relative, be it is as illumination or ignorance.

B. Here, the reference is to the three *Gunas*, or attributes, mentioned in many Indian scriptures and in the *Bhagvad Gita*. According to the scriptures, this existence or appearance is an interplay of the three *Gunas – Sattva,* or purity; *Rajas,* or royal; and *Tamas,* or lethargy – in a varied range of shades and tints.

Note 13) The Pathless Trail

A. This poem is not a translation or rendition of any work but has been inspired by the *Tao Te Ching,* by Lao-Tzu, which has many profound non-dual expressions.

Note 14) The Creative Cut

A. To decipher the meaning of Oneness, creator, creativity, creation, and illusion, it is important to know the meaning of three Sanskrit words: *Brahmaan*, *Braham*, and *Brahma.* There are several meanings of *Brahmaan,*which is used differently in each context. For instance, in some contexts it is deciphered as the formless appearing as form, which is neither born nor dies and neither creates nor is created. It is also known as the ineffable mystery or the energetic presence. Other meanings imply growth, expansion, impersonal universal spirit or soul, or sacred word, to name just a few. Here, in this verse the reference is to the word *Braham,* which means to wander or to seek the one that appears, and yet is not split in its seeking, so is not a separate entity. It also implies that it is the creativity that appears as the form and the illusion of a separate self. The word *Brahma* refers to the creator God of the Hindu trinity; however, it is evident that Gods are not individual entities with real stories, but simply symbolic representations or pointers – with apparent narratives – described in anthropomorphic terms. In the story of *Brahma* (the suggested creator), it is clear that there is no separate creator as is generally understood, but is apparent creativity in appearance. *Brahma's* consort is *Saraswati* (the one that appears as the sound, speech, art, recognition, to name just a few), which makes forms appear, as it is. In a well-known story, *Brahma* sires her – implying that speech would not be possible without creativity – and then chases her, implying that the attributes or instruments of speech, art and knowing, are used to create more form. This narrative suggests the self-sustaining attribute of this appearance, which constantly claims more and appears to be in creative mode. As Nanak states in *Japji,* 'None can know the end of this expanse, the more that is said the more comes to being'; for there aren't any solid static small forms in existence, only the formless or nothingness expressing itself as form and apparently seeming to appear as creativity, sustenance, and transformation, yet which is not affected by them. Here, floating fluidity is the pulsating, constantly changing and ever new aspect of this appearance, implying that nothing is solid or static. Finally, the illusory capability of seeming separation is referred to as *Maya* in many scriptures.

B. This seems to be the symbolic meaning of the allegorical Hindu story of trinity, wherein the creator (*Brahma*) falls in love with its apparent created manifestation and believes it has created this existence and owns it. It seems to imply that the illusory self believes that it is the doer, performer, or actor of the appearing act (which is ignorance). Hence, in one story from the Hindu texts, *Brahma's* fifth wandering head – which owns and chases the appearing creation – is cut by *Shiva* , later known as *Mahadev (*the illusory destroying presence, or the third God in the Hindu trinity, as per the story). The meaning of *Siva,* or *Shiva,* comes from the same root as *Sewa,* implying happiness, joy, and auspiciousness. It also means 'that in which all does lie' and implies the recognition (by none) that the form and formless are one; or formlessness appears as the form it longs to be. *Shiva* is also shown as half-masculine and half-feminine or nothing and energy – *ShivShakti* as one. *Shiva* is also the symbolic representation of the human form, as the human form is the minute representation of this entire appearance.(However, this is simply a non-dualistic translation or rendition of symbols or the allegories; one can interpret the scriptures as one wishes. No interpretation is right or wrong, nor is it ultimate, for no meaning is significant, as all is Oneness appearing as that expression.)

C. The parable of the vineyard workers from the Bible (New Testament, Matthew 20:1–16) seems to illustrate the irrelevance of the *karmic* theory.

D.

- A quote from the Heart Sutra (Buddhist text) states, though not in these exact words, 'Form is emptiness, emptiness is form (*sunyata*).'

- A hymn of Guru Nanak recorded in *Raga Asa* in the *Guru Granth Sahib* illustrates '*Gun eho hor nahi koi na ko hoya na ko hoye*' (the trait alone appears; there was none in existence nor shall one exist).

- In the Bhagvad Gita Chapter 3 (3.27), Krishna states: 'All the works are being performed by the traits of nature, but by the delusion of the ego, the act is attributed to the self.'

- In the Quran, *Surah Ya-Sin* – 36, especially verses (*Aya*h) 32–7, 41–7, 71–5, and 77–83 seem to illustrate this in a profound manner, especially the words *Kun (*Be) and *Kun Fayakoon* (Be and it is). This message and many of the symbolisms seem intuitive on the apparent unravelling of the veil of separation. There are other verses which point to the omnipresence of the One, like 2:255 and 24:35, the *Sura*h – 67 (Control or Sovereignty), and *Surah* – 112 (Purity of Faith). All of these make it clear that Oneness is infinite, ineffable, unknowable and that it alone has full sovereignty of the form and yet is untouched by its appearance and can never be known. (For the references,

I have listened to the Quran in Arabic, interacted with a few experts, and referred to translations by M.A.S Abdal Haleem and Muhammad Marmaduke Pickthall).

Note 15) Theatrical Delight

A. Here, the reference is to Sherlock Holmes, the fictitious character created by Sir Arthur Conan Doyle.

Note 16) The Wholesome Split

A. Here I have translated the hymn *Jao tum girvar tao hum mora ...* of Bhagat Ravidas, from the *Guru Granth Sahib*. It is recorded in *Raga Sorath* (p. 658). Ravidas, a saint from northern India, is known to have belonged to the Bhakti tradition. Though his exact date of birth is not known, he is known to have lived in the late fifteenth and early sixteenth centuries. His local works, such as *Panchvani,* are prevalent as folklore and some are recorded in the *Guru Granth Sahib*.

B. The Chukar partridge, known as the *Chakor* in Sanskrit, is found in the Middle East and South Asia. The bird is a symbol of unrequited love in South Asian folklore and literature; the legend is that it is in love with the moon and stares at it all night. Other legends believe it is a mythological creature that lives on moonbeams.

C. In many of the hymns of the *Guru Granth Sahib*, the word *Rahau* is used after a stanza or a line. Its meaning is given in the footnotes of the verse 'Merchandise'.

D. Here, the word 'I' seems to be the generic self and not a reference to the poet Ravidas, while the word *Jati* literally translated implies the generic properties of a species. It originates from the word *Jat,* which means 'to be born, to come into existence or become apparent' (*Sanskrit–English Dictionary*, Monier Monier-Williams.), though in Hinduism, *Jati* has come to be understood as the caste system, which has a defined hierarchy, and only certain castes are allowed in some of the pilgrimage centres. Ravidas compares this system to the formlessness and its appearance (the illusory self). He states that if the formless is the pilgrimage centre, then the self or the 'I' is akin to the *Jati* – the basic yardstick or measurement which believes it can attain the formless and therefore creates levels to attain it, not realising that it is an illusion which keeps itself intact by adding to its existence. *An introduction to Hinduism* by Gavin Flood succinctly explains the *Jati* system.(Cambridge University Press, 1996, pp. 58–61).

Note 17) The Creation's Story

A. This is the translation of the line *Aaḏ kao bismaaḏ beecẖaar kathiyale sunn niranṯar vaas leeya*, by Guru Nanak, from the composition *Sidh Ghost*. This composition is a dialogue between the Yogis and Guru Nanak on Oneness, recorded in the *Guru Granth Sahib* (p. 940).

B. The reference here is to the *Nasadiya Sukta*, a hymn from the *Rig Veda (*book 10, hymn 129), and in this account, I have given a summary of it. The poet poses a question about the creation, but then goes on to reveal the wonder of nothingness or formlessness illuminating as form, and finally ends it with that fact that it is unknowable. In the *Nasadiya Sukta* the waters indiscriminate seem to imply the floating fluidity or the vibrating, pulsating aspect of this appearance, suggesting that nothing is solid or static. And the last line of the verse, 'He surely knows or maybe He does not', makes it evident that this is unknowable. A few Indian scriptures are clear that there is no concept of time, but many poems from the ancient times were written in an obscure fashion, so to decipher them is challenging, also because the meanings of word have changed. It was the later texts, like a few *Upanishads* and *Vasishta Yoga*, that lucidly explained the concept of time, of it being non-existent or simply being an appearance of timelessness. Some of these texts go on to say that it is non existent yet seems to appear in a cyclic manner (an example given in the *Vasistha Yoga,* verse 1:27 compares time to a potter's wheel; and in verse 3:61, 'The infinite consciousness held in itself the notion of the unit of time equal to one millionth of the twinkling of an eye: and from the this evolved the time scale right to an epoch… The infinite consciousness itself is uninvolved in these for it is devoid of rising and setting (which are essential to all time scales) and it is devoid of beginning, middle and end.'

C. Dattatreya was an Indian saint. He is revered by the *Siddhas* (a sect of Yogis), and his *Avadhut Gita* is a masterpiece on non-duality.

D. Here, I have translated the verse *Yadi saarvisarvihhin iti...* (chapter 6, verse 6) from Dattatreya's *Avadhut Gita.*

E. Here, the reference is to the story of the churning of the ocean (*Amrit Manthan)* from the Hindu scriptures. On reading many scriptures, it seems obvious that some allegories were used to describe liberation or the appearing phenomena, which were later endowed with anthropomorphic qualities and termed as real stories with real Gods. If the stories are read by the etymological meaning of their words and the symbolism of the concept, then the interpretation implies that the macrocosm and microcosm are one. And the churning of the ocean is symbolic of the churning of the apparent illusion, to unravel that which is. The root meaning of some of the symbols is as follows. *Vishnu* is the impenetrable presence or the all-pervasive essence that appears as this appearance. *Narayan* translated as the path of waters, also refers to the energetic, pulsating, constantly changing and ever new aspect of form. *Lakshmi* is auspiciousness or riches of the appearance of form. *Shiva, or Siva,* has several meanings, such as auspiciousness, delight, joy and formless forming. It is also known as *Shiv* and *Shakti* (nothing and energy) at one and the same time – where energy is the appearing form of *Shiva* – or nothing being everything,. It also means the embracing presence in which all forms (seen and unseen) lie, and yet it alone appears as all the forms it longs to be. In later times *Shiva* was known as *Mahadev,* the third God of the Hindu trinity with *Parvati* as his consort, and *Skanda* and *Ganesh* as their sons, the latter meaning to count, implying value, and the former meaning the force to battle illusions. *Asur* (the demons) comes from the word *Asuh* (to throw, expel, or sunless, or to delight in evil), which is also a synonym of exhalation of breath. *Suran* (the gods) seem to be the elements in the form that make form appear and also a synonym for inhalation of breath. *Dev* means to shine implying that which shines in this play of light. *Ratna* (the jewels) are the auspicious qualities, herbs. Finally, the *Riddhis* and *Siddhis* are the qualities or powers or wish-fulfilling objects that appear on the churning of the ocean. The poison in the narrative seems to be the illusion of self which leads to suffering.

Now, if you read the allegories in this light, it is evident they highlight the illusory self or are a representation of the churning of an apparent illusion, to see the real. The *Amrit,* or the elixir of immortality, is the illumination (for no one) that immortality alone is, and that there is no birth and death, while the self is not a small entity but an illusory expression of Oneness; thus, the self can never acquire immortality, for immortality exists. I personally feel the concept of *Amrit Manthan,* or churning of the semblance of illusion, has parallels in many scriptures, albeit in a different manner. Thus, if read in this light, it is clear how the illusion of the self loves to conceptualise everything. Nonetheless, I feel most stories are dualistic in their approach, for there is no one existent to be liberated, as all is energy appearing as that form or all is formless forming.

Note 18) An Apparent Pilgrimage

A. *Ramayana* is an ancient Indian epic. A prince called *Rama* is prevented from becoming the rightful king of Ayodhya – an ancient Indian kingdom in the north of India – by family intrigue. He is exiled to the forests for fourteen years, accompanied by his wife, *Sita*, and brother *Lakshmana*. During the exile, *Rama's* wife is kidnapped by the erudite *Ravana*, the king of Lanka, and the whole story revolves around *Rama's* endeavour to release *Sita* from the clutches of the Lankan king. *Rama* is helped by several characters, the chief being *Hanuman*, who is considered an epitome of intelligence and devotion, and *Ravana's* younger brother *Vibhishan,* who defects to *Rama's* side and divulges many secrets that are the key to success in *Rama's* attack on Lanka. After an epic war, which results in the death of *Ravana*, *Rama* unites with *Sita*. The homecoming of *Rama* to his kingdom is celebrated as *Diwali* by many Hindus.

There are several versions of this story across India, with different depictions, endings, and later interpolations indicating its aliveness and local influence. The two popular versions are the original, by Sage Valmiki, and a later version by Goswami Tulsidas. Many believers feel that this story is an inner trajectory from ignorance to enlightenment, while others believe *Rama* was the incarnation of *Vishnu* – one of the main gods of the Hindu trinity – who came to earth to destroy evil. An etymological study of the word *Rama* shows it implies dark, giving delight, pleasing, to stop, to emit light, all pervasive presence, or 'causing rest', or rest that radiates as form or light, while *Sita* means the radiant light or form, a furrow or a line of a ploughshare, or the radiant goddess of agriculture or food. *Lakshmana* implies one with auspicious marks and to view, or witness, while *Vibhishan* means to abort. *Ravana* means sounding or crying, and his other name, *Dashanana,* implies to have ten heads. *Ramayana,* which literally means the path of *Rama*, seems to signify the appearance of Oneness.

Note 19) The Undying Death

A. This statement is in several spiritual texts, though it varies. In the *Guru Granth Sahib*, Guru Arjan elucidates that 'Nothing is born, and nothing does die' *(Sukhmani Sahib*). In the *Avadhut Gita,* Dattatreya says, 'I was not born, nor will I die.' Similar messages are found in the *Bhagvad Gita* (where Krishna reiterates the soul is free from birth and decay) and the *Katha Upanishad.* The texts use different words, such as self, nothingness, energy, or formless, to illustrate the one that is indestructible and yet appears as all is its appearance. Moreover, similar echoes are found in the other scriptures. Eating the apple, in the Bible, is the acquisition of knowledge, or the illusion of individual existence, while the Garden of Eden is the existence of immortality. Therefore, the illusion that there is birth and death comes from the apparent eating of the apple of knowledge, which is the seeming separation of existence; however, there is no separation.

Note 20) The Milky Way

A. A similar reference is found in the *Guru Granth Sahib*, p. 617, wherein Guru Arjan reveals that 'Inherently all vegetation has fire, and all milk has ghee in it; similarly, every being seemingly high or low, has the divine light, for the Master pervades the body of every living creature.' Similar references are found in the Hindu scriptures (both the references were brought to my notice by a friend).

B. Here, the reference is to the word soul, *Atman*, and cosmic soul, *Paramatma*, as mentioned in Eastern scriptures. *Aatman* is normally translated as the self or soul. However, it does not seem to imply the small or vast self, as is generally understood. It seems to be derived from the root *Aa,* which means to or towards; *An,* which is to breathe and *At* means to move or to go and *Va* to blow, and *Aap* to obtain. *Aatman* is also known as the principle of life or the energetic presence, which is already obtained, existent and omnipresent.

C. This seems to be the essence or rendition (not the exact translation) of verses 5,6,7 and 8 of Chapter 4 of the *Bhagvad Gita,* wherein Krishna says to Arjun that you and I have been born several times. In the context of these verses, it appears, as *Rishi Vyas* implies, that Krishna refers to the 'self' as the formless forming appearing as 'me' and 'you' and not Krishna and Arjun appearing as a small form. The self not being confined to a form is also evident in the Chapter 11 and 15 of the *Bhagvad Gita*. Furthermore, if one reads the *Mahabharata*, *Gita,* and *Bhagvata Purana* in combination, this message seems obvious. In these verses, it appears that the formless alone appears as form and as the illusion of separation of self and the other. However, if the teachings appear dualistic to the reader, then that is what is appearing, and no one has or can give an authoritative explanation for any scripture, or for life itself.

D. I have given the essence of verses 5,6,7 and 8 of Chapter 4 of the *Bhagvad Gita.*

'The self, is the formless forming,
At once – untouched, yet performing –
Alone – appearing as the 'me' and 'you',
Which seems to be in birth, anew,
(Though seems self-sustaining in its hue,
But is one appearing as two);
And when (it's) forgotten that performs
One alone. It rises as freedom's form,
To remind itself: life as it is (the natural norm),
Destroy the illusory bits,
But one alone does appear,
Untouched, yet as seeming pairs.'

The *Gita* also refers to the apparent illusion of the self – the 'me' and 'you' as self-sustaining in its hue. But when one reads verse 6 it immediately illustrates that the eternal, immutable formless alone appears as forms and as the illusory dress. The word *Yuga* has been used in this verse, and for an in-depth meaning of the word, please refer to footnote C in the verse 'Merchandise'.

A point worth mentioning is that the meaning of some words changes with time and situations. To give an example, the word *Dharma* initially meant firm, to uphold, naturalness or natural appearance, that which is as it is, or the natural order which is inherent for this appearance, or natural norm of each appearance (like lemon being sour or sugarcane sweet, or the *Dharma* of the fire being to burn and that of wind to blow). In the later times, several other meanings were attached to this word, one of them being righteous living or religious way.
A final point about the translation of the texts is that most songs of non-duality or emanating from the formless describe the same differently. However, many of them deem themselves to be *Param Idam* – the best that is, or last to come, for they emanate from nothingness or the immaculate source.

E. The scriptural symbolisms are interpreted very literally by many, who believe heaven and hell to be physical places in the skies above or below. On the apparent disappearance of the veil of separation, it is evident that the imageries are used to point at that which appears. For instance, peace and fulfilment are the paradise that always is, while the frantic seeking of this paradise or duality is to burn in the hells of suffering and separation.

Note 21) The Last Laugh

A. *Vada-Pao,* or *Vada-Pav,* is a popular snack and street food of Mumbai. Boiled and spiced potatoes are deep fried with a covering of gram flour batter and served with *Pav,* chutney, and green chilies.

B. *Moksha* and *Nirvana* are the Indian words for liberation, enlightenment, freedom, or salvation.

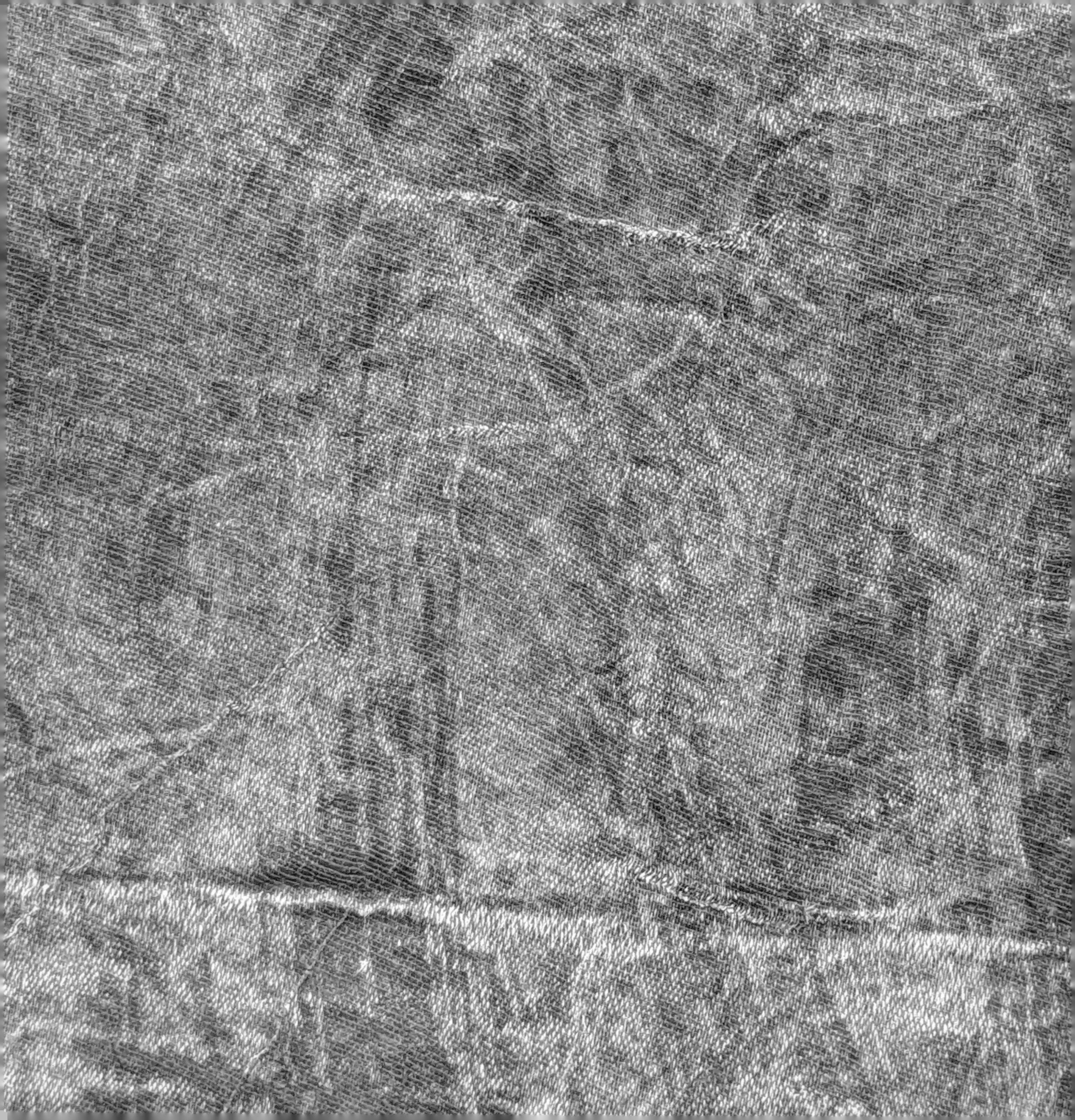

List of the artworks & illustrations

Artwork by Rehraas:

1. Camaraderie – The colourful corn is in clay on a vase.

Artwork by Sumaera:

1. The Unsaid Words – The mountain is in acrylics.

Artworks made by Sumita:

1. The Unending War – The onions are in watercolour on onion paper.
2. Chromatic – The lobster is in oil colours.
3. Metamorphosis –

   a) The lamb landscape is in wet felt, needle felt, and stitch.

   b) The lamb with bow and arrow is in appliqué, felt, machine quilt, and hand embroidery on hand-dyed cotton fabric.
4. The Rebelling Shadow – The crochet honeybee blanket is in acrylic yarn and amigurumi crochet toys.
5. An Apparent Pilgrimage – The custard apple is hand embroidery with watercolour on watercolour paper.
6. The Non-dual Election –

   a) The blackhole is in hand-embroidered in silk thread on hand-painted Lutradur.

   b) One of the eggs is in crochet.

Artworks by Darpana:

1. Ingress – Egress – Acrylic and ink on cartridge paper.
2. The Enlightened Tea –

   a) Watercolour and colour pencil on handmade cornflower paper (Lokta paper) from Nepal.

   b) Watercolour on handmade paper.
3. A Perfect Shape – Watercolour on handmade khadi (rag) paper.
4. Home –

   a) The aeroplane is in watercolour and pencil on water colour paper.

   b) The parrots are in acrylics, ink, and liquid gold on canvas.
5. Camaraderie –

   a) The bird is in acrylics and ink on linen canvas.

   b) The corn is in colour pencil on board.
6. The Unending War –

   a) The salt mill is in watercolour and ink on onion paper.

   b) The other is in watercolour on black card paper.
7. Frangipane Art –

   a) The feast of Epiphany is in acrylic, ink, and liquid gold on canvas.

   b) The spider and fly is in colour pencil on handmade paper.
8. The Leaning Pizza – The pizza is in acrylics and colour pencil on mixed media paper.
9. The Unsaid Words –

   a) All characters and flora and fauna is in watercolour on watercolour paper.

   b) Adult bamboo in colour pencil and liquid gold on Himalayan bamboo paper.
10. The Royal Duo – The characters are in watercolour

and gold ink on handmade *khadi* paper.

11. Merchandise –

a) The Golden Temple is in acrylics, ink, and liquid gold on canvas.

b) *Ek Ongkaar* calligraphy – gilding with pure shell gold.

c) *Japji* calligraphy – colour pencil on handmade fern paper.

12. Cook Create Compose –

Cook is in colour pencil and gold ink on *khad*i bougainvillea paper.

Create is in colour pencil and gold ink on handmade fern paper.

Compose is in colour pencil and gold ink on Himalayan bamboo paper.

13. Hail Energy – The apple is in pencil on handmade *khadi* paper.

14. Love's Salad –

a) The nun is in pen and liquid gold on cold-pressed paper.

b) Hand painted silk scarf.

15. The Shocking Tail –

a) The salmon, prawn and seaweed are in soft pastel on Japanese watercolour paper.

b) The calligraphy (*seijaku wo kiku*: listen to the sound of snow/silence) is on Himalayan bamboo paper.

16. The Unfulfilled Croissant –

a) The baguette is in watercolour on watercolour paper.

b) The croissant is in watercolour, gouache, ink, and pencil on rice paper.

c) The recipe is in calligraphy on handmade paper.

17. Comparative Culture – The banana, grape, fig, orange, and frozen yogurt are made in mixed media: acrylics, oil, fabric (tissue), and banana paper collage on canvas.

18. Iced Melody – Mixed media: watercolour, pastel, and acrylic paint on music paper.

19. The Unknown Stone –

a) The nut is in colour pencil on pastel paper.

b) The pear singing is in colour pencil and ink on cartridge paper.

20. The Seeking Lion – Soft pastel on handmade *khadi* paper.

21. Big Bang – Watercolour on watercolour paper.

22. The Timeless Song – Miniature-style painting is in shell gold, colour pigments, and watercolour, on handmade paper from Jaipur, India.

23. Chicken's Story – Water colour on *khadi* paper.

24. Neighbours – Watercolour and ink on handmade *khadi* paper with bougainvillea flowers.

25. The Holy City – Water colour on handmade *khadi* paper.

26. The Pathless Trail - The *wonton* is in colour pencil and watercolour on handmade *khadi* paper. The *wonton* cover is rice paper.

27. The Split – The mushroom and lychee are in watercolour on handmade *khadi* paper.

28. Eton Mess – Mixed media: collage on handmade *khadi* paper.

29. Pretty Peas – The peas are in colour pencil on watercolour paper.

30. The Creative Cut – The oil, ginger and garlic are in water colour, colour pencil, and gouache on mixed media paper.

31. A Natural Pimiento – The pimiento and peppers are in acrylics and ink on Egyptian papyrus (paper).

32. Theatrical Delight – Acrylics and ink on linen canvas.

33. The Hot Tom Yum – Mixed media; pen, ink, soft pastel, and pure shell gold on handmade *khadi* paper.

34. The Dreamy Treat –

    a) The cocoa bean is in ink.

    b) The Swiss chocolates are in colour pencil on printed paper.

    c) The marshmallow and fudge are in gouache and oil pastels on printed paper.

    d) The jellybeans, gobstoppers, and wine gums are in colour pencil on printed paper.

35. The Wholesome Split – The *moong* beans are in watercolour and colour pencil on cartridge paper. The calligraphy is in ink on cartridge paper.

36. Made for Each Other – The slices of bread are in water colour and colour pencil on *khadi* paper.

37. The Creation's Story –

    a) The chickpea is in colour pencil on pastel paper.

    b) The kidney bean is in colour pencil and watercolour on pastel paper.

    c) The chickpea and the kidney bean in the park are in watercolour and colour pencil on handmade flower *khadi* paper.

38. The Charming Spud – Mixed media: fabric, banana paper, paper, ink, soft pastel, and acrylic paint collage.

39. Priceless Refuge – The oranges and pomegranate are in watercolour and colour pencil on watercolour and handmade *khadi* papers.

40. The Undying Death – The tomato and knife are in pencil and ink on pastel paper.

41. The Milky Way – Gouache and ink on pastel paper.

42. Food for thought – The pastries are in watercolour and gouache on watercolour paper.

43. Non-dual Election – The egg and writing are in watercolour and colour pencil on pastel paper.

44. The Last Laugh – The potato and foods all are in colour pencil on pastel paper.

45. Boundless Transformation – The tea/ coffee cup is in acrylic and ink on linen canvas.

A variety of art materials have been used in this book. A few papers, pigments and art materials are from India, but most of the papers, paints, and the rest of the materials have been brought from the local specialist shops in the UK.

About the Author & Illustrators

Darpana

This book sings of the formless forming – the simple message that the formless alone appears as all forms, embraces it and yet remains untouched by it. My apparent story is pale in comparison to this song of unconditional, ineffable love.

Sumita *(1954–2022)*

The co-illustrator of the book did not sign up for this role. She was persuaded and convinced by Darpana to use her amazing artistic talents to make relevant artworks for the verses. Sumita in her own words was a multi-talented art teacher who lived in London.

Printed in Poland
by Amazon Fulfillment
Poland Sp. z o.o., Wrocław

18579914R00150